SPY IN THE SKY

A COLD WAR STORY OF ESPIONAGE, ROMANCE AND INTRIGUE

TOM ELSASSER

outskirts
press

Outskirts Press, Inc.
http://www.outskirtspress.com

Paperback ISBN: 978-1-4787-8007-6
Hardback ISBN: 978-1-9772-0266-6

PRINTED IN THE UNITED STATES OF AMERICA

For my wife Pat, and Suzanne, Mark, Matthew, Jamie, and Joan

Acknowledgements

To all who assisted me in writing *Spy in the Sky*, I offer my sincere thanks.

This book could not have been written without the help of Theresa (Terry) Hannah. Our paths first crossed quite by chance back in 1972 when I was a Naval Officer returning to the States on a Pan Am flight. It was the Officers' habit to write "good gal" letters to Pam Am for particularly competent flight attendant service, and I had written such a letter for Terry's outstanding service. When I hatched the plot for *Spy in the Sky*, I reviewed my correspondence from that era, hoping to find someone from Pan Am who could act as a subject matter expert. The letter I had written regarding Terry came up, and I was able to locate her in Chicago. She graciously agreed to help with the book and provided invaluable background information on Pan Am operations, and on the New York social scene in the 1970s. She reviewed the chapters as they were written to ensure every detail was accurate and offered suggestions on plausible plot lines. The value of her assistance cannot be overstated. Thank you, Terry, for the many, many hours you contributed to this effort.

When I started down the path to write this book, my classmate from the Naval Academy Class of 1964, Charlie Jett, was just finishing the very successful *Super Nuke*, a memoir of Charlie's time as a junior officer in the nuclear submarine program during the late 1960s and early 1970s. Charlie generously offered his guidance and encouragement, and without his help I could have never completed *Spy in the Sky*.

My initial manuscript was about one-third longer than what

is presented here and needed significant revision to get to a manageable size. Joan Rogers and Ken Nichols provided their editorial expertise, and succeeded in leaving the unwanted one-third of the first draft on the cutting room floor. The result was a much improved second draft, which was reviewed by several good friends who provided suggestions for plot improvement, character development, and a careful review of plot specifics. I owe them all a debt of gratitude, including Ed Schoenberger, my Naval Academy roommate, Sharen Finzimer, and Susan Gerrity. Hilary James also provided significant editing expertise for the final draft. Mal Wright, my shipmate and fellow depart-ment head on the USS Will Rogers, SSBN659, provided a most welcome final technical edit to ensure all things Navy were spot on. My apologies to anyone I might have missed.

The dynamic sister team of Elizabeth English (Gwen Rowley) and Janie Minogue provided invaluable assistance in proofread-ing and consultation to produce the book in its final form. Liz, an award-winning romance novelist, was able to steer me in the right direction concerning matters of the heart. Liz and I had many conversations and email exchanges regarding the softer side of character development and the non-technical aspects of the book.

A special thank you goes to fellow Naval Academy gradu-ate, Rick Campbell, who is enjoying a very successful career as a writer of fictional novels based on submarine warfare. His first novel, *The Trident Deception*, was a huge success and had a sig-nificant impact on this book. Following one of his book signings in Annapolis, I met Rick and a few friends for dinner. He asked me about my book and the opening that sought to hook the read-er. At that point my manuscript started with the Chapter One meeting, not the sinking of the K8. Rick told me he had made a similar oversight in the initial draft of *The Trident Deception*, and advised me never to start an action or thriller novel with a meeting—it just doesn't have any punch. As a result, I went back to the drawing board to find a factual, action-based event to open my story. The sinking of the K8 provided just such an opening.

Matthew Englebert and Nathan Novak, the two-man team that created the cover photos and many of the "on site" New York City photographs that appear on my website, deserve special thanks. The website, www.tomelsasserauthor.com, provides access to the photographs as well as additional background information on *Spy in the Sky*.

Of course, this book would have not been possible had I not graduated from the Naval Academy and served in the Navy. As a young Naval Officer my life and career were shaped by Admiral Rickover's program and the extreme sense of responsibility it instilled in each of us. The success of the Navy's nuclear submarine program is a testament to his vision and leadership. The various commanding officers under whom I served each had their own leadership style, and I learned something significant from each of them. However, they all had one thing in common: the ability to foster and develop a keen sense of personal responsibility that was the hallmark of the Navy's nuclear submarine program.

Finally, and most importantly, I thank Pat—my wife of 54 years. Pat and I have been together from the time I was submarine officer, and throughout a career comprised of varied work assignments. While I was on active duty, we moved 11 times in just under 11 years. I was at sea or on travel much of the time, but Pat had the situation well in hand, and we were able to raise five absolutely wonderful children. And now, I thank her for her patience while I wrote.

Prologue

Bay of Biscay
April 8 -11, 1970

"Fire in compartment three, fire in compartment three."

Captain Bessonov bolted from his state room and sprinted to the central command post. Even before his arrival, a second announcement came over the ship's speakers. "Fire in compartment seven, fire in compartment seven." When the fires broke out, Submarine K-8 was cruising quietly at 390 feet below the surface of the Bay of Biscay. Submarine fires while submerged were lethal; smoke and fumes had no place to go. Two simultaneous fires meant double trouble for the 135 crew on board K-8.

As the Captain entered the central command post the Officer of the Deck, Lieutenant Popovitch, slammed a terrified young seaman against the bulkhead. "Get to your damage control station, go fight the fire." Shouts of confusion grew louder as the seaman bolted through the water tight door; the sound of the general alarm was deafening and smoke from the adjacent compartment started to billow around the men in the central command post.

Bessonov instructed Popovitch to order immediate isolation of compartments three and seven to limit the spread of fire and smoke. Popovitch reminded the commanding officer that there were men in those compartments fighting the fires. Bessonov looked grimly at Popovitch. "There is no choice. We must contain the fires. Order the isolation."

In compartment three, Seaman Oleg Lukin was slowly being

suffocated by the acrid haze. As he struggled to find his way out of the compartment through the dense smoke, he heard an ominous clang as the water tight door slammed shut. A vision of his young wife and daughter flashed before his eyes just as he lost consciousness. Other crew members in the two isolated compartments had similar experiences as death approached. In just a few minutes, eight men lay dead. But the worst was yet to come.

For three days, Bessonov and the 51 members of his crew who had not been evacuated to a rescue vessel struggled to save the K-8. With both reactors shut down and the diesel inoperable, the crippled submarine was little more than an inert tube of steel under tow to a Northern Fleet port. Desperate attempts to remove the four nuclear tipped torpedoes were unsuccessful. Bessanov lamented the overall situation in his thoughts. *Why are we so far behind the Americans in submarine engineering and technical capability? Design and construction expertise are clearly lacking—the Americans are obviously much better at what they do. It is just that simple.*

The Captain's musing was rudely interrupted when the submarine suddenly took an up angle as the stern started to sink. Reports from back aft indicated the hull seals in compartments seven and eight had failed and sea water was rapidly filling both spaces. Bessonov shouted, "Emergency blow after ballast tanks!" However, the air banks were quickly exhausted and the sea won the ultimate battle for buoyancy, sending the K-8 on its way to the bottom some 15,000 feet below.

Drawing his last breath as K-8 sank beneath the waves of the Bay of Biscay, Bessonov thought, *What an unnecessary loss of additional life. The upper command of the navy and government are fools. Instead of trying to save the doomed K-8, attention would have been better spent launching an effort to find out why the American submarines are so superior.*

The Captain, his 51 brave crew members, and the eight initial casualties were soon resting in a watery grave on the bottom of the Bay of Biscay, many miles from Mother Russia. Once again Soviet technical expertise had failed its naval force, resulting in the loss of another submarine and death to its crew.

Chapter 1

It was one of those meetings that never took place. Each of the participants entered the bowels of KGB headquarters by a different path. This was intentional. Had it been known that the four men were meeting, the entire building would have been buzzing before they even had a chance to take their seats. Four chairs and a square table occupied the center of a soundproofed grey room with bare concrete walls. The single door could be locked from within, preventing intrusion by uninvited guests.

This no-frills setting had been deliberately chosen by Fyodor Mortin, head of KGB's First Chief Directorate. This was to be a bare-knuckle, no-holds-barred meeting. Also in attendance were Nikolai Gorsky, deputy for Covert Operations; Vladimir Kerchenko, head of the Third Chief Directorate; and Fleet Admiral Gorshov, overall commander of the Soviet naval forces.

The moment they were seated, Mortin got right down to business. "Comrades, yesterday I had a most unpleasant meeting with Yuri. In essence, he handed me my ass." Mortin had been in power long enough that with regard to intelligence matters, his word was absolute — and like most high-ranking officials, he felt entitled to refer to his bosses — Yuri Andropov and Leonid Brezhnev — by their first names.

"Yuri is concerned that all of you have been sitting on your fat posteriors since Leonid signed the ABM and SALT treaties in May. Some seem to think that détente is to be taken literally, and that we are supposed to enter into a holding pattern with the Americans and maintain our respective military positions that existed when the treaties were signed. The advertised purpose of the treaties is to ease world tension. Your collective inaction since the signing of those treaties seems to indicate you believe that to be the real reason behind Leonid's action.

"If you think that, you are all fools; the exact opposite is true. Our intention is to play catch-up if the Americans are stupid enough to hold the line on various aspects of their military position. Treaty rules need to be bent if we are going to get anywhere near a position of parity. This means finding out what the hell they are doing — and taking steps to put ourselves in a superior position."

Looking directly at the Admiral, Mortin continued, "I have a message specifically for you. What have you been doing to avoid future submarine disasters and improve the capability of our submarine force? It has been over two years since the sinking of the K-8 and Leonid is of the opinion that little has been done by the navy to correct the situation. We cannot continue to scatter nuclear torpedoes and reactors on the bottom of the world's oceans. What specific information do we need to steal from the Americans?"

The Admiral shifted uneasily in his chair. "Comrade, I will start working on your request immediately following our meeting."

This was vintage Mortin. He had been in his current position for only about a year, and already knew how to use a little bit of exaggeration to make a point. His audience heard: *Yuri is unhappy, and you better get your collective selves in gear, because my butt is really on the line, and I want to keep my job.*

Wrapping up, Mortin told them to reconvene on September 21st. All hands were directed to provide creative ideas for use by the KGB to improve the overall military posture of the USSR. The clear intent was to shrink the Americans' current lead in military effectiveness, with submarine warfare of particular interest. The USSR had appreciated America's military prowess as an ally during World War II, but times had changed, and now the Americans had gone too far. Sooner or later, they would regret holding a gun to the head of Holy Mother Russia.

Chapter 2

Prestwick, Scotland
September 14th, 1972

After three days inspecting a submarine in the Irish Sea, LCDR Max Millen, USN, was looking forward to his Pan Am flight back to JFK.

"Sure looks like you got up on the right side of the bed this morning, in spite of all the scotch we drank last night," said Doug Pritchett, one of the other three officers on the inspection team.

Max offered a sly smile. "Of all the airlines, Pan Am is the best by far. Care and feeding of passengers is a real priority."

Pan Am flight attendants were the best in the business. Navy teams that crossed the Atlantic every other week spent substantial time chatting up the crews on both Pan Am and TWA. There were, of course, unwritten rules. For example, if the goal was to have a winning record when flirting with female crew members: never come on strong, don't interrupt when they're really busy, be yourself, and don't press the issue if there's no apparent interest. If your pitch doesn't work on one young lady, try another. Max always made eye contact with the crew during the boarding process and noted the names of the prime candidates. He always returned a smile, and often offered a witty remark to indicate he was happy to be on board. An elite submarine jockey wouldn't be very attractive if he came across as a grumpy passenger.

Flight attendant flirting was like catch-and-release fly fishing.

At the end of the flight, parting was simple—a warm handshake followed by kind words about sharing pleasant conversation. Both deplaned and were thrown back into the stream of life. There were thousands of flight attendants, so almost no chance of ever meeting again. Once off the plane, the Navy guys rushed to catch a connecting flight to Norfolk, Virginia, and that was that. Little did Max know that this flight would not follow the usual pattern.

The four members of the inspection team rarely sat together; separately, they had a better chance of meeting interesting passengers and crew. Across the aisle was acceptable; those were desirable seats because they provided easy access to the galleys where the ladies worked. A quick trip to the lavatory and nearby galley when the seat belt sign was turned off provided a great opportunity to locate candidates for conversation. No chatting-up just yet, as the crew would be preparing beverage service—just a brief hello and encouragement to serve cocktails ASAP.

Max finished his visit to the lavatory and made a casual visit to the rear galley. The crew was busy readying the beverage carts; a brunette with sparkling eyes looked up and smiled. Max recognized her from boarding.

"Natalie, right?" he said. "I noticed your name while boarding."

The smile broadened. "You have a good memory."

"Some things are especially memorable. OK if I come back and visit after dinner service? My name is Max, by way of introduction."

"Well...maybe. It's a long flight; we're not always busy."

Max always capitalized on mild encouragement. "It's a date, then," he said, and she nodded.

Max was off to a good start. Just wait patiently through cocktails and dinner and then visit the rear galley after the crew finished eating. Another unwritten rule: Don't interrupt the crew during meals.

Back in his seat, Max leaned across the aisle and whispered to team member George, "What do you think of the one I was talking to?"

"Not really my cup of tea. I prefer blondes."

"You're too picky. The most important thing is whether they want to share conversation...and if they're fun to talk to."

George shrugged. Flirting on flights wasn't his idea of fun; he preferred to binge on sci-fi paperbacks. Max left George to his Isaac Asimov. He thought again about Natalie. Max appreciated a wide variety of women; however, Natalie was his preferred type: warm olive complexion and glossy dark hair. Italian, he guessed.

Back in the galley, Natalie thought about the Navy guy who had approached her. She felt confident he would come back, and found herself looking forward to his visit. Having a serious boyfriend, she was pretty reserved in her contact with male passengers — but things weren't completely rosy with her and Scott. Casual conversation wouldn't hurt, and Pan Am always encouraged flight attendants to take an interest in their passengers. The airline carried a flock of world travelers; many had at least one fascinating story. She wondered what Max would have to say for himself.

As she finished her last spoonful of crème brulée, Max surfaced at the galley door. "Buy a sailor a cup of coffee?"

Well, he certainly has great timing — I'll give him that, thought Natalie. "My pleasure — it's a fresh pot," she said.

Max plopped down. "If someone needs the seat, I'll get up."

Gentlemanly and practical — not bad, mused Natalie. She handed him a steaming cup. "I don't think we've been properly introduced," she said.

"My apologies, fair maiden. I am Maximillian Millen, Lieutenant Commander USN, at your service."

"Natalie Tomassi here, flight attendant. Pretty impressive, Mr. Max, what were you doing in Scotland?"

"Inspecting submarines. Teams of four fly around the world, making sure their power plants are safe to operate."

Natalie hadn't run across that before—he must be intelligent and detail-oriented to do that kind of work. She let her guard down, and over the next half-hour found he had a knack for asking questions without being intrusive. By the time the coffee was gone, Natalie had told him she was twenty-seven and had been flying for nearly five years. She had attended a Catholic all-girls high school and college. Having grown up in the Bronx in an Italian family she was fluent in Italian and had studied French in college. She lived in a one-bedroom apartment with three other flight attendants on the Upper East Side. They managed in such a small space with two sets of bunk beds.

"That's a lot like submarine life," Max grinned. "Officers are three to a stateroom, with triple-stacked bunks."

Natalie loved that Max was so open about his life and work. He had gone to a Catholic all-boys school in Philadelphia, and graduated from the Naval Academy in 1964—he was older than Natalie, but not by much. He lived in Norfolk, and submarines were the center of his career. She learned he worked with four-man teams that traveled to Europe regularly to inspect nuclear submarines. Max considered it a unique way to see the world at the government's expense.

As Natalie and Max talked, they found they shared a love of travel, good food, classical music, and museums. Natalie was used to her passengers taking the lion's share of the conversation with travel stories—she rarely revealed much of herself. And it was even rarer to find someone with whom she had so much in common. Who knew? Maybe Max was one of the unique guys who saw conversation as a prelude to the main event, not an obstacle.

The intercom phone rang; duty called and Natalie was needed forward in the red galley. Max returned to his seat. He tried reading *The Eiger Sanction,* but found it difficult to focus.

Chapter 3

Somewhere Over the Atlantic
September 14th, 1972

When Natalie arrived in the red galley, her roommate Caroline asked, "Well, what's he like? You guys were having a pretty intense conversation. What would Scott say?" Caroline and Natalie were very close. They often bid the same lines, so they spent a lot of time together.

Natalie gave a little laugh. She'd had four years of ups and downs with Scott. "Well when I look down at my left hand, I don't see a sparkle. Maybe it's time for a little competition—I think Scott has been taking me for granted. Don't jump to conclusions, though. I enjoyed talking to Max, but I don't even know him. He lives in Norfolk and travels just as much as we do." Then Natalie shifted focus and asked Caroline what she thought of Max's traveling companion.

"Sci-fi guy? He looks too nerdy for me."

"No, not him—the one Max was with when they boarded."

"Oh, that one! He was a doll…and just about the right size." Caroline winked at Natalie. "No matter what they say, size does matter."

Natalie grinned. "Well, I'll see what I can do. He's on the submarine team with Max, so I have to assume he's bright enough to hold up his end of a conversation."

About an hour later, Max decided to make an unnecessary head call and then visit the back of the plane. But when he got to the galley, Natalie was nowhere to be found. She must be somewhere up forward. He turned around and started for the red section galley. Natalie and Caroline were chattering brightly as they made coffee and tidied up. The conversation abruptly stopped when he poked his head in.

"Sorry if I'm interrupting."

Natalie smiled. "It's no bother. We can walk and chew gum at the same time."

"I bet. And you can probably carry on a conversation in three languages."

Natalie felt herself blush. Flattery was always pleasant. "Where's the rest of the team sitting?" she asked.

"Up forward. They're across from each other in Aisle 12." He looked at Caroline. "I wonder if you could lend a hand…I owe Doug and John a drink. Both of them would love a Scotch on the rocks with a can of club soda on the side."

Caroline made the drinks and took off, flashing a conspiratorial glance at Natalie.

"I'm not used to being chased all over the aircraft," Natalie said.

"Well, our conversation ended a little prematurely, and I was just looking for an excuse to pick up where we left off."

"I've got about fifteen minutes before the next service. Where were we?"

"I was just about to ask what you usually do for fun on the weekend."

"Well, you know New York—it depends on what's happening. Sometimes we go clubbing and dancing, or sometimes we go to MoMA or the Met."

"Have you been to Alice Tully Hall?"

"Oh, yes—for both the film festival and chamber music. I love it," Natalie said.

Max and Natalie traded ideas of a good time in New York

for fifteen minutes. Caroline returned from Aisle 12. Max asked, "I'd ask if they accepted the drinks, but I know sailors never turn down free booze."

"They were happy to see me with the Scotch, and in return, I got a lot of idle chit-chat. Doug is pretty nice—he said you two are roommates, and often partners in crime."

"Guilty as charged. Work hard, play hard—that's the code we live by. Or is it the code by which we live? I just hate those dangling prepositions."

Natalie, hands on hips, said, "OK, wise guy, we've got to get back to work. Seats, everyone."

Max turned to go and said in a low voice, "I'm really good at following orders, but is there time for another get-together between the end of service and prep for landing?"

"Probably. I'll see if I can fit you somewhere on my dance card."

Back in his seat, Max was too distracted to read. Natalie was so sweet, bright, and pretty—and best of all, she didn't act as if she knew how attractive she was. Max had lost count of the flight attendants he'd met, and he was not easily impressed. Natalie was special. Max figured he had one more move, but he wasn't sure what it should be. Jumping off to NYC for a few days would be a bit much. How about one day? Even that could pose problems, considering his schedule. Getting the first date would take some careful consideration.

Service was over, and they would soon be prepping to land. It was time for one last effort, so Max headed to the rear galley. Natalie was there, and fortunately, she wasn't very busy. She greeted him warmly.

"Hi there. Well, you certainly are a man of your word—return visit, as promised. I don't want to be rude, but I only have a few minutes."

"Well, I function best under pressure: Damn the torpedoes, full speed ahead. I have a favor to ask, and I won't be offended if you say no. Would you be willing to share your phone number with me?"

Natalie considered and didn't see any downside. "Sure, no problem. Let me grab a pen and paper out of my purse."

Without hesitation, Natalie offered the coveted piece of paper with that wonderful 212 area code. Max hid his excitement as he accepted the number. He expected to be shot down and given some reason why providing the number would not be appropriate. Max stowed the paper in his carry-on, buckled his seat belt, and got ready for landing. He felt reasonably confident that when he called — and it was definitely when, not if — she would agree to see him.

Sitting on the jump seat, Natalie wondered if Max would call. If he did, she could easily manage the situation with Scott. She daydreamed a little about what she and Max would do when he visited New York — and then she shook herself. She wasn't in the habit of sharing her phone number with strangers she met on international flights.

The plane landed safely. Max and Natalie went their separate ways…for now.

Chapter 4

All four team members from the Pan Am flight hopped on the bus to head over to the National terminal and lounge for complimentary drinks and snacks. The club staff was always happy to see the naval officers, who livened up the small lounge. Max and Doug were fortunate to be best friends as well as roommates, so they preferred to travel together, especially when going to inspections in Scotland and Spain. On the bus over to National, Doug and Max sat together, and the conversation turned to their favorite subject — women.

Doug wasted no time. "You didn't spread yourself around much on that last flight. Was she worth it?"

Max said, "I don't know where to start. I talked to her for more than an hour and half, and I couldn't get enough of her. I probably looked like a puppy dog, following her all over the plane. Every time we started to get on a roll, she had to go back to work. I haven't even scratched the surface, but what I've found so far is exceptional."

"It was pretty obvious you were interested. Not like you to put all your eggs in one basket; she must have been interested, too. What's she like?"

"Smart as hell, speaks French and Italian and has been flying with Pan Am for about five years. She's been to more places than I could possibly visit in four lifetimes. Get this: She lives in a one-bedroom apartment on the Upper East Side with three other flight attendants. One of her roommates is Caroline, the one who brought you and George the Scotch and sodas."

Doug snickered. "Sounds like submarine living—how do they do it, hot bunk?" Doug was referring to the submarine practice of assigning two men to one bunk when the crew was too large to provide an individual bunk for each man. The bunk-mates would be assigned different watch sections and then had to work out the sleeping schedule for themselves.

"Nope, they have two sets of bunk beds. I doubt they're all there at the same time. With one bathroom, can you imagine what goes on Friday night at about 1900 if they're all there trying to get ready to go out clubbing? It would be like four women in a blender—arms, legs, bras, panties, stockings, lipstick, hair spray, and perfume going in all directions at the same time."

"Maybe we should find a way to sell tickets. We'd make a fortune in less than six months and could retire early."

Max laughed. "Doug, you are one sick dude. But I'll admit the picture does boggle the mind." The bus stopped, and it was time to hop off at the National terminal. Max quipped, "Saved by the bus stop." The men wasted no time getting off the bus and piling into the National lounge.

Seated with drink in hand, Doug continued where he'd left off. "So, what else can you tell me? Is there any chance you'll ever see her again? You know how it goes—so many flights, so many flight attendants lost in a sea of zero possibility."

"If you manage to get a phone number, the odds are a lot better. For the first time ever, I got the guts to ask. I hope this isn't like the proverbial dog chasing the car—once he catches it, he doesn't know how to drive it."

Doug chuckled. "Well, it's not like you've never been on a date. However, she is somewhat GU—geographically undesirable. Both of you travel constantly, and you don't even live in the same state, much less the same city."

"Look at it this way. All of our European flights go through JFK. She starts all her trips out of JFK. That's a reasonable number of chances to engage a target of opportunity."

"My, my—you do get an A+ for logistical planning. Just don't forget to make a phone call when we get back to Norfolk."

The intercom announced boarding for the flight south. Max leaned back and smiled. This was the best day he'd had in a long time.

While the boys headed south, Natalie and Caroline were safely tucked away on the Carey bus headed through the Queens-Midtown tunnel on the way to the East Side Airline Terminal at 37th and First. From there, it was a quick taxi ride up to their apartment at 77th and First. Caroline leaned in close, unwilling to broadcast Natalie's personal business to the entire bus.

"I overheard the end of your conversation before we landed," she said. "I can't believe you actually gave our phone number to a perfect stranger. Have you thought about the impact on your relationship with Scott?"

"You know what I said on the plane about Scott. I think it's time to shake him out of his complacency. He keeps talking about waiting until he gets out of grad school before even considering marriage—and he hasn't even applied for grad school yet! Am I supposed to cool my heels for two years and hope it all works out? Anyway, I've had good experience with the military before— there was my guy from West Point. That didn't work out because of 'Nam. I think it may be time to give the Navy a chance."

Caroline was wide-eyed. "Slow down, Nat! You don't even know if Max will call."

"It won't be the end of the world if I don't hear from him. He's nice enough, and I hope he calls, but you're right; I don't know him. There is something special there, though. I guess that's why I gave him our phone number."

Natalie leaned her head back against the seat and let her eyes drift shut. Almost in a dream state, she thought, *This little flirtation might lead to something interesting.* The next thing she knew, Caroline was shaking her shoulder.

"Hey, Sleeping Beauty. We're here. Let's get off this bus and grab a taxi home. Did you have sweet dreams?"

Natalie flashed her charming smile. "It's too soon to know, but—you never can tell."

Chapter 5

New York City—Upper East Side
September 14th, 1972

As Natalie and Caroline took the elevator up to their 8th-floor apartment, Caroline was thinking ahead. "Hey, Nat," she said, "I'll make a deal with you. If you'll run down to the basement with our laundry, I'll run by the deli on First and make a quick list of available snacks for tomorrow night."

Natalie replied, "OK, I'll see what's in the fridge for dinner. I'm beat and really don't feel like going out tonight. I'll see what I can throw together to go with a Manhattan."

Since she and Caroline were the original tenants of the apartment, each had one of the bottom bunks and half of the closet on the side of the room nearest her bed. There were two dressers, and each of the girls had two of the four drawers. The tops were divided in half to accommodate a variety of cosmetics.

Natalie would live in a closet if she had to; having grown up in the Bronx, her lifelong dream was to live and work in Manhattan. For all intents and purposes, her dream was fulfilled—she worked around the world and played in Manhattan. Not bad for a twenty-seven-year-old from a Catholic all-girls college. Another distinct advantage was that her father operated Pietro's, a well-known Italian restaurant in Midtown. No matter how tight her budget was, she would never starve. Every so often, Daddy would make a run to the apartment with steaks and chops to stock the freezer.

Natalie was looking forward to Friday night, when she

was throwing one of her legendary parties. Growing up, she had been fascinated by *Breakfast at Tiffany's*. At the tender age of twelve, she wanted to go to parties in Manhattan, just like Holly Golightly. At that time, she had no idea how Holly earned her living. Oh, to be young and naïve again! Natalie was now old enough to throw her own Manhattan parties. Since she had been living in and around the city all her life, the guest list was always out of control for their 800-square foot apartment.

As soon as Natalie got back from the laundry, she mixed a stiff Manhattan for herself and a vodka martini for Caroline. She put Caroline's drink in the fridge and rummaged around for something to make for dinner. She found a big bowl of rice, an assortment of cooked vegetables, and a container of chicken scraps. She heated oil in a frying pan and began to brown an onion and some scallions.

Caroline burst through the door. "Boy, am I ready for a drink."

Natalie got out the soy sauce and a couple of eggs. "I'm way ahead of you. There's a vodka martini in the fridge for you, and I'm making chicken fried rice."

"Well, if I were Scott, I'd start thinking about making sure you don't get away," Caroline said. "He'll never find anyone else who brings as much to the table as you do." She had touched on a sore subject. Scott's continual procrastination regarding a long-term commitment was a recurring topic of conversation. "What about the guy on the flight today?" she persisted. "Any potential?"

"He's been in the Navy for about ten years. His work seems to require a high degree of smarts and responsibility. He has the gift of saying the right thing at the right time and is never at a loss for words. We seem to like the same things, and honestly if

I were making a list of what I want in a guy…he'd look good on paper."

"Bet you ten bucks he calls tomorrow. He was chasing you all over the plane. He wouldn't have asked for your number if he didn't intend to use it."

They had another drink, and settled in to watch an old black-and-white movie on TV. Tonight it was *Casablanca*, one of their favorites. After it was over, Natalie looked over at Caroline and said, "Of all the planes, and all the flights, he had to walk into mine. It has to be more than a coincidence."

Chapter 6

Frankfurt—New York City—Upper East Side
September 15th, 1972

The first-class passengers strolled leisurely to their seats aboard the Pan Am direct flight from Frankfurt to JFK. It was going to be busy for one of the flight attendants working the first-class section, but it had nothing to do with her official Pan Am duties. She was rather tall, with a white porcelain complexion set off by a blonde pixie cut. Easy to spot in a crowd. One of the passengers immediately took note, and touched her arm as she walked down the aisle in first-class. "Would you please hang up my sport coat. Take care, it is pure cashmere." She flashed him that Pan Am smile. "By all means, Mr. Merkel. I'll give it special attention." She helped him shed the elegant jacket and briskly walked to the forward closet.

The password and name match; he's the guy, she thought as she placed the jacket on one of the hangers. In the process, she deftly removed a small notebook from the right inside pocket and wedged it in the waistband of her uniform skirt.

The remainder of the flight was strictly routine. Upon arrival at JFK it was just a matter of one more transaction and she was home free. She glanced at her watch; the timing was perfect. She gathered her luggage and headed for the Carey bus stop, pausing a bit apart from the waiting crowd. Almost immediately, she was joined by another Pan Am flight attendant who set down her luggage next to hers and said, "I'm just in from Paris, how was your flight?" "Pretty much routine," she answered. A minute or two later the bus arrived and again she gathered her luggage. With a distracted expression, she deliberately took the girl from Paris's carry-on instead of her own. Once on the bus she felt a wave of relaxation and thought, *Almost finished, just a quick trip to Bloomingdale's to pass on these little treasures and mission complete.*

Apartment 8L ~ 400 East 77th Street

"Did you remember to get trash bags?" Natalie asked Caroline, as the girls efficiently unloaded the deli snacks, mixers, bags of ice, sleeves of plastic glasses, and packages of paper plates.

"Are you kidding? It wouldn't be a party without them," Caroline said. Their only hope of keeping the party under control was to make everything disposable and coax a chivalrous male guest to make a run to the trash room as the bags were filled; otherwise, their apartment would end up looking like the streets of New York after a three-week garbage strike.

"Are you hiding anything special this time?" Caroline asked.

"I'll never tell," Natalie teased. As the daughter of a restaurant owner, she had a more sophisticated palate than most of the guys who brought "vin du jug" to their parties. She often hid a bottle of good booze in one of her dresser drawers, and would discreetly mix herself "something drinkable."

Mia and Sabrina rushed in later than expected. Mia said, "It looks like we're having quite a few guests this evening. Is it okay if we go to the head of the bathroom queue? We're going to clear out and go clubbing."

Natalie nodded as Caroline picked up the ringing phone. "Hey, it's great to hear from you," she said. "I guess you guys got back to Norfolk safely." She mouthed the word "Max" silently to Natalie, who felt herself blush. "Here she is," Caroline said and handed over the receiver. Mia looked back and forth between the two girls; realizing that something interesting was going on, she stopped to listen in.

"Hi there, Mr. Max," Natalie said. "You're a man of your word, but then again—why ask for a girl's phone number if you aren't going to use it? What do a bunch of sailors do on liberty Friday night?"

"Well, we usually hang out at the Christian Science Reading Room; then we go for hot chocolate and spend a quiet evening at home. How about you?"

Natalie was surprised by the tingle of excitement she felt when she heard Max's voice. She tried to sound nonchalant when she replied, "We're a little more adventurous. We're having one of our locally famous parties at the apartment. I do hate to call you a liar, but I have to say I don't believe you about the Christian Science Reading Room."

Max chuckled. "Guilty as charged. How big is the party?"

"I've never actually counted. Probably around seventy-five—the apartment won't hold many more."

"To answer your original question, if we're in Norfolk on Friday nights, we usually head over to the Officers' Club at Little Creek or Fort Story. But listen, before I forget the reason for my call—I'll be coming through New York on Monday, October 30th. Can we make a date for lunch?"

No time wasted there, Natalie thought. "Good timing. I got my October schedule set up yesterday, and the 30th should be fine. We can firm up plans later."

"That's great. It's been quite a while since I was on the loose in New York. I'm not sure I'll know how to behave."

"Don't worry—I'll let you know if you're misbehaving. I hate to cut this short, but I have loads to do before the hordes arrive. Call me around the middle of the month. Bye for now."

Max said, "Bye yourself." As Natalie hung up the phone, her hand trembled just a little. She was aware that Caroline and Mia were watching, and she needed a moment of privacy. "I'll be right back…I just realized I left my schedule in my flight bag."

"What was that all about?" Mia asked Caroline, her face bright with curiosity. Of course, she knew Scott; it was unusual for Natalie to accept a date with somebody she just met on a flight. "Who's the bloke?"

Caroline answered, "We met these Navy guys on the plane yesterday. They're in the submarine service, and they fly around the world doing nuclear inspections, or something. Natalie and this guy Max really seemed to hit it off. His roommate Doug is no slouch either."

"Hmm. Maybe Sabrina and I would like to join that party if the rest of the crew wants to spend some time in The Big Apple," said Mia. "We've begun to go off our usual New York set a bit… too much of the same thing, you know."

Natalie overheard this from the bedroom and thought, *That's a bit different…usually Mia and Sabrina can't wait to get away from our parties and go clubbing with jet-setters. There's something about a man in uniform, I guess.*

She opened the closet and found her Pan Am carry-on on the floor next to Mia's. She searched for her diary, where she tracked her flight lines and schedule. She noticed that meticulous Mia's bag looked strange: dirty, and damaged in one corner. The handwriting on the crew tag was different, too…it didn't look like Mia's handwriting. Like some Europeans, Mia always put a line through the number 7, and this tag was written without it. Back in the living room, Natalie said to Caroline, "What do you make of that?"

"I'm not sure what you mean."

"I mean Mia jumping on the bandwagon and practically

inviting herself to spend some time with the Navy guys if they come through. You know how Mia is; she likes flashy Riviera playboys. If he has a tan and a tailor-made suit, it's good enough for her."

"I agree, but Mia's no fool. There's only so long she can play that game. We're not getting any younger—maybe she's ready to ditch the playboys and think seriously about her future."

"Well, anyone on Max's crew would be a good catch," Natalie admitted.

"I think getting all four of us and Max's team on a quadruple date would be a total hoot," Caroline said. "The more the merrier, I always say."

While Caroline and Natalie busied themselves with the final party prep, Natalie's thoughts were down in Norfolk with Max. It had been a fun phone call, and if nothing else, it confirmed that she wasn't wasting her time thinking about him.

"Hey, you—get with the program and open the chips and dip," Caroline teased. "You look like you're a thousand miles away."

Natalie smiled. "More like four hundred miles due south."

"You'd better get ready to act normal tonight. Scott's going to wonder why you're in such a good mood."

"You know I'm always extra nice to Scott when I get back from a trip," Natalie replied with a wink.

Mia and Sabrina were dressed to the nines. Natalie watched them strut out the door. *I wonder what they'll really think of the Navy men*, she thought. *Well, time will tell.*

Chapter 7

September 15th, 1972
Norfolk, Virginia

Max and Doug got back from their office on the CINCLANT compound around 1630, and Doug immediately turned on the tube. Most of the news was about the upcoming national election in November. George McGovern had no chance against Richard Nixon, and they were sick of the pundits trying to make something of the race.

Before Doug could change the channel, Max told him to wait, as a Pan Am commercial was starting. It was the one that played a catchy jingle with the words "Pan Am makes the going great." It showed a 747 taking off and then landing at all sorts of exotic locations around the world. Pretty flight attendants welcomed happy passengers with that spectacular Pan Am smile.

Max said, "Not only can I not get Natalie out of my mind—even the TV keeps her memory front and center. I did call her today to set something up. On my return from Rota I'm going to swing through New York, and we'll spend an afternoon together on the 30th. She seemed pretty enthusiastic so I'm really encouraged about the whole deal."

"Did she say anything about what Caroline thought of me, charming devil that I am?"

"Sorry, big boy, no news on that front. When I'm up there next month, I'll ask Natalie to float a trial balloon."

Doug said, "Roger—sounds like a plan. Speaking of action, what about tonight?"

Usually, there were three choices for Friday-night action. The "O" Clubs at the various bases: Navy at Little Creek and Oceana, and the Officers' Club at Fort Story. Then there was the "Body Exchange" at the Chief Petty Officers' Club at Little Creek.

Max said, "Let's grab some grub; shit, shave, shower, and shampoo, and be out of here by 1930. If we go to Little Creek for the singalong, we want to be there early enough to get a spot by the piano. Are any of the other guys going to be there tonight?"

"The Charleston trip got back around noon, and they drove. As you know, the captain doesn't like to fly, so they took two cars. My guess is Peter will probably be at Little Creek; he was on the Charleston team. Possibly he'll stop at the Body Exchange before coming to the O Club."

Peter was their resident wild man. Never married, he was a big drinker and notorious womanizer. He had a 1969 Corvette that he drove hard, and if there was a party going on, he'd find it—and if he couldn't find one, he'd start one. Travel with Peter on the team ensured a good time for all when they were "on the beach," Navy slang for being on liberty.

Max and Doug arrived at Little Creek on schedule. Pappy Walsh was a retired Navy musician, played a mean piano, and loved to lead the singing. It never got rowdy; it was more about the big mingle. However, Max's thoughts were elsewhere; he didn't even notice the overtures from a petite blonde sporting a summer tan. Max and Doug had been there about an hour when Peter rolled in—he was feeling no pain but still walking a straight line.

"What's up, guys?" Peter asked cheerfully.

Since Pappy was ready for his break, it was a good time to get an update from Peter. He had indeed come from the Body Exchange. The "Exchange" part of the name was a nod to the "Navy Exchange" or the "Post Exchange"—a store where you could get almost anything you wanted without going off the base. This was true of the Body Exchange. The women were a bit older, and the men hung at the bar waiting to make eye contact. It was a no-nonsense place; minimal conversation was required before a couple left and got down to business.

Doug said, "Peter, we didn't expect to see you here until much later. You didn't strike out, did you?"

Peter shook his head. "Never! I'm just really beat. It was a tough exam—they almost failed. The captain didn't feel like sharing the driving; he loves to drive the 'Vette on the open road. I think the exam took it out of him. The seas were pretty rough the entire exam."

Max asked, "Well, what did you guys do last night?"

"We went out to the Air Force Officers' Club—they have a killer seafood buffet with she-crab soup. It didn't disappoint. But the best part of the night came after dinner. This really cool chick came along, and we got drunk as skunks. She wanted to know what kind of car I drive, and I told her I had the 'Vette out in the parking lot. She said she'd always wanted to drive a Corvette. I didn't let her drive without first getting her name and number. Good insurance for a future visit. Anything interesting happen in Scotland?"

"Well, I think our young Max is in love," Doug said.

"Do tell!" said Peter. Doug gave him the whole story in detail.

Max held up a hand. "Let's not get too excited. You all know that my wife and I have been separated for six months, and it's not going well. I'd prefer that you not mention that fact if we're socializing in NYC. Just recently, my wife and I agreed that we would be free to see other people. We're never going to get back together. You know how it is, though; Catholic boy, divorce…I don't know how that's going to shake down. As far as Natalie is concerned, we're just two people who hit it off. I don't see it going anywhere serious, and I certainly won't take advantage of the situation. I just enjoy her company." He shook his head ruefully. "You guys probably can't imagine what it's like to be married to the wrong person. For her sake and mine, I wish we hadn't got hitched. But we did, and — well, let's just say it's been a while since I talked to a woman I really like, and who seems to like me. That's all I want from Natalie."

"Really?" said Doug. "With all that, you still made a date to see her in New York on your way back from Rota?"

"She's an exceptional conversationalist," Max said with a straight face. Doug and Peter laughed. "Seriously, though — I don't plan to put the moves on this girl. I do want to see her, and there's an opportunity for our entire crew. Get this, Peter — she lives with three other stewardesses in a one-bedroom apartment on the Upper East Side with two sets of bunk beds. Sound familiar?"

"Just like a submarine," Peter interjected. "Hey, Doug — did you get a crack at one of the Pan Am lovelies?"

"I think I made a good impression on Natalie's roommate Caroline. Plan is to go to NYC with Max in November and double date."

"C'mon, guys — you know how much I love New York. Take me with you," Peter said. "What are the other two roommates like?"

Max said, "We have no idea. They weren't on the flight. You can get an idea from the Pan Am commercial, though. They have unbelievably high standards."

"Doug, you run the schedule," Peter said. "Just put all of us on the Rota trip at the end of November. I'll even volunteer to be the writer, to sweeten the pot."

The writer was the hardest job on any inspection. It involved planning the drill scenarios and reading them to the ship's

company. At the end of the inspection, the writer read the results and findings before the team left the sub. Returning to
Norfolk, the writer had less than a week to get the final report
in for typing.

Max said, "OK, deal. This assumes that my date at the end
of October goes well. If we get our proposal out there early, we
should be able to arrange our schedules to get together at the
end of November."

They clinked glasses and Peter said, "You never know what's
going to happen when we all get together on the beach."

Just then Pappy returned and the party resumed. Max got
Peter's attention, "See the cute girl with the summer tan? Very
friendly—why don't you give her a whirl?"

The piano started up with "I Wonder Who's Kissing Her
Now?" and everyone joined in.

Chapter 8

New York City—Upper East Side
September 16th, 1972

Natalie's party wrapped up around 2 a.m. and goodbyes lasted a little too long for her taste. Finally, only Natalie, Caroline, and Scott remained.

"I'm going to leave you two love birds alone—I need my beauty sleep," Caroline declared, and considerately made herself scarce.

Scott and Natalie went into the kitchen. Pinning Natalie up against the counter, he gave her a long, deep kiss. Scott Junior started to pay attention. "Want to go over to my place? There are four here tonight, and it will be a zoo in the morning. Promise to come back tomorrow and help clean up the mess."

Natalie needed a moment; the Manhattans had made her thinking sluggish. She was still jet lagged; no matter how many trips to the other side of the pond, it always took a day or two to adjust. Finally, she said, "Scott, I really want to, but I'm still beat from the trip. Let's not tonight. I don't travel again until Tuesday, so we'll have all weekend."

The silence of Scott's dejection was broken by Mia and Sabrina coming home, chatting loudly in their clipped British accents. "Oh, great—Frick and Frack are here," Scott muttered. "As always, perfect timing. Right on cue." Natalie giggled; she liked Mia and Sabrina well enough, but after a few drinks, they verged on brassy.

Mia came into the kitchen. "Oh—sorry; rotten timing on my

part. I just need a glass of water to pop a few aspirin before hopping into bed."

"I'm with you," Scott said, trying to be gracious. "If I don't drink two glasses of water and take something, I'll pay in the morning."

Scott and Natalie headed into the living room and sat on the couch. Natalie caressed the back of Scott's head and whispered into his ear, imitating Holly Golightly, "Darling, you'd better get going. It's pretty late, and we have the whole weekend ahead of us."

Scott gave her a hug and a brief kiss. "I know the sensible thing for me to do is go home and get a good night's sleep. I have to start updating my résumé."

They crossed to the front door, put their arms around each other, and shared a satisfying good night kiss. Turning quickly, Scott was gone.

Natalie thought of getting undressed, but she was just too tired. Caroline was sound asleep, and the other two were already settled in. Natalie kicked off her flats and got under the covers. She still had a warm, floaty feeling from the Manhattans. She put her head on the pillow and thought, *I hope Scott wasn't too disappointed.* She closed her eyes, and much to her surprise her thoughts drifted to Max. She wondered about his night down in Virginia. He really was something—not just different from Scott, but different from all the guys she'd dated. He had definitely sparked her interest. Maybe that's what caused this luxurious, comfortable feeling. With a smile on her lips, she drifted into a deep sleep.

By 11:00, everyone was up and moving. Caroline made a big pot of strong coffee. There were bagels left over from yesterday's breakfast—a little stale, but just fine toasted and spread with butter or cream cheese. As Natalie waited for the bagels and coffee to make a dent in her hangover, Scott called and asked if she could come over around 2:00. Then they would plan the rest of the weekend. He was in a good mood and not holding a grudge from the night before. The extra down time until 2:00 was welcome; she considered doing some shopping before going to Scott's. His apartment was located catty-corner across 77th on the west side of First, and at times just a little too convenient.

"Hey, Caroline—what's up for today?" asked Natalie.

"There's a new exhibit over at MoMA; I'll let you know how it is. If it's worth it, maybe you and Scott could visit on Sunday."

"Thanks for the reconnaissance. Scott isn't really excited about art, but I'll run it by him if I can advertise your stamp of approval."

Pretty soon all four were ready to face the day. It was Natalie's and Caroline's responsibility to clean up the wreckage from the party, and Mia and Sabrina pitched in to help accelerate the process. Natalie was on her second cup of coffee when she overheard Mia talking to Sabrina in the bedroom.

"I'm going to Bloomie's and exchange this swimsuit. I bought it for a trip to the Caribbean next month, and my tits just don't seem to fit right. I don't want to be flopping all about." Bloomingdale's bag in hand, she was out the door. Sabrina, who had agreed to do the food shopping, was right behind her.

After the two British girls had left, Natalie said, "Doesn't that seem a bit odd? Mia is so precise. I find it hard to believe that she wouldn't try on a swimsuit before buying it—and if she did try it on, wouldn't it be readily apparent it didn't cover her rather ample bosom?"

"Sometimes Mia is a bit of an enigma," Caroline offered. "Take that bit about the Navy guys. Who knows what's really going on?"

Natalie pondered this. "It might be that she is considering

settling down…and I can think of one reason why the size of her breasts might have changed unexpectedly. I wonder if she might be pregnant."

Caroline stared at her. "Oh, wow — you're right. That would be really hard for her…for all of us, really. And you know, although she seems outgoing, she's hard to get to know. If she was in trouble, she might not tell us."

"I might be imagining things, but I think I'll run after her and see if I can catch up. Maybe she'll want to talk. If not, I'll have a chance to do some shopping before all the fall stuff is picked over. Nothing to lose, right?" She grabbed her purse and walked to the door. "Have fun at MoMA, and let me know about the exhibit. I'll probably be over at Scott's by the time you get back."

"Happy shopping, Nat," called Caroline, as Natalie headed out the door.

Natalie had a plan. She walked along 77th toward the subway at Lexington Avenue. Just as she arrived, a 6 train on the Green Line came along.

Natalie knew the store like the back of her hand. It was a constant struggle to keep her shopping habit to $100 a month or less; she had excellent and sometimes expensive tastes. Pan Am flight attendants maintained a certain air of sophistication, and clothes were an important part of the package. She knew that at this time of year, there was only one department where stylish swimwear would be available, and she headed right for it. She approached the first sales clerk she saw.

"I wonder if you can help me out. I was supposed to meet my roommate here at one o'clock — I thought — but after checking my diary, I have the time wrong. Have you seen her? She's tall, short blonde hair, very pale skin."

"I've been here since noon and haven't seen anyone fitting that description. Let me check with Joan. She's been here since

10." Joan joined the group and verified that she had not seen anyone resembling Natalie's description.

"Thanks heaps. I guess we really got our signals crossed," Natalie said. "You were both a big help. That's why I love Bloomie's — everybody is always so helpful."

I know I heard Mia tell Sabrina that she was coming here right away to exchange the swimsuit. I hope she's okay, Natalie thought. *Well, there's not much I can do about it now; I'll look crazy if I try chasing her all over Bloomingdale's. Maybe I'll be able to tell whether she's OK next time I see her at the apartment.*

Natalie visited the new blouse boutique for a look. She had 20 minutes to kill before visiting Scott for fun and games. Reluctantly, she walked away from the tempting selection and left through the exit that put her right on the platform for the Lexington Avenue subway. During the trip to Scott's, she thought about the events of the past few days. A lot had happened, on many fronts. Before she knew it, she was opening the door to Scott's building and on the elevator up to the third floor.

Chapter 9

The four men reconvened in the stark basement room. During the intervening weeks, Mortin had received additional clarification and was now ready to define the nature of the problem and get input from the group. He wasted no time getting to the point.

"Number one on the list is to improve the effectiveness of submarine operations. How the hell can we increase our 'strategic arms' effectiveness if, in the oceans of the world, the Americans always know where we are, and we have no idea where they are? Admiral, you may be able to track the *Nautilus*, *Sea Wolf*, and *Triton*, but you know that is not good enough. The problem is that we have no idea where their operational FBMs are on patrol. They just roam freely, ready to shove sixteen Polaris missiles up Holy Mother Russia's ass."

The three referenced submarines were over ten years old and clearly among the noisiest in the US nuclear fleet.

He continued, "Four years ago, John Walker waltzed into the Soviet embassy and handed us information on a silver platter—information related to just about every aspect of US submarine operations. None of us did anything to recruit him; he just walked in, and all you had to do was manage him as an asset."

Mortin still couldn't fathom why John Walker, Jr., prior Chief Petty Officer on the *USS Simon Bolivar*, had gone to the Soviet Embassy in DC to offer his services as a spy after he had been transferred to CINCLANTFLT staff in Norfolk. Better just to be grateful and not question.

"Despite this gift from the gods, we are no closer to the Americans from an engineering standpoint than we were five years ago. We have confirmed how good they are and how easy it is for them to find us. We are getting better, but they are also getting better, at a faster rate. We'll never catch up. We lost the K-27 in 1968, the K-8 in 1970, and the K-19 just can't get their shit together and avoid running into American submarines."

All those in the room were well aware of the tragedies associated with the three submarines. The radiation exposure rates for the Soviet crews were dramatically higher than those of US submarines. The reason was clear — the Soviet desire for fast, deep-diving vessels compromised their safety design. This translated to nuclear accidents, sunken submarines, and the continued overexposure of submarine crews.

Mortin continued, "Yuri wants an answer as soon as possible with a broad plan of action. You have two weeks to gather additional information. Admiral, give us a quick assessment of the situation, and given the short turnaround, please start us off with a recommended plan of action."

As the naval operation expert in the room, the admiral was the obvious choice to start the discussion. However, Gorshov did not appreciate being put on the spot.

Gathering his thoughts, the admiral said, "Walker can provide information derived from communication sources. Clearly, design documents and associated criteria are not included. His information is primarily in operations and communications, not engineering." This was an attempt to shift the initial responsibility to Mortin's deputy for covert operations. Temporarily, it worked.

"So, Gorsky—what do you think?" Mortin asked his deputy.

"Well, information of the type we need can be obtained through the use of human intelligence. You can't do an audio recording of an engineering diagram." Gorsky redirected the opening salvo, "So, Admiral, what sort of things do you require?" This was a tactical error, as the admiral's list was long and complicated.

"Operationally, the three biggest problems we face are reducing the sound signature of our submarines, increasing the margin of reactor safety, and reducing the radiation exposure to our crews. This information would normally be available from shipyards where the subs are built, from prototype reactors, and from operational submarines."

Gorsky said in jest, "So the solution is fairly simple: We just put some of our guys on the crews of operating American submarines."

Mortin glared at him, failing to appreciate the joke. "No. The pipeline to train a nuclear operator is more than a year. I don't think Yuri wants to wait that long. Try this: first, determine what groups make periodic visits to operational subs; next, find out whether we have illegals or operatives near shipyards, submarine bases, and nuclear prototype installations. With that information, we can determine how to use existing KGB operatives to recruit naval or civilian personnel in target groups. Priority would be personnel with vulnerabilities— those who could easily be turned to work for us." He looked at Gorksy and the admiral. "Any ideas how to identify the target groups?"

The admiral went first. "Walker served on two submarines before he turned—the *Jackson* and the *Bolivar*. We should ask for a summary of outside visitors to operational submarines, and their parent activities. He knows nothing about shipyards and prototypes; he was a radio operator. Move those activities to tier two."

Finally, Gorsky chimed in with something useful. "We'll make a list of all agents and illegals in close proximity to the parent activities. Based on the location of our resources, we'll find the best match between our agents and activities that periodically visit the subs. Walker should be able to provide a list of parent activities. I'll get Walker's handler to have him identify the visiting groups."

Mortin asked Kerechenko, "Vladimir, based on your experience — with the exception of your political hit teams, define the groups likely to conduct such visits to our submarines."

Kerechenko answered, "For the most part, these would be safety inspections for reactor operations and nuclear weapons handling, and sometimes teams to install special communications equipment. I would assume something similar exists with the Americans. Based on the time Walker served on submarines, no problem for him to provide an idea of the types of visiting personnel."

The admiral's eyes lit up. "I can see where we are going with this. What do sailors like best? Booze and sex. I'd put our best sexually trained agents and illegals at the top of your list."

This was a clear reference to graduates of the Soviet-run schools that recruited and trained operatives, mostly women, at their School for Scandal. These operatives existed among both active KGB agents and illegals, and used their acquired sexual skills to compromise and recruit future spies. Illegals were individuals under deep cover, trained in the USSR and then placed in parent countries, living normal lives until directed to surface and perform specialized espionage activities.

Mortin quickly closed. "Many good ideas now on the table –you have two weeks to sort out the best information available."

October 5ᵗʰ, 1972
KGB Headquarters, Moscow

Mortin opened the meeting with a subtle attack on Gorsky. "Well, Nikolai, I understand that Walker came into the Soviet embassy in DC on another matter a few days ago and that his handlers were able to carve out a few minutes to help you solve your dilemma."

Gorsky was more than eager to report on the Walker meeting. "In a very short period of time, Walker provided a wealth of information regarding the sources we require. Of the outside teams visiting operational submarines, only Nuclear Propulsion Examining Board — NPEB — is of any value. The weapons and communications teams focus on the forward end of the ship and rarely go aft of the reactor compartment. Even if we could turn one of them, it would be extremely suspicious if they were found in the engineering spaces."

"On the other hand, NPEB has access to all engineering spaces and every piece of documentation available on the operating units. In fact, they design the drills run during operational examinations. If we were able to turn an asset on one of the teams, he could direct certain drills or simulated casualties to be imposed during the examinations, and collect useful information during the response to the drill situations."

The admiral asked, "How many of these teams are there, and where are they located?"

Gorsky answered, "Walker is most familiar with the teams that work out of Norfolk, since they are located on the CINCLANT compound where he was working when he came to us. These teams conduct operational examinations of the FBMs in Charleston, Rota, and Holy Loch, as well as the fast attacks that are located in Norfolk, Charleston, and New London. Similar teams operate out of Pearl Harbor.

Mortin asked, "How can we hope to turn one of those guys? Clearly, they are well placed on their career paths and are probably loyal and dedicated officers, not strapped for cash or susceptible to ideology differences. It would be extremely difficult, if not impossible, to turn one of them."

Gorsky continued, "A strong possibility is the two American flag airlines that carry the teams to Europe and Guam to conduct the exams—Pan Am and TWA. Pan Am goes to London or Prestwick, and Guam. TWA goes to Madrid."

The admiral asked, "What good is the airline connection?"

Gorsky had all the answers. "We have several flight attendants in our employ at both airlines, used primarily as couriers. After recruitment, they attend the School for Scandal and are trained in the sexual arts. We are constantly on the alert for an opportunity to use them to bait a honey trap."

Mortin had what he needed. "Nikolai, reach out to the flight attendant network. It appears that a honey trap would work best. As with Walker, one asset can gather a hell of a lot of information. We meet again in two weeks."

Chapter 10

New York City—Upper East Side
October 30th, 1972

Max exited the Pan Am terminal and caught the Carey bus to the East Side Airlines terminal. A short taxi ride later and he was ringing the bell at 8L. The excitement of their first meeting was alive and well; anticipation for the coming visit was sky-high for both Max and Natalie.

Max felt a twinge of disappointment when Mia answered the door. Dressed in her uniform, she was ready to leave for JFK. "You must be Max," she purred. "I've heard a lot about you."

Natalie quickly appeared from the bedroom. "Glad you got here safely—any problems?" she said.

"Nope, your directions were perfect." He smiled at Mia. "Is this another of your lovely roommates?"

Natalie introduced them. "I'm off to London and points east from there," Mia announced.

Max looked her over—she nearly matched him in height, about 5'8". She would be perfect for Peter, who was 6'2". She was his type, too—voluptuous, blonde, a little racy.

"I don't mean to seem forward, but—one of the guys I work with is interested in meeting a Pan Am flight attendant," Max said to Mia. "If I bring him with me next time I swing through town, would you be interested? He's tall, good-looking, and knows how to have a good time."

"That sounds brilliant," said Mia. "Natalie and Caroline have quite convinced me that Navy men are worth meeting. Do keep me in mind when you're making plans." She gathered her things, and pulling her bags behind her was out the door.

The door had barely closed when Max gave Natalie a big hug, then stepped back and said, "Hi there! Can we rewind the tape? It was a little weird, with Mia here—I didn't feel right about saying hello the way I wanted to."

Natalie laughed. "I thought she'd be long gone. She was dragging her feet so she could meet you—she'd mentioned wanting to try a Navy guy of her own, after hearing about you. But enough about Mia—I have a surprise for you. My father owns a restaurant down at 45th and Third. That's where we're going for lunch, unless you have a better idea."

Max said, "Any ideas I had pale in comparison. Let me dump my luggage somewhere and make a head call, then I'll be ready to go."

Natalie showed him to the bathroom and continued to the bedroom to grab her purse. A quick look in the mirror showed her lipstick needed a touch-up. Taking one from the bureau, she noticed the stick was short, and the shade was all wrong—and the case looked odd. She realized she had Mia's lipstick, not hers. Touch-up completed, she went into the living room to re-trieve Max.

"How do we get there?" he asked.

"Well, we have a choice between fast and lazy. We could taxi and sit in traffic, or walk over to the Lexington subway. I'd vote for that—it's a short walk back to 45th from the 42nd street station. And it's a beautiful day." She gave Max her charming smile. "Fall is my favorite season."

"It's quickly becoming my favorite, too. Walking it is," Max said.

Natalie pointed out her favorite funky boutiques as they strolled along. Max couldn't resist buying an artsy pin that caught her eye—an Ann Klein knockoff, but affordable and striking. He said, "Something to remind you of our day in New York."

Natalie accepted, a little hesitant. Then she remembered *Casablanca* and replied, "We'll always have New York."

When they arrived at Pietro's, it was obvious that she was the boss's daughter, and well liked. As soon as they were seated Natalie said, "How about a tour? Lunch service is almost over; we won't be in the way."

"I'd be thrilled. I like to experiment in the kitchen; I'd love to see how the pros do it."

There was a flurry of activity in the kitchen—focused on pounding veal for the evening's entrées. Pietro's opened in 1932 and featured northern Italian cuisine with abundant options for steaks, chops, and the like. It had a "clubby" atmosphere, and according to Natalie, the clientele was a cross-section of New York's elite: journalists, advertising executives, business magnates, and entertainers.

Returning to their table, Natalie talked about growing up in an Italian family. She learned the language at an early age, and then majored in French at a small Catholic women's college in Purchase, New York. Her father, Nat, had only three years of formal education and came to the US when he was thirteen years old. He was determined that his only child would be well educated. Born on Christmas Day, 1899 he was now seventy-two. According to Natalie, he still worked long hours every day to ensure the "back of the house" ran as it should. When Pietro's opened, he split duties with his brother Pete (Pietro), for whom the restaurant was named. Uncle Pete had died a few years earlier. Much to his disappointment, Nat was not in the house that particular afternoon.

Max and Natalie had a lot in common. Max's grandfather was

a German immigrant who first owned a butcher shop and later was employed full time as a butcher in an upscale Philadelphia restaurant. Max had gone to an all-boys school, so he and Natalie shared many funny stories about "avoiding the near occasions of sin" and confessing in the box on Saturday afternoons. Max offered one of his favorite Catholic jokes: "It's OK to kiss the nuns, as long as you don't get into the habit."

It was as if they had known each other for years. The conversation was relaxed, with never an awkward pause. One thought or story led to another. Three hours flew by. At Natalie's suggestion, they ordered Dover sole and easily put away a bottle of Soave Bolla. Max asked Natalie to order the wine; his knowledge of Italian whites was pretty limited.

Max asked why she chose Pan Am over TWA. She laughed and said, "That's quite a story. Bottom line, I guess I wasn't what TWA was looking for. The interview was from hell. This older blonde woman, hair in a chignon, no smile, had me seated in front of her in a Manhattan hotel suite. She stared right at me and asked, 'Does your face always look like that?' I kid you not. I was floored. All I could think of was that I might have a blemish or two. I stared right back and said, 'Actually, it looks pretty good right now.' She had me hold my hands out in front of me, palms down, and walk back and forth in front of her. I don't think she gave a hoot about my personality or intelligence. It was a really stupid interview and I knew I wasn't going to get a job offer."

"I wonder what they could possibly have been looking for," Max asked. "In my opinion, there's no comparison between Pan Am and TWA when it comes to personnel and level of service — and believe me, I am a qualified critic. We fly to Europe three times a month, and alternate between the two."

After sharing a cannoli with a cup of cappuccino each, Max

said, "The day is off to a great start. I have three ideas for our next stop: MoMA, the Met, or a movie."

Little did he know that the Museum of Modern Art was one of Natalie's favorite places. Although their lunch was on the house, Max left a generous tip, which pleased her. Then they were off to see what MoMA had to offer. They shared a particular fondness for Picasso, and spent a lot of time viewing the pieces in the permanent collection, both sculptures and paintings. From there it was on to the postmodern artists and an animated discussion of the influence they perceived Picasso had on Matisse. The visit finished with a special exhibit that featured works of French Impressionists, from Monet to Manet.

Next stop, the nearby Four Seasons for a glass of wine and more nonstop conversation. The setting was spectacular, with a large square bar surrounded by small tables, and a large, lighted icicle-like fixture that hung above the center of the bar. As they sipped their wine, each thought: *This one is a keeper.* Comfortable and happy, it was as if they were a couple crazy in love, enjoying a day out on the town. They left hand in hand to hail a taxi for the trip uptown.

As they hopped out of the cab, Natalie wondered if Scott might see them together from his all-too-convenient vantage point across the street. Then she shrugged to herself; she and Scott were not engaged, and if he wanted an exclusive relationship with her, he would have to ask for it. As soon as she and Max got to the apartment, Max took her hands in his and kissed her lightly on the lips.

"I've wanted to do that all afternoon," he said. "You are something very special. Thank you for making this a memorable day."

She put her arms around him, gave him a big hug, and said simply, "Thank you."

Max looked at his watch. "I've got about an hour until I have to head to the bus terminal." Natalie put some Frank Sinatra on the cassette player and asked if Max wanted a glass of wine. "I never refuse a drink from a pretty lady," he said.

Natalie took an open bottle of white from the fridge, poured two generous glasses, and set them on the coffee table. Max accepted the unspoken invitation and sat down in the corner of the couch. She settled close to him and put her head on his shoulder. He put his arm around her, and she snuggled in. Frank was in the middle of a Cole Porter favorite, "You're So Easy to Love."

Max said, "How about some advance planning? I've looked at my November schedule, and it looks like on the 30th I'll be coming back from Spain with Doug. He and I could get a cheap hotel room somewhere close. That way, we could go out clubbing on the 30th and then hop on back to Norfolk sometime on the 1st. He'd like to see Caroline again, if you think that would work. Maybe you can check her schedule, and if it's OK he'll extend a formal invite. Our friend Peter wants to come along... Mia would be a great fit for him."

"Sounds like a plan. Just give me a call when you're back in Norfolk, and we'll confirm," Natalie said. Max drew her close and gave her a long, probing kiss. Both started to feel that little tingle, though it was far too early for anything more than kissing. But one kiss followed another, and Frank was now on to "Fairy Tales Can Come True."

Max brought them back to reality. "I'd better get going—I'm already booked on the last flight for tonight." He gathered his luggage, and paused at the door for one more embrace and a deep kiss.

Natalie looked into his eyes and said, "Give me a call to let me know you got home safely."

Max replied, "You got it," and was out the door.

Chapter 11

Rota, Spain – New York City
November 30th, 1972

It was one month to the day since Max and Natalie had seen each other. They talked on the phone and did some focused planning at both ends to ensure the coming evening would be a success. Max thought of Natalie often during the intervening month; Natalie came to realize Max was completely unlike Scott and different from the other men she had dated.

The trip from Rota to JFK was the trip from hell. First, there was a 90-minute van ride over bumpy roads to Seville, an Iberia flight to Madrid, and finally the 7-hour flight back to the States. During the van ride, Max, Doug, and Peter talked about the evening ahead.

Doug laid out the strategy. "Peter, one goal is to give Max some alone time with Natalie. They'll have dinner together while we get appetizers and drinks at the disco; then join us later for dancing and a night of fun—at a table for six."

Max said, "We're going to an intimate French bistro on 86th. I'll tell you guys all about it in case you ever get back here with romance in the air."

Peter chimed in, "First things first. What do these girls look like?"

"No worries—they all far exceed Pan Am minimum standards. Natalie and Caroline are about 5'6" with dark-brown hair. Caroline is a real head-turner, and Natalie has that girl-next-door look. Both are of Italian descent and speak the language fluently. Mia is at the opposite end of the spectrum — tall, blonde hair, skin like porcelain. Hey Peter, thanks for volunteering to be the writer on this trip. I appreciate there's no pressure for me to get right back to Norfolk."

"Tell me more about Mia," Peter said.

Max answered, "I've met her only once. She had a firm handshake and was keen on our night on the town. Natalie mentioned that she and their other roommate Sabrina usually date the playboy types — so you'd better uphold the finest standards of the submarine service."

"No problem there," Peter said. "I can party with the best of them."

Before they knew it, the three men were getting out of the taxi at 85th and First at a small, nondescript hotel. The rooms were small and affordable, and each had his own. Peter insisted on it, "Just in case I get things lined up for the big score," as he put it.

After a quick shave and shower, they met in the small lobby. Max said, "The girls want us at their place right away for drinks and snacks. After the disco, Doug and I have agreed that he and you, Peter, will not go back directly to the apartment, so that Natalie and I can have some time alone. You can take Caroline and Sabrina to PJ Clarke's on Third for a night cap — or maybe take a carriage ride in Central Park. They'll have blankets… might be an opportunity to get up close and personal. Please be on your own for at least an hour and a half. Guys, make sure you knock loudly when you drop off your date."

Doug said, "We can't go empty-handed. During the taxi ride, we passed a liquor store on First. Let's stop there, pick up some wine, and speed walk down to their building."

Sparing no expense, they made three selections: a chilled Taittinger Brut champagne, a Chablis Gran Cru from Burgundy, and finally a St. Émilion from Bordeaux. A very excited Max and his little crew soon found themselves at the door of Apartment 8L.

Natalie opened the door, and Max was met by the wonderful scent of "Y" by Yves St. Laurent, and the best Pan Am smile in the whole world. The party had already started. Caroline and Mia were on the couch with glasses of white wine and a wonderful cheese board on the coffee table. Caroline was as Max remembered her—a real head-turner, indeed. Mia was another matter. Absent the Evan Picone tailored powder-blue uniform, she had on a low-cut, scoop-neck dress that really meant business. Mother Nature had been kind to Mia in the bosom department. Max glanced at Peter; it looked like his eyes had just popped out of his head.

Natalie covered gracefully and said, "I assume you are Peter? Please say hello to Mia."

Mia offered her hand, while Max and Doug gave their dates an affectionate hug. Natalie thought, *Boy, that feels good. It's been a while.*

"What have we here?" Caroline asked, nodding toward the brown bags set on the coffee table.

Each of the guys identified what he had brought, and when the Taittinger was announced, Natalie said, "Oh, I think we need to get right into that—we have some stemmed sherbets in the kitchen."

Max replied, "I'll meet you in the kitchen. I'll be happy to pop and pour. I won't let you enjoy a busman's holiday tonight."

Natalie lined up the sherbets on the counter, and Max went to work. He deftly removed the foil and cage and carefully eased out the cork without spilling a drop.

"Bravo!" exclaimed Natalie. "Most guys would have the cork in the other room and part of the bottle all over the floor. That just wouldn't do, in the world of Pan Am inflight service."

They chuckled while Max filled the sherbets and Natalie delivered them to the living room. Cocktail hour went well. The champagne disappeared quickly, and they made a significant dent in the Chablis. All three couples seemed to be enjoying each other's company — the conversation was light and humorous, and everyone had a warm feeling from the high-end French offerings.

Suddenly, Natalie looked at her watch and said to Max, "We've got to get going; we have a dinner reservation in fifteen minutes."

Caroline said, "You guys just leave, and we'll take care of all this stuff. There is still a little white to finish off, God forbid it should go to waste."

While Max and Natalie were putting on their coats, Peter asked, "What's next on the agenda?"

Caroline said, "We're going to head over to Hippopotamus at 62nd and First to grab some appetizers and commandeer a table for six. The disco gets going around nine, and we're all up for some serious dancing."

Max and Natalie left, and the others lingered to finish the opened wine and cheese board. Doug and Peter gave each other a quick "thumbs up" while the ladies were gathering their purses and coats from the bedroom.

After a pleasant hand-in-hand walk, Max and Natalie arrived at Café du Soir, an intimate French bistro. Since Natalie was fluent, ordering was a breeze. They chose a bottle of Sancerre and shared a plate of escargots, taking turns picking the garlic-laden morsels out of their shells, mopping up the pungent butter sauce with crusty bread.

Natalie remarked, "Thank goodness we are both having a heavy dose of garlic — no chance of offense on either side."

Each ordered cassoulet; his with rabbit, hers with chicken.

For dessert they shared a tarte tatin cut with cups of strong espresso. Max had never been to Paris; he hoped that this evening wouldn't be as close as he ever got.

"Tell me about Hippopotamus," said Max. "Why did you choose it?"

"Well, you said that you love to dance, and really wanted to go to a hip club in the city. Hippopotamus is as good as it gets. If you want to see and be seen, that's the place." Natalie chose not to mention that she also loved to dance…and Scott didn't.

"We'd better get moving," Max said. "I can't wait to get out on that dance floor."

He had been holding her hand on and off during dinner—it felt good to softly stroke the back of her hand and gaze into her eyes, encouraged by Edith Piaf's poignant voice wafting from the stereo. This was only their second date, yet it felt as if they had known each other for years. Max felt a pang of regret as he gallantly pulled Natalie's chair out for her and took her coat from the maître d'. If only he had been able to wait until she came into his life—if only he were not in the messy throes of a failed marriage. There was no point in dwelling on that. Their friends were waiting for them, and Natalie, her eyes shining, was clearly ready to go.

Chapter 12

Natalie sat close to Max in the taxi and leaned her head on his shoulder. The bottle of Sancerre was history; warmth and affection were running high.

"You'll love Hippopotamus," Natalie said. "They play a wide variety of music, wonderful for dancing."

Max said, "You are New York City born and bred; if you don't know the best places to dance, who does?" Max thought a night of dancing was the best kind of date. Mixing fast and slow numbers, you got a chance to do a little bit of everything. Interaction during slow dances gave a clear indication of how the evening was going.

When Natalie and Max walked in, the party was well underway. Doug and Peter had procured a table close to the dance floor so there would be no need to fight the crowd. Being a Thursday, the clientele was increasing but still manageable

When they sat down, Doug asked, "How was the restaurant? What did you guys have?"

Don Mclean's "American Pie" started up. "Sorry, buddy," Max said. "It will have to wait—that's a great song for dancing. Come on, Natalie. Let's hit the floor."

Natalie was impressed; Max was an above-average dancer with lots of enthusiasm. He was OK at "no touch" dancing, but when they did a modified '50s jitterbug, he really shone. Growing up in Philadelphia, Bill Haley and the Comets had played at his high school. Max realized that if you couldn't dance to rock-and-roll in the '50s, you were viewed as a dud by the opposite sex. Who would ever invite you to a dance at a girls' school, if you couldn't dance? It was much the same with Natalie, having grown up in the Bronx. Being a good and willing dance partner at high school hops was the key to an active social life.

The fast numbers warmed them up, and there was no thought of sitting down when Roberta Flack started with "The First Time Ever I Saw Your Face." It was noisy and crowded, but Max managed to make himself heard over the din.

"When I walked onto that plane and saw you, I thought, *I'll bet that lady is really something special.* I had my sights set on you even before the plane took off. I'm glad you didn't shoot me down."

Natalie thought, *It wasn't quite like that for me. He is growing on me, though. For him, it might have been love at first sight, if you believe in that sort of thing.*

They decided to stay on the floor for "I Can See Clearly Now," and certainly the music was moving the night in the right direction. At the end of the song, all six were on the dance floor; when it was over, everyone returned to the table.

Right on cue, the waitress arrived. The guys all ordered Scotch and soda. The girls finished off a bottle of California white and ordered another. Peter was clearly the most at ease, probably one or two drinks up on Doug, and was the life of the party. Mia seemed hooked. He told a few colorful Navy jokes, yielding laughs from everyone. Natalie and Max just listened; they were intent on dancing most of the time.

About midnight, Natalie realized she hadn't enjoyed herself this much in a long time. A night of dancing at a New York club was as good as it got, and Max was proving to be the perfect companion. The music turned to "Precious and Few." Max knew the song, but was not really familiar with the lyrics. One phrase caught his attention: "Precious and few are the moments we two can share." *That pretty well sums it up,* Max thought.

As the song ended, Natalie suggested they return to the apartment. Back at the table, Max told the group, "We're heading out—it's pushing one o'clock."

Doug took his cue. "You two go ahead. Peter and I will settle up when we're ready to leave."

Without fanfare, Max and Natalie were out the door, into a taxi, and on their way to 8L. When they got to the apartment, Max embraced Natalie and gave her a long, deep kiss. He held her for a long time, feeling her lean back against his arm, her body light and supple. Finally, he said, "That was some evening, and it's not over yet. Buy a sailor a drink?"

"What would you like?"

"You know, I am dying for a Manhattan. I would have ordered one, but I was afraid they'd screw it up."

Natalie countered, "We've both had a lot to drink. How about some coffee, and we save the Manhattans for next time?"

He nodded, and Natalie brought coffee into the living room. She put her favorite Frank album on the turntable—"September of My Years."

Max asked, "Why in the world aren't you engaged or married? Either you're single by choice, or someone here in New York is really missing the boat."

Natalie wasn't sure where Max was going, but she dove right in. "I've had a serious boyfriend for four years. If he asked me to marry him, I would say yes. However, he's currently unemployed, and is considering entering graduate school in January. I think he feels a need to be established before we get married, so for now I guess we'll wait."

Max considered this. "You might think about laying down the law and forcing a decision. It would be a tragedy to waste four years of your life hoping for something that might not even happen, and then end up starting from square one." Max was sincere; this wonderful woman deserved a commitment. He could not imagine what her boyfriend was thinking.

"That's probably good advice. However, I'm an Aries, and we're not good at taking advice," Natalie said lightly. "Let's drop the subject. This is our night, and I don't want to spoil it."

Natalie put her arms around Max's neck. She gave him a long kiss, pressing her entire body against him. Max went limp for a moment, but finally returned the kiss and embraced her long and hard. He wanted to touch her as a lover would, but resisted the urge. Natalie's head was spinning—she felt a shock, an excitement she hadn't felt in a long time. Frank was crooning "Hello Young Lovers" in the background. What could be more appropriate—unless it was "Once Upon a Time," which came on two songs later. Max and Natalie kissed and cuddled without speaking.

Max broke the silence. "I'd better get going. Can we have breakfast tomorrow before I leave?"

Without hesitation, Natalie said, "OK, call me about 9:30. That should be enough sleep; let's grab something out on First."

Natalie helped Max with his coat, and looked deep into his eyes, "Thank you for an absolutely perfect evening."

One more kiss and Max was out the door. Natalie leaned against the door and closed her eyes. Max was so different from any man she had ever known. What did that mean to her, and her relationship with Scott?

Walking to the elevator, Max wondered about the long-term boyfriend. Natalie was affectionate with him, and it was clear she was still considering her options. However, Max couldn't offer a relationship with real potential. He needed to proceed carefully and not lead her on, even accidentally. The reality was he enjoyed her company immensely and was willing to provide an added dimension to her life, for as long as she would allow.

Chapter 13

New York City—Upper East Side
November 30th-December 1st, 1972

Leaving Hippopotamus, Doug asked Caroline, "What's the next stop on the Big Apple Midnight Tour?"

Triple dates were fine, but Caroline clearly understood that Natalie wanted "alone time" with Max. Doug was an excellent conversationalist; Caroline didn't mind spending time with him. And as a Navy submarine officer, Doug was a unique experience.

They walked to PJ Clarke's on 63rd Street where there was still a late-night crowd. Fortunately, Doug found two seats at the bar. Caroline ordered a Kahlua and coffee; Doug ordered brandy.

She looked at Doug and said, "I've been doing most of the talking tonight. Tell me a little bit about you and the Navy."

"I'm just one of a whole bunch of Navy Nukes trying to keep the world safe for democracy."

"And how do you do that?"

"Well, it all goes to the current duty station. Right now, what we're doing is important but not very exciting. We inspect operational nuclear submarines to make sure they're safe. The subs we inspect are the ones that are out on the front line. There are two types: FBMs—Fleet Ballistic Missiles, or Boomers, as they're called—and fast attacks."

"What's the difference?" asked Caroline.

"The Boomers carry sixteen Polaris missiles, and the claim is that from the middle of the Atlantic, the weapons system can land a warhead at home plate in Yankee Stadium. The Boomers just roam around the ocean and stay away from the Russians. The fast attacks are more versatile. I can't provide specifics; just use your imagination."

Doug told Caroline about growing up in California and going to the Naval Academy. His next assignment would be as an executive officer — or XO — in about nine months.

Shifting gears, Caroline said, "Max seems to be quite taken with Natalie. They were having a terrific time on the dance floor."

Doug said, "Well, Max really does like to dance. Throw a pretty, intelligent girl into the mix, and he's in heaven. He talked about her a lot over the past few weeks."

Caroline did not offer anything regarding Natalie's feelings for Max and was relieved that Doug didn't ask. It was well after 1:00 now, and Caroline asked, "Should we think about getting home?"

Doug said, "I'm no party pooper, but in less than a week I've been to Europe and back and at sea for three days. I'm pretty beat, so — let's head back."

When they arrived at the apartment, Doug closed the door and said, "Thanks for a wonderful evening. How about a repeat performance?"

Caroline answered, "Well, right now our schedules are crazy, and the holidays are coming. Maybe we can arrange something in the New Year." She came close to Doug, put her arms around his waist, and invited a good-night kiss.

Doug complied and said, "Perfect ending to a great night."

Caroline opened the door and blew Doug another kiss as he went on his way. Natalie appeared in living room and said, "Looks like you had a nice evening."

"I did," Caroline said. "How about you?"

"The best in a very long time," said Natalie. Tired and happy, they crawled into their bottom bunks.

Mia and Peter decided a carriage ride in Central Park would be a terrific idea, despite the chill in the air. Mia assured Peter that the blankets would be more than adequate—and she would do her best to make the ride comfy-cozy. Peter had another Scotch before leaving the disco and was feeling the effects of a night of serious drinking. They were both in a silly mood, giggling like high school kids at each other's jokes.

Peter was a farm boy from Wisconsin who received his commission through the NROTC program at the University of Wisconsin. As one of the top engineering graduates, he was actively recruited by Admiral Rickover's program. Leaning back in the carriage, the scent of the horse brought back memories of his grandfather's farm. He thought it odd that such memories would surface in New York City.

Mia was busy arranging the blanket to keep out the cold. Suddenly, Peter realized that Mia had covered them to conceal her busy hands underneath the blanket. He grinned, unbuttoned Mia's coat, and put his hand down the front of her low-cut dress. He had wanted to do that all night; several times he had left the dance floor fully aroused after she pressed her luscious body against him. Mia turned to him, gave him a deep kiss, and let out little moaning sounds.

Things were heating up, and Peter said, "Hey, slow down. How about we go back to my room and do this thing right?"

"That's the best idea you've had all night. Aren't you quite the cheeky monkey?" Mia teased. She stopped what she was doing, just in time. They relaxed a little while Mia nibbled on his earlobe and tickled his ear with the tip of her tongue. Peter let her heavy breast fall out of his hand, and moved to slide his fingers between her legs. Mia moaned, and it was obvious she was ready for the next act in their little drama.

When the carriage ride ended, they hopped into a waiting taxi at the south end of Central Park, and soon found themselves in Peter's room at the hotel. The door was barely closed before clothes started coming off. Neither said a word. Mia obviously spent a lot of time shopping at those little boutiques in Paris — her lingerie was exquisite, including her black silk underwire bra trimmed with delicate lace. He told her not to take it off; it really turned him on.

All in one smooth motion, Peter was flat on his back, and Mia was on top of him. She was confident and in control. Before he knew it he was inside her, and she had a firm hold on his hips. She began to move against him; a few moments of delirious excitement later Peter exploded with pleasure. They lay together in each other's arms for a long time. Finally, Mia said, "How about a night cap? I have some Hennessy mini-bottles in my purse. I'll get some glasses; let's toast a wonderful evening."

Peter clinked glasses with her and swallowed his drink. Ten minutes later, he felt an irresistible urge to sleep. His head fell onto his pillow, and he was deeply unconscious. Mia went right to work. She found his carry-on in the small closet and rifled through his documents. She took all the documents into the bathroom and removed her Minox camera from her purse. She locked the door and laid the documents on the toilet seat one by one. She worked slowly and efficiently. Having no idea what was important and what was not, she photographed everything Peter had in his bag. It took her nearly an hour.

Back in the room, Peter hadn't moved a muscle. She carefully replaced the documents and returned his carry-on to the closet. She took a small card out of her purse and wrote: "Peter, darling. Call me. Love, Mia." She propped it against the lamp on the night table, gave him a little kiss on the lips and whispered, "Sleep well, sweets."

When she returned to 8L, Natalie and Caroline were already sound asleep. Hiding the Minox inside her pillowcase, she joined her roommates in the Land of Nod.

Chapter 14

New York City—Upper East Side
December 1st, 1972

Natalie and Caroline were on their first cup of coffee when the phone rang.

"I wonder who it could be at this hour, after a night out on the town?" said Caroline, teasing Natalie.

"Right on schedule with Navy precision—I wouldn't have expected anything less," replied Natalie, "Miss Golightly's residence; Holly speaking."

"Would Holly be free for breakfast?" asked Max, not missing a beat. "Let's forget Tiffany's, maybe some cheap place down on First?"

"Oh, darling, how divine, how soon can you get here?"

Back to reality, Max said, "As long as it takes me to walk down from 86th—I'd expect fifteen minutes. Is it OK if I drop my luggage there? Our flight isn't until two o'clock, but I want to leave plenty of time to get to JFK."

"It's a date," said Natalie. "There's a spot a few blocks away on 75th that has reasonable food; the morning rush will be over when we get there."

Natalie greeted Max with a peck on the cheek. "Dress warmly," said Max. "There's a cool breeze blowing off the East River." He dropped his luggage and helped Natalie on with her coat.

Mia appeared in her bathrobe, yawning and stretching. "Hey,

mates — thanks for making coffee. I really need it. God knows how long it will take me to get back to the land of the living."

"Well, at least you don't have anything pressing today," Natalie said with a smile.

"I wanted to hop the tube down to Bloomie's," Mia said. "Shopping is always pressing!"

"In case you're gone when we get back — it was great to see you again, Mia," said Max. "I think we all had a terrific time last night."

"I agree," she replied. In a flash, she had crossed the room and was giving Max a goodbye hug that lingered too long. Natalie was not amused.

"Tell Peter I had a smashing time last night," she said.

"Likewise," said Caroline. "Give my regards to Doug. It was such a great night for everyone."

As Max and Natalie walked to breakfast, Peter and Doug entered a coffee shop on 85th Street. Peter had a mild but nagging headache, and his depth perception was off — he reached past his cup twice before he managed to pick it up.

"How did you enjoy Mia?" asked Doug.

"She was fantastic — no better word for it. I couldn't have asked for a more perfect evening. Only problem was that after the big score, I must have passed out after we shared a night cap. I really missed sharing post-coital bliss. However, she left this on the nightstand."

Peter gave Doug Mia's note. "Well, that's pretty encouraging," Doug said.

With a wicked smile, Peter said, "I guess I made a pretty good impression. Future prospects look good."

"Are you going to call her before we leave?"

"I don't want to appear too anxious. I think I'll call her shortly after we get back. That would show strong interest without seeming desperate."

Doug nodded. "I think you got it. She gave you pretty strong encouragement. My situation is just about the opposite. I'm not sure how Caroline feels about another date. She suggested pushing things off until after the first of the year. I might be over-analyzing, though. There could be good reasons for her reluctance to commit: the coming holidays, our crazy travel schedules—maybe even a boyfriend in NYC."

"Don't read too much into it. Just go with the flow," said Peter.

"Easy for you to say; the flow is always in your direction. However, I'll give it a shot and try to set up something for January."

They ordered a hearty breakfast, accompanied by many cups of much-needed coffee. Their plan was to have a leisurely morning and get to the National lounge in plenty of time to catch the 2:00 flight. Max was on his own and would meet them at JFK.

Max and Natalie ordered eggs Benedict, home fries, and plenty of coffee. Max said, "I'm glad you suggested coffee rather than Manhattans last night. I think we would have paid for it this morning!"

"Sometimes discretion is the better part of valor. Hopefully there will be an opportunity to enjoy a Manhattan in the future—or maybe not. Only time will tell. Speaking of the future, what does the Navy hold in store for you?"

"I've been lucky so far in my career. The next step would normally be back to sea as the navigator on a Boomer or a fast attack. However, I think I might apply for the EDO program …that means Engineering Duty Only. One candidate is chosen every year and—if it's me—it would mean minimal sea duty for the rest of my time in the Navy, and better still, a trip to MIT for a degree in marine engineering." Max smiled and asked, "And what about you? What does your future hold?"

Chapter 15

New York City—Upper East Side
December 1st, 1972

"**M**y future is less uncertain," Natalie answered. "I'll keep on as a flight attendant for as long as I can. It's really the best job in the world—why would anyone want to stop doing it? I get to live in New York, and the rest of the world is my playground. The pay and benefits are pretty good."

"Can you keep flying if you get married? I know the initial requirement is that you have to be single."

"You can stay on; they have a decent policy for maternity leave. Pan Am does value its experienced flight attendants. As I mentioned last night I want to get married, sooner rather than later. The problem is that there's a lot of uncertainty with Scott, my boyfriend. He's unemployed at the moment and I really don't understand why he decided to give up a really terrific job at Smith Barney.

"He's a smart guy from a good family and has a lot going for him. His undergraduate degree is from Princeton with an American history major. A girl could do a lot worse than Scott. I know he wants to get his MBA, but so far he hasn't even finished the application. He has enough money saved to live comfortably now, but it won't last forever. If he does enter graduate school in time for the January semester, it will still be two years until he graduates. Knowing Scott, he wouldn't want to get married before completing his MBA."

Natalie stopped abruptly, aware that she had answered in

much greater detail than she had intended. Max gave her a sympathetic smile. "How do you feel about waiting for Scott?" he asked.

She sighed. "I need to think about it. The good news is that I'm happy and secure in my job with Pan Am—no uncertainty there. The rest of it will have to be worked out pretty soon, though."

Max took her hand. "Relationships are not a one-way street. I think some serious conversation is in order to determine how much flexibility Scott really has. More information needs to be on the table before sketching out a path forward. The current plan simply doesn't seem to be in your favor. But I don't mean to lecture. On to more pleasant things—such as when I can see you again."

Natalie hesitated. She wasn't sure what to make of her friendship with Max. They enjoyed each other's company, but neither of them was ready to move heaven and earth to be together. Max knew there was nothing he could offer to replace Natalie's long history with Scott, so he felt comfortable advising her to get a commitment. Even though his feelings for Natalie were genuine and growing, he felt the best situation would be for her to resolve things with Scott.

"My schedule in December is pretty busy," she said. "In order to get off for Christmas and New Year's Eve with my family, I had to bid a line that has a lot of days in the air. I would really like to see you again before the first, and I'm not blowing you off. I just don't think it will be possible."

Max said, "I have one or two trips up to New London next month. I can always stop in New York for a few hours on the way back. Do you have your calendar with you?" Natalie gave Max a list of the days she would be available. "I'll give you a call, and we'll see what we can work out. We'd better get going back to your apartment so I can retrieve my luggage."

When they got to the apartment, Caroline was gone, but they could hear Mia in the bedroom. Natalie called out, "Hey Mia, Max and I are here; he'll be leaving in just a few minutes."

The implication was clear: *Please stay in the bedroom for a few minutes and give us some alone time.* Max helped Natalie off with her coat and they gathered his luggage.

Natalie moved close to him. She rested her head on his shoulder and said, "Thank you for a truly wonderful two days. I can't remember when I've had more fun jammed into such a short time—last night at Hippopotamus was terrific in every way." Even before he kissed her, Natalie felt that little flutter in the pit of her stomach. The long kiss was meaningful for both of them.

Max thought, *What did I do to deserve this? She is so special.* They stood staring at each other for a moment, each wondering how they could feel so much in such a short time. One final hug and Max was on his way.

When she heard the door shut, Mia came into the living room. "Hi, Natalie—looks like you had a smashing time. It appears that Max truly cares for you. Not to rain on the parade, but Scott called while you were at breakfast. I told him that you and Caroline went out to eat—I didn't know where—and that I would tell you to return the call as soon as you got back."

Natalie called right away; it was clear everything was OK. Scott was job hunting, so he was busy with the Friday *New York Times* want ads. His message for Natalie was simple—could she come over? Maybe they could go for a walk.

As Natalie got ready to leave, Mia was putting on her coat. "I'm headed over to the Lex tube—first stop, Bloomie's," she said. "Depending on what I find, it could be on to Saks, Bergdorf, or wherever. Not sure when I'll be back."

"Did you get your swimsuit exchanged the other day?" Natalie asked.

"They didn't have that same design in my size, so I took a rain check," Mia answered easily. Natalie chose not to challenge her, although she knew perfectly well Mia hadn't tried to exchange the swimsuit. What Natalie didn't know was that as they spoke, Mia had the film from the Minox in her purse, ready to deposit at the dead drop.

Natalie was out the door just a few minutes behind Mia. She crossed over to Scott's building and took the elevator up to the third floor. She felt conflicted, unsure how to straighten out her thoughts. She loved Scott, but with Max entering her life, there was suddenly an added dimension, and she wasn't sure how to handle it. Scott greeted her warmly and suggested a walk. Lunch and "other things" could wait until they were back at the apartment. They walked east on the north side of 77th toward John Jay Park. A cool breeze blew from the East River and Scott put his arm around Natalie to shield her from the cold.

Natalie glanced over at the south side of 77th. To her surprise, she saw Mia with the wind at her back walking briskly westward. Natalie instinctively grabbed Scott and pulled him into a convenient doorway, his back facing the street and his tall frame hiding Natalie. She put her arms around his neck and gave him a series of playful little kisses, watching Mia out of the corner of her eye. What was Mia up to? Why did she tell Natalie she was going to Midtown when clearly she had a different agenda?

"What was that all about?" asked Scott.

"I just needed a little warm-up. I've missed you," Natalie said. Sure that Mia was fading into the distance, she took Scott's hand and resumed their walk.

"Well, I'm certainly happy to oblige," Scott said.

When they got to the park, Natalie noticed a small waist-high chalk mark on a light pole at the entrance to the park. It was a bit odd, because there were no other chalk marks anywhere near the light pole, or in fact anywhere else. She decided to keep this thought to herself, and filed it away in the back of her mind along with all the other odd occurrences surrounding Mia. There might be a logical explanation, but Natalie didn't have a clue what it could be.

Chapter 16

New York City—Norfolk, VA
December 6th-7th, 1972

When the USSR consulate closed in August of 1948, all espionage activities in and around New York City were managed from the United Nations (UN) mission located at 136 E. 67th Street. Those attached to the UN mission had diplomatic immunity, just as if there were a consulate in the city. KGB operatives were assigned official titles, but their primary function was espionage. This included case officers (or "handlers") who oversaw intelligence gathering activities. Ivan Ivanovich was assigned as the cultural attaché; in reality he was the handler for flight attendant assets working for Pan Am and TWA. Assets had code names—known only to the handler and a select few KGB officers. Reports contained only code names to avoid identification of the assets. Ivan assigned the code name "Songbird" to Mia.

Yakov Malik, the permanent resident who managed the overall UN mission, had been in place since 1968. One of his primary responsibilities was to manage the handlers and direct overall espionage activities in New York. Ivan managed the flight attendant network from New York since several of the assets were based there; handlers also operated out of London, Hong Kong, and other major cities. Malik was most enthusiastic to meet with Ivan regarding Songbird's December 1st delivery.

"Songbird is to be complimented for her extremely high level of initiative," he said to Ivan. "How did all this come about?"

"It's quite a story," Ivan said. "Mortin put out a general

memo that all assets should be on the lookout for opportunities to compromise US naval officers. I passed that on to the flight attendant network. Songbird was one of those I reached first. She told me that her roommate had made the acquaintance of several naval officers based in Norfolk. I told her to keep on top of the situation and take advantage of any opportunity to get close. What happened next was a bit of luck. Three officers were coming through New York on November 30th, and she managed to arrange a date with one of them. At the end of the evening, she had sex with him and then drugged him.

"She went through his luggage and copied everything, not knowing what was in the documents. I reviewed the film, and what I found was rough notes from an operational inspection for reactor safety. In addition, there was administrative material that included the names of all inspectors, both in Norfolk and Pearl Harbor."

"How valuable is the information?" asked Malik.

"I don't know; it is quite different from anything Walker has provided. I forwarded all of it to Mortin, and he and the little submarine team issue are evaluating it. The asset has potential, but the information itself is not highly sensitive."

Malik asked, "What is the next step?"

Ivan said, "We need to proceed with caution. The asset does not know he has been compromised. Songbird told him she is interested and urged him to stay in contact. The beauty is that he comes through New York two or three times a month on his way back to Norfolk from overseas. It will be easy to encourage a romantic entanglement. He is not married, so there's no blackmail angle there. However, he has compromised Atomic Energy Act material. This is a significant violation from a security standpoint. It is an angle we may be able to exploit.

"She has been trained in the sexual arts at our School for Scandal, and from what I understand this guy will really enjoy the ride. On their next date, she will give him plenty to drink and get him talking in broad generalities about his duties. This should include significant operational and engineering aspects of submarine work."

Malik asked, "Does Mortin have an idea what information his team needs?"

"Gorsky is working hard to formulate leading questions. We can't make Songbird a nuclear engineer in three weeks, so good questions will be vital. One option is to drop the bomb on Neutron — that's what we're calling the asset — and confront him directly. Then our guys can be specific in regard to the needed information. In any event, Songbird will be his handler and convey information to us through a dead drop."

Malik chuckled. "You're calling a nuclear sub engineer Neutron? That's amusing. If we try to turn him too early, he could blow up your entire network of flight attendants. The only thing Neutron has done wrong at this point is fail to properly secure his inspection notes."

Ivan leaned in. "I will meet with Songbird in the very near future. I'll tell her to make a date with Neutron as soon as possible. She should get him boozed up and encourage him to talk about anything related to nuclear submarines. I'll caution her to back off if she feels any resistance. I'll get back to you with an update after Songbird and Neutron meet."

Malik said, "Excellent — caution is our watchword. We don't want to screw this thing up, considering its superb potential."

December 8th, 1972

The phone rang as soon as Natalie got in the door from her Paris turnaround. "Hello, this is Natalie," she said, expecting to hear Max on the other end of the line.

"Hi, Natalie. It's Peter. Thanks again for putting together that great night on the 30th. I bet you've guessed that I'm calling for Mia."

Natalie hid her disappointment. "Let me check," she said cheerfully. She heard Mia in the bathroom and called in, "Peter's on the phone. Can you talk?"

Mia emerged, smiling and took the phone from Natalie. "Hello, ducky—I'm so glad you called. Are you in New York? I'd love to see you again."

Peter was pleased by this warm reception. "No such luck, but I'll be through New York on my way back from London next Wednesday, the 13th. How does that look for a night on the town?"

"Perfect. I get back on the 12th and don't have to go out again until the 15th."

"Tell you what—how about booking a mid-range hotel near your place? If Pan Am gets a discount, maybe you can save me a few bucks, and I'll reimburse you directly."

"I'll take care of everything. Just call me when you land. You can come right here to our flat, and then we'll go to your hotel."

This was music to Peter's ears. No pretense and no wondering what he could expect at the end of the evening. "That sounds fabulous. I'll call as soon as we hit the ground at JFK. Bye for now."

"Bye, love—can't wait to see you." Mia hung up, surprised by her sense of excitement. She had a job to do, but Peter was fun and good-looking. She enjoyed his company, and was willing to bet that his lovemaking would be better the second time, if he eased off on the booze. She had handled many assets, but none she cared for.

Natalie smiled. "Sounds like you made quite an impression on Peter. He called you back even before Max called me."

Mia saw through the bravado and spoke kindly. "Don't be too downcast. You and I both know that Max will call. Anyone can see he is very taken with you."

I sure hope so, Natalie thought.

Chapter 17

New York City—Norfolk, Virginia
December 9th, 1972

The phone rang and Natalie felt a tingle race through her—she was sure it was Max. She had thought of him constantly during the past week, despite working the Paris flight and seeing Scott. Not even Scott could keep Max off her mind.

She decided to answer with a bit of fun. "This is Holly. How may I help you?"

Max replied, "I'd like to speak with Natalie, but if she isn't around, I'd be happy to chat you up, Miss Golightly."

"You stinker! Just because I was on a trip to Paris, you'd throw me over for Holly?" Natalie teased.

"Timing's been rough," said Max. "Right after our date last week, I went on an exam to Charleston, and by the time I got back, you had already left for Paris. We need to do a better job of communicating our schedules."

"I'll vote for that," said Natalie.

"I really want to see you before Christmas, but I know your schedule is crazy. You said you had to do it that way to have Christmas Eve and Christmas Day off, as well as New Year's Eve."

"You have a great memory. However, I do have a few days here and there; maybe we can put something together. What is next week like for you?"

"I have an exam in New London next week, and we are driving because Captain Callaghan hates to fly. We wrap up on

Wednesday the 13th, and normally I would ride back with the guys on Thursday — but I'd just as soon avoid a crappy road trip. How about I book an early flight down to JFK? I can catch a connector back to Norfolk later in the day. It wouldn't be a long visit, but better than nothing."

"I have an idea," said Natalie. "I'll catch the bus out to JFK, and we can have breakfast at the Pan Am terminal. They have great food in the upstairs dining room. I can easily hang out until you have to catch your flight back to Norfolk."

"Are you OK with that? I'd be perfectly happy to make the bus trip."

"Don't be silly. I have plenty of free time during the day; you're the one who has two plane rides to get home. I can snooze on the bus or read. Really, it isn't any trouble at all."

"Natalie, you are a doll. That makes my day a hell of a lot easier all the way around. I'll give you a call when my flight is booked and let you know my arrival time. By the way, I think Peter will be in town the day before on the 13th to see Mia. He seems very interested. I don't mean to snoop, but what's your take on the situation?"

"You know, I'm glad you asked. If I were you, I'd warn Peter to proceed with some degree of caution. A Navy guy is totally out of character for Mia. She normally gravitates toward international playboys with a lot of cash to throw around at clubs. Peter obviously has a wild side, but still, he doesn't fit the mold. Maybe her taste is improving, but...I don't know. I wouldn't want to see your good friend get his heart broken."

Natalie considered telling Max about the unusual happenings, but decided against it. All she really had was an unsettled feeling, and Mia's having claimed she was going shopping and going somewhere else instead.

Max said, "I'll have a heart to heart with Peter, but I'll be subtle. I'm sure he's perfectly capable of taking care of himself, but I'll suggest he ask a few pointed questions so he can gauge where things might be headed."

Max and Natalie exchanged goodbyes, and he assured her he would call on the evening of the 13th. They shared a warm, pleasant feeling inside as they hung up.

Soviet Mission to the United Nations

Gorsky felt compelled to travel to New York on behalf of Mortin to ensure the proper handling of Neutron. He had a diplomatic passport that allowed him to travel openly as a member of the Soviet cultural mission. The CIA knew who he was, and he wasn't fooling anyone.

It was a one-on-one meeting with Ivan, with no need for Malik to attend. Gorsky took an aggressive posture regarding the pursuit of the KGB's new asset. Ivan, reflecting on Malik's words of caution, reined in Gorsky a bit to keep him from blowing up both Neutron and the entire flight attendant network — nicknamed the Stork Club. Gorsky felt pressured to make a big score to ensure that he and Mortin maintained their positions.

"Gorsky, we need to proceed with a high degree of caution," urged Ivan. "Neutron does not know he has been compromised. If we expose ourselves too early, he can run directly to NIS or the CIA and blow the whistle on Songbird. The only thing he has done wrong so far is to leave some Atomic Energy Act information unprotected and screw a KGB agent. That's not enough to get him completely under our control."

Gorsky replied, "I'm willing to ease off in the beginning, but once we get Neutron on the hook, I want this thing to really roll along. We'll screw him and his career to the wall if he doesn't give us what we want."

"We've just had a bit of good luck." Ivan said. "Neutron told Songbird to book a room in Midtown when he comes to New York on the 13th, next Wednesday. We'll have Songbird check in early and send our teams to rig the room. We'll set up audio and video surveillance in advance; that way, Songbird can concentrate entirely on our asset without worrying about triggering collecting devices. We'll provide lots of good booze so she can get him drunk right from the start."

Gorsky asked, "What is the plan for gathering information?"

"That is where you come in," said Ivan. "We need leading questions for Songbird to ask Neutron. The idea is to get him talking about the kind of information available on every inspection. Do you want to brief Songbird directly, or should I continue to handle her?"

Gorksy wanted to be involved; however, the first rule was that every barrier between asset, handler and control should be maintained whenever possible. Therefore, he declined to do the briefing. Gorsky knew that if Songbird learned his identity, the information would have significant value for US intelligence services if Songbird were ever turned. Ivan agreed to one more meeting with Songbird before the 13th to provide her the leading questions.

Chapter 18

New York City
December 13th, 1972

Peter hustled off the plane into the TWA terminal, found a pay phone, and immediately called apartment 8L. "Hello, who is calling, please?" came Mia's sophisticated British accent.

"It's Peter. I'm just about ready to grab the Carey bus into the city. I can't wait to see you."

"Everything is arranged—I booked a room at the Penn Garden down on 7th, near Madison Square Garden. I got the Pan Am rate, so I hope it won't break the bank."

"Anything would be better than that fleabag we stayed in last time," said Peter. "I know Natalie got what Max asked for— close and cheap—but that's not good enough for us. I'm sure the price is perfectly OK at Penn Garden."

Mia said, "Why don't I just meet you at the hotel? It isn't sensible for you to come all the way up to the flat. I'll see you in the lobby; most likely I'll beat you there."

"That's a great plan. See you soon."

"Cheers—can't wait," said Mia.

Natalie and Caroline overheard. Natalie said, "Sounds like Peter arrived."

"He did, and we're planning a splendid time. I expect I won't be back until late tomorrow," said Mia.

"Hope you both have a wonderful time," said Caroline.

"We haven't any particular plans, other than to spend time together. I'm sure we'll have a posh dinner somewhere tonight or tomorrow. I really do fancy him. He has so much more to him than the chaps I usually see." Mia thought, *It should be a lovely two days, despite my job.*

Natalie said, "I'm so happy things are working out. Such a nice bunch of guys—I guess there really is something to this 'officer and a gentleman' stuff."

Mia picked up her Pan-Am carry-on, and was out the door. As soon as she left, Natalie said to Caroline, "Maybe she really does like him. She seemed excited—more so than with her usual dates. I shouldn't be so judgmental; maybe she's changing for the better."

Caroline said, "I think you may be right. I never thought she quite clicked with us, but wouldn't it be great if Peter fixed that?"

"It would. Did I tell you that I'm meeting Max at the Pan Am terminal tomorrow morning? He really wants to see me, and that's the best we can do until I leave for Caracas on Friday. I'll see Scott late in the day tomorrow, so it works out all the way around. Since Scott is currently unemployed and still hasn't decided about grad school, he's around all the time. It doesn't seem to be bothering him, but it's getting on my nerves."

Caroline said, "Nat, we've been down this road many times. I'll just say a prayer that it all works out for you. I know you want to get married sooner rather than later."

Mia left the building and stopped at a pay phone on 77th. Her message was brief. "His plane was on time. I am meeting him at the hotel in a few minutes." Mia finished her walk over to Second, hailed a taxi, and gave the driver the address of the Penn Garden.

Mia and Peter weren't the only ones looking forward to what would happen at the hotel. Earlier in the day, the KGB team installed a voice-activated audio system, along with a camera that would record all activities on the bed. They left a bottle of champagne chilling in a bucket to get the party started—this would be Mia's explanation for checking in early. They also left a bottle of Peter's favorite scotch, and several bottles of French white burgundy along with a nice selection of pâté and cheeses. No need to leave the room for a long time, and the KGB would be recording every word.

Mia arrived at the hotel well before Peter; she went up to their room to drop off her carry-on. There was no sign the KGB had visited, except for the wine, scotch, and snacks. She laid out a sexy negligee on the bed—an unmistakable invitation to events yet to come. She picked up a copy of *The Economist* and returned to the lobby.

About half an hour later, Peter arrived and saw Mia waiting for him. She popped up and gave him a big hug and kiss on the cheek. "Sweetheart, we're all checked in. We can go right up to the room." Like an obedient puppy dog, Peter followed her to the waiting elevator. As soon as they were in their room, Mia locked him in a deep embrace with a kiss that made no mistake about her intentions.

Peter was pleasantly surprised—snacks and enough booze to survive a two-day lockdown, and one of the sexiest things he had ever seen, laid out on the bed. "Where do we start?" he asked. "You obviously did a lot of planning."

Mia said, "Let's start with the champagne. We have almost two full days…no need to rush things." After another long, deep kiss, Peter made his way over to the ice bucket. "Let me do that," said Mia. "I've had years of practice. I promise not to spill a drop." Mia had on a casual scoop-neck dress, and when she leaned over, she made sure Peter got a good view of the deep cleavage barely contained by the black lace bra she had bought on her last trip to Paris. As they nibbled on the snacks, Peter could not help letting his gaze stray down the front of her dress. She caught him peeking and winked at him.

They finished the champagne in short order, accompanied by delicious bites of crackers with pâté or cheese. Mia made sure Peter had more than his fair share of the champagne. As a result, he was feeling very mellow. Mia knew where this would end up, and she didn't want to rush things. She knew Peter's thoughts, but she wanted to take it slow and tease him. The last time everything was too rushed; she had to seal the deal and give him the knockout drops. She had practically ripped off his clothes and jumped him once the door was closed.

"Tell me a bit about you," Mia purred. "Last time we met, we didn't do much talking."

"Not much to tell," Peter said. "I grew up on a farm in rural Wisconsin. I did fairly well in high school, and with Nam starting up, I found out I could get a Navy scholarship to the University of Wisconsin. After graduation I was strongly encouraged to apply for nuclear submarine service. I had the usual Admiral Rickover interview, and eighteen months later, I found myself on my first sub, in charge of the electrical division. After two more sea tours, here I am."

"Who is Admiral Rickover?" asked Mia.

"He's the Father of the Nuclear Navy, and he personally interviews every officer assigned to the program. I've done pretty well so far, and my next assignment will be back to sea as an executive officer. I've always had to do a little extra to keep up with the Academy guys—my career is very important to me, and I want to put in at least twenty years, so I can retire. I already have eleven years invested."

At this point, Peter had enough talk. He moved next to her on the love seat, put one arm around her, and kissed her. He put his other hand down the front of her dress, eased one breast out of her bra, and shifted his mouth to her exposed nipple, licking and sucking lightly. Mia had not expected this. She moaned involuntarily—she didn't even have to resort to her scripted sounds of arousal. Just to make sure they were on the same page, she reached down between Peter's legs. He was hard under her hand, so she undid his zipper and began to stroke him in a gentle but insistent rhythm. By this time, Peter had exposed her other breast, and was dividing his attention equally between them, while Mia nibbled on his ear and neck.

Mia thought, *I think I'll truly enjoy this.* By all indications, Peter was a good lover. She decided to let him take the lead, rather than being the aggressor.

Peter glanced over at the bed and said, "Let's slow things down a bit. I want to enjoy every moment. How about we get more comfortable? If you go into the bathroom and slip on that little thing on the bed, I'll meet you under the covers."

Mia did not need any encouragement. Peter was completely naked when Mia joined him. Thanks to the champagne and foreplay, they were both fully aroused. They started touching each other all over. Mia took Peter's face between her hands and gave him a probing kiss, and then started tracing down his chest with little nibbling kisses. Peter slipped his hand under the waistband of her negligee and removed the flimsy garment. Before too long, it was apparent that no more teasing and kissing would be necessary.

Foreplay is great—but when you're ready, you're ready, Peter thought. Remembering last time, he whispered, "How about I get on top this time? I want you to lie back and enjoy this, and not do all the work."

Mia nodded in delight—she could feel waves of pleasure crashing over her, and just to lie back and enjoy being made love to for a change was a very welcome thought. Peter gently rolled over on top of her, his tongue flickering over her nipples. She guided him inside her, moving in ecstasy beneath him. They were both already so aroused that it did not take long before both were satisfied.

As they lay next to each other afterward, Mia said, "Darling that was lovely — so sweet and so gentle."

Peter said, "I wanted to make it special for you. I haven't been able to stop thinking about you since the last time we were together."

This was business as usual, but Mia's feelings for Peter were quickly becoming real. This was a red flag; she needed to get her emotions in check. It was time to get back to the business at hand.

"I've thought about you, too. I want to hear about your trip that took you away from me for such a long time," she said with a little pout.

"Before I get started, I need a scotch and soda," said Peter.

"I'll get it for you. Just wait right there. I'm going to open some white wine," said Mia.

Drinks in hand, they toasted the start of Peter's visit to the Big Apple.

Chapter 19

New York City
December 13th, 1972

"We have a driver that picks up the four of us in a van at the base BOQ in Rota and then drives us all the way to Seville over some terrible roads. Then we grab an Iberia flight to Madrid, finishing with a TWA flight back to JFK. I don't have to tell you that TWA flight attendants are nowhere near as much fun as you and your friends."

"What happens when you're on the submarine?" asked Mia. "I know all about flying—I do it all the time. Going to sea on a submarine is exciting."

"Well, what we do isn't all that exciting—mostly safety checks," said Peter. "All the inspections are pretty much the same. We get on the sub early in the morning, go to sea, and submerge. We look at how three different watch sections respond to the various planned drills; that way, we get to evaluate all of the nuclear operators on the ship. That's about it."

Peter took a long pull of his drink and could feel himself relax even further.

"Why does that take two or three days?" asked Mia.

"Well, besides the drills, we have meals, read, and sleep— that takes up the rest of the time. Seriously, we do a document review and interview most of the nuclear operators. When all three phases are complete, we compare notes, and the guy assigned to write the report puts everything together. We present our findings to the ship's captain when we return to port."

"Who writes the report?"

"The captains never do it, so it rotates among the three junior members of the team. I lucked out this time and someone else is the writer—last time, it was me. It involves a lot of work, but I only have to do it one out of every three trips. Enough about my boring job. What about you?"

Peter finished his Scotch, and Mia got a refill before she started her story. She wanted to probe further and ask additional questions, but Peter had put the ball squarely in her court. She would look evasive if she ignored him and pushed the questioning back to the inspections.

"I was born in East Berlin in 1945," said Mia. "According to my parents, those were terribly difficult times. As you are aware, due to the Soviet occupation, things were far from what you would call normal urban living. My parents were academics at what is now Humboldt University in the eastern sector of the city. When the Russians invaded, there was rape and pillage everywhere. My mother was approached by a rogue band of soldiers, and was spared only because she was six months pregnant with me. Some women, pregnant or not, were not so lucky.

"As my parents tell the story, there was very little food, and the electricity was on only a few hours every day. Food was hoarded and hidden; otherwise the Russians would just come and take it. Eventually, in 1946, the university was opened and my parents resumed their teaching duties, but things were still very difficult due to the shift to Soviet ideology. The Western Sector was jointly occupied by the Americans, French, and British, but we were restricted to the Soviet sector. With the help of some academic friends from the West, we fled to England. This was well before the Wall was built, so it was not as difficult to escape. After the American equivalent of high school, I attended the University of Manchester and graduated in 1969. My area of study was mechanical engineering."

"Really? Why did you go to work for Pan Am?"

Mia poured two more generous drinks. "You can guess why. Imagine me, trying to find a job as an engineer in London. It's a male-dominated field, and I had certain—assets—that made it difficult for people to take me seriously. I had a friend who was hired by Pan Am because she's proficient in French. Since I grew up speaking German, she encouraged me to look into it. One of Pan Am's requirements is foreign language fluency. The interview went very well, and here I am.

"Things were expanding in the East, and there was a need for additional flight attendants based in Hong Kong. I was anxious to see more of the world, put in for a transfer, and it was granted. While based in Hong Kong, much of what we did was fly the 727 for the R and R trips out of Saigon for the US and other military personnel. As the war was coming to an end, I saw a posting at the New York base for someone fluent in German, so I again applied for a transfer. As soon as I got here, I saw an advert for a shared flat on the Upper East Side. And the rest, you already know."

"Wow what a story—a lot more impressive than Farm Boy From Wisconsin Joins Navy." Peter drained his glass. "You know, I feel like such a dog; you must think I'm just like all those guys who wouldn't take you seriously because of your—assets."

Mia sensed an opening and skillfully played her advantage. "I didn't tell you about my engineering background straightaway because I do tire of people rolling their eyes, as if I couldn't possibly be telling the truth. But I trust you, darling. I trust you to respect my mind."

"Of course I do," Peter said, worried that he had underestimated her. Mia knew he was a party animal; he wasn't used to caring what his partners thought of him. However, he was already invested in his relationship with Mia—his eagerness and his tenderness both told her as much.

"Tell me more about your work," Mia cooed. "Listening to you brings back such lovely memories of being at University. I love the stimulation." She drew out the final word slightly, giving it a suggestive edge.

Peter, his inhibitions lowered by alcohol, immediately took the cue: the way to this woman's bed was through her brain, and if that was what she wanted, he was hooked enough to give it to her. She asked numerous leading questions about the submarine drills: who made up the scenarios, what kinds of documents were reviewed, and even what kinds of problems were pervasive in the general operation of US submarines. On their face, the questions were benign, and she did not press for specifics. Ivan had directed her to keep him talking; they would sort out the importance later.

As a reward for Peter's unwitting compliance, and to cement the idea that treating her as an intellectual equal would pay off for him, Mia decided it was time for another round of lovemaking. Since Peter had so much to drink, he needed assistance to perform. Mia's School for Scandal education by the Soviets was not wasted, and Peter eventually rallied to answer the bell. Afterward, they lay in each other's arms, touching and exploring. Peter had not felt this good in a long time.

The exercise had caused Peter to sober up a bit. Out of nowhere, he said, "I'm famished. Those little snacks won't be enough to fill the void in my belly. I read something in a magazine about a really top-notch restaurant in Midtown—some funny name—La Grenool?"

Mia laughed. "*Grenouille*," she corrected his pronunciation.

"Let's give them a call and see if they can sneak us in at the end of the evening. It can't be too far away — I think it's on East 52nd."

The restaurant did have a late table available and they both enjoyed one of their best meals ever. The room was classic French opulence, gleaming with silver and damask. The elaborate flower arrangements were gorgeous, though without fragrance, to avoid interfering with the scent and taste of the food. Mia and Peter both felt as if it was a celebration, though for entirely different reasons.

As soon as Mia and Peter left the hotel room, the KGB team retrieved the audio and video feeds. The recorded tapes were taken immediately to the Soviet UN Mission for evaluation. Ivan was pleased — everything was going according to plan.

Chapter 20

New London, CT—JFK Airport
December 14ᵗʰ, 1972

"**M**ax, you get an A for creativity," Captain Callaghan said. "I have to admit, this is the first time I've ever heard of a breakfast date at the Pan Am terminal, without flying Pan Am."

Max was the object of gentle ribbing this morning, since he was not going all the way back to Norfolk with the group. The team had agreed to drop him at the New London airport to catch the early-morning commuter to JFK.

"I have to give Natalie the credit—it was her idea," Max said. "She assures me that the food is first rate, with built-in entertainment—planes taking off and landing every thirty seconds."

A cheerful chorus of "Have a safe flight!" came from the team as they left Max standing curbside at the small terminal. Once inside, Max confirmed that the flight was on time and called Natalie from a pay phone.

"The flight's on time," he said. "We land at 8:45. I should be at the terminal no later than 9:00."

Natalie felt a little flutter of anticipation. "It will be great to see you. Thanks for making the effort."

"*Au contraire, ma chérie,*" Max replied. "It is I who should be thanking you for agreeing to hop on a bus and take an early-morning ride out to JFK just to see me."

"Speaking of which, I'd better get going. See you in a little while."

Both were filled with anticipation about the unconventional date. Two weeks had passed since the wonderful night at Hippopotamus; each thought a lot about the other, wondering what the future would hold.

Natalie arrived first. When she saw Max at the entrance to the restaurant, luggage in hand, she waved excitedly; each of them broke into a broad smile. Max walked over to their table and wrapped his arms around her. *Boy, does she smell good*, Max thought. She had on a subtle application of "Y," her favorite, and Max remembered it from their last date. Their embrace was a bit more than a casual hello, but the kiss was comparatively chaste. No need to embarrass themselves in front of the early-morning travelers.

"How was your flight?" asked Natalie.

Max shook his head. "I'm no fan of those puddle-jumpers. Give me a 747 any day—especially if *you're* on it. I'm glad I don't have to take that flight on a routine basis." They took their seats and immediately the waitress brought over coffee and menus. "Give us a few minutes," Max said. "We're in no hurry."

Natalie liked that Max was practical and always seemed to say the right thing. Nothing was worse than an overly attentive wait staff when uninterrupted conversation was the order of the day.

"I'm so glad we could get together," Natalie said. "It was really sweet of you to interrupt your trip to Norfolk. This works out perfectly and gives me tonight to get my act together for the trip to Caracas tomorrow." The truth was that she needed some time for Scott; he would think it odd if she went missing in action the night before a trip.

"I just screwed up," Max lamented. "I shooed away the waitress before I could order drinks. I'm up for a Bloody Mary—how about you?"

"I'll have a mimosa," said Natalie. "It's great neither of us has to drive. We can have a few drinks and really enjoy ourselves."

Max tracked down the waitress and ordered their drinks.

"What are your plans for the Christmas holidays?" asked Natalie.

"I've got an exam next week, and then I'll head up to Philly just before Christmas to spend some time with my parents. I'll probably hang around there until after the New Year. How about you?"

Natalie answered, "I practically had to kill myself just to get Christmas and New Year's off. Check this out." She took out her diary and began to recite her itinerary. "Tomorrow I do a Caracas turnaround and return one day later. On the 18th a Santa Domingo one-day, on the 21st a Bermuda one-day, on the 23rd a Trinidad one-day — and then I wrap up the month with a four-day between the 26th and the 29th through Amsterdam and Vienna."

"Please stop!" said Max. "My head is spinning. I can't believe we managed to fit in our little get-together. Take a look at your diary for January. I'm coming back through New York on the 27th from London. Will you be around?"

"No conflicts with my Pan Am schedule. Give me a call mid-month, and we'll set everything up. Also, don't be shy about asking me for another breakfast date. This early-morning thing is turning out to be a lot of fun." By this time, they were well into their second cocktail.

Max felt his heart sink a little. If he wasn't careful, he would lead her to believe he was a relationship prospect. He didn't have the strength of will to refuse to see her — he was drawn to her as to no other woman in his life. But he wanted to make sure she wasn't investing too much in their friendship. Gritting his teeth, he asked, "Have you and Mr. Main Squeeze made any progress regarding your future together? Has he applied to graduate school yet?"

Natalie shook her head. "Scott is still sitting on the fence. We haven't had a serious conversation on the issue since the last time I saw you. To be honest, Scott and I haven't had the steadiest relationship during these past four years. Let me fill you in a little more on the situation."

Max was sure he didn't want to hear this with an alcohol-fueled buzz. "Hold on for just a minute—let's order breakfast while there's still time." He signaled the waitress. Each ordered an omelet, with a side of fruit, and a basket of croissants with butter and jam.

Max's head cleared a little once he'd sampled a croissant. He couldn't imagine why Scott wouldn't leap at the chance to marry Natalie. He didn't want the booze to do the talking for him—he felt at risk of telling her Scott was an idiot. But with food in his stomach, he was confident that he could be discreet.

"So—what's up with you and Scott? Whatever you feel comfortable telling me," he said.

"After dating for two years, I addressed the commitment question. I pushed too hard, and Scott decided we should cool it for a while and not see each other. Reluctantly, I agreed. He obviously wasn't ready to make a commitment. I was really hurt and thought it would be a good time for a transfer. I remember sitting on the jump seat with a friend shortly after this happened, and her gently trying to warn me that maybe this cooling-off period was Scott's way of breaking up with me. I didn't want to believe he could be so cruel, but after thinking about it, I put in for a transfer to San Francisco.

"About a month later, I was on my way to Second Avenue, looking really cute in my galaxy gold Evan Picone uniform with the bowler hat. I was going to take a bus or train down to the

East Side Terminal. I ran into Scott, and all the feelings were still there. He asked where I was going, and I told him London. He asked when I would get back, and if he could call me. Without thinking, I said, 'Sure.' I couldn't believe how automatically I'd fallen back into the old pattern, but I knew then I wasn't done with Scott. I still had too much invested. So I gave up on San Francisco, and we started all over again. Please understand; he is a good investment.

"During the past two years, we've become a lot closer, if you catch my drift. However, my feeling is that although we have advanced romantically, there's been no progress on the commitment front. Until graduate school gets resolved, I don't think anything will change."

Max thought for a minute and said, "Well, now that I know more, my opinion still hasn't changed. If you really think he's the one for you, I believe you should consider forcing a decision—maybe wait until January to give him more than a fair chance to apply to graduate school. But I just can't see any benefit to you in waiting another two years for him to make a decision."

Natalie was suddenly uncomfortable, having told Max so much about Scott. What would Scott think, if he knew she was confiding in another guy? "I'd like to change the subject a bit," she said.

"Sure," Max agreed.

"Peter seems quite taken with Mia, and I don't want anything bad to happen to your friend. I know I mentioned this, but it's really nagging at me. It's not just that Peter isn't Mia's usual type…it's that her behavior has been erratic lately. She'll make a point of telling me where she's going, and then by chance, I discover that wasn't where she went at all. Something is going on, and whatever it is—I'm worried she's not being straight with Peter."

"OK, I'll poke around the edges a little bit," said Max. "I don't know anything about Mia except that she's British, flies for Pan Am, and used to be based in Hong Kong."

"I don't know much more than that myself, and I live with her," said Natalie. "She's kind of a mystery."

"Well, I like a good mystery. I'll see what I can find out. Fair enough?"

She nodded, and they turned the conversation to their shared interests—fine dining in New York and abroad, favorite museums around the world, popular and classical music. Max learned she had been involved with a West Point grad, and it hadn't worked out. The Army guy was gone, Scott wasn't stepping up to the plate…maybe Max had a chance….*Hold on!* he cautioned himself. *My marriage is unresolved. I can't be thinking along these lines.* But he couldn't help it.

His experience with Natalie was like love at first sight, something Max didn't think existed. What was his responsibility here? As long as she didn't seem to be taking it too seriously, surely there was no harm in their continuing to see each other. He had encouraged her to nail down her status with Scott. He'd done everything to support her stable future, so—he wasn't going to second-guess his yearning to be with her.

After almost three hours, Max walked Natalie to the bus stop. As soon as they got there they embraced and kissed, not wanting to miss an opportunity for at least one kiss before she left. Shortly thereafter the bus came, and they hastily exchanged goodbyes. Max looked after the bus and gave a little wave as it pulled off into the distance. Soon, his loop bus came for the ride to the National terminal. He felt like Natalie took a piece of his heart back with her to apartment 8L.

Chapter 21

Moscow
December 18th, 1972

T he time for action was at hand. Mortin met with his team of three in the basement room to evaluate Songbird's two data dumps and press for a plan of action. "Ivan's report is divided into three parts: First, a summary of the documents taken; second, a summary of the inspection notes; and third, all salient points taken from the transcript of Songbird and Neutron's conversations. First, let's discuss the actual documentation retrieved."

The admiral was ready. "The most valuable information is the Board's inspection schedule for the first half of 1973. We can glean a wealth of information regarding the operational schedule of the fast attacks and FBMs in the Atlantic fleet. If we are trying to determine the identity of a given sub, the inspection schedule will enable us to project or eliminate certain possibilities. In trying to match a sound signature with a given submarine, the known location of a sub being inspected is of extreme value.

"Projecting the overall FBM schedule is invaluable. Based on the inspection schedule and Neutron's future assistance, we may be able to ascertain the schedule for the entire Atlantic FBM fleet. Eventually, Songbird will need Neutron to provide specific information. And Walker may be able to gather helpful information from message traffic coming out of CINCLANT headquarters in Norfolk. Gorsky, we'll need your help."

Mortin responded, "The admiral is right, Gorsky. Please take these needs and put them at the top of the list for required intelligence—we must develop a verified inspection schedule for the Atlantic fleet for the latter half of '72 and '73."

Gorsky said, "OK, got it. Regarding the inspection notes, they give us insight into how the inspections are formulated and conducted. In essence, the inspection team has operational control of the ship for almost an entire day. In the future, Neutron can create drill scenarios that yield beneficial operational information. Neutron can then record the informational data and include it in his post-inspection report to us."

Mortin put a question to the group. "What about existing documentation onboard the ship? How much access would Neutron have?"

Kerechenko saw his opportunity to contribute. "I reviewed the actual transcript of the conversation of December 13th-14th, supported by Ivan's excellent summary. The crews being inspected fear the inspection teams. Not only is it important to pass the inspection, but the ships are evaluated in relation to their peers. Members of the crew are only too willing to cooperate. Neutron would have carte blanche regarding access to onboard records and documentation. He needs only a private place to review and photograph."

Gorsky thought he saw an opportunity. "Getting Neutron on the hook is the key to success—the sooner the better. During the next scheduled meeting between Songbird and Neutron, one of us should make it a threesome and lower the boom."

Mortin was calm but furious with Gorsky. "I appreciate your enthusiasm, but that is one of the stupidest things you have said in a long time. When you were in New York with Ivan and the resident, they made it quite clear they want to proceed with extreme caution. The Stork Club belongs to Ivan, and it has taken him years to set it up. If Neutron pushes back hard, we may lose Songbird and the entire network. The problem right now—as has already been explained to you—is that the only leverage we have with Neutron is his getting drunk, screwing a KGB agent, and mishandling Atomic Energy Act classified information—mostly just handwritten notes."

The admiral supported Mortin's view. "Neutron is too valuable to have him compromised this early in the game. We don't even know what kind of incentives appeal to him. My sense is that he would like to keep his position in the Navy and, like Walker, will act as if everything is normal…possibly even rise to the rank of submarine commander. What a coup that would be—to have the CO of a US submarine among our network of agents. Fyodor, do the resident and Ivan have any suggestions?"

Mortin responded, "We will have Songbird create situations that allow us to edit the audio and videotape to manufacture compromising evidence. For instance, we can develop a freeze frame of money being exchanged. It would be impossible to tell who was giving and who was receiving; just that money was being transferred. Also, we can edit the audio transcript to make it appear Neutron is giving sensitive, classified information when answering benign, open-ended questions.

"To turn Neutron in the future, we might have Songbird appeal to him for help out of a difficult situation…maybe using the excuse that *the bad guys made me do it*. If we're lucky, Neutron will be a typical American male with a hero complex. However, now is not the time for such an approach."

Mortin was ready to conclude. "In summary, I am going to send the results of our meeting to Ivan and tell him to provide Songbird appropriate direction for her next meeting. For the present, she will continue to keep Neutron in the dark. Gorsky, verify the '72-'73 inspection schedules using other channels. We will reconvene after Songbird and Neutron's next meeting. Any questions?" There being none, Mortin gathered his notes and was gone.

∽ 98 ∽

Chapter 22

New York City—Norfolk
Early January 1973

Mia picked up the ringing phone. It was Monday the 8th of January. Ostensibly, the call was from her mail order book club. The voice asked if she wanted the latest offering to be delivered on the 14th. She said OK, and added she looked forward to receiving the book. The real intent was to set up a meeting with Ivan later that day. The code words were "offering" and "the 14th." Her response of OK meant that she could accept the meeting. "Offering" translated to the designated meeting place in Van Courtland Park, and the 14th translated to 1400 on the 24-hour clock—or 2:00 in the afternoon.

Mia's trip was uneventful, as she really did not have to ensure that she was "clean" when she arrived for the meeting—meaning that she was not being followed. The number 4 northbound train on the Lexington Avenue subway ended at the Woodlawn Station, right near Van Courtland Park and a short walk to the designated meeting place.

For Ivan, the trip was complicated. He changed subway lines several times and ended up on the 4, with an exit at the Woodlawn station. He arrived with a bag of nuts and seeds, and sat on his usual bench near the entrance to the park. The birds would come, and he enjoyed feeding them. He placed a copy of the *New York Times* on the bench near him. At exactly 2 PM, Mia came walking along with a carefree manner. She approached the bench and asked, "Do you mind if I join you?"

Since it was the dead of winter, there were few people in the park, except for an occasional jogger—a perfect situation for a brief conversation.

Ivan said, "You are to be complimented on your excellent work. Continue to shield Peter from the fact you are working for us. Before revealing our actual intentions, we must ensure he will not turn us in to the CIA or FBI. He must be faced with a decision that dictates it will be better to cooperate with us than to admit his wrongdoing and take his punishment. We are not at that point yet. Inside the newspaper are your instructions for your next meeting. Certain questions are to be asked exactly as stated; these are clearly marked. This will allow us to edit the audio so that Peter is in a compromising situation. If he is drunk enough, he won't remember exactly what he said. It will be difficult for him to argue that the tape is not accurate.

"Also, please ensure that you pre-pay for the room. When he reimburses you, be sure you accept the payment at the foot of the bed, so we can get a good still shot of money being exchanged. Finally, the emergency dead drop in John Jay Park should not be used again. If there is need for a dead drop, use the one here in the park. It is a long trip, but the one at John Jay is too close to your apartment. Are there any questions?"

Mia said, "I understand my questions should be leading and innocent. If he suspects anything, I'll back off immediately. Peter and I have not set up another date; the holidays intervened and our schedules didn't align. I'll call him and casually set something up as soon as possible. I don't want to appear overly aggressive, but I know he will jump at the chance if I suggest time together. I'll book exactly the same room, for 'sentimental reasons.' I know it will be easier for the team to equip the same room. When I have his arrival date, I'll phone it in."

Ivan was pleased with her complete understanding. "Mia,

as always, you have grasped the situation perfectly. I have no further instructions, except to say good luck with setting everything up—when you are ready, we will be ready. Please be on your way."

Mia got up, folded the newspaper, and retraced her steps from the park. The entire exchange took no more than five minutes. Mia felt conflicted because of her growing feelings for Peter. At least the KGB would continue to shield Peter from what was actually going on. She thought, *As long as that is the case, perhaps there is some way that this can work out for the good of everyone involved — except, of course, the Soviets.* The more they delayed exposing the operation to Peter, the longer she would have to figure out how to beat them at their own game. She shook her head. *That's dangerous thinking, Mia. You have to be extremely cautious.*

As soon as Mia returned to 8L, she called Peter. "LCDR Peter Bronson, please," she said to the yeoman who answered. Peter immediately picked up and said hello. "It's me. How are you?" said Mia.

"Mia—what a pleasant surprise, it's great to hear your voice. I was just thinking of you."

"I really want to see you soon here in New York. Let's compare schedules." Mia rattled off several two-day periods, and Peter said he could come on the 17th and 18th. "This is brilliant," Mia said. "I'll set everything up, just like last time. I'll even try to get the same room. Call me as soon as you land at JFK on the 17th, and we'll meet in the hotel lobby."

Peter was floating on air, and readily agreed to the plan. He was looking forward to an instant replay of the two best days of his life.

"OK, Peter darling, looks like we're all set. See you in the lobby on the 17th," said Mia, ignoring the pang of guilt as she hung up the phone.

Chapter 23

Mia felt trapped. Her growing feelings for Peter were in conflict with the job she needed to do for the Soviets, and there was no way around it. She had the list of questions from Ivan. The damn tape would be rolling, and she had no choice but to ask the questions. Peter would either provide information of minimal use to the Russians, or reveal information that would allow the Soviets to blackmail him. Ivan cautioned her at their meeting that she needed to perform well, despite the huge success she had achieved by finding Peter in the first place.

She had no stake in the Cold War; her motivation going forward was self-preservation and the remote possibility that things between her and Peter might work out. Her growing feelings for him defied any rational explanation—they were two people from vastly different cultural spectrums. In her short life, she had known many men and had consciously avoided any kind of romantic attachment. The School for Scandal had seen to that.

A number of factors contributed to her unique attachment to Peter. He was tall, thin, and very muscular, with intense dark eyes and wavy dark hair. Although his looks were appealing, there was much more to her attraction—it was his American personality, his evident integrity, his drive to succeed, his simple upbringing on a Midwest farm. He had earned everything, unlike those she usually dated when not on a job for the Soviets.

Upon reflection, she detested what she had done to Peter

their first night together. Her own self-interest required her to take the Navy story to Ivan, and now she was right in the middle of it in a way she could never have envisioned. There had to be a way out, but she didn't have a clue what it was.

All the arrangements for their second hotel-room tryst were in place. Getting the still shot of the money exchange might be tricky if Peter didn't suggest it; maneuvering him to the foot of the bed would be the easy part. He would eventually offer to reimburse her, but it might happen when they were out at dinner, walking in the park, or wherever. Worst case, she would just have to ask before they left the hotel room — "before we forget," or "I have a few unexpected expenses." There were ways to handle it that wouldn't arouse any suspicion on Peter's part.

All during the trip from Rota to JFK, Peter thought only of his upcoming time with Mia. They had settled into a comfortable routine. He would give her a call from JFK and then go straight to the hotel. He was the writer on this last inspection, but John had offered to take the documentation back to Norfolk so the yeoman could start typing up the rough notes, to help Peter meet the report deadline.

The team joked with Peter when they hit JFK. "You'll probably be in the sack before we're even on the plane back to Norfolk," Doug teased. The officers on the Board weren't really a kiss-and-tell bunch, but they were so close and perceptive that nothing escaped their attention. If somebody was not going back to Norfolk, something had to be up. And of course, the ongoing liaison with the Pan Am ladies was big news, rather than a big secret.

Mia was unlike any woman Peter had known. She was stunning — tall, voluptuous yet fit, with that delicate-featured, pale face set off by naturally blonde hair and sky-blue eyes. He loved her British accent, which made her sound upper-class. Yet he sensed there was something melancholy deep inside her, which made him yearn to know more.

Despite his growing feelings, fleeting concerns bothered Peter. He didn't know the implications of her British citizenship. Naval officers with high security clearances were continually cautioned about close contact with foreign nationals. He should probably talk to the NIS folks back in Norfolk, if he were considering a serious relationship.

Peter's main goal was to be given command of his own submarine. This drove him to perform professionally at the highest level possible. He was on the right track—his membership on the Board all but assured the path to command. If his relationship with Mia put that in jeopardy, then there was no question of what he would do. He had dedicated too much time and effort to his naval career to give it up for love, no matter how wonderful Mia might be.

As soon as he landed, he called Mia from the nearest pay phone.

"Hello, sweetheart," said Mia. "I can't wait to see you. Everything is ready over at the hotel; you can come straight up to the room. Do you remember the number?"

Peter said, "You bet—609. What great memories! Do I need to pick up something on the way there—wine, cheese, or anything?"

"No, darling; everything is arranged, same as last time. Just bring your handsome self. You'd better get going. We'll have plenty of time for a chat when you get here."

"I'm good at following orders," Peter said slyly. "I'm on my way. See you soon!"

Mia left 8L and stopped at a pay phone on 77th to make the

required call. She got to the hotel well before Peter and went right up to the room to slip into something a little more comfortable — a see-through number acquired at an upscale boutique in Paris. The French really knew how to make a woman feel like a goddess when it came to lingerie. A modest application of Rive Gauche, and she was ready to welcome Peter back to New York. He had mentioned on his last visit it was one of his favorite perfumes, and she was prepared to do any little thing to please him.

When Mia opened the door and Peter saw her exquisite curves outlined in softly clinging black silk chiffon, his mouth literally dropped open. He recovered quickly and said, "Mia, you look absolutely gorgeous."

As soon as he was in the room; she put both arms around him, pressed herself against the full length of his muscular body, and gave him the kiss he had imagined all the way from Rota. She probed his mouth with her very active tongue, and Peter became immediately aroused — the scent of Rive Gauche accelerated matters.

"You wore my favorite perfume — you remembered," he said, nuzzling her neck.

"I love it too. It really puts me in the mood," she murmured. But she had to think of her job, the real reason she was there. "How was your trip?" she asked.

"Pretty routine," said Peter. "The only thing is that I'm the writer on this inspection and I'll have a little extra work to do when I get back to Norfolk. Let's not talk business, though — do I see a bottle of champagne peeping out of that ice bucket?"

Mia nodded but was immediately alert, because his comment meant there would probably be documentation in his bag similar to what she had found during their first date. Since his remark was on tape about being the writer, she had no choice but to try to photograph as many documents as possible. This was a new wrinkle, but she knew how to handle it if the time came.

She gave him a big hug. "Why don't you take off your coat and hop on over to the loveseat. I'll bring the champagne."

Years of flying with Pan Am gave her some advantages. By the time Peter shed his coat and put away his luggage, Mia was waiting for him at the cocktail table with champagne and two glasses. As soon as they toasted and drank their first glass, Mia tried one of the easier questions.

She put her hand on his knee. "I worry about you when you are out at sea. Is it safe to be so close to the nuclear reactor on those inspections? Do you ever worry about negative health effects from radiation?"

Peter chuckled. "We all wear film badges that track our radiation exposure on a monthly basis — I've probably received more radiation from flying than I ever have on board a sub. It's a common concern among civilians, but the newspapers blow it all out of proportion. I'm perfectly safe."

Mia stroked his cheek and gave him a little kiss. "That makes me feel so much better. When I was at university, they painted a very bad picture of nuclear radiation exposure. I'm so glad your exposure is low." *Not much more I can do with that one*, thought Mia. If she asked about specific values, that would surely rouse suspicion. Any Russian scientist worth his salt could easily translate Peter's remarks to actual radiation levels and values.

They had another glass of champagne, and Peter was starting to feel the glow. He pulled her to him, gave her a deep kiss, and fondled her breasts through the sheer material of her negligée. He could feel her nipples harden under his fingertips, and at the same time, she was exploring his fully aroused manhood. Before he knew it, she had unbuckled and unzipped his pants and was skillfully massaging him.

"Peter, let's move over to the bed. Just lie back, and I'll plea-sure you."

On the way to the bed, they left a trail of various articles of clothing. Peter lay back as instructed. Mia had a bit of a wild side to her even before she graduated from the Russians' School for Scandal. She was the school's star pupil, since by nature she was uninhibited and liked to experiment sexually. Fellatio was a cor-nerstone of her technique, and her expertise made Peter moan and writhe like never before in his life.

When it was over, Peter stared at Mia, wide-eyed. "How in the world did you learn to do that?" he asked.

Mia smiled. "Just doing what comes naturally, darling. I have a naughty mind."

Peter pulled her on top of him and looked into her eyes. "Well, I promise that before my visit is over, I'll return the favor. I'm pretty naughty, myself. I hope you won't mind."

"I'm quite certain I won't mind," she said.

Peter said, "Why don't I grab a quick shower and shave. I've been traveling for almost ten hours and I'd like to get rid of the road dust. Just relax until I get back — you deserve a rest after all that hard work."

As soon as the bathroom door was shut, Mia sprang into ac-tion. She opened his carry-on, but there were no documents. She searched frantically through both pieces of luggage but found nothing. What could have happened to all the documents? She would be in trouble if she didn't produce as much information as possible. The only thing of interest she found was an enve-lope with her name on it. That might make the money shot a bit easier, but she had to think of a way to make him present it to her in view of the camera. She slipped back into her negligée, curled up on the bed, and waited for Peter.

The door opened, and a cloud of steam preceded his arrival.

He had a towel wrapped around his waist and was drying his curly dark hair with another towel. When he got to the bed, Mia pulled his towel off. "What are you hiding under there? Do you have a prezzie for me?"

That was all the invitation Peter needed. He got onto the bed next to her, and things started all over again. Peter was as good as his word and pleasured Mia as promised. Because of her growing feelings for him, Mia didn't have to fake her delight. She thought, *He has good instincts, but I will be able to teach him a few things. In many ways, this relationship has real potential.*

She ran her fingers through his slightly damp hair afterward, as he lay next to her with a look on his face that made her writhe inwardly with guilt—he was happy that he had pleased her. She hated what she had to do.

"Did you bring me anything from Spain?" she cooed.

"All I could find were some beautiful black lace mantillas, and somehow I just couldn't picture you in church, so I passed. I do have something for you, though." He went over to his luggage and retrieved the envelope with her name. "I almost forgot—this is reimbursement for the room, snacks, and booze. There should be more than enough to cover everything."

Mia jumped off the bed in joking anticipation and met him at the foot of the bed. She held on to the envelope for just an extra second before she took it from him. Mission accomplished.

Chapter 24

New York City
January 17th-18th, 1973

Mia put the envelope in her overnight bag, tucking it in among some sex toys that might see action during Peter's visit. "Thank you, darling," she said. "I hope you took into account the Pan Am rate at the hotel."

Peter got a serious look on his face, took both of Mia's hands in his, and looked directly into her eyes. "I have a concern that I need to discuss with you," he said.

Mia's heart sank. Had he noticed that something was out of place when he retrieved the envelope from his carry-on? Her mind was racing as she tried to maintain her composure. "What is it? Wasn't I good in bed this time?"

Peter pressed his naked body up against her and whispered into her ear, "You silly thing. All I was going to say is that I'm about ready to pass out if I don't get some food. All I've had to eat today was a bag of nuts and a measly in-flight lunch. With all our exercise, I've worked up quite an appetite." Mia inadvertently moved against him in relief. Peter said, "Slow down—much more of that and we'll end up back in bed instead of at a restaurant...and you'll be responsible for my death from starvation."

"Sorry—I'm so relieved my lovemaking is still up to par. I have a nice surprise planned for dinner. Natalie made a reservation for us at her father's restaurant, Pietro's. It's a short taxi ride away, and they'll hold our table until we get there. Now that I know how hungry you are, we should be on our way."

With an appreciative eye, Peter watched Mia get dressed. She wasn't trying to arouse him, but just watching her lacy French underthings slide up her body was enough to get a rise out of any red-blooded male. To top it all off, she put on one of her favorite scoop-neck dresses that showed enough cleavage to get attention wherever she went. The crowd at Pietro's was in for a visual treat. Having her on his arm made Peter feel like a king.

When they arrived at the restaurant, they were greeted warmly by Leo, the maître d'. "Just a minute, I'll get Nat. I'm sure he'll want to say hello and show you to your table."

Nat appeared in his chef's whites and toque. He gave Mia a quick hug. "How are you, my dear?" he asked with his slight Italian accent. "And who is this handsome young man?" Mia introduced Peter, who basked in Nat's fatherly warmth; he made everyone feel like family. "If you're looking for a dinner recommendation, the veal marsala is always a favorite, and our steaks are all prime cuts," Nat said.

He took Peter and Mia to a special table by the window. The waiter arrived promptly; Peter ordered a double scotch on the rocks, and Mia a glass of Gavi di Gavi. Peter ordered the scampi appetizer and Mia had melon with prosciutto. They took Nat's recommendations; Peter had sirloin strip steak, and Mia chose the veal marsala with mushrooms. The waiter recommended a bottle of Chianti Classico, that they finished with no trouble. Mia made sure that Peter had the lion's share, and when it was gone he ordered another glass.

During dinner, Mia tried to keep the conversation focused on her, because she didn't want Peter to talk about the world of submarines until they were back at the hotel, on tape. She relayed stories told to her by her parents about how much the Germans hated the Soviets, and how brutal they had been to people in the Eastern Zone. She told stories about her travels

and interesting people she met flying Pan Am. Peter was enter-
tained, relaxed, and happy.

"What a wonderful meal. No wonder Max fancies Natalie—
Pietro's is a terrific fringe benefit. Does anything on the dessert
menu catch your eye?"

"The spumoni is nice," said Mia. "Let's split it—we can get
espresso or cappuccino to go with it, and finish things off with a
glass of Sambuca."

"You've obviously been here before," said Peter, finishing
his Chianti.

"Natalie's father is very good to us. He keeps our freezer
stocked with steaks and chops, as well as other goodies. We all
appreciate his generosity."

Once back in the hotel room, Mia had a plan to gather the
needed information. The first order of business would be to
make Peter a stiff scotch on the rocks to further reduce his inhibitions. Next, she would ease him into talking about submarine
operations in general and then his specific ambitions as a naval
officer. Based on Peter's answers, she would try to maneuver
the conversation toward the specific questions Ivan had given
her.

There were four questions remaining, so if she could get to
three of the four, they would probably consider that she had
done a competent job. She made a conscious decision to hold
off on any sexual activities until after the submarine Q and A.
Pillow talk about submarine systems would be too much out
of context after lovemaking. Also, once her business with Ivan
was out of the way, she could really concentrate on creating an
atmosphere for lovemaking. She looked forward to rewarding
herself for a job well done.

"Let's settle down on the love seat and I'll make you comfortable," suggested Mia. She took off his shoes and gently

massaged his feet for a few minutes. "You've had a busy day, coming to me all the way from sunny Spain."

"Oh, that feels really good—I'll give you two days to stop," joked Peter, taking a sip of his scotch. "Mia, I want you to take some time to relax, too. Why don't you sit next to me?"

She curled up on the love seat. "I feel as if your job is so much harder than mine—after all, I just fly around to exotic locations, making people happy. But you...do you really enjoy it? It seems that before being assigned to the Board, you spent some dreadfully long periods of time at sea, away from civilization. Don't you miss being in touch with the outside world?"

"Well, it's true that the fast attacks are pretty isolated. But the FBMs, or Boomers, get news all the time. On my last Boomer, we were up to date in real time with what was going on."

Mia acted surprised. "How is that possible, unless you surface?"

"Well, we can't do that, or it would be easy for the bad guys to find us," Peter said with a chuckle. "Suffice it to say that we manage, and if I told you how, I'd have to kill you. I don't want to do that—it would mean no more sex tonight, and I was really looking forward to round three."

"You are so funny. Of course, you can't give away any secrets; then they wouldn't be secrets anymore."

"What secrets do you have, Mia?" asked Peter.

"I have a few secret surprises in my overnight bag," she replied. "I'll reveal them to you in time, if you're good."

The probe on submarine communications continued off and on for the rest of the evening. Mia was able to get all the required questions in, but although Peter's answers were straightforward on the "what;" he provided no specifics on the "how." Mia found herself frustrated by knowing only that the Boomers stayed in constant communication, without any explanation of how they did it. She could only imagine how much more frustrated Ivan would be.

Once the Q and A was over, Mia kept her promise and brought out her overnight bag. "Recognize any of these things?" she asked with a naughty smile.

"I've seen some of them advertised in men's magazines, but this is my first time up close and personal," said Peter. He had no idea where this was going, but he was happy to be along for the ride. Before they finally got to sleep that night, Peter discovered that some of those little things really worked, and in certain instances were labor-saving devices.

When they woke up the next morning, they made love again—just them, no toys. This allowed for individual expression and further exploration of their individual sexuality. Afterward, they decided to go over to the Four Seasons for the famous breakfast buffet.

They were hardly out of the hotel before the KGB team was all over the room, retrieving the audio and video tapes. The tapes were immediately delivered to Ivan, whose team of analysts went right to work. Within four hours, the analysis was complete, and a summary report prepared. Copies of the raw data and the summary report were put in a diplomatic pouch for the next flight to Moscow. Less than ten hours later, Mortin, Gorsky, and the team were poring over the information that Songbird had gathered. She had done her job; however, it was immediately apparent that Neutron had not provided any actionable intelligence.

Gorsky spoke first. "It is obvious that we will have to raise this effort to the next level. I don't believe Neutron is suspicious, but it is clear that he is cautious, talking to a foreign national. Either consciously or subconsciously, he is wary of saying too much, no matter how drunk he is. The absence of the inspection documents is not a concern—I think Songbird is playing it straight. The simplest explanation is that Neutron sent the documents back to Norfolk with one of the other team members. I doubt we missed anything of significant intelligence value."

Mortin said, "Gorsky, I think you gave an accurate summary of the situation. I agree that more aggressive action is needed to take this operation to the next level. Take two weeks to put together a plan. At this time, we don't even know when Songbird and Neutron are planning to meet again. When we have that information, we can develop a timeline. Some creative thought will be required from all of you. Gentlemen, we will reconvene in two weeks."

New York City
January 21st, 1973

Late in the afternoon of January 21st, Natalie had just awakened, following a 6:00 a.m. arrival from a trip to Africa, when the phone rang. Automatically she said, "*Pronto*," as she picked up.

It was Max, who replied, "Natalie, I hear the Italian in you coming out—and that's my favorite part, *carissima*."

Just to be smart, she answered, "*C'est moi, mon chéri.*"

"No, I want the Italian part, not the French part. Now that we have exhausted my entire vocabulary in both languages, how about English? If my calendar is correct, you just got back from a pretty good trip to Africa, *n'est-ce pas?*"

Natalie laughed at his little joke. His timing was perfect; Natalie had promised to be over at Scott's in an hour; she would have hated to miss Max's call.

"I'm just terrific. It was a pretty easy trip with no problems and lots of beach time in Monrovia. How about you?"

Max said, "Well, to tell the truth, I wish I had been more

attentive about wishing you a Merry Christmas and a Happy New Year. The entire month was a little crazy, and then I went to Philly to visit my parents, and before I knew it Christmas and New Year's had come and gone. I tried calling the apartment, but there was no answer. I wasn't very persistent."

"Don't be so hard on yourself; I didn't do a heck of a lot better. You saw my December schedule—I blinked, and before I knew it, it was 1973. We can make up for it when you visit on the 27th."

"That sounds perfect. Unfortunately, I have to be back in Norfolk early on the 28th for an all-hands farewell luncheon at the Officers' Club, so I'll have to catch a late plane on the 27th."

"We can hang out here at the apartment. Everyone will be gone, and we'll have the place to ourselves. We never run out of things to talk about, and we'll have a whole month of news to catch up on. If I don't talk to you before the 27th, just call when you land at JFK."

"Perfect," said Max, "I can't wait to see your smile and claim a belated kiss under the mistletoe—don't take it down until after I leave."

"I've never had a guy ask me for anything like that before," said Natalie with a laugh.

"I'm a unique guy," replied Max.

Yes, you are, thought Natalie as she hung up the phone.

She was on her way out the door to see Scott, partly to congratulate him on his successful admission to Columbia. He'd just walked into the registration office with his Princeton credentials and secured a slot in the Finance and Economics focus in the MBA program. This would mean two more years of waiting for Natalie, though she was pleased that Scott finally took action to resolve his "unemployment." He still hadn't asked her to marry him—and until he did…well, she couldn't get Max out of her mind, and she couldn't wait for the 27th.

Chapter 25

New York City
January 27th, 1972

Max's elevator ride up to 8L seemed to take forever. The little flutter in the pit of his stomach was already there as he knocked. Natalie flung open the apartment door, put both arms around his neck, and gave him a series of soft, teasing kisses.

"Hey, give a guy a chance—I haven't even put down my luggage."

Once inside, Max tossed his bags aside and returned her affection, putting both arms around her, lifting her off the floor, and giving her a 360° spin before setting her down and returning the kiss.

"Seems like you missed me," said Natalie.

"You can't imagine how much," Max replied. "How about a little dance before I get my coat off?"

It was not a coincidence that Frank was singing "Once Upon a Time," since Natalie had put her favorite albums on the turntable in anticipation of Max's arrival. The request for a dance was a surprise, but in keeping with Max's overall approach to life—seize the opportunity when it presented itself. Natalie pressed her whole body firmly against Max's solid frame during their little dance. She thought, *I just can't believe how good this feels. This is what I have been missing for the last six weeks.*

"How about some wine?" she asked. "I have two bottles of your favorite Sancerre in the fridge. The glasses are already on the table."

In the blink of an eye, the glasses were filled, bottle back in the fridge, and Max and Natalie assumed their usual position on the couch. Max put his arm around her, and with his free hand gently tilted her pretty face upward so he could kiss her. Natalie responded by running her hands up and down his hard, muscular chest. He felt so good to be with. She was not shy, and did her share of exploring during the kiss. When they finally separated, Max broke the silence.

"You know — I've been meaning to ask you about your work and your trips. I go to the same places all the time and want to live vicariously through your travels. What are some of your favorite or most interesting trips?"

"You've hit on it just right; there is a difference between favorite and interesting. Let's start with interesting. I took one of my very good friends to Moscow during the spring of last year. It wasn't exactly a favorite destination, but it sure was interesting. Moscow is a very depressing place. The average American has no idea how bad things are over there — not enough of anything, except maybe vodka."

Max wondered why she didn't tell him who she took on the trip, though he figured it must have been Scott. Occasionally he had daydreamed that he and Natalie would be able to meet in some exotic locale — Casablanca would do just fine, as far as he was concerned. He couldn't decide whether to leave the mystery companion question alone or pursue it. He decided on the latter.

"So, who was the 'very good friend' you took with you to Moscow?"

Natalie decided to toy with Max a bit. "Do I detect a hint of jealousy? Would you like to take a trip with me sometime to a faraway place? Where would we go, if you had your choice?"

"Someplace I've never been, which is a pretty wide field. But you're changing the subject — who was your traveling companion?"

"You silly thing—it was Daddy, of course. Actually, what made the trip interesting was that Daddy has a friend there who's also a client, employed as an AP reporter. The food in the restaurants was inedible, except for the caviar and black bread. But all was not lost. We were invited to his apartment a couple of times for dinner and his lovely new wife from New Zealand was an excellent cook."

"Moscow doesn't sound like much fun...just interesting. Where have you enjoyed going?"

"Believe it or not, I'm in Teheran fairly often because that trip goes through Rome, and as an Italian speaker, I bid that line often. It's an interesting city, out of the norm for an American tourist. One of the accidental benefits of the trip is the ability to buy caviar—and I mean the real Caspian Sea sturgeon variety—at rock-bottom prices. I usually pay $6 for 300 grams—it is just one level above grand theft larceny. My friend Celeste and I have the system down pat. The pilots all know that she loves to shop for a variety of things, in addition to the frequent caviar purchases. During one trip, we scurried off to purchase some particularly attractive brass barbecue skewers. As we hurried back to the plane, one of the pilots said, 'Here come the merchants!' I guess he nailed that one. I've never been one to pass up a bargain."

"Wow—it sounds like the trip would be worthwhile just for the caviar...but of course, I'd want to go only with you. All this food talk is making me hungry. Can I steal something from the fridge? And I think we need that second bottle of Sancerre."

"I'm way ahead of you. There's a platter of nibbles Daddy sent from Pietro's and some other things I picked up at the deli earlier today. Why don't you open the wine; I'll put the goodies on the table, and we'll have a little lunch."

Max grabbed her around the waist, gave her a little kiss, and said, "You think of everything. I guess you believe the old adage that the way to a man's heart is through his stomach. I plead guilty to being a sucker for that one."

Max opened the second bottle of excellent wine, which was making its effects known, as both of them were feeling relaxed and carefree. Once lunch was well underway, Max decided to acknowledge the elephant in the room. "How are things with Scott?"

"Believe it or not, there has been movement. He was able to enroll at Columbia, starting at the Business School this semester."

"How do you feel about that? I assume this means another two years before you find out whether there's a wedding in your future."

"The good news is that there seems to be a plan. The bad news is that I still have to wait another two years. A lot can happen in two years. You don't see a ring on my finger, do you?"

Max replied, "I'll give it to you short and sweet—it looks like you've decided that he's the one. He broke it off once—why, I'll never understand—and fortunately for him, you didn't get away to San Francisco before he came to his senses. You took him back without question. That was two years ago. Now, he wants another two years. If I were you, I wouldn't give it to him—at a minimum, you should ask for a commitment to marry, date to be determined."

Natalie knew Max was right. Enough was enough. However, the situation had been complicated by Max's arrival on the scene. If nothing else, their brief relationship had demonstrated to her that she could care for someone other than Scott. She and Max had never actually said they loved one another, but all the signs were there. Max had so many desirable qualities that were compatible with her values, and she could see no impediment to their having a long-term relationship.

However, he had never tried to sweep her off her feet. He had been a perfect gentleman, even though she had decided after the night at Hippopotamus that she would go to bed with Max if she had the chance. But he was holding back—why, she didn't know. If only he would give her a reason to reconsider her relationship with Scott, the future would open up for them. Instead, he seemed invested in pushing her back toward the familiar.

They were done with lunch, so Natalie said, "Let's go back to the couch and relax a bit. Your advice about Scott is, of course, very reasonable. I just want to make sure I do the right thing. Looks like you'll have to leave in about 45 minutes, if you want to catch that flight. We don't need to spend that time talking about Scott. The situation is clear to me."

Max and Natalie and the bottle of Sancerre moved back to the couch. Natalie had put a collection of recent hits on the tape player. Strains of "We May Never Pass This Way Again" by Seals and Croft filled the air as they settled next to each other, Max's arm around Natalie and her head on his shoulder.

Chapter 26

As the tape drifted into Carole King's "You've Got a Friend," Max and Natalie's kisses got deeper and longer, interrupted only for an occasional sip of Sancerre, which only helped to move things along. Things heated up on the couch, and before long, Natalie was lying on her back and Max was kneeling on the floor next to her, cradling her face in his hands and returning her soft, frequent kisses.

Max gazed into her eyes. "Do you know how happy I am just to be here in New York with you, even if it is only for a little while?"

Natalie didn't know what to say, so she said nothing; instead she put her arms around his neck, pulled him to her, and gave him another series of soft kisses. Max felt his heart squeeze painfully—what had he done to deserve the affection of this incredible woman? *Oh, why couldn't she have come along seven years ago?* he wondered. Carol King continued to help the agenda, singing softly, "Will You Still Love Me Tomorrow?"

Max's knees started to protest, so he eased himself back up onto the couch next to Natalie. She could feel that he was fully aroused as his body pressed against hers. She wasn't wearing anything underneath her soft cashmere sweater, and her nipples were getting plenty of attention from Max's chest as he moved against her with gentle intimacy. He knew this had to end soon; he had to get to JFK and back to Norfolk. But it was torture to tear himself away from her. *Sooner or later, this situation will get resolved*, he thought, though he had no idea how or when.

Natalie was tantalizingly aware of the bedroom only a few steps away. She wasn't sure where this was headed, but they'd gone further than ever before, and any doubts she'd had about Max's interest had been swept away. But he was still a model of self-control and respect, which only increased her admiration and affection. She was obviously inviting his attentions—what could possibly stand in their way?

Suddenly, she knew.

Natalie stopped kissing him. "Max, are you married?" she asked.

Max's wheels were spinning. "How did we get on that subject?"

"I asked."

Max felt his heart skip a beat. "You're asking me now, when I have to leave in five minutes to catch a plane?" He saw from her face that she had guessed the truth; there was no way out now. "I'm separated," he admitted.

"Thanks for being honest," Natalie said with a sigh.

It was bad news, but she was relieved to know. It explained why he had seemed unnaturally restrained, and why he had not more vigorously pursued a relationship with her. For a few moments that seemed to stretch into an eternity, they just lay in each other's arms on the couch, not saying a word. Natalie was both happy and unhappy; her feelings for him were too strong to let things continue to limp along. Serious decisions in her life would be based on knowing whether a future with Max was a possibility, or if she needed to push Scott to make a commitment. Her two viable options were now down to one—she would have to decide very soon how to approach Scott.

Carole King was spot on again, singing "It's Too Late." The

irony was not lost on either of them. Finally, Max broke the silence when the song ended. "It has been a fabulous five months. You are so very special to me, and I really want you to have the happiness you deserve. Push the agenda with Scott, and if he isn't interested, move on. Life is too short. Now I'd better get moving, or I'll miss the plane. I have no idea how bad the afternoon traffic will be."

"Thank you so much for everything," Natalie said. "You have been a perfect gentleman, and I admire you for that."

Even though he was sure he knew the answer, Max dared to ask, "Would you consider marrying someone who is divorced?"

"No," Natalie replied, even though that wasn't quite true. It was the right answer in the moment, however.

Time was now becoming a problem. Max threw on his coat and held Natalie in his arms for one last long kiss. "Travel safely," she said.

"Thanks," he said.

He was upset to leave on such a sour note, and Natalie knew it. After she closed the door softly behind him, she thought long and hard about the entire afternoon. She had promised Scott she would come over later, so she got herself together and was quickly on her way. Scott had no idea what was in store for him.

Max was feeling pressured; it would be touch and go to catch his flight. As he sat in the cab, he realized that he should have just let this one go and tried to book the next flight to Norfolk— he knew there was at least one more. The traffic was heavy, and he was in danger of missing his Carey bus connection, so he told the driver to take him directly to the National terminal at JFK. For some reason the Queens-Midtown tunnel was jammed, and the minutes were ticking away.

When he arrived at National, he sprinted up to the departure gate. Fortunately, the plane was still there; unfortunately, the door was shut. They would not open it for him despite his show-ing his military ID and pleading "operational necessity." No dice. It was back to the waiting area with his bags, his thoughts, and a two-hour delay. He finally got up the courage to call Natalie, but there was no answer. He assumed, correctly, that she was over at Scott's, but he would never have guessed the drama unfold-ing while his unanswered call was ringing at 8L.

Max had a lot of time to think while he waited. He bought a book but couldn't focus on it. His thoughts kept going back to Natalie and the events of the afternoon. He was feeling a lot of Catholic guilt, even though he hadn't actually lied to her; he just hadn't told her the whole truth. He had convinced himself that his marital status didn't matter; she had a serious boyfriend who would surely marry her eventually. Max told himself he was just a pleasant diversion…her last fling before she tied the knot. He had been careful not to lead her on, and he hadn't pressured her for physical intimacy.

Nevertheless, the afternoon's events weighed heavily on him. Why had she chosen that precise moment to ask such a cru-cial question? There were many possible answers, not the least of which was that if he had lied convincingly, he was sure they would have ended up in the bedroom, and he would have re-booked for the early-morning flight to Norfolk. He would never have lied to her, though, no matter how tempted he was by the prospect of sleeping with her. He still believed in honor.

Back in New York, Natalie wasn't wasting any time. She went to see Scott, who was expecting her, but not what was about to happen. She got right to the point.

"Scott, I am breaking up with you. It's been really beautiful, but it's over. I'm happy that you're back in school and getting on with your life. Don't bother calling me to ask how I am; you can be assured that I am in good health and getting on with my life.

If you want to ask me to marry you, call me. Otherwise, we have nothing more to say to each other. That's it. Goodbye."

Scott just stared at her, expressionless. He knew she was serious. She didn't give him her schedule; she had already made their relationship too easy for him. She didn't expect him to call with the restriction she had just laid out, but if he did want to reach her, he would have to work for it. He should have seen this coming; she had made no secret of the fact that she was unhappy with his having quit Smith Barney with no immediate backup plan, and of course there had been the temporary breakup two years ago.

"You've been pretty clear," he said. "I think I get the picture."

With that, Natalie gave him a chaste kiss on the lips and was gone. When she left Scott's apartment, her step was lighter and she felt an enormous degree of relief. She took a walk over to John Jay Park and looked out over the East River for a long time. She knew she had done the right thing; enough was enough. Her feelings for Max made it easier. She noticed that the chalk mark on the light pole at the park entrance was gone—probably park maintenance had cleaned it off.

When she finally got back to the apartment, she poured one more glass of wine and sat down to contemplate the events of the afternoon. She was convinced that Scott would never call, and she certainly wasn't going to call him. The ball was squarely in his court. Let him waste time in grad school for two years—by that time, she was convinced, she would have found someone else and moved on. If nothing else, Max had proven to her that she could really care for another person besides Scott, which made it easier to give him her ultimatum. If he couldn't step up to the plate, maybe someone just as good or better would come along. She believed she would see Max again, but they had left things too much up in the air to be certain. He had her number, though. And then there was the issue of Mia and Peter. Maybe they should discuss that at least one more time—it still nagged at her.

She busied herself getting ready for her next Africa trip, looking forward to some more beach time in Monrovia. She had a lot of traveling and fun planned for the next several weeks. She wondered whether Max had made his plane. He was very special to her; even if he was separated and working through a failing marriage. That didn't change her deep feelings for him. As for Scott, it was about time he decided what he wanted to do with the rest of his life, and whether she was going to be part of it.

Chapter 27

Doug noted that Max was moping around, not saying much. He put an affectionate arm around Max's shoulder. "Hey, buddy—I know it was a pain in the ass to come back for Callaghan's farewell luncheon, but there will be plenty of other nights to stay over in New York with *beaucoup* opportunities to hang out with Natalie."

Max stared at the floor. "Well, you got that one wrong 100%."

"What happened? Did she ditch you? I know you really like her, but there are a ton of girls in the New York club scene. What do you say we head up to NYC soon? We don't have to stay in that same fleabag hotel—maybe Mia can get us a rate at that Pan Am layover hotel."

"I'm not too keen on New York without Natalie," said Max.

"What happened?"

Max shrugged. "We were going hot and heavy on the couch, when out of nowhere she asked if I was married. I couldn't lie to her, so I told her the truth—that I'm separated. It all happened right before I had to leave."

Doug looked puzzled. "Why would she drop a bomb like that?'

"I guess it's my own fault. I should have told her a long time ago. Since she had a main squeeze, I figured it didn't make any difference—I was just a guy who was fun to go dancing with once in a while. I didn't expect to fall for her. I thought she really wanted to marry the guy, so it didn't matter. Now I think there's more to it, but there was no time to talk. I had to take a taxi to JFK, and even then, I still missed the plane. I tried to call her during those two endless hours I spent in the National lounge, but nobody was home, so I gave up."

Doug fixed a pair of Bloody Marys. "Here, this will straighten you out. I guess it will be up to Peter to be the standard-bearer from here on in Camp Pan Am."

Max munched a celery stick. "I've been meaning to talk to you about that. I know Peter has a great track record using the farm boy act, but Mia has been around the block a few times. Natalie said she often exhibits unusual behavior. No details yet, but she's worried Mia may not be playing it straight."

Doug dropped in a little more Tabasco. "We know she's a foreign national; with our clearances, it's not the smartest thing in the world for Peter to do. When you and I were dating Caroline and Natalie, there was a chance that we could keep an eye on Mia, but now—nothing."

Max finished his celery stick. "Let's corner Peter after the luncheon today and pump him for information. Natalie's concerns are reason enough. We'll start with the fact that Mia is a foreign national; even though she's a Brit, it's still a problem."

New York

When Natalie was up first on Sunday morning bouncing all over the apartment making coffee and prepping for breakfast, Caroline knew something was up. Caroline stretched and yawned, joining Natalie in the kitchen. "OK, Nat—what's up? I know Max stopped by yesterday. Did something happen?"

Natalie put her hands on her hips. "Well, I was a very busy girl yesterday. First, I found out that Max is married but separated.

As soon as he was out the door, I marched my little self across the street and broke up with Scott—I mean really broke up; I told him not to bother calling me unless he is ready to propose marriage. The whole thing took less than ten minutes."

Caroline burst out laughing. "Natalie, it's the 28th of January, not April 1st. What really happened? Did you and Max slip between the sheets?"

"I'm dead serious; it happened just the way I told you. Getting rid of Scott is a huge weight off my shoulders. I skipped all the way down 77th to the park and just looked at the river for a long time. I knew I'd done the right thing. Max is another matter; I am sad about the situation. He asked me if I would consider marrying a divorced man, and I lied and said no. We never even discussed the particulars of his situation—I don't know whether he has children, but I am not equipped to deal with a ready-made family. I completely blindsided both of them. Scott was practically speechless; Max just gave me a big hug and was gone. I doubt I'll hear from either of them."

Natalie wiped a little tear from her eye. "Max never did anything wrong. I asked, and he told me the truth. I guess he figured since I had Scott, he was happy to keep seeing me until wedding bells started ringing. He did me a big favor. He made me realize I could really care for someone other than Scott. Once I knew that, breaking up with Scott was a piece of cake. Scott, on the other hand, has had a bunch of chances. His latest grad school caper will delay any thought of marriage for another two years. An ultimatum was clearly in order."

Natalie got out her little red book and started making notes. "I seriously doubt Scott will be in contact, so I'm going to make some calls later today. Let's see—Victor the banker might have moved on by now, but it won't hurt to try him. There's Bill the reporter with the Associated Press; there's Dick, who works for

Westinghouse and sells commercial nuclear power plants. Do you think three is enough for starters? I'm going to let them know I'm available. If they call while I'm on the Africa trip, just make notes and tell them I'll return the call when I'm back in town."

Caroline's jaw had dropped open while Natalie was on her rant. "Well, Nat—I think three is just fine, even if it does seem a little soon...you just broke up with Scott yesterday, after all. However, I can see you're a woman on a mission; I'll help any way I can."

Mia entered the kitchen and caught the end of the conversation. "Sounds like I'm the last contestant in the Navy game. The problem with Peter is our schedules are going in opposite directions for most of February. Our next date is pushed to the end of next month."

Norfolk

The luncheon for Captain Callaghan was at the Officers' Club, Main Navy in Norfolk. Compared to the farewell parties for the lieutenant commanders, this was a fairly tame affair. The club itself was frequented by admirals and generals and did not cater to more junior officers. Doug, Max, and Peter sat together; copious amounts of alcohol made the staid affair tolerable. When the luncheon was over, all were feeling no pain. It was easy to convince Peter to stay for another round of drinks. To ensure discretion, they assembled in a quiet corner of the enclosed porch. Doug led off, telling Peter about Max's fall from grace. Peter knew that things had fizzled out between Doug and Caroline; so now it was apparent he was all alone in the Pan Am playground on First Avenue.

Doug tapped Peter's forearm. "Hey, guy—how much do

you know about Mia? Where's she from? And what do you two talk about? On the surface, it doesn't seem that you have much in common."

Peter set down his drink. "She was born in East Berlin, and when she was a baby, her family fled to the UK. She went to Manchester University and studied mechanical engineering. She's technically very savvy and loves talking about submarines and what we do on the Board. I keep the conversation general, but she always has a lot of questions. Now that you mention it... we don't talk about much else."

Doug exploded, "Are you fucking insane? You are dating a foreign national born in East Berlin, and all you talk about is submarines?"

Peter smiled. "Well, not really—we do spend an equal amount of time talking about and having sex. I just assumed she is a British citizen, since she lived there most of her life."

Max shook his head. "When are you seeing her again? I think we all need to go and have a talk with NIS."

"We haven't worked that out. Our February schedules have us limited to a wave at JFK, going in opposite directions. You know tomorrow I leave for a double at Holy Loch, and won't be back for over two weeks."

Max recalled Natalie's concerns. "Peter, as soon as you get back, we are going over to NIS. In the interim, make a list of all the things you talked about. Don't talk to anyone about this. Probably nothing to worry about, but best to get out in front of it before the shit hits the fan."

Chapter 28

Moscow—New York City
February 1ˢᵗ-4ᵗʰ, 1973

Mortin was late to the meeting, which was unusual. While waiting, the admiral provided his insight. "I met with my technical and operational staffs. They put together specific needs Neutron must obtain. If the information from the tapes is correct, Neutron has the ability to design drills for our use and record the data as certain operational parameters change."

Mortin burst into the room. "I had a last-minute meeting with the chairman. He has huge expectations from today's get-together. Gorsky, I hope you have a solid plan of attack."

Gorsky exuded confidence. "We must turn Neutron as soon as possible and already have him well set-up. We have a photograph of him accepting an envelope; the technicians inserted a dummied close-up of a model's hands with a stack of hundred-dollar bills. Further, they altered and spliced the audio tapes to make it appear that Neutron is providing sensitive information. The most damning evidence is the photographs of the documents Songbird collected during their first meeting."

Mortin leaned forward in his chair. "Excellent work, Gorsky—excellent work. How will we actually get Neutron turned?"

"We decided first to try the soft sell. The next time Songbird and Neutron are together, she will tell him the Russians made her do it and that we have amassed evidence against him. She will offer excellent monetary compensation and a continued sexual liaison. To make the offer palatable, he need only work for the Soviets until a specific amount of information is gathered. At that point, both he and Songbird will be released from further obligation, and can have a life together. Of course, this is completely untrue; once we have him, he is ours for as long as we want him.

"If this doesn't work, she will tell him the KGB will be in touch with a much less favorable offer. His choice is to work for us or endure public shame. Either way, his goose is cooked. She'll tell him we have contacts in the leftist media that are more than willing to disgrace the US Navy.

"What we don't know is when this will happen. Songbird told Ivan their February schedules are completely incompatible. However, to move things along, Songbird asked Neutron to arrange a fairly open schedule in March."

Clearly, Mortin was pleased. "Excellent! Just Excellent! In the interim, Admiral, I want a complete list of information for Neutron to gather."

This was the admiral's moment to shine. "Before our meeting started, I told the group we already started such an endeavor. We will now accelerate developing a final wish list. In the end, it may require creative thought by Neutron, but he is a pretty smart guy. He'll just have to perform to save his ass."

Mortin was beaming. "We will reconvene immediately after Songbird and Neutron's next meeting, when he is turned. Gorsky, travel to New York, meet with Ivan, and between the two of you arrange the best way for Songbird to execute the plan."

New York

Natalie got back to 8L from her Africa trip at 8:00 a.m. on February 4th. "Hey, Caroline—I'm going to nap until mid-afternoon. Make sure I'm up in time for us to get to the Four Seasons for happy hour free bar food. This will help me reset set my internal clock and then go to bed at the normal time. Did anyone call?"

Caroline presented the note pad from the phone table. "Two out of three ain't bad. Victor and Bill called. Dick did not. Their return numbers are here. I told them you wouldn't be back till tomorrow. By the way, you look fabulous with your West Africa tan. You'll have to beat them off with a stick when you go out clubbing."

Natalie did a glamour girl pose. "Do you really think so? I am available, so to speak, and I'm going to enjoy it. I'm off to dream of things to come."

Oddly enough, Natalie thought of Max, rather than things to come. As she drifted off to sleep, she wondered how he was doing. She got up at 3:30 and hopped into the shower. She chose an outfit and put on enough makeup to attract attention from the quiet, more affluent crowd at the Four Seasons. She and Caroline spent about an hour catching up, and were in a good mood when Mia returned home.

Mia picked up the ringing phone. "This is the book club calling for Mia Beck. Is she available?"

"This is she."

"Oh, very good," said the voice on the other end. "We regret to tell you that the normal selection is not available this month. You can either decline, or accept the alternate selection, that will be mailed out on the 5th."

"That is perfectly acceptable. Thank you for calling and telling me, rather than just sending something out. Goodbye for now." Mia rung off.

Caroline nudged Natalie. "I thought for sure that was Dick, making it three for three."

Mia said, "Is the shower free? It looks like you girls are all ready to go. I'm popping off to Beekman Towers to meet Sabrina and some friends."

Caroline and Natalie decided on another glass of wine before confronting commercial happy hour. Before they were finished Mia appeared, wearing the scoop-neck dress she wore the night the Navy guys visited. The view was spectacular and would certainly turn heads at Beekman. With a quick "Cheers!" she flew out the door.

"We'd better get going, if we want a seat at that wonderful square bar," Natalie said. She and Caroline touched up their lipstick, and they were off for fun and frolic in Manhattan.

Natalie was first into the bar area when they got to the Four Seasons. She immediately did an about-face and said to Caroline, "I've changed my mind—just go with it; I have my reasons. Let's go over to the Plaza. The bar isn't as interesting, but the crowd is just as good—maybe better."

Caroline grabbed Natalie's arm and murmured, "What's going on?"

"I thought I saw Dick at the far end of the bar. This is our night out, and I don't want to talk to him and leave you stranded. We haven't talked in over a week."

"I don't mind—I like Dick," Caroline said.

Natalie was adamant. "Really, I would rather go over to the Plaza."

The reality was Natalie had caught sight of Mia with her short blonde hair and familiar dress. Across from her, leaning in close, was a man who looked vaguely familiar. Natalie tried hard to place the man from the sea of faces she encountered on a daily basis while flying. Someplace on a plane…where had she seen him? She needed time to think, and a side trip to the Plaza was the best she could do at the moment. She and Caroline got there, ordered two white wines, and toasted Natalie's newfound freedom. Caroline could tell Natalie was distracted.

Suddenly, Natalie remembered where she had seen the face.

It was on the trip back from Moscow with her father in the spring of 1972. One of the flight crew snapped a candid shot of her and Daddy standing in the aisle, and she was fairly certain the face across from Mia was in the background — the photo was one of her favorites, and she looked at it often. She also remembered that the man had spent a lot of time chatting with a particular flight attendant.

"Oh, damn!" exclaimed Natalie. "I promised my mother I would stop by late today, and I completely forgot about it. Let me make a quick call to apologize and tell her I'll be there in about an hour. I'm really sorry, Caroline. She wasn't specific about why she wanted to see me; I think it may be something about Daddy's health that she didn't want to discuss over the phone. He's still at Pietro's, so this would be the perfect time to see her. Do you want to stay here or share a taxi? If we taxi, I can hop out and get the subway at Lex."

Caroline looked perplexed. "Let's grab a taxi; when you get back from your parents', maybe we can watch a late-night movie and make popcorn."

Natalie gave her a big hug. "Caroline, you are the best friend ever. Thanks for understanding. Let's go."

Natalie hopped on the Dyer Avenue Line, number 5. It was only two blocks to her parents' house on Yates Avenue from her stop. She still loved this neighborhood where she had grown up on a quiet, tree-lined street with a mix of duplexes and single-family homes. Theirs was a single, with an oversized lot that had plenty of space for playing games when she was a kid.

Although she called ahead, her mother was surprised to see her. Natalie rarely just showed up. With a big hug, her mother said, "What brings you all the way out here on a Sunday evening?"

Natalie smiled. "Mother, it's the silliest thing, — one of my friends is making a trip to Moscow in a few weeks, and I wanted to show her some of the pictures that Daddy and I took when we were there last spring. Are the albums in the usual place?"

"They are. Do you have time for a coffee and something sweet before you go back to your apartment?"

"Of course. But I may have to make a phone call first." Natalie easily found the album and quickly leafed through the familiar photographs. There at the end of the trip section were two candid shots of her and Daddy on the plane, with a man's face clearly visible in the background. She knew she wasn't mistaken; he had made a nuisance of himself with the crew, so he was easy to remember.

With the album under her arm, she said, "I have to go upstairs for a minute to make a phone call. I'll be just a few minutes, and then we'll have that cup of coffee." She got out her little red book and dialed Max's number in Norfolk. Doug answered, and she greeted him warmly and asked for Max, who came on the line immediately.

"Hi, Max. It's Natalie. How are you doing?"

"Not so good, really. I'm feeling guilty about the way things ended between us. I really am sorry."

"I'd like to talk to you about all of that, but that's not why I called. Maybe we can straighten things out a bit later. Right now I really need to see you on a non-romantic matter. Can you get up to New York tomorrow?"

"Sounds serious. You know I would do anything for you, but tomorrow is impossible — I have to finish my current report by the end of the day and get it turned in for typing…the deadlines are serious business. I have the rest of the week free; I'll get Doug or Peter to do the final proof. Will any other day do?"

"This is insane, but — I leave for Paris late tomorrow. I'll see if I can get you some kind of ticket that will put you in Paris on the 6th, if you can get as far as JFK."

"Let me talk to Doug. He's pretty much the boss of the schedule." Back on the line, Max said, "Doug said we can swing it. Call the office tomorrow — you have the number, right? — and let me know about the ticket to Paris. If you can't manage it, I'll work something out with our travel office. If you don't mind my asking — what the hell is this about?"

"Mia and Peter. I don't want to say anything more. It pertains to our breakfast conversation at JFK. I'll call tomorrow and make final arrangements. For certain, we'll meet at the Hôtel de la Terrasse in Montmartre. You know I wouldn't ask unless this was really important. Time is of the essence; I need to get you involved as quickly as possible."

"You have really piqued my interest; let's talk tomorrow."

Polite goodbyes and the conversation was over. Max thought, *A few days in Paris with Natalie? I can think of worse things.* Even if he just helped with her problem, they would probably have a nice dinner somewhere, and then relive their night at Hippopotamus at a Paris disco.

For Natalie, it was a chance for the closure she desperately wanted. There would be no romance; they had already been down that dead-end road. But she still felt a need for closure.

Chapter 29

Norfolk—New York City
February 5th, 1973

The Board office on the CINCLANTFLT compound was a modest space, considering it housed three senior Navy captains and nine lieutenant commanders. Administrative support consisted of two senior enlisted yeomen who managed report preparation and routine paperwork. Travel was handled by the central travel office.

There were no individual offices. The captains shared a large open office with a door, each having a desk. The junior members were in their own space on the other side of a small central area where the yeoman worked. Max had one of nine cubes, each with a desk and phone, separated from its neighbor by a flimsy government partition. Everybody knew everybody's business; privacy was illusory at best.

Max called Natalie mid-morning. Natalie said, "I have information on our flights—and thank you for humoring me."

Max said, "If I read you right, we need to meet in person and as soon as possible."

"Yes—and I have good news and bad news. The good news is that we'll be able to meet the day after tomorrow in Paris, on the 7th. The bad news is that you have to pay for your own ticket. To get you a good price, we're not on the same flight. I'll work the daily JFK-Paris flight 114, leaving at 8:30 p.m. tomorrow. You're on the daily JFK-London flight 002, leaving at 6:45 p.m. Then you have a short hop from Heathrow to Orly, leaving at 10:00 a.m. Flight 002 is our most prestigious flight; you'll be fascinated when the crew lists the stops for our 'Round the World Flight.' I just love rattling off all the romantic, exotic cities. Just make sure you get off at London," said Natalie with a little laugh.

Max scribbled the information on his notepad. "Sounds pretty straightforward. Once I get to Orly, what's the cheapest and best way to find you?"

"I recommend you take a bus to the Gare du Nord station closest to Montmartre, and then you can take the Métro. Or you can take a taxi—the address is 12-25 rue de Joseph de Maistre, in the 18th arrondissement, Montmartre. I'm sorry I couldn't get you a companion ticket; they're available only for immediate family."

"So, if we could get married between now and tomorrow, we'd be in business in more ways than one."

"That wouldn't work," Natalie said, playing it straight. "There isn't time to get to Vegas and back and still make our flights tomorrow. And then there's the issue of the paperwork before we could even consider a marriage license."

Max chuckled, "Yep, I did forget a few little details. Once again, our timing is not optimum. But seriously, it will be good to see you again and come to closure in a more civilized manner. Our last time together left a lot to be desired. I have the flight details, and I'll get our travel office to issue a ticket based on the booking you made. I'll book a return to JFK on the 9th. I think you said you have a free day on the 8th until you dead head to Milan. This gives me plenty of time to get through the report I'm working on—I can use the extra time. Anything else?"

"That's about it. If there are any changes on either side, let's communicate via telephone. I hate to drag you all the way across the pond, but it really is urgent."

Max was so absorbed in talking to Natalie that he was unaware of Peter in close proximity. Naturally, Peter was curious. He pulled up a chair in Max's cube.

"Yo Max; that sounded pretty serious. I thought it was over a week ago, and now you're trotting off to Paris. What's up?"

Max felt anxiety rising in his chest. What should he tell Peter? It was far too early to break this thing wide open without seeing what Natalie had to offer. Natalie's information would determine how they approached NIS regarding their concerns. Max decided to give Peter just the surface information.

"She wouldn't tell me; however, I trust her judgment. She's not a drama queen, and in the few short months we were together, the emotional level of our relationship was pretty solid. She is smart as hell; if she tells me she needs to discuss something face to face, I take her at her word. Why Paris? I can't get up to New York today or tomorrow, since I have to finish this report. She's working a trip to Paris that leaves tomorrow, and was able to book me a flight through London that gets to Paris on the seventh."

Peter put his hand on Max's knee. "Sounds like a bit of international intrigue to me. There are a whole lot of worse things that can happen to a guy than a day in Paris with someone as pretty as Natalie. To add to the package, she speaks fluent French. What more could you ask for?"

"I'd be lying if I said I'm not looking forward to the adventure. I still have strong feelings for her, and if there's a way for me to help her out of a jam, I'm in. She is very special."

Doug joined the conversation and offered support. "Max and I discussed the situation last night," he said. "Despite an apparent air of secrecy, we decided that prudence dictates that Max should get together with Natalie as soon as possible. If she says something is important, then it is. Hey, Max—how about a game of squash right after work? It will help you relax and get your mind off this stuff."

"You're on, Doug," said Max.

After their squash match, Doug took Max aside in a quiet corner of the locker room. "You were right not to open a can of worms. Just pretend you don't know why Natalie wants to see you. If whatever she has to offer is real, we don't have to tell Peter we knew anything in advance when we trot him over to NIS. If whatever Natalie has is a big zero, then we'll save ourselves a lot of grief with Peter. Regardless, the issue of Mia being a foreign national will have to be addressed."

Soviet Union United Nations Headquarters

Gorsky met Ivan at his office, the day following his meeting with Mia at the Four Seasons. Ivan said, "I would have preferred to present the current situation to Songbird. I have been her sole handler these past several years, and I really do feel I am better equipped to handle this matter. How did she take what you had to offer?"

"She clearly understands the situation. Obviously, she would prefer that the soft sell will work, but she has her doubts. Without presenting hard-core evidence to Neutron, she fears he will not take her seriously. If this is the case, she will turn him over to one of us to close the deal. We have a few weeks to think this over. It appears that they will not meet until the beginning of March. We just have to sit and wait."

Chapter 30

New York City—Paris
February 6th-7th, 1973

Natalie was ready to leave for Paris and the unknown when Mia returned unexpectedly early. Natalie had hoped to avoid Mia before leaving for JFK, and for a moment was at a loss for words. Recovering, she said, "Hi, Mia. I thought I was going to miss you. I'm off to Paris with a rare day off, then dead head to Milan to work a charter back to JFK."

Natalie stared at Mia for a moment, thinking, *What secrets are you hiding behind those blue eyes? The next few days may tell the tale.*

Mia gave Natalie a little wave. "Have a brilliant time in Paris—see you in a few days."

"Thanks," said Natalie as she closed the door. *It might be fun; it might not. At least it will be interesting.* She didn't tell anyone she was going to meet Max—not even Caroline. It was best no one know the true reason for her trip. It would only lead to some very uncomfortable questions, with no acceptable answers

Natalie left in plenty of time to make her 7:00 report time. When she was finally on the bus, her mind was racing a mile a minute. As expected, Scott had not called, but Victor and Bill had. That was nice, but they weren't Max. As for the situation with Mia, all she wanted was to hand the whole mess over to Max. He was smart and level-headed and would know just what to do with the information in her luggage. Where would the picture end up? NIS? CIA?

To complicate matters, her strong feelings for Max remained, but his marital status was a deal breaker. Waiting for a final divorce decree was more uncertain than waiting for Scott to finish graduate school. To add another degree of uncertainty, she didn't even know whether he had children. If so, that would be the final nail in the coffin. However, her feelings for Max were not like a light switch that she could turn off. He had too much going for him.

Finally, swirling in her mind were all the unusual occurrences associated with Mia even before she appeared at the Four Seasons with the man from Moscow. Natalie made a mental list so she would be organized when telling Max the story.

Natalie arrived at the crew lounge early, with time to be alone with her thoughts. She was ready to board the plane and get to work. It was time to be a first-rate flight attendant, which she really enjoyed, rid herself of the Mia business, and eventually find a life partner. With a spring in her step, she walked down the jetway to the waiting 747. She loved flying on these new jumbo jets with all their wonderful features.

Max flew up from Norfolk in plenty of time to catch Flight 002 to London. It was on time, approximately two hours before Natalie's flight left for Paris. Max had his suspicions about what was going on with Mia, but had no idea what had pushed Natalie to demand an instant meeting. Peter's association with a foreign national was trouble enough; if Natalie had something concrete, Peter might be in very hot water.

Then there was the matter of his relationship with Natalie. Their time in Paris would allow them proper closure. No doubt she would eventually move in the direction of having a talk with Scott. He would be a fool to let her go. Max was in love with her, but there was no point in saying so, since he wasn't free to act on his feelings. Once the Mia stuff was out of the way, they could enjoy a day or two in Paris. Seeing The City of Lights for the first time with Natalie by his side would be heavenly. A little bit of intrigue, sweetened by a dash of romance. "Precious and few are the moments," indeed. It was their song, even if their relationship was over.

Max deplaned at Orly and followed Natalie's directions that ended with a three-block walk to the Terrasse Hôtel. He asked if a room had been reserved in his name. Indeed it had; Mlle. Tommasi had reserved a room for him at the Pan Am rate. He was to call her room as soon as LCDR Millen checked in.

Right after Max surrendered his passport, the clerk made the call. Natalie appeared almost immediately, looking just as fabulous as ever. She was dressed in a tan miniskirt, a color-matched cashmere sweater with a Hermès scarf, and loafer-style shoes with a chunky heel. He loved her sense of fashion; she was never overdressed but always stylish and classy.

Her smile was devastating, and he melted. "Max, it is really important that you came." They shared a long embrace and the required three French air kisses on each cheek. It felt like a lot more welcome was needed, but the lobby wasn't the place for it—even though this was Paris.

Max said, "Let me dump this bag in my room. Come with me, and we can get right down to the reason I'm here—it will be private there. I think it best we get that out of the way as soon as possible."

Once in his room with the door closed, there was an awkward moment. They just stood there looking at each other, not moving. Finally, Max said, "I think one of your soft kisses would be in order." Natalie obliged, and Max felt the tingle first in his chest, and then all over. Natalie didn't want to let go, but finally they broke the embrace and Max said, "OK, we'd better get down to the business at hand, or we may never get there."

Max retrieved a steno pad from his carry-on. They took a seat at the small desk in one corner of the room. "Let's start from the beginning," he said. "I have a few of the pieces, but it will be easier if I don't interrupt your train of thought."

Natalie pulled a pile of index cards from her purse. "OK, here we go," she said.

Chapter 31

Paris
February 7th, 1973

"It all started when Mia invited herself to our date night at Hippopotamus and showed an unusual level of interest in you and your naval officer friends. Clean-cut men just aren't Mia's type. She normally prefers shallow, playboy types. Certainly, she and Peter had sex on their first date, which is totally in character.

"Even before that, a series of unusual things happened just after you and I met on the Prestwick flight. Mia and I share a bedroom closet. Right after she returned from her trip, I noticed the Pan Am bag she put away was rather beat up and didn't look like hers at all. I really didn't think much of it at the time.

"The next day, she told me she was going to Bloomingdale's to exchange a bathing suit that was too small for her. I thought it was odd because she's usually so picky and just wouldn't come home with something in the wrong size. I thought she might be pregnant, and was worried she didn't have anyone to talk to… she's always been a little hard to get to know. I decided to go after her and see if I could offer some support. But when I got to Bloomie's, I found out she never visited the swimsuit department. It was strange she would lie about the swimsuit.

"The night we went to Hippopotamus, just before we left the apartment, I went to refresh my lipstick and grabbed Mia's by mistake. The stub was short, and the case looked odd. Since we use the same brand, I thought it peculiar that the cases were different.

"Then, the next day after we had breakfast, Scott and I decided to go for a stroll over to John Jay Park. Mia had left the apartment before us and said she was going to 77th and Lexington to catch the subway. But as we were going east to the park, I saw her coming toward us in the opposite direction. I quickly pulled Scott into a doorway so Mia wouldn't see us. When we got to the park, I noticed that one of the light posts had been marked in white chalk, which struck me as strange since there were no kids nearby playing with chalk and there were no other visible white marks anywhere else. And I certainly hadn't seen them the last time I was in the park.

"The most recent occurrence was similar to the others. As before, Mia announced she was going one place and then went somewhere else entirely. Just two days ago Caroline and I went to the Four Seasons for a cocktail and I couldn't believe my eyes when I saw someone sitting with Mia having drinks. Since Mia had told me she was going to meet some friends at Beekman Tower, she was the last person I expected to see there. She was sitting with her back to us and I realized that the man she was with looked vaguely familiar although I couldn't place him at the time. I hustled Caroline out of the bar and we high-tailed it over to the Plaza.

"On the walk over, I realized why the man looked familiar — he was on the flight back from Moscow when Daddy and I were there last year. The crew took two candid shots of me and Daddy on the plane, and I'm certain the man with Mia at the Four Seasons is in the background of the photo. I remember he was obviously Russian, and spent a lot of time talking to one particular flight attendant. I have copies of the pictures for you; you can give them to your people for analysis. So — what do you think? Am I crazy, or is something going on?"

Max took the pictures. "You're not crazy, and something is definitely going on. Not to be overly dramatic, but it's possible that Mia is a spy, working for a foreign government. Because the man on the plane was Russian, chances are it's the Soviets. They have their own nuclear submarines and are desperate for information on any aspect of US submarine operations…and guess what? She's dating a submarine inspector. According to Peter, she asks a lot of innocent questions about subs and his work. Since she has a mechanical engineering degree, he thought that was the root of her interest. However, based on what you have told me, her interest in Peter's work is not at all innocent. Let me tell you what I suspect accounts for Mia's strange behavior.

"At the very least, she may be working as a courier. That would explain the Pan Am bag mystery: she was probably instructed to swap identical bags so vital information could safely be delivered. Someone with the other bag clearly put it on the ground next to Mia's and she then picked it up ostensibly by mistake. Once back at the apartment, she transferred the contents of the Pan Am bag to a Bloomingdale's bag and then swapped it again when she went to the store.

"As far as the lipstick is concerned, it's configured so that a dummy bottom and can hold a small roll of film or a micro-dot. She received the phony lipstick on one of her trips; all she had to do was unload the bottom and pass the contents to her handler in New York."

Natalie was transfixed by the explanations, "I feel so stupid! I should have come to you far sooner with all of this."

"Don't be so hard on yourself." Max put a reassuring hand on her shoulder. "It was better you waited and gathered additional information. By being natural, you avoided arousing suspicion and were able to gather additional pieces of the puzzle. You handled things just right."

"What about the trip to John Jay Park? What was that all about?"

"This is a real concern and I'll explain why: it happened the morning after she spent significant time alone with Peter. Because we know he passed out, it seems obvious Mia took something from Peter that she immediately passed on to her handler. No doubt there is a dead drop somewhere in John Jay Park. A dead drop is a place where a package is left for later pick-up. That was the purpose of the chalk mark on the light pole — Mia made the mark to alert her handler that something was in the dead drop."

"What kind of places are used for dead drops? How do the spies avoid things falling into the wrong hands after they're dropped?"

"Good question. Drops are usually in remote places. John Jay is off the beaten path, and far less busy than Central Park. Spies try to use hidden but normal-looking places, such as a loose stone in a wall or a hollowed-out rock or stump."

"Why are you so concerned about Mia making a dead drop after her night with Peter? Is the information really that important to the Russians?"

"Smart girl — that would be my guess. It's probably the start of a whole new operation for the Soviets. At this point, Peter has no idea what's going on — he took Mia, the sex, and her interest in his work at face value. We took him aside at the farewell luncheon and told him to keep his mouth shut for now about his relationship with Mia. When he gets back to Norfolk in about a week, I'll get together with him and we'll go from there."

"What happens when you get back to Norfolk? What a mess — is there anything else I can do to help?" Natalie was genuinely willing to get involved.

"For openers, I'll take the pictures and your entire story to the NIS office on the Norfolk compound. The first thing will be to run the photographs through various databases, concentrating on the Russians. The results of the search will dictate what comes next. At this point, I suspect—you, me, Doug, and Caroline—will somehow be involved in future activities. Mia knows all of us; introducing another set of players would be problematic. NIS and CIA are very clever, and I don't want to speculate about next steps. Suffice it to say that at some point you will probably be contacted about any future involvement. Can you think of anything else?"

Natalie took Max's hands in hers. "I want to discuss the last time we were together, and clear the air. We need to reach closure like responsible adults."

Max said, "I agree with you, and I have a proposal. Let's pretend while here in Paris that we are boyfriend and girlfriend just like before January 27th. Nothing heavy, and the same rules as before, if you catch my drift. Let's enjoy Paris, without outside worries. At dinner tomorrow night, we'll put all our cards on the table. Then, as you suggested, we can come to closure. How's that for creative thought?"

"You always have the best ideas. Let's plan tonight's dinner and our evening over lunch." Natalie gave Max a big hug. "I knew I could count on you to do the right thing—in so many ways."

"I need to grab a quick shave and wash off the road dust before lunch. Give me a few minutes. I'll pick you up at your room and we'll go on to lunch. I'm starving."

"You poor thing," said Natalie, kissing the stubble on his cheek. "Please don't take all day in front of the mirror—I've got some great ideas for tonight. See you in a few."

True to his word, Max knocked on Natalie's door less than fifteen minutes later. He was greeted with a knockout Pan Am smile as Natalie's face glowed with anticipation.

"Buy a sailor a drink?" It was an old line, but Max always got a kick out of it.

"You have a deal. The first glass is on Pan Am, and after that, you're on your own," said Natalie with a sly smile. "Let's try the rooftop restaurant. If we hustle, we'll get there before lunch service is over."

When they arrived rooftop, things were winding down; however, the staff assured them they could get lunch. They ordered a bottle of Sancerre—a couple glasses of wine would help the post-luncheon nap sorely needed to reset their internal clocks.

"Everything on the menu looks great; let's eat light. I want to enjoy dinner tonight," said Max. "The fresh oysters look good, and I'll have Salade Niçoise. How about you?"

"Oysters for me as well, and Quiche Lorraine. I can vouch for the food—and of course, Sancerre makes everything taste better."

The oysters were ice-cold, served with a wonderful tarragon vinaigrette. They disappeared quickly, and Max and Natalie attacked the main course.

"What's the schedule for tonight?" asked Max, sipping his wine.

"I booked us on the 8:30 Bateaux Mouches dinner cruise. It ends right around 11:00, just as the Paris disco scene starts up. Maybe we can fit in some dancing, if tired old Max is still game."

She gave Max a brochure describing the dinner cruise. "This looks terrific," he said. "Let's take the Métro and make this a real adventure. With your French and my superior directional skills, we'll have no problems. If boarding starts at 8:00, what time should we leave the hotel?"

"Let's meet at 7:00 and have a glass of wine at the hotel bar," said Natalie. "Changing subjects—I've been thinking about our conversation earlier today. What is going to happen?"

"Assuming you're talking about Mia and not us, there are a few possible outcomes." With the restaurant empty and the wait

152

staff out of earshot, Max felt comfortable sharing his thoughts. "If Mia is what we think she is, the first step would be to confront Peter and have him break off the relationship—and that would be that. The damage would be limited to whatever Peter told her in person, and the stuff she left at the dead drop. However, I don't think NIS and the CIA will stop there. They would consider how best to utilize Peter's relationship with Mia. My guess is she's not the only Pan Am flight attendant working for the Soviets—the exchange of carry-on bags tells us that much.

"The CIA will want to infiltrate the Spy in the Sky network." Max cleverly coined a name for Mia's little group that he assumed existed. "If Mia can be turned, there are a number of ways to use her as a double agent and feed the Soviets bogus information. Peter would continue to be involved, and his relationship with Mia would continue. Ironically, the US would turn the tables on the Soviets. Keep in mind this is just conjecture on my part. Once I'm back in Norfolk with the photographs, the wheels will really start to turn."

"Is there a possibility I'll need to be involved? I'm willing to help, but I don't know what I can do."

Max smiled. "Don't worry about it just yet. If the CIA tries to infiltrate the network, your knowledge of Pan Am operations will be invaluable. I'll pass along the information that you're willing to help."

They finished the Sancerre and decided a short walk before an afternoon nap would be in order. They enjoyed a twenty-minute stroll around the neighborhood, through the Place du Tertre with its bevy of sketch-pad artists, and then on to the steps of Sacre-Coeur with its scaly, white Asian dome. It was Max's first taste of the sights Paris had to offer.

Back at the hotel, Max walked Natalie to her room. There was the now-customary awkward pause, followed by a hug and brief kiss. The boyfriend-girlfriend charade was working, and the good feelings were mutual. They were going to live in the moment, and not dwell on the future.

They met at the hotel bar at 7:00 and shared a glass of sparkling sauvignon blanc before setting off on the next chapter of their little adventure. Natalie was understated but elegant in a silk blouse, mini skirt, and shoes with a low heel, suitable for walking and comfortable for dancing. The Métro had them boarding the boat just a short hour later. Their table was perfect, adjacent to a large window with a great view of Paris.

As far as Max was concerned, everything about the cruise was perfect: the best dining partner ever, a wonderful description of the brightly lit sights of Paris as they passed, and a delicious meal paired with delicious wines. The live music put the finishing touch on a beautiful picture. The conversation sparkled, easily avoiding Mia and Peter, and their own unorthodox relationship. They had so much in common, even down to their taste in food and wine—except that Max loved good red wine and Natalie drank only white—and that didn't matter at all in the grand scheme of things.

The two and a half hours flew by and, before they knew it, the boat was tied up at the pier adjacent to the Pont de l' Alma. Finding a taxi was easy, and Natalie told the driver, in French, that they wanted to go somewhere for dancing—not too pricey. The driver smiled, and fifteen minutes later they were in each other's arms, dancing, with memories of Hippopotamus flooding both of them.

During the ride back to the hotel, Natalie put her head on Max's shoulder, and they held hands. The first of their last two days together was almost over. They picked up their keys, and Max walked Natalie to her room. Standing in front of her door, Natalie said, "Thank you for a perfect evening—the best night out since we were together at Hippopotamus."

They looked at each other for a long time, their arms around each other. Finally, Natalie gave Max a soft kiss on the lips. "*Bonne nuit, mon cher.*"

Max held her close and said, "I guess that means good night. Suppose I wanted to say *Sleep tight* to you in French? What would I say?"

"*Dors bien. Dors bien, ma chérie,*" Natalie murmured.

Max picked up immediately and said, "*Dors bien. Dors bien, ma chérie.*" He gave her one last kiss, deep and long. Natalie kissed him back. "How does breakfast at nine sound?" asked Max.

"Fine." Natalie turned and opened her door. She glanced back, gave a little wave, and smiled. Max returned the wave, walked toward his room and heard the sound of Natalie's door softly closing.

Under the covers in their respective rooms, neither could think of much else than the other. One day left, and each was determined to make it unforgettable; then it was time to do what should have been done two weeks ago ... say goodbye to Natalie and Max in love, and step into a more platonic friendship.

Chapter 32

New York City
February 7th, 1973

The tension between Gorsky and Ivan was much in evidence during their meeting at the UN Mission to discuss the Neutron-Songbird situation. Ivan's main concern remained preservation of the Stork Club. If his asset was not handled properly, the very existence of the network would be threatened. Gorsky, on the other hand, was motivated by self-interest and the desire to advance his standing within the KGB. Mortin's pressure to quickly deliver the needed information only added fuel to the fire. Unfortunately for Ivan, Gorsky had the political advantage because of his close ties to KGB leadership.

"How was your meeting with Songbird?" he asked Gorsky. "I still think your meeting at an emergency location here in Manhattan was ill-advised. Far better you made the trip to Van Courtland Park and met her on our usual bench. I realize you are running Operation Neutron; however, the Stork Club remains my responsibility. The two operations must dovetail, not be at odds."

Gorsky, arrogant as ever, replied, "Stop acting like a worried mother with her daughter on a first date. I considered it of primary importance that the significance of the operation be impressed upon Songbird, and that she clearly understands the options being considered. We will lose the entire month of February to move the operation forward. I wanted to ensure she is available to meet with Neutron as soon as possible, and accommodate his operational schedule."

Ivan folded his arms, "OK, let's deal with this one piece at a time. How do we make sure she is available? There is no guarantee that the line she bids for March will be compatible with Neutron's schedule."

"I solved that quite easily. She will bid a line for March that includes two weeks of leave at the beginning of the month. In the event she does not get leave, she will just call out sick. Either way, she will be available to meet with Neutron any time during the first two weeks of March."

Ivan was not convinced. "This assumes that sometime during the first half of March, Neutron will be coming through New York."

"Don't worry about that. He is hot to see her, and he has bargaining power with his schedule. He helped out with scheduling problems in February, and that is why he was traveling most of the month."

"If you say so—it seems you have that aspect of the operation under control." Ivan unfolded his arms. "Tell me about the options you presented and her response."

"I provided everything in the newspaper swap. Included is the documentation needed to present option number one." Gorsky removed a stack of papers from a file folder. "Here is what I have given her, and how it is going to work. If required, she will present four things: a copy of his photographed documents; a money exchange shot with a stack of hundred-dollar bills; video stills showing them in compromising sexual positions; and finally a doctored transcript of a conversation in which he appears to reveal classified information."

"OK, I'm tracking. What next?" Ivan was slowly coming around to Gorsky's point of view.

"She will tell him her real story—that she has been forced to work for us, and we have her father under house arrest in

East Berlin because of his efforts to support German unification. Without her ongoing cooperation, he will be placed in prison, either in the DDR or shipped off to Lubyanka. If she doesn't co-operate, she will never see him again. Neutron thinks she was raised in England. She'll tell him the truth—she was raised in East Germany and her family never left. We gave her language training and deep cover to pass as a Brit."

"How will she present the package to ensure the best pos-sible outcome? A lot seems to depend on her sales ability—of course, persuasion was part of her training," said Ivan.

Gorsky answered, "At the outset, it will be an emotional ap-peal based on his apparent feelings for her. Briefly, he will be asked to work for us in exchange for freedom for herself and her father. Neutron is to perform six missions and gather informa-tion on US submarine operations. He will be compensated hand-somely for his cooperation. At the conclusion, he will derive the following benefits: first, Songbird's father will be released and free to travel; second, her responsibilities will cease with respect to the Stork Club; and finally, Neutron will be released from any further involvement in intelligence-gathering. Of course, this is all a smokescreen; as soon as he completes his first mission, we will have him firmly in our grasp and will then milk him for all the information we can get."

Ivan was still skeptical. "This guy isn't stupid. The deal seems too good to be true. What if he declines to go along and threatens to blow everything up?"

"Songbird will tell him the deal is reasonable because we are desperate for information; we are willing to pay without too many demands. He will be able to pursue his ambition to com-mand his own submarine, and they can enjoy a life together with a little extra cash in hand."

Ivan worried about Neutron's level of cooperation. "I don't

believe that will convince him. This remains a very dangerous situation, especially if he turns around and blows the whistle on us."

Gorsky lowered his voice and said, "If he will not cooperate, I'll burst through the door, send out Songbird, and take matters into my own hands. I know he has a strong desire to succeed — to prove that although he's a farm boy, he is as good as the Academy men. I'll tell him that if he does not cooperate, we will leak the evidence gathered to the left-leaning, anti-military press here in the US and abroad. He will be right in the middle of a worldwide firestorm as a result of the successful Soviet penetration of the US submarine service. No matter what he does, his career will be over. He will be disgraced as an officer.

"With Songbird out of the room, I'll tell him that unless he cooperates she will be taken to a location between East Berlin and Moscow, never to be seen again. The reason for her disappearance is to hide the truth; it will then be his word against the evidence. He will be in a lose-lose situation — cooperation will the only viable option. I will offer a one-time chance to get all the benefits from option one, but he must decide then and there. A delay in decision means all the incentives are off the table."

"Gorsky, I have to hand it to you — the plan is compelling," said Ivan. "However, much hinges on Songbird's ability to close the deal. It is in her interest to encourage him to choose option one. His willingness to cooperate serves everyone's best interest. We will be in better control if he is not resentful about our approach and his decision. How can we help her succeed?" Ivan paged through the documents.

Gorsky had all the answers. "We told her to think about it and practice precisely how to make the initial approach. She is to engender a lot of sympathy for her situation — if he really does care for her that may swing the deal. If she is uncertain about her preparation, we have offered to conduct live training in the hotel room where they meet. The familiar surroundings will help create a level of comfort and hopefully increase her confidence in selling option one."

"I'm impressed," Ivan admitted. "The plan might actually work and not adversely impact the Stork Club. What next?"

Gorsky took back the papers. "By the last week of February, we will know about her leave request. If granted, she will immediately contact Neutron and set the date for a get-together here in New York."

Ivan had to agree with Gorsky's approach; he did not have the political clout to do otherwise. Songbird was one of his best assets; if anyone could pull this off, it was she. Gorsky felt overly confident his plan would succeed; however, his arrogance often clouded his judgment. In the end, it all depended on Songbird's ability to sell a very difficult product.

Chapter 33

Paris
February 8th, 1973

Fortunately, the young lady who answered at the front desk spoke excellent English when Max made his call to Doug at 0700. She understood perfectly, and efficiently put through a trans-oceanic call to the Board offices in Norfolk. The chief yeoman immediately put Doug on the line.

"Hey, buddy—how's Paris? Is it as romantic as everybody says it is?"

Max decided to have a little fun. "Doug, you know this trip is strictly business. I haven't given the romantic aspects of the city a second thought. Natalie and I had an interesting conversation, followed by an early dinner. After that, it was straight to bed for me. I was so jet-lagged, I barely made it through dinner without falling asleep."

Doug laughed. "Yeah, and if I believed that, you could sell me the Chesapeake Bay Bridge Tunnel. You know, I wasn't born on the 4 to 8." This was an old Navy saying equivalent to "I wasn't born yesterday"; the 4 to 8 was the first watch before the start of the normal work day.

"My, you are wide awake," said Max. "Let's make this short and sweet. First, I'm flying back early tomorrow, and will get back to Norfolk late on the 9th. Next, I think you should talk to the guys across the parking lot, and schedule a little get together for drinks as soon as I get to the compound. I think Peter is still on the road so he won't be there. Oh, I forgot to tell you—I took some great photos of Paris before I hit the hay, and I can't wait to show them to you. How does all that sound?"

"Perfect—I'll set up a little party for late on the 9th."

"If there isn't anything else, I'm going to ring off and stop spending my hard-earned money on this call. See you late tomorrow."

The call was prearranged code worked out before Max left for Paris. "The guys across the parking lot" meant NIS. "Having drinks" indicated they needed to meet as soon as possible. Reference to a photograph meant he had photographic evidence to be run through a recognition database. Peter being out of town meant that he was not invited to the meeting. The phrase "hit the hay" meant that Natalie was willing to help with the situation if she could. As soon as Max hung up, Doug walked over to the NIS office and set up a meeting late on the 9th. While there, Doug gave NIS a broad-brush picture of the Peter/Mia situation.

Once the call to Doug was over, Max concentrated on the important business of sharing the day with Natalie. The boyfriend-girlfriend masquerade was working well; he looked forward to an unstructured day enjoying Paris with his favorite person. He tried to suppress the reality that this would be their last day together, but the words kept coming back: "Precious and few are the moments...." He refused to let that put a damper on the day.

He got to the restaurant ten minutes early and sat alone thinking about his conversation with Doug and the possible unpleasant outcomes. Natalie was halfway to the table before he noticed her. She was wearing a striking red sweater that set off her dark hair and glowing skin. To complete the ensemble, she had a navy-and-white herringbone miniskirt, a long white cashmere scarf, and chic red shoes.

"Hey, sailor," she said with a brilliant smile. "Penny for your thoughts?"

Max stood and embraced her. "Well, since you asked, two things. First, you look absolutely fabulous. Second, I just got off the phone with Doug, and I have an update. Doug and I will meet with NIS when I get to the compound late tomorrow. I gave him a coded mini-brief of the situation. That's about it. On to what you have planned for the day. I forgot to ask—what's the difference between the Right Bank and the Left Bank?"

The waiter appeared with the coffee, croissants, and fresh fruit that Max had ordered. Natalie nodded her approval and said, "This is perfect. Thank you.

"So—the difference between the Right Bank and Left Bank. Right now, we are on the Right Bank, or Rive Droite, and that is the area north of the Seine. The Rive Droite style is elegant and sophisticated. The Left Bank, or Rive Gauche, is the smaller section of Paris, and historically has been known as the artistic part of the city, where many famous artists and writers lived— Picasso, Matisse, Hemingway. It used to be significantly cheaper for food and lodging than the Right Bank, but those days are gone.

"I've put together a tour that starts at the Arc de Triomphe and ends at la Tour Eiffel, with all my favorite places in between."

"What's for lunch?"

"Slow down, I'll get to that. Right before lunch, we'll cross the Seine and visit Notre Dame on the Île de la Cité located in the middle of the river. From there, it's over to the Quartier Latin, which includes the Sorbonne where the students hang out. Our first stop will be an inexpensive Algerian restaurant—dining there is an experience in itself. That's it for now. I want some of the tour to be a surprise."

"OK. I'll leave it all in your very capable hands. I have one request—let's take a pass on the Louvre. There's just too much there, considering our limited time."

"You are a mind reader," said Natalie with a wink. "We'll walk past it as we leave Tuileries Gardens, but we'll just keep on going. Some day, when you have a lot of time in Paris you can give the Louvre the attention it deserves."

Max glanced under the table at Natalie's shoes. "I heard we might get snow flurries this afternoon. I'd hate to see you ruin those wonderful red shoes."

"I have boots with me — I'll just slip them on before we leave. Time for one more cup of coffee, before we go."

Fifteen minutes later, they donned coats, boots, and gloves and were on their way to the Métro stop. It was a straight shot from the Clichy stop to the Arc de Triomphe, where they spent a few minutes admiring the architectural marvel. Next, they wandered down the Champs-Élysées toward the Place de la Concorde. As a cycling fan, Max had one up on Natalie. This stretch was familiar to Max because it was where the Tour de France finished every year. He explained the importance of the Tour and the last leg. After a casual walk through the Tuileries, they found a bench near the Louvre.

Max said, "Wow, what a city — beautiful things around every corner. Can you imagine how devastated the Parisians were as the Nazis marched right through the Arc de Triomphe?"

"Those were terrible times for the world. I'm so glad you are one of those dedicated to preventing another world war. I've come to understand how important our submarine force is in helping to maintain peace. I guess I never told you, but I'm really proud of you and what you do."

Max's head swelled two hat sizes. "Wow thanks, Natalie — that means a lot. I know you are absolutely sincere. Very few people really understand what we do and the sacrifices we make."

Natalie put her arm around Max, moved a little closer, and

gave him a hug and a kiss on the cheek. Max tingled inside. Natalie always knew exactly what to do and say, at just the right moment.

"OK, lazybones, on to our next stop," she teased. "Next is something off-beat, that I know you will really enjoy. Let's take a cab to the Les Halles neighborhood and save a little energy."

They soon found themselves in front of a store called E. Dehillerin. Natalie explained it was a professional cookware store, established in 1820. It gained fame in the United States because of Julia Child, who shopped there and provided a lot of free advertising. The store carried a full line of equipment, but was especially well known for its line of copper pots.

Natalie and Max were both drawn to the copper pommes anna pan; the top fit right over the bottom. Each half had small brass handles, and when the dish was cooked, the pan would be inverted for serving. Unfortunately, the pan was the last one in the store. With a dramatic sigh, Natalie agreed to relinquish the pan to Max.

"I will live without this, knowing how happy it will make you," she said. She began a futile negotiation with a salesman. "Puisque c'est la dernière que vous avez — vous allez nous faire un prix n'est-ce pas?"

The salesman shook his head in mock despair. "Eh ben justement, comme il ne m'en reste plus qu'une, je vais probablement l'augmenter, non baisser, le prix! Désolé, mais mon prix reste le même."

"What was that all about?" asked Max.

"I told him that since it was the last one in the store, we should get a discounted price. No go — he jokingly replied that since it was the last one, he should charge more. Unfortunately we have to pay the asking price."

They toured both levels of the store. "If I had known, I would have brought an extra suitcase," said Max. "Maybe it's just as well—I would have blown my budget for the next three weeks."

Since Natalie and Max were both raised Catholic, the next stop had special significance. Max was in awe of Notre Dame, as it was one of the best of the magnificent European cathedrals. He insisted on lighting a candle for them and said a quiet prayer for their mutual happiness and health.

"When is lunch?" he asked. "We didn't have much breakfast, and I've worked up an appetite."

"OK, next stop—lunch. We'll go over the bridge to the Left Bank."

After a short walk, they were in the Quartier Latin. Natalie told Max that there were dozens of inexpensive couscous places run by Algerian immigrants. They chose a place frequented by students from the Sorbonne; it was like the Tower of Babel, with animated conversations in many languages. They ordered traditional Algerian fare—lamb with a generous portion of couscous and pita. The place was progressive and served wine, but wanting to be fully alert for the rest of the day, they drank tea. Max was amazed at how low the bill was.

"OK, time to walk off lunch," Natalie announced. "Let's go through the Luxembourg Gardens." Natalie explained that during the warmer months, the gardens were crowded—but today, with the threat of snow, they had the place to themselves. Sitting on a bench, they snuggled close, taking in the scene. Max thought the whole thing seemed a bit like the musical *Brigadoon*—they were Fiona and Tommy, and at the end of their enchanted day, they must face the consequences. He couldn't resist sharing this with Natalie; she immediately understood. She looked up at him and gave him a tender kiss on the cheek.

She tugged gently on Max's arm and said, "Let's find a taxi to get us over to the Rodin Museum. It's the next to last highlight on today's tour — and it's one of my favorite places in all of Paris."

Looking up at the cloudy sky, they were sure there would be snow before the sun set. After a short ride, they found themselves among some of the most significant sculptures in the world. There was an indoor museum and an outdoor sculpture garden that was open even in winter. Max was amazed at the collection, and Natalie's knowledge. The pieces in the garden included *Balzac*, *The Thinker*, *The Gates of Hell*, and *The Burghers of Calais*. As they stood in front of *The Gates of Hell*, Max remarked, "I hope to avoid this place in the hereafter; however, the detail and variety of the scenes is just unbelievable."

Once inside, they stopped in front of *The Kiss*, and could not resist the urge — they put their arms around each other and enjoyed a soft, prolonged kiss in front of the sculpture. Max thought, *I wonder how many couples have done that?* Then he remembered they weren't really a couple, and felt a pang of the loss that was to come.

When they left the building, a few flakes of snow began to flutter from the sky. They took a taxi to the last stop of the day, la Tour Eiffel. The winter weather had thinned out the crowd of tourists, and before they knew it, they were off the elevator at the top of the tower. The view of Paris was spectacular in all directions, and the falling snow made the scene look like a Christmas card. Max felt the scene etch into his mind's eye — he didn't need a camera.

He turned to Natalie and put his arms around her. "I'll remember this forever," he said.

Her beautiful smile was wistful now. "So will I."

Chapter 34

Paris
February 8th, 1973

Back at the hotel bar, they shook off the snowflakes before settling into red velvet chairs on either side of a small marble-topped table. They ordered Kentucky bourbon with a side of ginger ale.

"We have a La Casserole booking at 7:30," said Natalie, still brushing snow from her dark hair. "It's right here in Montmartre, behind the Sacre Coeur. A pleasant walk in spring, but I think we'd be better off taking the metro tonight."

Max took her hand. "You're the expert, Natalie—that's the only reason I invited you to Paris for this little get-together." They both laughed.

"Let's meet in the lobby around 6:45. I'm ready for a little nap—how about you?"

"Sounds perfect. I'm really looking forward to our dinner. Why La Casserole?"

"The owner and chef, Bernard du Boise, was Eisenhower's personal chef when the general was in Versailles. The place is American-friendly, and offers traditional French food. The décor is incredible—you'll find one of just about everything on the walls, hanging from the ceiling and even in the loo. A visit to the bathroom is a must; you'll laugh out loud at all the outrageous stuff they have in there. They close down for two days in the summer to take everything down and dust the place."

Max walked Natalie to her room and they paused by her

door. "I guess we'll have an interesting conversation at dinner," said Max, taking her hands. "Playing boyfriend and girlfriend has been terrific; I'm glad you agreed to it. As they say in basketball—no harm, no foul. See you at 6:45."

Because of their careers, both were always punctual and arrived simultaneously. Max caught his breath at the sight of Natalie in a cream-colored silk blouse over a French lace camisole. There was still a light dusting on the streets and sidewalk; Max watched Natalie's stylish boots making small prints on the pavement as they strolled to the Métro.

La Casserole was as Natalie had described it—festooned with an endless assortment of stuffed animals, plants, doo-dads, fish nets, seashells, pots, pans, feathers, flags, and banners. No room for even one more thing on the walls or ceiling. "Wow," said Max, as he marveled at the vast assortment of junk. They were soon seated at a quiet corner table where they ordered a glass of champagne while they looked at the menu.

They had oysters and escargots to begin; Natalie chose beef carpaccio and veal cutlet with spring vegetables. Max ordered salmon gravlax and sea bream with clams and asparagus. They agreed to share their meals so each could enjoy a taste of both and ordered a bottle of Montrachet to accompany their entrees.

"Before we get really serious," said Natalie, picking up a glistening oyster, "I just have to ask—what will happen to Mia? I realize this isn't the time or place, but can you tell me anything at all? It really has been bothering me."

"It depends on what the spooks find out—who she's working for and exactly what she's been doing. Her motivation and personal situation also enter into the equation. If the CIA really nails her, she'll be given an opportunity to cooperate. There's not much more I can say—here, or anywhere else".

"Quelle mess," said Natalie. "When we get back, I guess this will be a situation unlike anything we could have imagined. Speaking of situations, I'd better get started with my half of our story."

Max shook his head. "My part isn't complicated."

Natalie took Max's hand. "I'm certain you didn't have any idea of the depth of my feelings for you. You were always a perfect gentleman; you never came on strong in any way. This is only our fifth or sixth time together and yet in that short time, I feel I really know you. Something about you just resonated with me, whether it was our similar backgrounds, my admiration for your Navy work, or—just you...caring, kind, and smart.

"Since you could easily have invited me to Norfolk and didn't, I suspected you were married. I started to wonder the night after Hippopotamus, when you literally swept me off my feet—you are one of the few men I have met who enjoy dancing. Believe it or not, that really meant a lot to me.

"Then came January 27th. I just had to ask if you were married. I was very close to taking you to the bedroom and I couldn't unless I knew the answer. I appreciated your being truthful with me—I knew you would be. When you asked if I would marry someone who was divorced, I said no, which wasn't completely accurate. I wondered at the time why you asked, but we were so rushed because of your plane—everything was left up in the air. For me, though, the important issue was resolved.

"You're not going to believe what I'm about to tell you. First of all, you have to understand that my intense feelings for you helped me to realize that I could care for someone other than Scott. That realization spurred me on and you were barely out the door on the 27th when I took my little self across the street to Scott's apartment and broke up with him. The whole thing took less than five minutes. I told him not to contact me unless he intended to propose marriage. You knew about the situation with Scott after our various discussions—and you were right. I put the ball squarely in his court, but not because you said I should. My feelings for you let me know there could be life beyond Scott, so it was easier to let him go."

"Scott would be insane not to take action," said Max. "If you still haven't heard from him after two weeks, I guess he must still be on the fence...he must have a lot of issues to resolve. Last time it was his suggestion to break up, so I guess he doesn't like the shoe being on the other foot. I bet something will happen when you get back to New York.

"Now for my side of the story. I was taken with you from the first time I saw you on the flight from Scotland.. I've flirted with a lot of flight attendants, but I have to say that yours was the only phone number I ever asked for—and I was surprised when you gave it to me.

"My intentions were honorable from the outset. I wasn't looking for a serious relationship, because my marital status was unresolved. Hence, my behaving like a gentleman. After you gave me your number, I envisioned dates in New York City and maybe even here in Europe if our schedules allowed. So I called, you accepted, and we had that amazing day… and the night at Hippopotamus. I think that evening had the same effect on us both, but of course I couldn't tell you how I felt. It was too early, and I wasn't free to be with you. The breakfast at JFK confirmed that we were both willing to think outside the box, just to see each other.

"Then came January 27th. You really blindsided me, but once you asked, I realized there were things going on that we'd never talked about. You had a right to know and I felt guilty about not being up front with you. You told me everything about Scott and the ups and downs of the relationship. I believed deep down that the two of you would end up married. That was how

I justified my decision to stay silent about my marital status. As long as you were happy to share a small part of your life with me, I was willing to go along for the ride.

"I missed my plane to Norfolk and might as well have stayed at the apartment to sort through everything with you then and there. But now, I'm not sure there is anything to sort out. I'm still married and we're both Catholics. I knew you probably wouldn't marry a divorced man, and when I asked, you answered as I expected. Even though now I know you might consider it, there's still too much uncertainty in both of our lives. My marriage is ending, but not over. Your situation with Scott isn't entirely resolved.

"You have to believe my marriage didn't limit my feelings for you then, or now. You are unlike any woman I've ever known, and I want only the best for you, whether I can be in your life or not. For your sake, I hope Scott comes to his senses."

Natalie knew that every word was true. She was particularly touched by his sincere desire to see her happily married. Her thoughts tumbled out.

"Max, what you just said — that's the reason I have such strong feelings for you. You are such a wonderful man. You clearly put me and my happiness before your own and I admire that so much."

Max flushed a bit. "Hey, take it easy. That's just how I feel; there's no ulterior motive in telling you my thoughts. But I must admit that you blew me away with your comments about your feelings for me. Truth be told, I never thought I could win your affection. I am unbelievably flattered and grateful to learn that you care for me." That having been said, Max changed the subject. "I'm dying for dessert. How about you?"

Natalie looked at him and laughed. He had just taken their most intensely tender moments from the last five months and brought them back to earth with one sentence — and she loved him for it. Max was tenderness and reality wrapped up in one wonderful package. He signaled the waiter and requested the restaurant's most decadent dessert, two spoons, and two cappuccinos.

A few snowflakes had started to drift down again, and Natalie took Max's arm to avoid slipping as they walked to the Métro. Once again they found themselves shaking off snowflakes in the hotel bar. They agreed to an after-dinner drink; neither of them wanted the evening to end. Natalie ordered a Grand Marnier and Max had cognac. They sipped their drinks slowly and their glow from dinner intensified. They went over the highlights of the last two days, focusing on the most unforgettable moments. Then it was back to reality.

"I'm sure you will be contacted after we return to the States, either by me or the spooks," Max said. "Except for official contact, I realize this is just about it for us." He blinked back tears. "You need to get on with your life, whether it's with Scott or someone else."

Natalie was glad that Max put it out there with no equivocation. "You're right, so there's nothing more to be said," she agreed. "Our relationship ended the best way it possibly could have — thanks to Peter and Mia. We couldn't have planned it better if we'd tried."

Max signed for the drinks and said, "Guess we'd better get to our rooms since we're both flying in the morning. How about a coffee in the AM? I think you said the crew bus picks you up at 7:30 — how about sneaking me aboard the bus in your luggage? Just about the easiest way for me to get to Orly."

"Be in the lobby a little before 7:30; I'll do everything I can. You can't go to the crew area at Orly, but we'll drop you somewhere convenient for check-in."

"Thanks." Max walked her to her room. At Natalie's door they held hands, facing each other, for a long time. Finally, Max said, "I hate long goodbyes." He took her face in both his hands, kissed her softly on the lips and turned to go. Natalie caught his arm, spun him around and gave him a searching kiss, her tongue parting his lips. Max had both arms around her; she could feel him getting hard as she pressed up against him. Natalie felt her heart racing—she should have just let him go. This was danger-ous; they wanted each other too much.

Max came to the rescue. "Now that we've had a proper good-bye, I really have to go."

He turned away and walked down the hall. With a slight shake of her head and a wistful sigh, Natalie opened the door to her room, not realizing that Max had looked back to watch her. Door closed, Natalie sat down on her bed, motionless. She wondered if what she had just done was totally unfair—but her desire for him was real.

Suddenly, there was a soft knock. She jumped up and opened the door just a crack. There stood Max with a bottle of cham-pagne and two glasses. "Share a drink with a sailor?" he asked with a sly smile.

Natalie threw the door open wide. "Get yourself and that lovely bottle of champagne in here!"

Max set down the glasses, opened the bottle, and poured. He had kept the bottle in a bucket of ice while they were at dinner, so the temperature was perfect. "To a wonderful two days in Paris—and to us," said Max.

"Yes, to us," responded Natalie.

They set the glasses down, and both instinctively knew what would come next. Their kisses were gentle, sweet, and yearn-ing. They looked at each other with an intensity that outweighed caution. It seemed so right.

Max unbuttoned Natalie's blouse and slipped it off, along with the French lace camisole. She reached down, unbuckled his belt, and unbuttoned his trousers. Her scent aroused him even more—she still had faint traces of "Y" in all the right places. Before long, they were lying on the bed. Memories of January 27th came rushing back, but the questions and desires of the past weeks would now be put to rest. They took turns undressing each other. Nothing was rushed. They knew this would be their one and only time together. They took turns kissing each other for a long time.

Finally, Max couldn't wait any longer. He said, "I want to look in your eyes and kiss you while we make love."

It was as if they had always been lovers, responding to one another with unspoken intuition, each wanting to please the other, which only increased their own delight. Afterward, glowing with sweat and sweet satisfaction, they lay in each other's arms for a long time. Then, they slipped under the covers. Natalie lay on her side, and Max took a spoon position behind her, pressing his body against hers. Before long, both were sound asleep. It had been a perfect day.

At 6:00, a soft ringing woke Max. He had set his wind-up travel alarm for half an hour before Natalie's wake-up call at 6:30. He reached over and lightly massaged her back. She opened her eyes and turned to face him, pressing her body against him.

"Do we have time?" she whispered in his ear. "What time is it, anyway?" Her hands were already all over him.

"You know how I like to plan. I set my little alarm for six, so we have half an hour. I suggest seeing how much we can get done in the allotted time…you are just going to have to finish what you started," Max said, caressing her.

Max couldn't help thinking how beautiful Natalie was, even half-asleep, makeup smudged from the night before. He couldn't get enough of touching her, and she felt the same about him. Like the night before, they started slowly, savoring every moment, but intensity built quickly. Natalie's mind was racing — Max was such a wonderful man and fantastic lover. How could she let him go? She knew she had to, but she would give him something to remember.

"Thank you — for so many things," he said, brushing strands of hair out of her eyes. "These were two utterly perfect days."

"I agree. We made the most of the time given to us." Natalie lay on top of him, kissing him softly. At that moment, the phone rang, bringing them back to reality.

Max dressed quickly. "See you for coffee in a few," he said.

When Natalie joined him, he was ready for her at a small table for two. There was a cup of coffee waiting for her, along with a croissant and a small dish of fruit. To the end, Max was a perfect gentleman. The glow on their faces clearly indicated what had happened in the past twelve hours; there was no need to summarize their mutual feelings. "Be back here at 7:20," said Natalie. "I won't have any trouble getting you on the bus." She finished her coffee and gave Max a kiss on the cheek.

The rest of the morning was uneventful. They sat next to each other on the crowded crew bus, their bodies touching. Even though it was over between them, the physical contact filled them with inner warmth. The bus dropped Max at a public access location, and before long, he was on Pan Am Flight 115, ready to depart for JFK. At the same time, Natalie was on her dead-head flight, making provisions to take off for Rome on the continuation of Flight 114. As Natalie and Max were flying in opposite directions, their thoughts remained on each other. There was a lot of uncertainty in the coming weeks; but no matter what happened — they would always have Paris.

Chapter 35

D oug was waiting for Max in the deserted Board offices. "Well, buddy, how was your time with Natalie?" he asked eagerly.

Max wasn't going to indulge him. "It was great to mix business and pleasure, but the business part is what's important now. Are the spooks ready for us and the photographic evidence?"

Doug snapped his briefcase shut. "They're waiting for us over at the Comm Center. Let's get going."

The stiff February wind blowing across the compound made their unsettling errand even more chilling. Two NIS personnel were waiting for them: Mr. X, a civilian, and LCDR Y, a former submarine officer.

Mr. X took the lead. "I understand you have photographic evidence that may be of value. Let's start with that." He pushed an intercom button and a chief petty officer promptly appeared. Max handed Mr. X the two photographs he had received from Natalie.

Mr. X got out a communications form and started making notes. "When and where were these taken?"

Max replied, "As far as we can determine, they were taken on March 15th, 1972 on a Pan Am flight from Moscow to Frankfurt. Natalie Tommasi, who provided the photographs, is in the foreground along with her father, Nat Tommasi. Our mystery man is in the background. Natalie is confident the same man met with her roommate at the Four Seasons in New York, just 5 days ago. Based on observations she made during the flight from Moscow she's quite sure our mystery man is Russian.

Mr. X handed the completed form and the photographs to the CPO. "Get this information over to the facial identification network. Assign our inquiry priority basis."

"Aye-aye, sir," said the CPO, and was on his way.

"Well, Max — where do you want to start?" asked Mr. X.

"I think it best to give you the background on how I first met Natalie's so-called roommate."

"For now, you may refer to her and everyone else by their real names. Our reports will protect their identities. Neither you nor Doug will know the code names assigned. Neither of you is to discuss any aspect of this inquiry outside this room — this applies to senior Board members as well. We will brief them in accordance with their need to know and notify them that we may need ongoing cooperation from both of you. Provision may be required for temporary relief from your normal duties."

Mr. X looked directly at Max, "No one knows where this will end up, but we appreciate your initiative in responding to Natalie's concerns. We understand you have borne all the expenses to date; but don't worry, you will be suitably reimbursed. Now, let's start at the beginning."

Max sat back in his chair. "I first met Natalie on a flight from Prestwick. We had a low-key relationship and dated about once a month. Early on, her roommate Mia, also a Pan Am flight attendant, expressed an interest in meeting my naval officer friends. One weekend, we planned a nightclub outing for me, Doug, and Peter — LCDR Bronson. The date was November 30th of last year. The next morning we learned that Peter had gone back to the hotel with Mia, had sex and then passed out. I didn't think too much about it at the time, but in retrospect, this was totally out of character for him—he can drink and party into the small hours without missing a beat.

"Jumping ahead from the notes I took during our February 7th meeting, early in the afternoon of December 1st Natalie and her boyfriend Scott went for a walk over to John Jay Park, going east on 77th. On their way there she saw Mia coming towards them in the opposite direction. This was odd since Mia had told Natalie she was going to take the Lexington Avenue subway downtown. The subway stop is west of First where their apartment is located. There was no reason for her to be coming from the direction of the river and the park. When Natalie got to the park, she noticed there was a white chalk mark on a light post near the entrance—it caught her eye, because it looked so strange. I put two and two together and concluded that Mia had put the information she stole from Peter in a pre-arranged dead drop in the park."

Mr. X interrupted, "What was the general nature of the conversation the six of you had on the night of November 30th?"

Doug said, "We all had wine at their apartment; then Max went to dinner with Natalie, while Peter and Mia and Caroline and I went ahead to the club. There was very little Navy-specific conversation, but the girls knew that we traveled frequently to Europe to conduct safety inspections on Atlantic fleet submarines."

Mr. X looked up from his notes. "OK, I think I have a clear picture so far. What else caused Natalie to be suspicious of Mia?"

"It started with Mia's interest in me and my fellow officers," said Max. "Right from the get-go, Mia wanted in on the party. This was out of character for Mia, who normally prefers

European playboy types, not clean-cut naval officers. Later, other things alerted Natalie. She noticed Mia's Pan Am carry-on was older and more beat-up than her usual bag—my guess is that Mia made a bag swap on a return trip from Europe. The very next day, Mia left with a Bloomingdale's bag saying she was going to exchange a bathing suit, ostensibly because she bought the wrong size. Natalie decided to discreetly follow Mia to see whether something else was going on that Mia might want to talk about—long story short, Mia never went to the swim suit department.

Mr. X stopped writing for a moment. "Did you and Natalie talk about all of this as it was happening?"

"When she and I had breakfast at JFK early in January, she said that Mia's interest in Peter seemed odd, and she encouraged me to keep an eye on the situation, lest Peter get hurt. But she didn't have any hard evidence. When she saw Mia with the mystery man at the Four Seasons and recognized him from the Moscow flight, she told me it was urgent that we meet."

There was a knock on the door. Mr. X said, "Come." The CPO entered and handed him several flimsy pieces of thermofax paper. "Dismissed," said Mr. X, and the CPO departed immediately. Mr. X surveyed the room with a concerned expression. "Gentlemen, we have a real problem on our hands. We have an 85% recognition probability that our man is none other than Nikolai Gorsky—as far as we know, he is head of KGB covert operations. God only knows what kind of information Mia gathered from Peter during their time together. Direct contact with agents at the Gorsky level spells big trouble. The next step is to get Peter in here ASAP. Doug, when will he be available?"

"He gets back day after tomorrow from Europe. Normally, he would not come into the office the same day he returns stateside. However, I can get a message through Pan Am to the senior member on the same trip and tell Peter to come to the Board offices directly from the airport when he lands in Norfolk. We'll bring him over here late in the day on the 11th."

Mr. X put everything in his briefcase. "Both of you come with him on the 11th. Do not discuss this matter outside of this room, not even with the senior members. If they press you, have them contact me directly." Mr. X handed out business cards. "If you think of anything in the interim, bring your notes to the next meeting. Max, what's your take on Natalie?"

Max said, "I told her that she was to remain 100% silent on this matter until she hears from us. If she was smart enough to bring this to me—she's smart enough to follow orders."

"Good," said Mr. X. "Give me a call when you have Peter's ETA here at the compound. Don't hesitate to call if anything changes. That's it for now—I'll see you guys on Sunday. And remember, total radio silence."

Max and Doug looked at each other and said in unison, "Loose lips sink ships—we get it."

Mr. X smiled. "See you day after tomorrow."

Chapter 36

New York—Norfolk
CINCLANTFLT Compound
February 11th, 1973

Peter had no idea what the hell was going on. The Pan Am purser on the flight from London gave him a cryptic note from Doug that said simply — "Upon arrival NORVA, proceed immediately to the Board offices on the Compound." He checked with his teammates and the senior member; nobody knew anything. Suddenly, it hit him like a ton of bricks. He recalled Doug and Max's concerns regarding Mia; so as soon as he landed he tried to call her.

As luck would have it, Mia answered the phone at 8L. "Peter, I can't believe it's you! I was just about to catch the bus to JFK. I have great news. I applied for leave the first two weeks in March, and I'm sure it will be granted. I am so hoping you will be able to visit me here in New York, if only for a few days. February has been awful. I've missed you terribly."

Everything seemed normal, so maybe Mia wasn't the problem after all. "That's great news," said Peter. "When I get back to the office, I'll check my March schedule. I can't wait to hold you in my arms."

"Sounds delicious — but I really must get going. I'll be back in New York for a few days starting on the 16th. Call me then. Goodbye, darling — I must ring off."

Peter felt better after his conversation with Mia, but he couldn't dispel the nagging feeling that something ominous awaited him at the Compound in Norfolk. He picked up his 'Vette at long-term parking, and headed immediately to the Compound. Since it was early evening when he arrived at the office, he was not surprised to see only Max and Doug.

"Hey, Peter. How was your trip?" Doug asked in a neutral tone. Max offered a similarly bland greeting.

"What's with the cloak-and-dagger stuff?" Peter tried to be upbeat. "My head is kind of spinning — What's this immediate recall all about?"

"We're not going to mess with you, Peter; this is serious. The spooks are waiting for us now over at the Comm Center. We can't tell you any more until we meet them in the secure conference room."

Peter looked at the floor and shook his head. "This has to be about Mia...and it can't be good. I just spoke to her before I left JFK. We were planning a nice get-together in NYC early in March. I guess that's not happening."

Doug and Max just shrugged and motioned Peter toward the door. As soon as they were in the conference room, they met someone who introduced himself as Mr. Z, of the CIA. X, Y, Z all addressed Peter informally by his first name which made the meeting seem a little less ominous.

Mr. X took the lead in defining the ground rules. "Peter, as I'm sure you've surmised we've already met with Doug and Max on this matter. It involves your relationship with Mia Beck. Doug and Max have provided most of the background. We will be asking specific questions about the times you were alone with her. You are not to discuss any aspect of this unless you are in this room. Any questions so far?"

Peter shook his head. "No questions. Let's get started — fire away."

Mr. X looked at his notepad. "We know that you and Mia

spent part of the night in your hotel room on November 30ᵗʰ. You told Max and Peter you had sex with Mia and shortly thereafter 'passed out.' When you awoke the next morning, she was not in the room, but other than a headache, you felt more or less normal. Is that correct?" Peter nodded. "Did Mia give you anything to drink?"

"Right after we had sex, she said she had some brandy. She produced two airline-sized bottles and asked if I wanted a night cap. We had been drinking heavily all night, so I accepted without giving it a second thought. In retrospect, I realize that it was shortly after that I passed out. The next thing I knew, it was morning. She left a note for me on the nightstand, thanking me for a great evening and suggesting another date."

"Do you remember discussing anything with her that would border on classified information—about submarines or national defense?"

Peter took his time and thought hard. Finally, he said, "Not at that time. All of our conversation that evening was general. We talked about my duties on the Board and in broad terms about our inspections. I told her a bit about my personal life."

Mr. X asked, "Did you have any documents with you of a sensitive nature?"

Peter shifted uncomfortably in his chair; he felt waves of tension coming from Max and Doug. "I was the writer on that inspection. In my carry-on, I had the handwritten notes from the inspection and all other material that pertained to the assignment," he admitted. "Also, there were other documents that, although not marked classified, could be considered sensitive because they detailed Board operational procedures. Other than that, nothing was particularly sensitive." Clearly Peter was trying to be as thorough and forthright as possible.

"We will need copies of everything that could have been in

your carry-on," Mr. X said, emphasizing the gravity of the situation. "Please err on the side of providing too much information. If you think the documents could have been there, please provide copies. I am going to give you our current thinking; that may help you answer the remainder of my questions. We strongly suspect that Mia is an agent acting on behalf of the Soviet Union."

The color drained from Peter's face, and a mist of sweat gleamed on his brow. "How—how certain are you? I have to admit that I feel strongly about her and it's difficult for me to grasp what you've just told me. I understand that anything's possible and I'm willing to cooperate, it's just that…it's just…." The room fell silent for a moment as Peter struggled to regain his composure. "Of course, you will have my full cooperation. If you want me to terminate my relationship with her, I'll do so immediately."

"Oh, no—what we want is quite the opposite," Mr. X said. "But I'm getting ahead of myself. We have confirmed through photographic evidence and Pan Am flight manifests that Mia met recently in a New York cocktail lounge with a high-ranking member of the KGB's covert operations. This evidence came to light purely by chance; we did not have either of them under active surveillance.

"Doug and Max are here because they have background information about your relationship with Mia. Please do not even consider they blew the whistle on you; rather, their assistance on background was critical. You need to trust them implicitly; mutual trust is essential if we are to limit the damage and turn this entire matter to our advantage.

"We have additional questions related to meetings with Mia after December 1st. Please describe where the meetings occurred, what you did, and anything that happened which might be considered suspicious.

Peter was no longer quite so pale. He took out his handkerchief and mopped his face. "I think I understand — can I get some coffee? This may take a while, and I just got off a transatlantic flight from Europe."

LCDR Y pushed the intercom button. "Hey, Chief — put on a fresh pot and bring it in, along with six mugs, cream and sugar."

"Aye-aye, sir," came the reply on the squawk box.

Peter grabbed a notepad and started in. "I'll have to double-check my calendar for accuracy, but we had two get-togethers, both in NYC, about a month apart, in December and January. Mia reserved Room 609 at the Penn Garden Hotel; she met me there when I arrived from JFK. She had the room pre-stocked with booze, champagne, wine and hors d'oeuvres. The second time we met, she'd made sure we had the same room — for romantic reasons, according to her. We had sex several times during each visit and we drank pretty heavily."

Peter, now aware of the gravity of the situation, distanced himself from his emotions and related the facts as clinically as he could. "During the first meeting, our conversation was about our feelings for each other, my naval career, and a general discussion of the submarines we inspected, and where they are located. However, during our second meeting, her questions became more pointed. She has a degree in mechanical engineering so her questions seemed logical coming from an educated engineer. If they became too specific, I joked and said, 'If I told you that, I would have to kill you,' and laughed it off.

"If I had known then what I know now, perhaps some of my answers would have been vaguer. I never provided any specific parameters, locations of identified submarines, or any technical information that is not available with focused research in unclassified sources. Thinking back on it, her questions on the second visit did seem to be agenda-driven…that is, she did have a range of specific, focused topics."

There was a knock on the door, announcing the arrival of the coffee. Once all were suitably fortified, Mr. X resumed the discussion. "Peter, when you search your calendar to nail down the meeting dates, try to marry the topics of inquiry with the specific dates. To help you, we'll provide a list of general categories to trigger your memory as to her specific questions. This will give us an idea of the type of information the Russkies are looking for. Did you reimburse her for the room and amenities — how was that handled?"

"During the first get-together, we had dinner at a very high-end restaurant, at my suggestion. I asked her the room rate and the approximate cost of the food and booze. She said she wanted to contribute to the cost of the weekend and, after considerable objection on my part, she agreed to accept the total for the room and amenities, less one half of the cost of the dinner. She was quite insistent on paying for some portion of the visit, so that was how we settled it. I didn't want a discussion about expenses during my second visit, so I got together sufficient cash and gave it to her in an envelope shortly after I got to the room. She thanked me, and took it without further discussion.

"We did not meet in February; our schedules were incompatible. But I called her from JFK before coming back here today — she answered just as she was leaving to catch the bus to JFK. She told me she had requested leave for the first two weeks of March and asked me to arrange my schedule so we could spend a few days in New York together. I told her that it shouldn't be a problem, since I was on the road so much in February. I agreed to contact her on the 16th or 17th to arrange for our March meeting."

Mr. X looked up from his notes. "Peter, you have a lot of homework to do, and I think we've done enough for tonight.

Just to review what you need to do: first, we need a copy of everything that could have been in your bag on November 30th; second, we'll need the exact dates of your two subsequent meetings with Mia; and third, you need to fill out the topical analysis sheet I am giving you. You are not to discuss any of this outside of this room.

"Our initial thinking is you will continue your relationship with Mia; however, your relationship will be of an entirely different nature. We're considering having you turn her into a double agent and are looking at transforming your security breach into a significant opportunity to feed the Soviets false information.

"No one expects you to do this on your own; we'll be with you every step of the way. However, you are going to have to play your part very well to maneuver her into the position we want. Looking down the road, you must put aside your true feelings for her, but at the same time use her feelings for you to our advantage. We'll be in contact about our next meeting. Any questions?"

Peter couldn't believe what was happening. It was just too much to process. "I'll probably have a hundred questions, but for the moment, I'll just try and digest all you've told me and think it through until we meet again. As XO, I guess Doug will be in charge of my exam schedule so he can coordinate with you guys to make me available when you want to see me."

Doug broke in, "Peter, I'll handle your work schedule; if we need to put you on leave, no problem. Max and I have started gathering generic documents; you concentrate on the specific materials requested."

Mr. X said, "Peter, why don't you get going—get some rest, and dig into your homework first thing tomorrow. I'd like Doug and Max to remain behind. They'll catch up with you tomorrow at work. Come in late, as you normally would after returning from an overseas trip." Mr. X gave a final warning: "Remember, discuss this with no one. No leaks allowed if we are going to win this one and save your butt."

After Peter left, Mr. Z took charge with the CIA perspective. "Gorsky wouldn't be involved unless they thought they had a big fish. However, they're relying on the potential rather than the actual. The room at Penn Garden was obviously bugged and everything that was said and done there is now on video and audio tape. They have copies of what was in Peter's bag; once he reconstructs that for us, we will know exactly what they have. We'll be one step ahead since they don't know what we know.

"The next meeting between Peter and Mia must take place in Norfolk. We'll turn his apartment into a first-rate TV studio. The Soviets are ready for a big move to turn Peter, and they want it to happen in Room 609. We're banking on the fact that they'll allow Mia to come down here and meet with Peter first. We'll create a scenario of operational necessity that keeps Peter state-side and out of New York the first two weeks of March. We now know that she'll be on leave.

"Initially, we'll schedule an exam that takes Peter through New York in early March. At the last minute, we take Peter off that exam, backed up with some Max-Natalie communication. We keep Peter here in Norfolk during the two weeks in question, during which he invites Mia down for a long weekend. This will keep the Soviets off balance. If they choose to keep her out of Norfolk, we'll have to devise an alternate plan. If there's no choice but for them to meet in Room 609, we're still one step ahead, and we'll cross that bridge when we come to it. Let's give Peter two days to regroup, and have another late-night session here on the 13th. We'll be in touch."

Chapter 37

New York City—Norfolk, Virginia
February 11th, 1973

Mia was miserable during the bus ride to JFK. She was happy to have heard from Peter before she left the apartment but their conversation only brought back the sickening reality that she must try to turn Peter into a Russian spy. She had genuine feelings for Peter and was sure his affection for her was real.

Despite her betrayal, she had to convince Peter that his role as a spy would not mean there would be no future for him. After six assignments, they would both be released by the Soviets and her father would be given his freedom. She must convince Peter that they would then have a chance to spend the rest of their lives together. She only hoped their relationship would survive her deception. The Soviets had offered to train her in the subtleties of flipping Peter but Mia decided she would try her own approach.

An appeal to their love for each other seemed to be her best chance. The real danger was that Peter would not cooperate and she would end up God knows where with Peter disgraced and his naval career at an end.

The most difficult thing to explain would be why she involved him in the first place. It had been completely self-serving at the outset. Now, her only choice was to be completely honest. She would tell him she had initially thought that if she could bring a big enough piece of intelligence to Ivan, she could bargain for the release of her father and herself. But then along came Gorsky with his aggressive approach, and it was now apparent that Ivan had no control over how the situation would be handled. The short-term offer of six assignments and eventual release was close to what she had initially intended but it was now clear that it was Peter who held the key to success. It was going to be very difficult to convince him that cooperation was the only way out of the terrible situation she had created.

Back at the Pan Am terminal, Mia found that her two weeks' leave had been granted. She immediately found a pay phone and dialed the familiar number.

"Book club," said the voice that answered.

"This is Mia Beck," she said. "I will be in New York during the first two weeks of March and I'd like you to send both the primary and alternate selections. I'll have a lot of time for reading and I want to be sure the books are available when I start my vacation."

"Thank you so much for giving us your preferences. If there are any changes, please call."

Of course, it was all code. The Soviets wanted to know immediately if her leave was granted—mission accomplished. Her reference to the alternate selection told them that Peter knew about her time off. "If there are any changes, please call" meant that she was to notify them if Peter couldn't meet her at which point she would receive further instructions.

With the call out of the way Mia felt a modicum of uncertainty lifting. However, her anxiety remained. She had three weeks to figure it out. Peter would call when she got back on the 16th, and they would set the date for their next get-together. She glanced at her watch and realized she was now running late. During the flight service briefing, she could barely concentrate on the passenger count, meals to be served, special situations, and anticipated flight conditions. One of her crewmates brought her back to reality. "Come on, Mia — it's time to get over to the plane — only 45 minutes until departure."

Mia picked up her carry-on and hurried to the waiting aircraft, forcing herself to focus on her legitimate job and trying to forget the clandestine work that was going to command such a high price.

Norfolk

When Peter got to his apartment, he poured himself three fingers of neat Scotch. He needed to do some serious thinking — not so much about his homework assignment as about his relationship with Mia. Why had she compromised him in the first place? Obviously, she hadn't targeted him specifically; he just happened to be in the wrong place at the wrong time...and he'd had all those documents with him. He was in over his head; the spooks' plan was the only apparent road to salvation. But turning the tables on Mia and the Soviets was not going to be a walk in the park.

The question lingered...why work for the Soviets? Ideology didn't seem like a valid answer; that left money or some kind of external pressure. Money could be a motivator. She certainly liked the finer things in life — certainly more than her Pan Am salary could provide. However, that seemed too simplistic. Mia was outgoing and beautiful; if she wanted money, she could marry it. No, there was more going on than that.

Up until three hours before, he had been convinced that their feelings for each other were genuine and growing. Now, he wasn't so sure. Spies lied — why not Mia? Maybe he'd just been fooling himself. Fantastic sex didn't equal love, though love often made fantastic sex better. He had to separate those two things in his mind — but at the same time, what if he was right, and she cared about him? If that were the case, he could use those feelings to convince her to work as a double agent. That would put her in danger, but then again, she was the one who had started down the road of international intrigue, so why not take it in another direction entirely.

The Soviets had trained her well and the CIA could use that to their advantage. The idea of feeding them a bunch of bogus information gave Peter a sense of satisfaction. With the help of the spooks, maybe he could turn a security breach into a counter-espionage windfall. However, his love for her or vice versa was not the most important part of the equation. He needed to instill fear of what would happen if she didn't cooperate with the CIA. He had to set aside his feelings for her and paint a picture where the only possible outcome was unconditional cooperation. The spooks had three weeks to help Peter develop a convincing pitch.

He retrieved the worksheet from the meeting. Sleep would not come if he didn't at least get started on filling in the information. The dates of the meetings were easy; all he had to do was consult his travel log. Looking at the suggested topics, his conversation with Mia during their second meeting came flooding back. He pulled down her leading questions and put them in the appropriate categories. He would take as much time as he needed — there was no need to rush to the office in the morning. Doug and Max had started gathering the "generic" information; he would then verify if what they collected was sufficient.

Peter's glass was empty, so he splashed in some more Scotch and added an ice cube. Enjoying the calming effect of the booze he set about jogging his memory and committing the facts to paper. In less than two hours, he had finished and was pleased with the results. He would edit his efforts in the morning. Fortunately, what the spooks needed was second nature to him — recalling and recording information is what Board members did for a living.

He popped a sleeping pill and didn't bother to set the alarm. Just before drifting off to sleep he had a vision of sharing his bed with Mia in just a few weeks…knowing their time together would not be at all what she expected. Of course the sex would come first, but soon Mia would see the depth of his anger and then, he mused, would come the really hard part.

Well, sweet Mia, we're going to have an interesting night, he thought before falling into a deep sleep.

Chapter 38

Back in New York, Natalie felt as if she had been gone for years instead of just a few short days—so much had happened. Her time in Paris with Max had been like something out of a storybook, with a perfect yet bittersweet ending that only proved how right they were for each other…no, how right they would have been, if the fates had been in their favor. She would have to learn to cherish the memory without regretting what might have been. And she wondered what was going to happen to Mia and Peter's relationship. There was no point in thinking too much about that, either. She trusted Max to do the right thing with the information she had given him; the matter was now out of her hands.

Exhausted and agitated, even a glass of Chablis did little to help her relax and she finally drifted into a troubled sleep. She was abruptly awoken at 1 a.m. by the phone ringing in her ear and, much to her groggy amazement, she heard Scott's voice on the line.

"I need to talk to you," he said. "Come on over."

Really? Natalie thought. *That's not going to happen. There might have been a time when I would have gone running to him but not anymore; those days are over.*

"If you want to talk to me, you can come over here," she said.

"I'm on my way," replied Scott.

She didn't really believe it until he knocked on the door and, dressed in a tatty old nightgown and feeling slightly ridiculous, she opened the door.

"I've come over to ask you to marry me," Scott said.

Great timing, thought Natalie. "I'll have to think about it," she said.

Clearly that wasn't what Scott expected to hear, but he kept his cool. "OK," he said. "Let me know what you decide."

Earlier in the evening, he'd been to dinner with his Uncle Frank and Aunt Betty and asked for their approval. Scott's father had died when he and his twin brother were just fifteen and Frank had become their father figure. Frank's opinion of Natalie was that she was "pretty nifty" —not exactly a ringing endorsement, but sufficient to give Scott the impetus he needed to formally propose.

Natalie told Scott that she and Caroline were leaving for Puerto Rico in a few days, and she would give him her answer when they returned. She gave him a quick kiss on the cheek and said goodbye. Scott, who had been sure Natalie would say yes right away, trudged back home feeling confused and disgruntled.

Despite the fact that Scott had finally proposed, Natalie now had enough misgivings to make her want to think things through before giving him an answer. Even though she couldn't be with Max, he had nevertheless caused her to reflect on the true nature of her feelings for Scott. If Natalie could feel so strongly for someone other than Scott, was he really "the one"? Four years of ups and downs had left lingering doubts. Confronted with uncertainty, she decided to do the only logical thing. After a good night's sleep, she would go up to the Bronx and talk it through with her parents.

The next morning when Caroline came into the kitchen, she immediately sensed that something was going on. "It looks like you have some news—I can't wait to hear about it" she said, as Natalie handed her a cup of hot coffee.

"You won't believe what happened at 1:00 a.m. this morning. Scott called and wanted me to go over to his apartment. I told him to come over here if he really wanted to talk to me. He walked in the door and proposed marriage."

"I'm staggered." Caroline set down her coffee cup with a bang. "We both thought there was less than a 50/50 chance of that happening. What did you tell him? I sure hope you didn't turn into a blathering idiot."

"*Au contraire, ma chérie,*" said Natalie with a little smile. "I told him you and I are off to Puerto Rico tomorrow and that I'd think about it and let him know when we get back."

"Good for you," said Caroline. "But what are you going to tell him?"

"I'm not sure. He did exactly what I told him to do; he called me when he was ready to propose. But I'm still not sure. There's no future for Max and me, but he changed the way I look at life and permanent relationships. I do love Scott even though we've been off and on for four years. The question is whether I love him enough to make a permanent commitment. I'm going to talk it over with my parents this afternoon."

"Great idea. I know your dad likes him, but your mother isn't much of a fan. Between the two of them, though, they're bound to give you sound advice."

After the familiar subway ride to the Bronx and the usual short walk, Natalie was greeted warmly by her parents as soon as she walked in the front door. "I have some important news," she said. "And I think we need to sit down and talk."

Her father said, "I have a little time before I have to go to Pietro's, so sit down and let's hear all about it"

Natalie didn't waste any time. "At 1:00 a.m. this morning,

Scott came over and asked me to marry him and I'm not sure what to do."

Her father, always intuitive, asked, "Is there someone else?"

Natalie didn't mince words. "There is someone very special but he's married…though separated."

Nat's face was full of compassion as he looked at his only child. He smiled sadly and gently shook his head knowing how hard the situation must be for her. She had invested a lot of her life in Scott and had told them she loved him.

Her parents gently reinforced what she already knew: that a man separated, but not divorced, could bring untold complications in the future—still, the decision was ultimately hers.

She told them that she and Caroline were off to Puerto Rico for a short vacation and that she would decide what to do once she got back to the city. When Natalie left her parents' house, she was still undecided.

Chapter 39

D oug got a call at work on Tuesday the 13th letting him know that the next meeting with the spooks would be at 1800 that same night. He let the intelligence team know that the preliminary research had been completed and that the requested materials would be available at the meeting.

It had been a restless two days for Peter, but he was slowly wrapping his mind around the reality of the situation. His anger with Mia persisted, but he had a nagging feeling that there was more to the story than her simply being recruited by the Soviets. *One step at a time, he thought, I need to get my act together for my next meeting with Mia.* Getting her turned was his primary responsibility and anything else he could find out during the process would be icing on the cake. Any thought of pursuing their romance was off the table now and unlikely to be a possibility in the future. Peter was painfully aware that he had to pull this off or be disgraced and out of the Navy. If the whole mess could end up as a counter-espionage coup, Peter might just be able to retain his integrity.

The team of six took their seats around the conference room table. A pot of coffee was ready for them, in case it ended up being a long night. Peter, Doug, and Max opened their briefcases and put the requested documents on the table.

As usual, Mr. X got things rolling. "OK, guys, please tell me how many copies there are of these documents?"

Peter answered, "This is the only copy of the worksheet that I completed. As far as my rough notes, other than the copy you have before you, only the originals exist in a file that contains all materials related to that inspection."

Doug pushed his pile across the table. "These are all generic documents that change routinely as procedures and information change. The most serious information—though it isn't Atomic Energy Act restricted data—is a summary of Board procedures, a short summary of upcoming inspections as well as the names of all Board members gathered from both the East and West Coast distribution lists."

Max said, "None of this could be considered actionable intelligence per se, but it's all part of the bigger picture. If the Soviets were able to keep pulling the thread, they could piece together information of some value. Clearly, we need to stop that from happening, and given the opportunity, feed them false information that will send them barking up the wrong tree."

"OK, we accept that." Mr. X was paging through the information. "Peter, I have your completed forms regarding the categorized questions. Based on your three meetings with Mia, please summarize in your own words what you think are her main areas of interest."

Peter ran his hand through his curly hair. "Well—first, she was pretty interested in what we actually did during inspections. I was probably a little too forthcoming on that issue. I explained that we tested watch sections through drills, did an intense records review and interviewed most of the officers and nuclear-trained crew. She seemed particularly interested in the fact that we could impose drills and cause a change in actual reactor plant operation as a response. The other areas where she poked around the edges were the radiation levels and perceived health effects, submarine communications procedures, sound-quieting measures, the basic differences between fast attack and FBM operations and, finally, the safety margins and whether we ever had—or covered up—reactor accidents. The questions themselves were leading and non-specific. I kept my answers basic, and she was careful not to press for details."

Mr. Z leaned forward in his chair. "I want to shift gears now and discuss her perceived motivation. Peter, do you have any thoughts in this regard?"

"I have given that a lot of thought. I ruled out ideology, since there is no love lost between the Germans and the Soviets. She does like the finer things in life, so obviously money could be a motivating factor. She buys nice clothes but lives very modestly in a one-bedroom apartment on the Upper East Side that she shares with three other stews, and they sleep in two sets of bunk beds…not exactly a lavish lifestyle. That would leave some kind of external pressure—maybe they caught her doing something she shouldn't have and are keeping her on a short leash, or maybe they have threatened her with something far worse, perhaps even imprisonment. The problem with that thought, though, is that given the nature of her job, she could easily plan to escape the Soviets by dropping off the grid in some far corner of the world where they couldn't find her."

Mr. Z said, "What do you know about her family?"

"They are native to what is now East Berlin; they got stuck when the Allies and Soviets carved up the city. They suffered quite a lot during the initial Soviet occupation when Humboldt University closed and they had no source of income; Mia's pregnant mother narrowly escaped being raped by the Russian soldiers in 1945. In the late '40s, when Mia was a baby, they fled to England and have been there ever since. According to her story, she was educated at the University of Manchester. I don't think she has any siblings."

"Peter, you need to dig deeper into her family situation the next time you see her and try to nail down her motivation for working for the Soviets." said Mr. Z. "We have ways to relieve pressure on reluctant spies, if we know which buttons to push. Her willingness to share that information will depend on how afraid she is of what might happen to her."

Peter shook his head, resigned. "I'll do my best to find out what you need to know; at this point, I have no idea how she will respond. How do you guys see this whole thing going down? Are we going to discuss that tonight?"

Mr. Z said, "That is the next item on our agenda, unless anyone has pertinent questions for Peter at this point. I think we have a pretty accurate picture of what information the Soviets have and what they're looking for. That will help us to stay one step ahead of them." He looked intently at Peter. "OK, here's the basic plan. Give her a call on the 16th when she returns stateside and arrange to meet her in NYC as soon as possible after the first of March. Tell her to make arrangements at the same hotel and that you will come up two days before you are due to leave from JFK for Heathrow. You have to act like everything is normal and be as affectionate as usual in your conversation.

"The day before you are to travel to NYC, you will call and tell her that you have to leave the next day for an inspection on a submarine based here in Norfolk — somebody got sick, and you have to take his place. However, you'll be back in port in two days, and you want her to come down to Norfolk and meet you as soon as you are back. Paint a picture of fun for three or four days — going to Williamsburg and Yorktown, seeing the sights. Tell her there's a pop concert at the Scope and that you'll be able to go dancing at the O Clubs. Create an agenda that should have her chomping at the bit to be with you, since she has two weeks' leave and no work-related obligations. Apologize profusely for the Navy pulling the rug out from under the NYC visit, and tell her you are really trying to make it up to her."

Mr. Z paused to fill his coffee cup and then started in again. "We're going to rig your apartment like a TV studio. Everything you do and say will be recorded—we will do to her what the Russians did to you. Once you're alone with her, start off as you normally would, drinking and having sex. At a vulnerable moment, when she least expects it, spring the trap. Accuse her of being a Soviet spy, and hit her with the following facts: *The CIA is all over you — they have pictures of you meeting with a Soviet intelligence agent in the cocktail lounge of the Four Seasons in February and that's just the tip of the iceberg. Don't deny it; the evidence is overwhelming.* We don't actually have anything else, but what I've just told you is absolutely true and she knows it.

"Tell her the choice is up to her—work for the United States or go to jail for espionage. What happens next is up to her. We're guessing she will cooperate and you will then be able to find out why she's working for the Soviets. If she denies everything, throw her out of your apartment and tell her she's going to be followed as soon as she leaves. Her life will not be her own. We'll take it from there. However, I don't think that will happen. If she really does love you, she's been feeling remorse all along and will be more than willing to cooperate if she thinks we'll be able to keep her safe once she starts working for us."

Peter looked down at the table. "That's some pretty heavy stuff. I guess it's up to me to gauge her reaction once I've given her the ultimatum. If she denies everything and spews a lot of BS, out the door she goes, luggage and all. If she breaks down, what do I tell her about the next step?"

Mr. Z replied, "The most important thing is for you to get her agreement that she will work for us and will do anything within reason that we require of her. As soon as she agrees, tell her that during the next couple of days, while she's in Norfolk, we will outline the basic procedures going forward. You will be her handler; she is comfortable with you and we'll teach you how to function effectively in that role."

Mr. X added, "We do, however, see a few possible problems. Initially, the Russians will probably push back hard and not want her to come down here without having her under their thumb. If she hedges on the invitation, push hard to get her to agree to the visit. The Russians are likely to realize that if she doesn't agree, you will get suspicious, and that you two will eventually end up back in NYC so they can complete their planned operation. So, if she insists that she wants you in NYC after the Norfolk inspection, agree with her, but let her know you are not happy and you don't understand why, with two weeks' leave, she can't just hop on a flight down here.

"If you have to go to NYC, we will put Plan B in play, which is to disrupt the action in the usual room and have you moved to another room before the Soviets have a chance to set up their monitoring. We don't think it'll come to that, but we can deal with it if we must. Peter, take a few days to absorb all of this. After you speak with Mia on the 16th, we'll want to know how the conversation went. We don't expect any drama until we attempt to shift the venue. Once there's a firm decision as to where the meeting will take place, we'll give you a final briefing."

Mr. Z said, "Peter, do you have any more questions? Keep in mind that we will have at least two additional briefings before you see Mia again."

He was clearly ready to wrap things up and Peter was only too happy to call it a day. "No, I think I have it. It really is a tough situation, but it's clear what has to be done." Peter pushed back from the table. "I keep my own emotions and feelings in check but use her feelings for me to secure her cooperation. Is that about right?"

"Yes, and now you may leave. We have some logistical matters to discuss with Max and Doug regarding your schedule and potential future counter-espionage efforts." Mr. Z stood up and offered his hand. "We'll be in touch."

Once Peter left, everybody refilled their coffee cups. Mr. Z continued to speak to the group. "What is everyone's read on Peter? Is he going to be able to pull this off?"

Max was the first to respond. "Peter is a smart and resourceful guy. He clearly understands what's at stake and I think he has better than a 90% chance of succeeding. Doug and I know him very well and I think he'll be able to turn Mia and work effectively as her handler."

Doug nodded. "I agree. Plus, we'll have two more sessions with him before the big meet and can ask some pointed questions to make sure his head is in the right place."

Mr. Z clasped his hands behind his head and leaned back in his chair. "There's another matter we need to discuss before we conclude and that has to do with Natalie's potential role as we go forward. She is one smart, perceptive and cooperative lady. At a minimum, Max, I think you need to close the loop with her and let her know she has been extremely helpful—and that you are the only person with whom she is allowed to discuss any aspect of this matter. She needs to continue watching Mia's behavior from afar, without rousing any suspicion. Additionally, she needs to know that some wheels have been put in motion but that we cannot tell her the specifics. She just needs to continue to be alert. Max, this conversation needs to happen face to face. There is to be nothing in writing; this is not appropriate material for the telephone on an unsecured line. Do you have any ideas as to how you might meet up with her?"

Max considered the question. "Once we had breakfast at JFK. As soon as she's back in NYC, I'll call and find out her schedule. If I'm going through JFK on a trip to Europe, it would be a piece of cake for her to hop on the bus and meet me at the Pan Am terminal. I'll let her know it's 'official business.' Otherwise, I could always fly up on National to JFK to meet her if she happens to be on her way into or out of the country. Either way, we'll make it work."

"Max, that's spot on. Doug will work to arrange your schedule." Mr. Z got up and indicated that the meeting was at an end.

Chapter 40

Norfolk—New York City
February 14th-16th, 1973

After a restless night, Max woke up early on Valentine's Day. He longed to call Natalie and say he loved her—but instead, the call would be all business. The conversation would be brief and to the point.

Max went for a five-mile run to clear his head. When he got back, Doug was rattling around making breakfast. Max tossed the morning edition of *Virginia Pilot* on the kitchen table.

"Yo Doug, I'm going to shower and make a call before heading to the office. I need to reach Natalie and set up an in-person meeting. She should be back from Europe, but I think she and Caroline are leaving for a week in Puerto Rico."

Doug put his arm around Max's shoulder. "Hey, buddy—are you OK with all this? I know the romantic part of the relationship is over, but having to see her could open an old wound."

"No worries; we parted on terrific terms. I told her that I would provide closure on the Mia-Peter situation. She'll be expecting to hear from me eventually, though not on Valentine's Day. I'll just keep a stiff upper lip and get through it like a trooper."

"Good luck, and take as much time as you need. Don't call too early; I'll see you when you get in."

Max called at 9:00. He felt a tightness in his chest as he dialed Natalie's number. She picked up on the third ring—a good sign; she was probably already awake.

"I would be remiss if I didn't lead with Happy Valentine's Day — even if the call is 90% business, 10% social," he said.

"Max! It's great to hear your voice. However, this sounds serious. What's up? Oh, and — Happy Valentine's Day to you, too." Natalie decided not to tell Max about Scott's proposal, at least for now.

Max took a deep breath. "Natalie, there's a matter we need to discuss face-to-face. I don't think I need to elaborate. One of us will have to travel to the other, and the office has green-lighted me to come to New York. The meeting should happen as soon as possible."

"Your timing is impeccable," said Natalie with a little chuckle. "Caroline and I have a late-morning flight to Puerto Rico tomorrow — how about an instant replay of our last breakfast at JFK? If you can't make it tomorrow, the Navy may just have to send you to Puerto Rico. Tell me if you can get to the Pan Am terminal tomorrow morning, and I'll be out as early as necessary."

Max plowed ahead. "How about sometime between 8:00 and 9:00? Does that time fit in with your Puerto Rico flight? I know there's an early National flight that can hit the window. I'll give you a call with my exact arrival time."

"Closer to 8:00 would be better, but I can live with as late as 9:00. Just let me know your flight number and ETA, and I'll be there."

The morning meeting was a good thing, as far as explaining Scott's proposal. She was sure Max would be supportive. He told her in Paris that Scott would be a fool not to propose.

"OK — that sounds perfect," said Max. "I'll call back with my flight information. Thanks for being so cooperative — see you early tomorrow."

"Max, I really am looking forward to seeing you, no matter the reason. Au revoir until tomorrow."

February 15th, 1973

Natalie was already seated when Max arrived. She gave him an enthusiastic wave as he appeared at the hostess' station. He looked a little tired — obviously there was a lot going on, or they would not be meeting on such short notice.

Max started with a little humor. "We have to stop meeting like this," he said. A big hug was in order, and just a peck on the lips. They both thought it felt good to touch each other again, if only for a moment. Natalie had picked a table in a quiet corner and had breakfast waiting for them. The room was deserted. Max was grateful that they wouldn't have a waitress interrupting things. He poured himself a coffee and spread marmalade on a croissant.

"I'm glad we can get this out of the way before I leave for vacation," said Natalie. "I have some news as well, but let's get the official business taken care of first. I assume this has to do with the Mia-Peter situation?"

"As always, you're on track," said Max. "For security reasons I can't tell you everything — but we may need your help as we go forward." Max moved closer to Natalie and lowered his voice. Anyone watching would think he was about to whisper sweet nothings into her ear. "Long story short — Mia may not be acting in the best interests of the United States. My remarks will be pretty cryptic, but I know you'll be able to follow. Now give me a little kiss on the cheek to throw off anyone who may be watching, and I'll tell you as much as I can."

Natalie did as requested, with a little smile. "OK. I'll do my best. I'll interrupt only if you lose me completely."

Max thought for a moment. "Doug and I had a terrific get-together with the guys, and they wanted me to extend a big thank you for all that you did to make our party a huge success.

Everything you did was very helpful, and they were able to name all the players in our game. The most important thing for you is to behave normally, but take note of anything out of the ordinary, just as you've been doing. Your approach has been perfect."

Natalie nodded, so Max continued. "If you're still willing to help, the guys may want to come to New York and meet you. Daddy's restaurant would be a good place; they've heard about the food, and they're always happy to mix business with pleasure. Is there a private dining room we could use?"

Natalie picked up the thread. "As I told you in Paris, I'm willing to help in any way I can, but there may be complications. I'll explain when you're finished. There are no private dining rooms, but Daddy has a little office on the third floor, and I'm sure that could be set up for a meeting. When you contact me, we'll try to arrange a little get-together at a time that fits with my schedule. Otherwise, I'll just take note of anything unusual. And as we discussed in Paris, everything will remain strictly between us."

Max shook his head in amazement. "You never fail to quickly grasp the situation. That's about it—just sit tight and wait for a call. It could take a week, a month, or never happen at all. Oh, by the way—Peter is still infatuated with Mia, and I think he may be coming up to see her early in March. If you happen to bump into them, just act like nothing is going on. Now, I think you had some news for me? I'll just hand you the mic."

Natalie blushed slightly. "I guess I'll follow your lead and not beat around the bush. When I got back from Europe, Scott came over in the middle of the night and proposed. I told him I would think about it, and when Caroline and I get back from Puerto Rico, I'll give him my answer. That's it: no drama, just a straightforward marriage proposal."

"Well, you know what I think. First of all, my sincere congratulations—I'm not in a position to counter Scott's offer, despite how I feel about you. This is what you've wanted for a long time, and finally, Scott has come to his senses. You should accept as soon as you get back to New York. Is there any reason why you wouldn't?"

"No, not really. I guess it hasn't quite sunk in yet. I was convinced he wasn't going to come around, and that I would start over again as a single girl, without the distraction of Scott being around. As we discussed in Paris, my relationship with you turned everything upside down and convinced me that Scott was not the only person in the world I could love or think of in terms of marriage and a life together."

Natalie reached across the table and took Max's hands in hers. They just looked at each other for a long time without speaking. Max felt his eyes filling up; a single tear formed in the corner of Natalie's eye and ran down her cheek. Max took out his handkerchief, softly dried Natalie's tear, and blotted his own eyes.

"Max, I'll never forget you," said Natalie. "In a way I couldn't have expected, you have turned my life in the direction I always wanted it to go. Words can't express how that makes me feel about you, despite the love I have for Scott. Thank you for being the very best kind of friend and always doing the right thing during the six months we shared."

Max put away his handkerchief. "You know I'm so very happy for you. Scott is a lucky guy, and after your four years together, I'm sure he knows you quite well and will do everything he can to make you happy. Even though I haven't met him, I wish you both every possible joy that life has to offer." He squeezed Natalie's hand and let her go. "I don't know where this other matter is going to end up; things could be resolved in any number of ways. However, it's apparent that you and I will continue to be in contact. Even though you're engaged to Scott, you can't tell him about any of this. If the two of you do get married, the guys will have to think through the approach if you are still involved. Are you OK with the idea of keeping secrets from Scott?"

Natalie nodded. "I understand the ground rules. If it becomes difficult, I'll certainly tell you. At that point, I may need to reconsider my involvement. Is there anything else we need to discuss — anything at all? Caroline will be here in about fifteen minutes."

"How about I walk you to your departure gate? I'd love to see Caroline again, and my National flight doesn't leave for another two hours. After I drop you off, I'll go have a stiff drink to celebrate your pending engagement. I'm not much for crying in my beer."

Max paid the check, and they were on their way with their carry-ons in one hand, holding hands as they walked toward the departure gate. When they got there, Caroline was waiting with a cheerful greeting for Max. When they boarded, Caroline went ahead leaving Max and Natalie standing there looking at each other. They shared a lingering hug, and it was apparent that Max wanted a final kiss as he moved his face close to Natalie's.

"Well, I guess it's OK — I'm not officially engaged yet." What followed was one of the deepest, most meaningful kisses they had shared in the past six months. That one kiss seemed to say everything they could not express. Natalie turned away and walked slowly to the jetway, but before she disappeared, she turned and gave Max a little wave and that devastating Pan Am smile.

Chapter 41

Mia was full of trepidation as she walked into 8L. She couldn't wait to hear Peter's voice on the phone but was wracked with anxiety over the awful situation in which she now found herself. If she was going to protect her father, she had no choice but to do as the Soviets demanded. At fifty-eight, he had many good years ahead of him. He was her only family; her mother had died of pneumonia ten years earlier, and Mia was their only child. He had always supported and encouraged her and, because of her considerable abilities in mathematics and science, she had chosen to follow in his footsteps and become an engineer.

But the terrible truth was her family had never escaped East Berlin. She had taken her degree at Humboldt, not Manchester. While she was at university her father, Karl, became involved with the German reunification efforts. When this was discovered by the Russians, they unceremoniously threw him in prison and withdrew his teaching credentials. Mia was not implicated, but when the KGB hatched the idea of infiltrating Pan Am with Soviet couriers, Mia was an obvious candidate. They leveraged her father's imprisonment as a means to gain her cooperation. Because of Karl's considerable skills as a teacher and researcher, the Soviets would let him return to Humboldt if Mia agreed to work for them. Karl would be under constant surveillance, though, and not permitted to travel. If either of them made a false step, both would land in an East German or Soviet prison.

Mia was sent to the School for Scandal and became fluent in English, with a British accent. They created a deep cover story that she was a British citizen and falsified records to show she was educated at Manchester. This dovetailed nicely with her first Pan Am postings in London, then Hong Kong, and finally New York. She also spoke fluent German with either an American or a British accent.

Her initial assignments were relatively benign but, as her talents became obvious, they honed her skills even further. Unaware of the Soviets' real treachery, she naively believed that using the initial documents taken from Peter, she would be able to negotiate a better deal for herself and her father. In reality, all it did was to get her more deeply involved in one of the most critical aspects of the Cold War. She was unaware of the Russians' need to acquire inside information related to the US Navy's nuclear submarine program.

She remained distracted with anxiety as the phone rang and almost tripped in her haste to answer—she knew it had to be Peter. "Mia speaking," she said, with a little quiver in her voice.

Peter replied, "Welcome home, traveler. It's great to hear your voice. I missed you so much. I've got some great news about when we can get together—just a few weeks away."

"Oh, sweetheart, you have no idea how much I've missed you. Wherever I was in the world, you were the last thing on my mind before I fell asleep."

Peter didn't have to fake excitement. Their sex was some of the best he'd ever had—and if it all worked out, he hoped it would continue albeit on slightly different terms. "I've been able to arrange a great schedule," he said. "I can come to New York on Friday, March 2nd and won't leave for Europe until the evening of Monday the 5th. That means almost four full days together in New York. Start planning right away—the sky's the limit."

Mia couldn't believe her good fortune. The Soviets wanted a meeting as soon as possible and Peter had just solved the problem for her. "That's fantastic. I'll get on it first thing tomorrow. I'm here for two days before I leave on assignment." Having Peter's visit coincide with the start of her two-week leave was absolutely perfect. She wondered if it was really necessary to spring the trap on their first day together. She hoped Ivan would have some ideas about how to make the turn successful and as painless as possible. "What kinds of things would you like to do" she asked, "besides the obvious? Do you like museums, or classical music? I want you to have the time of your life."

Peter settled into his role. "I'll leave it up to you — whatever you want to do will be fine with me. But, for starters I'd like to go back to Pietro's and La Grenouille for dinner, and Sunday brunch at the Four Seasons."

"It will be a smashing visit — you won't be disappointed. Let's speak again when I get back. Call me any time after the 22nd. I'd like to chat a bit more but I'm so jet-lagged I can hardly put two words together."

"Sure thing, Mia — I'm going off myself to get some shuteye. I'll touch base as soon as you get back. Sleep tight."

"Goodbye, darling — talk to you soon."

Next came the required calls to their respective handlers. Mia went to her usual pay phone on 77th. Ivan picked up on the third ring and Mia said, "It is all arranged for Friday the 2nd and we'll be together until late on the 5th. I suggest we meet sometime in the next two days."

Ivan replied, "How about noon tomorrow, usual spot?"

"Perfect. See you then."

Four hundred miles south, a similar conversation took place. Peter called Doug. "It's all arranged for the 2nd, as we discussed. Will there be another meeting?"

"Plan for an after-work get-together at the usual spot," said Doug. "I'll confirm tomorrow as soon as I get to the office."

New York—Norfolk
February 17th

Mia followed her usual route and arrived at five minutes past noon in Van Courtland Park. Although it was a cloudless, sunny day, it was very cold and the park was almost deserted.

"Congratulations on arranging the meeting with your naval officer so promptly. However, I'm not clear on what it is exactly you need— additional training perhaps?" Ivan's tone was not disapproving, but merely curious.

"I thought it best you understand the situation. Peter will be here for almost four full days. Given the amount of time we'll be together, I wanted to know if I should I present the proposition right away or spend a day heightening his affection and attachment to me first? If my approach doesn't succeed, or if he delays making a decision, we need to give some thought as to how and when you and Gorsky will get involved."

Ivan rubbed his chin thoughtfully. "You have raised an interesting point. There is so much riding on this; I would like to discuss it with Gorsky before giving you guidance on the matter. We may be able to use the length of his visit to our advantage. If we can get him turned early, we might be able to get some intelligence from the inspection he plans to make right after his visit. Was there anything else?"

Mia moved a bit closer and lowered her voice. "Only that I want to be clear on the options if I try to turn him and fail. We can meet in person, or you can drop me written instructions."

Ivan folded his paper and stood up. "We'll be in touch in plenty of time."

Mia remained on the bench after Ivan departed and watched the pigeons finish the seeds Ivan had so generously scattered on the ground.

Norfolk

At the end of the work day, the committee of six assembled in the secure conference room. Mr. Z started the discussion. "Well, Peter, what do you have for us?"

Peter exhibited a bit of self-confidence. "This is what I put out there. I told her I would arrive on Friday the 2nd and wouldn't leave for Europe until late in the day on Monday. I pitched a wonderful time in New York and told her to plan a four-day blowout. Everything seemed perfectly normal when I spoke with her—just two lovers planning a romantic long weekend. She'll get back stateside on the 22nd and I told her I'd be in touch to finalize our plans."

Mr. X weighed in. "OK, so far, so good. Let's keep in mind that our goal is to get Mia down here and turned before Peter meets with her in New York, where the Russians no doubt want to turn him. When you speak to her on the 22nd, everything must go forward as if your weekend in New York is on track. On Thursday the 1st, you will call and tell her that you have an unexpected inspection here in Norfolk the next day—you will say that one of the team got sick and you are the replacement. Apologize profusely, and then pitch the whole Norfolk vacation plan as the only way you can see her this month. Tell her to book a flight that arrives here late on Monday and say that the Board gave you the whole week off to make up for the change in plans."

Max raised his hand, which Z acknowledged. "Max, what's up?"

"An entire week off is too much; it may raise the Russians' suspicions. I think Peter should tell her that he has shore leave on Tuesday and Wednesday, but on Thursday his team has to drive to New London to do an inspection that will finish late on Saturday. Peter should keep in his back pocket the possibility he could fly to JFK after the New London inspection to spend Sunday and Monday in New York with Mia. If, or when, Mia pushes back about Peter not coming to New York, he will offer the counterproposal to come visit the following Sunday. That should give the Russians a consolation prize and remove any objections to Mia's coming to Norfolk. If their plan is to turn Peter, they will still get to spring their trap when he gets to New York — a week late, but of course Mia will already be turned here in Norfolk."

Mr. Z said, "I see your point, and I think that will work. We should be able to manipulate the Russians. They certainly won't want to raise any suspicion by pushing Mia too hard about the Norfolk visit." Everyone nodded in agreement.

Mr. X said, "Peter, you really need to sell the Norfolk visit when you call her. Force a decision by the end of the day on Thursday and tell her to leave her flight arrival information at the Board office when arrangements are completed. Tell her you'll pick her up in your 'Vette at the airport when she arrives. Make it sound like a done deal.

"If she tries to turn you down, really hedge and pretend to be suspicious. Make the argument that you can't wait to see her and since she's on vacation, you don't see any problem with her coming down here for a romantic meeting with you — even offer to pay for her airline ticket to Norfolk. Break down every possible objection she may make."

Mr. Z said, "I don't think there will be any need for us to meet until March 2nd, when we know who is going where. After that, we'll have the whole weekend to plan. The ideal situation is that Mia comes to Norfolk, gets turned, and then the following Sunday, Peter goes to New York; the Russians may take a shot at turning him, but we'll still be one step ahead. It is a bit complicated, but I think we have the Russians in a damned if they do, damned if they don't situation. If Mia absolutely refuses to come to Norfolk and Peter has to go to New York without her being turned here in Norfolk, we'll make contingency plans accordingly. "Peter, any questions?"

"No. I'll pull the plug on my visit as we discussed and when I have her decision, I'll call Doug, and we'll go from there."

Peter stood up, pleased with himself and the plan's progress. Mr. X offered his hand and closed the meeting. Earlier, before Peter's arrival, Max had met with Mr. X and Mr. Z. He told them about his conversation with Natalie, her clear understanding of the situation, and that her father's restaurant would be available as a meeting place. He didn't tell them about Scott's marriage proposal; he would wait to tell the spooks when, and if, she accepted.

Chapter 42

Ivan opened the secure telephone line that linked the UN Mission in New York with KGB headquarters in Moscow. Gorsky answered immediately.

"How did your meeting with Songbird go?" he demanded.

"I'm happy to report that it went very well indeed. She has already arranged a meeting with Neutron. Since she was granted her two-week leave, he immediately arranged his schedule to be in New York on Friday, March 2nd and stay until the 5th. However, Songbird did raise an important point."

"What was it? I thought everything was on track with the plan we outlined."

"Our plan had Neutron in New York for two days but he will now be with Mia for almost four. The point she raised was one of timing. At which point should he be approached with the proposal? If she were to continue the soft sell for a day or two before we get involved she might have a greater chance of success. On the other hand, if we are able to turn him early, we might be in a position to gather useful information from his scheduled inspection due to begin after he leaves New York on the 5th."

"It's certainly constructive thinking on her part; I'm glad she raised the issue. I think an early direct approach is still our best plan. If we turn him early, we can brief him regarding the intelligence we want, and he can start right in once the inspection begins on the 6th. I'll gather the group here and have them prepare a list of all the documents they want photographed. If Songbird turns him early, it will give us time to provide him a mini-camera and teach him how to use it."

Ivan responded, "I'll contact Songbird as soon as she returns and tell her what we've decided. I'll arrange with your people here in New York for the camera and training. Also, we need to establish his method of communication with us at the end of each mission. We'll teach him how to make identical exchanges once he returns to New York."

Gorsky replied, "Excellent, excellent. I'll get my teams up to speed at once. Any other questions or comments?"

Having none, Ivan quickly concluded. "This seems to be it. I'll be in touch after the 22nd."

Gorsky gathered his notes. First order of business was to get the admiral to update the Navy's wish list. Gorsky's aggressive approach was alive and well at KGB headquarters.

Langley—Norfolk

As requested, Mr. X contacted Mr. Z via secure line at his office in CIA headquarters. Mr. Z asked, "X, what's your take on the situation to date? Do you see any pitfalls or immediate needs not addressed?"

"Two things come to mind," Mr. X replied. "First, there's Peter. These Navy Nukes are a bunch of smart guys and, although counterespionage isn't usually their bag, they learn fast and perform well. We'll be watching when Peter tries to turn Mia and we can always step in if things start to go south. The tricky part will be Mia's supposed turning of Peter in New York with the Russians watching. They'll both have to pull off a thoroughly convincing performance.

"Second, there's Natalie. I think there's significant potential there. We can use Max as a kind of handler; anything we need, we can pass to her through Max. This brings up an interesting point: we're going to need a secure means of communication for our growing operation in New York—something that does not involve any formal US government location. Natalie and Mia's apartment is clearly out of the question. However, I liked Max's idea of using Natalie's father's restaurant."

Mr. Z continued the thought, "In addition to a potential meeting place, why don't we consider dropping a secure line into her father's office? Even if we never use it, having it there keeps us one step ahead."

Mr. X chuckled. "My thoughts exactly! Max will need a secure way to communicate with Natalie. If we do get Mia turned, Natalie can use the line in emergencies or for certain communications. She can spend time at the restaurant without arousing suspicion."

"How should we make the overture to Natalie's father?" asked Mr. Z.

"The key is to run everything through Max. It will be up to him to test the waters. The pitch to her father will be short and sweet—the Navy has an operation in the New York area and there's a need for a 'special telephone line' for secure communications. If we get a green light from her father, we'll turn it over to our experts as to method."

Mr. Z said, "I'll talk to my team and get their thoughts. If it's a go, we'll direct Max to make the initial overture to Natalie; if it goes well, he can pitch the father."

"Sounds like a plan Z—let me know if and when you want Max to go forward. Stay in touch."

With a click, the line went dead.

February 22nd, 1973

As soon as Mia walked into her apartment, the phone rang. It was Peter, calling to let her know that plans for his trip to New York were on track. They chatted affectionately for a few minutes and then Mia rang off. She changed out of her uniform and went to her usual pay phone.

She identified herself using a prearranged code and was directed to go immediately to the designated dead drop in Van Courtland Park. Without returning home, she headed straight for the subway. Ivan had decided that the John Jay Park dead drop could only be used in emergencies; it was just too close to her apartment.

Mia retrieved a small package from the dead drop and returned to her apartment. With Natalie and Caroline still in Puerto Rico, and Sabrina on the road, Mia had the apartment to herself. She unpacked the message from the dead drop, got a magnifying glass, and read the tiny print. The message was straightforward—attempt to turn Peter as soon as possible. If she was unsuccessful after a soft approach, she could expect intervention from the Ivan/Gorsky team. However, if she were successful in turning Peter, she was to train him in the use of the mini-camera and tell him that a list of documents to photograph would be forthcoming. Further instructions for Peter would be passed on during his time in New York. Any problems, she was to contact Ivan for guidance.

For Mia, the day of reckoning had arrived. She was in a box and had no options. If she failed, she was aware all hell would break lose. She felt she had a good chance of turning Peter with the soft sell; there was a defined close-out clause with the six mission concept.

After Peter completed six missions, she could only hope the

Russians would be true to their word and that both she and her father would be released to lead a normal life–and that Peter's role as a spy would end. Any question of she and Peter having a life together was totally up in the air. For now, she had to put on the performance of her life and just hope it would be good enough.

Chapter 43

Puerto Rico—New York City
February 18ᵗʰ-28ᵗʰ, 1973

Natalie left for Puerto Rico with her head spinning. Two unresolved issues were at play now: Scott's pending marriage proposal and uncertain involvement with Max in resolving the Mia issue. She could use Caroline as a sounding board concerning Scott, but anything about the Mia situation had to be held strictly under wraps. Despite this inner conflict, she and Caroline managed to behave like high school girls on their first vacation away from home. After a week of harmless flirting, dancing and fun, they returned tanned and ready for whatever lay ahead.

Maybe Scott was watching the entrance of 400 East 77ᵗʰ, because as soon they opened the apartment door, the phone rang. Natalie picked up, and it was Scott. "How—how was your trip?" he asked, clearly uncertain and anxious to know Natalie's decision.

"Suppose I come over and tell you?" she suggested. He eagerly agreed.

"Well, I'm off to seal my fate," she announced to Caroline. Arriving at Scott's, she was happy to see he appeared nervous. *Good. He needs to stop taking me for granted,* she thought.

"Hi, darling. I'm accepting your proposal." He opened his mouth, but before he could speak, she went on, "I did a lot of thinking and planning while in Puerto Rico and I've decided that I want to get married in the same church where my parents were married back in 1928 — Our Lady of Peace on East 62nd. It's Victorian Gothic, not too big, and I've already found out that we can have it on May 6th."

"May...of 1974?" said Scott, incredulous.

"No, you silly thing, May of 1973."

"But that's only ten weeks away!"

"That's right, so we'll have to start getting organized straight away. You'll need to take care of the groomsmen and best man. Mother and I will go wedding dress shopping on Saturday, and Caroline and I are already working on the bridesmaids' list. We need to find a place for the reception, of course, but I was thinking perhaps the Regency Hotel ballroom or the St. Regis roof. We'll go to City Hall to get our marriage license and then afterwards we can go to Altman's to register for china and crystal. That will still give us enough time to pick out our wedding rings."

"Do you want to...have breakfast at Tiffany's, Miss Golightly?" Scott said, in a desperate attempt to slow down the speeding train of Natalie's wedding planning.

She smiled. "No. I want to be different and try Cartier's. I'm going to head back home now so you can get started on your part of the arrangements. Isn't this exciting?"

She gave him a big kiss of encouragement and scampered out the door, leaving no time for Scott to have second thoughts or weasel out of the marriage. Hopefully his stunned look would morph into enthusiasm once the initial shock subsided.

Just as she got back to the apartment, Max called. She gave him the good news about formalizing the engagement. Max was genuinely happy and told her so, then quickly shifted into business mode.

"This is going to seem a little unusual, but please go to a nearby pay phone with relative privacy. Take down this number—call collect, and we'll be talking on a secure line here in Norfolk. Can you call within fifteen minutes?"

"Absolutely. I'm on my way." Natalie grabbed her coat and rushed out the door. When she got on the line to Norfolk, Max started right in.

"Natalie, here it is in a nutshell—the operation needs a secure means of communicating with you on a routine basis there in New York. The spooks would like to install a secure line in your father's office at Pietro's and the intelligence team wants to come up and meet with the two of you. Please tell your father that the government has an ongoing operation in the New York area and needs a method of secure communication—and that you implicitly trust the people involved. He has no obligation to do so, of course, but please encourage him to at least meet with the intelligence team."

"What should I do when I have his answer?"

"Call me at the office and we'll set up a secure call like today. If the answer is yes, please provide a few dates and times that would work. We'll start as a normal lunch engagement and then drift up to the office to discuss the serious business I outlined."

"Since Scott and I are formally engaged, are there implications?"

"For the time being, tell him nothing, just as before. Your involvement remains unchanged—observe Mia for any unusual behavior. If the secure line gets installed, use it to communicate. If greater involvement is needed from you, we'll be in touch."

"Got it. I have to dash. As soon as I have Daddy's answer, I'll call you."

"Thank you—and again—congratulations. I know the two of you will be very happy."

Max was sincere, but the words nearly choked him. At least Natalie would be in his life for a little while longer, even if it was only business.

Chapter 44

Peter took a deep breath, finished his Bloody Mary and picked up the phone. He had run over this tough sell countless times and had his pitch down pat. Short and simple, convincing and not contrived: this was a matter of Navy operational necessity. The consolation prize was a trip to Norfolk.

Mia answered on the third ring. "Peter! I thought it might be you. I'm so excited about our upcoming weekend."

For Peter, her opening could not have been better. "Mia, I'm afraid I have really disappointing news. We'll have to delay our time together for a few days. One of the guys caught the 'flu, and I'm the only one available to take his place. The worst part is, the team goes to sea from Norfolk tomorrow."

"Oh, no! This is dreadful. Can't you do anything about it?"

Scared of the Russians, are you? thought Peter. "I've pulled every string I could and talked to everybody here in Norfolk. It was such short notice; I couldn't make other arrangements. But, to his credit, the senior member was very sympathetic. I have to stay in Norfolk next week, but he gave me the following Monday, Tuesday and half of Wednesday off. It would be super if you could come down to Norfolk late on Sunday. I'll be back from the sea in time to pick you up at the airport. You won't have to leave until Thursday morning. What do you think?"

"That's nice of the senior member, but still—this is terrible. I so wanted a long romantic weekend with you in New York.

Isn't there any way you can still do that, early next week? Even if you come for only one or two days, it would be better than not coming at all."

Peter was ready with his counter-proposal. "As long as we're together, why does it matter whether it's in New York or Norfolk? I thought you would be excited about seeing where I live and work. It's not possible for me to leave Norfolk. On-call duty obligations require that I stay here until I leave for Thursday's exam—but I'd still have a lot of free time. There's a whole list of fun things to do."

Mia tried one last time to save the New York visit. "But darling, all of the arrangements have been made. I reserved our usual room and bought tickets for several shows. I'm just so disappointed."

Peter continued to remove obstacles. "I'll reimburse you for all the tickets. Just give them to one of your roommates, with my compliments. Go through Pan Am and see if you can get a domestic airline deal. Put the cost of the tickets on my tab. Please say yes—I really want to see you next week. It shouldn't be a big deal for you to travel down here; it's a short flight compared to your usual. I'm beginning to wonder whether you really want to see me. If you agree to come here next week, I'll see if I can arrange to come to New York sometime during the remainder of your vacation. That way, everybody will be happy."

Mia knew she couldn't make that kind of commitment without the Russian's approval, but Peter's doubts about her wanting to see him made her frantic with worry. She had to convince Ivan that either he agree to the Norfolk visit or risk losing Peter altogether.

"Of course I want to see you—and come to Norfolk," she said. "I'm sorry for being such a goose; I was just thinking of all the plans I'd made and how I wanted to spoil you with the most brilliant weekend. But you're right; it would be lovely to let you spoil me in Norfolk. I'll see what I can do with airline arrangements. Give me a few hours, and I'll call right back. Will you be at the office?"

Mia knew exactly how the system worked when flying on a domestic carrier but she needed to buy time and touch base with Ivan.

Peter sensed her resistance crumbling, but had to seal the deal. "I'll be here at the office and will wait to hear from you. I'm really hoping this all works out."

"Me too," Mia said weakly, and rang off.

As soon as he got to the office, Peter went to Doug's cube and said, "Hey, let's head over to the gym for a game of squash." They grabbed their gear and started out for the gym, their game an excuse to stop in at the Communications Center's secure room.

"During the call to Mia, I used every comeback in my bag of tricks to try to make her believe that her continued objections were making me think that she wasn't all that keen to see me after all. Finally, she agreed to investigate options to travel down here on a domestic airline. Of course what she's really doing is checking with her KGB handlers. She said she would call back in a couple of hours."

Back in New York, Mia's brief panic subsided as she figured out her next move. She knew the KGB wouldn't like the idea of a trip to Norfolk, but she couldn't afford to antagonize Peter. As soon as she had her thoughts together, she headed to the usual pay phone and called the special number.

"Hi, it's me—is he available?" she said to the voice that picked up. This was code for an immediate conversation with Ivan. In less than a minute, he was on the line.

"It sounds like it's something important," Ivan was clearly concerned.

"Just a little disappointment." Mia tried to sound casual. "My boyfriend can't come to New York tomorrow and wants me to visit him in Norfolk on Monday. I tried hard to change his mind, but you know how it is with the Navy. I couldn't push too hard, because he started to question my commitment to see him. I put him off a bit, but I need to give him an answer as soon as possible. He goes to sea tomorrow."

Ivan had to think fast. Gorsky would be furious at this change in plans, but Ivan had faith in Mia. However, he needed all the details before he approached Gorsky.

"I think we should talk this over, before you act hastily," he said in a fatherly tone. "Let's meet by the river in about half an hour."

This meant meeting in John Jay Park, at their emergency location. "I'll see you there," said Mia, obviously relieved to shift the responsibility to her handler.

Mia found Ivan sitting on a bench, feeding the pigeons. Their exchange was efficient; Mia recounted the entire conversation with Peter and said again that he seemed to be questioning her sincerity. He couldn't come to New York as planned and was adamant about her going to Norfolk. She told Ivan that he had left the door open a tiny crack with the promise to try and arrange a quick New York visit before the end of her two-week leave. Ivan noted that perhaps he could use this as a bargaining chip with Gorsky—she would agree to go to Norfolk only if Peter would guarantee a quid pro quo trip to New York. Mia agreed that this sounded like a reasonable proposal. If she could pull it off, Ivan felt he could sell it to Gorsky. Time was so short; he didn't see any other option.

Mia needed to check the domestic flights from JFK to Norfolk and get tentative flight information but not commit to anything until Peter agreed to the compromise. If Peter didn't agree to come to NYC, then she would tell him she needed more time to think it over. At this point, the next step in the little drama would be up to Ivan and Gorsky. Ivan knew that Gorsky would never agree to a "something for nothing" negotiation. If Mia could close this deal, it would mean their plan to turn Peter would only be delayed a few days. Their next move depended on the outcome of Mia's conversation with Peter. Ivan was not looking forward to calling Gorsky. He would have to emphasize that, as Songbird's handler, he had to make an on-the-spot decision, trusting in her experience and ability to secure the arrangement.

As much as he would have liked to wait until Mia talked to Peter and could confirm the compromise, Ivan knew that if it didn't work out, Gorsky would be furious and could cause real trouble for him down the road. By calling him immediately, Ivan felt he would be able to maneuver Gorsky into thinking it had been their joint decision. In a sense, the quid pro quo depended on Mia's ongoing "relationship" with Peter, as well as her ability to work out a lovers' compromise. Ivan needed to impress on Gorsky that it wasn't just a matter of them issuing an order to Songbird to make Neutron come to New York, and that it called for a certain degree of finesse – a skill rarely found in Gorsky's tool box.

As soon as he got back to the Soviet UN Mission, Ivan got Gorsky on the line in Moscow and explained the situation. As expected, Gorsky was furious and refused to allow Songbird to go to Norfolk. Gorsky hated it when things didn't go his way and was known to become irrational when they didn't.

Ivan was ready for this. "OK, suppose I tell her that, and as a result, Neutron kills the whole relationship because he smells something fishy? After all, they are supposed to be lovers, and by refusing the visit, she would be acting like a spoiled child instead of a mature woman in love. Neutron is not stupid. We ordered her to get the two weeks' leave, and now we are telling her she can't use it to go to him. It makes no sense. Bear in mind, there is no down side for me if your demand ends up killing their relationship. Your operation will be over, but the Stork Club will still be intact. Comrade, I think you should reconsider your position and let me handle this as I see fit."

Ivan knew he was on dangerous ground, taking such an aggressive posture, but he was tired of Gorsky's bullying and felt that being blunt might shock him into agreement. Gorsky was so ambitious that the prospect of this extremely important operation being put in jeopardy had the desired effect. There was a long pause on the line—there was no way Ivan was going to break the silence and back off.

Finally, Gorsky acquiesced. "Ivan, I see your point. The plan does have merit. As long as we eventually get him back in New York, we can proceed as originally intended."

Ivan grinned into the phone. "Very well. Let me see how Songbird's conversation with Neutron evolves. If she gets him to commit to come to New York during her vacation, we'll just let things take their normal course. When he comes to New York, we'll put our initial plan into operation."

Gorsky couldn't resist a small shot at Ivan. "Let's hope she's as good at negotiation as you say she is. Keep me informed."

Mia gathered several flight options from JFK to Norfolk. Since Peter had hinted that he might possibly arrange a visit to New York while she was still on leave, she believed she could get him to agree to the quid pro quo. With her proposal and flight information in hand, she called the Board office in Norfolk. Peter was back from the Comm Center, waiting for her call.

Mia was cheerful and upbeat. "Hello, darling. I've been a very busy little girl. I have an idea and a proposal. You said that you might be able to come to New York before the end of my leave. If you absolutely promise that you will, I'll come to Norfolk. I have the flight information but I'm not going to purchase a standby ticket until you agree to my little proposal. What do you think? Me there, you here – double the fun, what could be better?"

Peter was relieved and couldn't resist loving how cute she was when she put her foot down. Obviously, the Russians had seen the problem with her continued refusal to come to Norfolk. He had managed the situation perfectly.

"Well, I have a plan I think you'll like. When I leave Norfolk next Thursday I'll end up in New London on Sunday. Max told me about a similar trip when he took a Pilgrim flight from New London to JFK to meet Natalie. I'll just do the same and end up in New York a week from Sunday. How does that sound?"

Mia was relieved to get this behind her. She might even enjoy the trip to Norfolk with no official duties. Just a few days of fun and sex—what could be better? She would just put the New York visit out of her mind for a while and enjoy her vacation.

Her response was bubbly. "Oh, darling—you are wonderful. It's perfect."

"Don't forget to keep track of your expenses. On Sunday night, I'll be waiting for you at the airport when you arrive. We're going to have a fabulous time."

"I'm so happy that this is going to work out, Peter. It just goes to show that problems are easy to solve when two people really care for each other."

After this comforting bit of amateur philosophy, they ended the conversation since ostensibly Peter had to go to sea the next day. Immediately, each of them scrambled to tell their respective handlers what had transpired. Ivan was pleased with the details provided by Mia, which confirmed his faith in her as an operative. All he and Gorsky had to do now was move their plan from March 2nd to March 11th. A delay of one week was nothing in the grand scheme of things. He was sure Gorsky would be pleased with the outcome.

As soon as Peter put the phone on the hook, he and Doug headed over to the secure room in the Comm Center. They initiated a conference call with Mr. X and Mr. Z. Peter relayed in detail the events of the day. They noted Mia's arrival time and told Peter they would let him know the details of the set-up to turn Mia. During the coming weekend, surveillance experts would visit his apartment and make the necessary arrangements to record all aspects of Mia's visit. Peter was uncomfortable being on camera at the discretion of the CIA, but he had no choice. His greater concern was getting ready for his next performance; it was going to be the role of a lifetime, with no room for error.

Chapter 45

Norfolk, Virginia
March 4th, 1973

Mia and Peter were full of anticipation, but for very different reasons. For Mia, espionage and the business of turning Peter were off the table for a whole week. They had been apart for a month and she missed the feel of his firm, strong body against hers and longed to feel his hands caressing her again. She packed an assortment of naughty French lingerie and a variety of sex toys with which she planned to keep Peter aroused for the entire visit.

Peter, though, had never had an assignment this difficult and with so much riding on the outcome. This new role was totally out of character for him. He was a good-natured man who had never experienced conflict with friends or lovers and had rarely told even little white lies. The very idea of turning Mia into a double agent made his head spin. He had rehearsed his approach over and over. The spooks gave him a certain amount of leeway but the bottom line was clear–turn Mia and do it now. The CIA wanted to get her fully indoctrinated into the dos and don'ts of working for "the Company," without wasting any time. The one positive in the process was that, as a trained operative, she already possessed the basic elements of successful spycraft.

Peter's overall responsibility was straightforward: confront her with being a Soviet spy, and then turn her into a double agent. But Peter had no idea how much resistance Mia would offer. Then there was the issue of their romantic involvement.

As it stood now, he realized that the line between love and hate was blurred given that Mia had not hesitated to entrap him. He couldn't ignore his strong attraction to her, but had to keep everything in the proper perspective. Being a realist, Peter was only too aware of the challenge that lay ahead. Approaching the Norfolk airport, his mind was working overtime; *I hope to hell I can pull this off. I'm going to need all the luck I can get.*

He saw her before she saw him—she was hard to miss: long winter coat casually left open, scoop-neck top, miniskirt, boots. A casual observer could mistake her for a fashion model. She had her carry-on trailing behind her; no checked luggage meant they could get going immediately. She threw her arms around Peter and slid her tongue between his parted lips. Her body pressed against his, Peter was immediately aroused.

Mia pulled away, gazing at him with what could be easily mistaken for love if only he didn't know she was a spy. "My darling," she cooed, "you have no idea how much I've missed you. I can't wait to make you feel good all over."

Careful, Peter thought. His response to her was so immediate, so instinctual—he had to keep his wits about him. "Mia, I thought about you every day," he said. She kissed him again, but Peter broke away. "If this keeps up, we might end up having sex right here on the sidewalk. Let's hop in the car and head to my apartment."

Off they went, the roar of the 'Vette's engine covering Peter's involuntary groans as Mia's clever hand explored his lap. As soon as they were inside his apartment, Peter helped Mia off with her coat and was teased by the scent of Rive Gauche, his favorite perfume. He flipped on the tape player to serenade her with his homemade mix of '70s hits. Then he went to the 'fridge to retrieve some expensive French champagne, courtesy of The Company. Two glasses stood beside an assortment of crackers and European cheeses. Next to the champagne was a can of whipped cream—this was new territory for him, but maybe tonight was the right time for a sexual dessert.

Seeing the champagne, Mia said, "Sit on the couch and relax. I'll pour." Within seconds, the bottle was open and she was bending over the coffee table, pouring champagne, and giving Peter an unobstructed view of her pink silk bra, trimmed with black lace. She settled down next to him and they drank a toast to their time together.

"What do you have planned for my visit—besides the obvious?" she asked with a wicked smile.

"Maximum flexibility—we can go to the local O Clubs for dinner and dancing, take a ride to Yorktown or Williamsburg, go for a walk along the oceanfront in Virginia Beach, and maybe catch a pop concert at the Scope on Tuesday or Wednesday night. The weather is supposed to be reasonable, but a little windy."

Mia put her arm around him, kissed the nape of his neck, nibbled on his earlobe and whispered, "Whatever you decide will be just perfect."

They kissed, drank and nibbled. With the bottle empty, both were feeling warm and uninhibited. Mia's top was off and Peter alternated between kissing her breasts and her lips. Under her miniskirt he saw that she had on silk panties that matched her elegant bra. Still fully clothed, Peter found himself flat on his back on the couch, with Mia grinding against his full erection. His plan had been to make the pitch to turn her once they were in bed, but now he was having second thoughts. *Maybe I can wait until tomorrow*, he thought. Everything felt so good; he hated to spoil the moment. Maybe some more champagne would help him follow through with the plan.

"Mia, let me get another bottle of champagne—I was keeping some for tomorrow night, but I made a point of stocking up!"

Peter disentangled himself and retrieved the second bottle. When he returned, Mia was sprawled on the couch wearing only pink silk and black lace. Peter filled their glasses. More kissing and drinking, and in the blink of an eye half the bottle was gone. *Hey, buddy – get your shit together*, he thought. *If you don't get this over with pretty soon, the CIA will probably break the door down.*

As if on cue, Mia jumped up and went to her carry-on and pulled out a zipper bag. "Look at all the goodies I've bought for you, darling! " Peter gazed inside and saw an assortment of feathers, clips, vibrators, handcuffs—even a short-handled riding crop. "Let's get over to the bed, and give a few of these a test drive," said Mia.

Peter had little experience with using the accoutrements in the bag—in fact, his last date with Mia had been his first venture into the world of sex toys. However, the sight of the riding crop gave him an idea.

"Great," he said and led her into the bedroom, where she undressed him. They lay on the bed and Peter quickly pulled off the pink silk and black lace. Both fully naked, Peter was clearly fully aroused. "Get on your hands and knees," he said sternly, retrieving the riding crop. Mia did as she was told and Peter started giving her little taps with the crop on her firm, white bottom. Mia whimpered softly and suddenly a switch flipped in Peter's head—he started to release his pent up anger. His strokes got harder, and small red welts appeared on Mia's creamy skin. She let out little screams with each stroke but didn't try to stop him. His level of excitement and arousal was beyond anything he had ever experienced. Finally, he put down the riding crop and entered her from behind. Mia started bucking like a wild animal; just as Peter was about to climax he withdrew and roughly pushed her on her back. She threw her legs around his waist, pulling him into her; her arms locked around his neck, and drawing him down. They moved in rhythm, each pushing the other toward orgasm. Then it came in crashing waves of pleasure for both of them, seemingly endless, surge after thrilling surge.

Peter was still inside her when he grabbed her head in both hands, forcing her to look straight into his eyes. "Why the fuck are you spying for the Russians?" he hurled at her.

Chapter 46

Norfolk, Virginia
March 4th, 1973

I n an instant, Mia's expression changed from ecstasy to utter confusion. This was the last thing she expected. Obviously, she and the Russians thought Peter was entirely clueless. Mia had to craft a response; however, she needed to buy time. Not knowing if Peter was serious, she feigned ignorance.

"I have no idea what you are asking; why would I do something like that? I love you."

Peter did not move a muscle. He held her face, staring into her eyes. "I guess that's the real question," he said. "If you do love me, why would you do such a terrible thing?"

After a long silence, Mia tried again. "This must be some kind of a joke—where did you ever get such an idea? I hate the Russians and what they did to my family after the war. Working for them now makes absolutely no sense. Either you're crazy, or you've received very bad information."

Peter considered his next move. He had to tread lightly since he personally had no direct evidence against her. Keeping it general was his best option, "I'm not crazy—you're the crazy one. If you hate the Russians, why would you help them and ruin my naval career …why would you do that? Tell me why, Mia."

It was the moment of truth for Mia. Her love for her father, and willingness to protect him at all costs, were at the core of her conflict. However, if Peter's feelings for her were as real as she thought, she could use them to craft a believable reply.

Her mind racing, she constructed a story with some elements of truth, some of fiction. If Peter accepted and supported her offering, it might just keep her out of an American jail.

"Please let me up, and I'll tell you the whole story." A tear trickled from her corner of her eye. "I need something to drink," she said.

Peter retrieved their glasses and the half-full bottle of champagne. She took a deep swallow and started right in.

"I'll try to be brief; please ask questions along the way. The story about my family going to the UK was fabricated by the Russians after my recruitment. They gave me a false identity and an assumed residence that supported a deep cover story. It was far easier to be hired by Pan Am as a Brit than as an East German. I attended Humboldt University, and it's true I studied mechanical engineering. My academic records from Manchester were fabricated and never comprehensively checked. Since I had an excellent education and demonstrated competence, there was no reason to look further.

"It all started when the Russians threw my father in prison and used that as leverage to recruit me as a spy. In return, they gave him a certain degree of freedom in East Berlin and allowed him to continue to teach at Humboldt. Initially my duties were as a courier; however, at times I did information-gathering from targeted individuals. As far as you and I were concerned, I took the opportunity to steal documents the first night we were together. The Russians got very excited because of their interest in the US submarine program and accordingly developed a plan to recruit you to spy for them. Along the way, I really did fall in love with you. Trying to solve all the problems at once, I put together a proposal that would free me and my father, while at the same time allow you and me to share a life together."

Peter had no idea where truth stopped and manipulation

started. "I'm amazed the Russians would cut any kind of deal—from what you've told me, they hold all the cards. What did you propose?"

Mia met Peter's eyes. "I sensed they were desperate for submarine information—so I proposed a limited number of missions to get them the information they needed and open the door to other avenues to obtain additional intelligence. I proposed six defined missions where you would gather targeted information requested by the Russians. At the conclusion of the missions, my father would be free to travel outside of East Germany, I would no longer have to spy, and your involvement would be at an end. If you refused my overture, they would then use all the information they had fabricated to make it look as though you had been spying for them all along. They would ruin your life and your career in the Navy if you refused to cooperate. If you agreed to cooperate, they were willing to discuss substantial compensation."

"How and when was this all supposed to happen?" Peter remained skeptical that the Soviets would agree to such a deal once they had him on the hook—unless they were so desperate for sensitive information that a limited scope of involvement with significant potential had a high degree of appeal.

Mia said, "It was all planned for our long weekend in New York. Your schedule change put them in a tailspin—that's why I had to negotiate so hard to ensure you would come to New York. Please understand I really do love you. The described plan was the only way I could see our relationship surviving. Since you found out the truth before I had a chance to tell you, it's probably hard for you to believe me. I wouldn't blame you if you hate me. It all started when I photographed the documents I found the first time we were together. The wheels were put in motion, and I couldn't stop them."

At that moment, Peter did hate her. He wanted to believe her feelings for him were real, but spies lied all the time, and the whole story might just be a creative effort to salvage the Russians' operation. It was also possible that self-preservation dictated she turn him when he visited New York next weekend. He didn't know what was true. It would be interesting to see what the spooks thought—but in a way, it didn't matter. Their plan to turn Mia was not affected by the story she just told him. The bottom line remained—the Soviets were desperate for any intelligence related to the US submarine program.

It was Peter's turn to play his hand. "Mia, I see a way out for you, but it's not what you and the Soviets envisioned. We are going to present you with some options, and if you accept, there will be risk involved. But we know you can handle risk—after all, you agreed to spy for the Russians in the first place. You are one smart lady; by now you have probably figured out what's coming next. The only way you can survive your betrayal is to become a double agent and work for the United States."

Mia was well trained and not stupid, and so far, Peter had not tipped his hand or shown her conclusive proof the Americans had a strong case against her. She was not going to go along so easily. "How do I know your government has proof of what it is alleging? What happens if I simply walk out of here, move from New York, and stop working for Pan Am? Why should I put myself in more danger than I'm in at present, by working as a double agent?"

Peter was one step ahead of her. "Apparently, everything is driven by your father's situation. If you walk out of here, you will have no value to the Soviets. Why would they offer any consideration to your father? If you leave Pan Am, he'll be back in prison the next day. However, if you agree to work for us, the CIA is pretty creative. No promises, but I'm certain there are ways to deal with your father's situation, especially since he's not in prison."

Mia immediately saw the logic of Peter's argument. "I'm not saying yes, but I must understand how this will work. Me as a double agent may not be the great benefit you imagine. I don't have access to information; up until I met you, I acted mostly as a courier, and didn't even know what I was carrying."

"You are going to have to trust me." Peter put his arm around her and gave her a hug. "I don't know exactly what's in store for you; that will be revealed if you agree to work for us. I can tell you this much: what we expect isn't substantially different from what you're currently doing. Going forward, this will involve us going to New York and ultimately convincing the Soviets you have successfully turned me. For you to function effectively as a double agent, I will have to appear to be working for the Russians. Unfortunately, we need your answer tonight. You cannot discuss this turn of events with anyone but me and the agents running this operation. You can ask questions, but I can't guarantee answers. What are your initial thoughts?"

Chapter 47

Norfolk, Virginia
March 4th, 1973

S till rattled, Mia tried to calm down and regain whatever composure she could muster. With precious little time to weigh the pros and cons of such a momentous decision, she looked questioningly at Peter.

"But what will become of us?"

Peter had not expected this: either he could use their ongoing relationship as leverage or he could put things on a strictly professional basis. Perhaps, though, he could engineer a way to have it both ways.

"Mia, I was really falling in love with you. But when the truth came out my feelings for you changed radically. Then the spooks figured out how to flip the situation around and save my career. So, as you can see, either you agree to cooperate or our relationship will be completely over and the consequences hard to predict.

"If you do agree to work for us, I would like to think that time will heal the hurt you've caused me. Be that as it may, if we do go forward we must absolutely convince the Russians that our love is real. This means living and acting as lovers, regardless of how I feel about you now or in the future."

Mia suddenly realized they were still completely naked, not an ideal situation for such a serious conversation. "I'm feeling a little strange," she said. "Let's get under the covers and talk." Peter nodded and they slid under the sheets. Mia continued, "What else do I need to know?"

Peter knew that what came next was probably pretty obvious. "If you agree to cooperate, you will be subjected to a complete debriefing by our intelligence services. Most importantly, they will need to know everything about your network of flight attendant spies. You cannot lie to them. For us to trust you, you must be completely honest…about everything."

Mia had expected this. Double agents had two primary functions: telling everything they already knew, and acting to the detriment of their former handlers. This 180-degree turn would allow the United States to gain the upper hand in this particular intelligence-gathering game. It would be vital to make their former handlers think that nothing had changed. That was the beauty of a double agent—the bad guys were continually being blindsided.

"OK, Peter, I really have no option, do I?" With those few words Mia crossed a line that would undoubtedly put her in considerable danger. "What about my father? Will they try to help?"

"Let's hold off your father's situation for a moment. There are a number of things I have to review with you before turning you over to the spooks tomorrow. First, do you understand that there will be no turning back now that you have agreed to work with us?"

"Yes, I do. But you must understand, too, that I shall now be in considerable danger if the Russians even suspect they're being duped. Tell me, who or what are the spooks?"

Peter laughed. "That's what we Navy guys generally call the guys in the intelligence services. You'll meet an assortment of them; which agencies they work for is not important.

"Mia, the US is trying to stay one step ahead of the Soviets. We'll feed them what we want them to have, not what they really want. Tomorrow you will receive a very thorough debriefing.

Try to answer every question in as much detail as possible. Ask questions, especially how you need to handle yourself in specific circumstances. For now, though, I need some vital information. Please summarize exactly what was supposed to happen in New York next Sunday."

With a little smile, Mia asked, "May I have some more champagne? This is going to be a bit difficult." Peter obliged, and Mia started her story. "Things would start off as normal when we met in our usual hotel room. At some point, with them listening, I was to tell you that the Russians have hard evidence implicating you as a spy. If you didn't agree to work for them, they would leak the false evidence to elements of the left-wing press. Since the information would clearly imply you were spying for them, your naval career and entire life would be completely ruined. In reality, the only real evidence is a copy of the documents I photographed that first night."

Mia bolstered her courage with another sip of champagne. "I was to tell you there are a bunch of doctored tapes and photographic evidence that would be used to support their case. My soft sell would mean your commitment to complete six missions. Once completed, you and I would be released to have a life together, and my father would be free to move outside East Germany. If you refused my overture, then my handlers would come into the room and present the hard sell. And then the entire matter would be taken out of my hands."

"If I did agree to your proposal, how was the whole thing supposed to work?"

"It was to be very straightforward. You would provide the Russians a list of scheduled inspections, and they would provide the intelligence they wanted gathered on each trip. You would be given a mini camera, and I would train you in its use. They would make provisions for you to dead drop, or hand off the film after each inspection. It was to be a pretty simple operation—only you and I would be involved, no need for an additional handler. If you refused the soft sell, I'm not sure what would come next."

Peter clasped his hands behind his head and leaned against the headboard. "What you just told me is pretty much how we thought the Soviets wanted it to work. In their view, as long as our relationship continued, it would be an easy operation to manage—no new players—you and I would run the entire operation. The simplicity works in our favor as well; it makes it comparatively easy for us to deceive the Russians.

"Step one—your soft sell will be seen to have been successful. It won't be necessary for us to follow a script or rehearse. You will present the proposal as you intended, and I will have a normal, very angry response—bordering on the violent. Eventually, I will reluctantly agree because of the limited nature of the assignment and the possibility that we might remain together.

"Step two—the operation will be tailored to suit the needs of the spooks. Here's what I think—as soon as the Russians send you the information they want for a given operation, you will photograph it before passing it on to me. The information will be passed to the spooks even before I officially get the list from you—time is of the essence. In the future, you will be told how to manage the transfer of the pre-inspection information to the spooks."

Mia snuggled her naked body up to Peter. "This is beautiful in its simplicity. If everyone does their job properly, the risk should be minimal. However, you haven't talked about the situation with my father."

Mia felt good against his body, and Peter did not push her away. "I'm not in a position to make any guarantees about your father; however, that's the area where the spooks really excel.

Tomorrow, tell them everything about your father's circumstances—no matter how insignificant. They will do everything
they can to resolve the situation. Those guys are really creative;
however, these things do take time and you'll have to be patient."

"I know you'll do everything you can to help, despite my
bad behavior. I really do love you," Mia purred, her hand taking
charge of Peter's increasing interest. Although he was angry, he
couldn't resist her. Before he knew it, her head was resting in
his lap, her soft lips caressing him. Peter could not believe her
expertise in giving pleasure as his hips undulated in climax, rewarding her efforts.

Peter thought, *This is going to be one hell of a ride. I have no idea
how it will end — I hope it will be all right, but for now, all I can do is
just hang on tight.*

The spooks listened to everything and were pleased with
Peter's performance. They still didn't fully trust Mia, but things
were off to a good start. Once Z heard Mia give her commitment to cooperate, Max got a call to get in touch with Natalie. He
needed to find out whether she had spoken to her father about
the operation. When he called the apartment, he was pleased to
find Natalie at home.

"Hi, Natalie," said Max. "How is engaged life treating you?"

Natalie was expecting his call, and was right on top of things
as usual. She had visited her father over the weekend and presented Max's request for assistance with the use of his office.

"So far, so good. We're pretty sure the wedding will take
place in early May. But I know that's not why you called. I did
talk to Daddy, and he would be happy to meet with you to
discuss what you need. Any day next week will work, and he
said the best time to visit would be for a late lunch. I may be a
little hard to reach so feel free to call him directly to set up the
meeting. If I need to be there for the lunch, Monday through

Wednesday will work. If you make arrangements with Daddy, just let him know if I need to be there."

"Great job of seeing to everything—it reminds me why I like you so much." Max couldn't resist a tiny flirt. "I'm pretty sure we can get up there one of the days you are available. I have to clear the actual day with the others involved. I really appreciate your efforts."

"You're welcome. I don't mean to rush off but, as you can imagine, I'm somewhat overwhelmed at the moment. Maybe I'll see you in a few days. *Bonne nuit*, Max."

"*Dors bien*," he replied, and Natalie hung up the phone. It was good to hear his voice, and so sweet that he remembered their good night exchange from Paris.

Chapter 48

Norfolk—New York City
March 5th, 1973

The CIA suspected the KGB might track Mia to Norfolk. Therefore, it was essential that her movements be exactly as expected. Accordingly, Mia needed to spend substantial time at Peter's apartment and also enjoy normal social activities in the Tidewater area. An extended visit to a military complex was out of the question; it would raise numerous red flags for the KGB.

Staying one step ahead, the CIA took a short-term lease on a vacant unit in Peter's building. It was perfect for conducting electronic monitoring of Peter's apartment and would serve as a base of operations for Mia's debriefing. Mia and Peter spent Sunday night in his apartment as expected—nothing unusual about that. After breakfast, Peter delivered Mia to the spooks in the leased unit. Present for the debriefing were Mr. X and Mr. Z, as well as LCDR Y. Peter gave Mia a little hug after the introductions and offered one last bit of advice.

"Just remember all the things we discussed last night and everything will be fine. Provide as much detail as you can in all your answers."

Mr. Z put his hand on Peter's shoulder. "Peter, we'll give you a call when we're ready to break for the morning. Then you can take her out for a nice leisurely lunch." Peter nodded and left, closing the door quietly behind him.

Mr. Z opened the meeting. "I assume Peter explained exactly what is expected of you and how the operation will be run once the Russians believe he has been turned. Do you have any questions in this regard?"

Mia tried to get comfortable in her chair; it was going to be a long session. "Peter made everything quite clear. I understand that the logistics have yet to be finalized regarding delivery of the information from the Russians to you before I give it to Peter prior to each inspection. Regarding my father, I understand that in return for my cooperation, you will devise a plan to free him from his current situation. I realize this will take time and I must be patient. To help you in your planning, I will tell you everything I know about his employment and living arrangements. So, shall we get started?"

The spooks agreed the debriefing would consist of three parts: the CIA would first proceed to gather information about the KGB's worldwide operation using the flight attendant network; NIS and the Navy would explore the technical aspects of what the Russians wanted regarding nuclear submarine operations; and, finally, they would probe for information regarding Mia's father.

Mr. Z was very efficient and got most of his questions answered in the four hours before the lunch break. The tape would be analyzed by CIA headquarters at Langley and possible follow-up questions formulated for Tuesday's session. Z was able to learn dead-drop and meeting locations, methods of communication between handler and agent, types of operations conducted and the approximate extent of the network. It appeared there was virtually no contact between individual members of the network. With the exception of others Mia had met in the School for Scandal, she had no idea who or how many there were. Besides New York, the major Pan Am hubs were London, Frankfurt, Honolulu, Berlin, Los Angeles and San Francisco; Mia assumed the network included agents in those locations, with handlers posted at corresponding embassies or consulates. Mia identified Ivan and said he was posted at the Soviet UN mission. Mia described her meeting with Gorsky, but didn't know his real name and assumed he was based in Moscow. He appeared to be Ivan's superior. This confirmed what the CIA already knew, and they didn't need to probe further.

Peter picked up Mia and they headed to his favorite seafood restaurant in Virginia Beach. The highlight of the lunch was a dozen Chesapeake Bay oysters for each of them — a special treat that Mia had clearly earned. Their conversation was cordial; it was going to take some time before their relationship returned to normal.

Meanwhile, Max made contact with Nat at Pietro's. They hit it off immediately and their conversation soon took on the tenor of two old friends chatting on the phone. Max didn't know how much Natalie had told her father about him, but it must have been positive. Max asked if Wednesday would be a good day for the team's visit. Nat invited them for a late lunch, and said he would personally plan the menu; afterward, they could meet in Nat's office. Max thanked him profusely, and couldn't help but mention how wonderful Natalie was — of course, Nat agreed.

LCDR Y was well prepared for the afternoon session. Mia's engineering background made it easy for her to recall in detail the various categories of technical information the Russians sought. She reiterated that they had told her to approach Peter with leading questions in specific areas: engineering safeguards, radiation exposure, quieting efforts, and communication procedures. She was not to ask for specific values or parameters, but rather, through open-ended questions, attempt to have Peter inadvertently reveal sensitive or useful information. She was instructed to ensure Peter had plenty to drink to lower his inhibitions. Mia told X and Y that it was reasonable to assume that these same technical areas would be the focus of the Soviets' "wish list" of information for Peter to gather once he was turned. She described the contrived exchange of money and how she set it up to look like Peter was being paid off.

At this point, discussion turned to her father. Mia provided handwritten notes detailing his situation. The notes explained where he lived, where he worked, his daily routine and how his movements were monitored. Mia didn't think his private life was closely monitored, but since he did not have the proper identification, he was prevented from moving freely inside the DDR, or even outside East Berlin. If he violated the terms of his agreement with the Soviets, it would be back to prison for good. X, Y, and Z listened intently to Mia's story and clarified small details that would help the CIA in their planning efforts. Satisfied they had what was needed for the present, Mr. X concluded the debriefing for the day.

Peter picked up Mia, and the group told them to enjoy the remainder of the evening out on the town. Mr. X contacted Max and learned that the team was set up to meet at Pietro's for a 2:00 lunch on Wednesday. Mr. X told Max to meet him at the Comm Center at 1800 to discuss the Wednesday meeting.

Chapter 49

Max was ready with a fresh pot of coffee when X, Y and Z breezed into the secure room right on schedule. Max couldn't hide his enthusiasm.

"I had a great conversation with Nat, Natalie's father. We're going to start lunch at two and he has promised us a very special meal, so bring your appetites. I anticipate Natalie will join us for lunch and the meeting. Immediately after lunch, we'll adjourn to Nat's third-floor office. I didn't discuss any specifics but my sense is he will be a willing participant."

Mr. Z took charge. "Based on what Mia has told us, here's what I envision once the Russians believe Peter has been turned. Prior to each inspection, the Russians will give him a list of the information they want him to photograph. He would then return either the film or the camera itself. If we're going to provide the Russians with false information, they have to believe that what we're giving them is authentic. I have some ideas about how to do that but would like your input."

Max spoke up first. "We need to get a head start on the requested information before the actual inspection takes place. Between the time Mia gets the list and delivers it to Peter, we need our own copy so we can prepare the phony documents while Peter is in transit. Clearly, this is a challenge."

Mr. X leaned forward. "Why don't we just give Mia a Polaroid camera and, as soon as she gets the list from the Russians, she makes a copy and sends it directly to our team via voice or fac-simile over a secure line. If Nat agrees to let us install the secure line in his office we will be able to create the fake documents as soon as we receive the information from Mia.

LCDR Y weighed in. "Right—once we have the list in hand it will be essential to create the bogus documents immediately. We need a team in place to create the material in order to completely mislead the Russians. It must seem absolutely authentic."

Max was all over that one. "A team must be preassigned to Peter's inspections whose responsibility it is to create the false documents. One person should be positioned in advance at the sub's home base. Here stateside, the Navy and CIA can assist in putting together the phony responses to the Russians' wish list. On the last day of the exam, Peter will photograph all the prepared information. The advance man will keep the hard copy of the created documents and return them stateside to be archived."

Mr. Z said, "So far this is a good assessment—however, a few caveats. The information about this operation must be com-partmented. The sub under inspection is to be told nothing about what's going on. Our operation will be limited to the ra-dio shack; because of the inspection, the sub's officers will be too busy to bother asking questions. The stateside team will not be told why the documents are being created or where they will end up."

Z slowed his delivery for emphasis. "With the exception of a handful of very highly placed CIA and Navy officers, those who know every aspect of this operation will be limited to those of us at the table, and Doug. Others will know bits and pieces but not enough to put it all together. This is intentional and brings me to the issue of the advance man. This position is so sensitive that only Max, Doug, or Y can be used in that role."

Max chimed in, "Also, the advance man can participate in the on-board examination by performing any of the functions expected of a team member. Since Peter has two jobs to do while on board, the extra man can help pick up the slack for the exam. Obviously, Peter and the advance man will form a team to prepare the documents for photographing. Two heads are always better than one."

Mr. X pulled closer to the table. "I think we now have this figured out on the operational side. It will be up to me and Z to organize the background teams who can create the bogus data. Mia has already told us the general areas of the Russian's technical interest so we can anticipate the kind of information they want. Next, we need to plan for our meeting with Nat on Wednesday and more importantly create a procedure for getting the advance copy of the wish list to us in Norfolk.

"Once lunch at Nat's is over, we will propose placing a secure line in Nat's office. Since he already knows Max is in the Navy, it should be enough to tell him that we need a Midtown communication site to support an ongoing operation. If Natalie agrees to help, she will be the primary user of the site. We can have it operational before the end of next week."

Max said, "Getting the information from Mia to Nat's office for transmission remains a challenge. I have a tentative plan that depends on Natalie's willingness to help: if she agrees, then our biggest problem will be coordinating everyone's schedules."

Mr. Z looked concerned. "Max, what is your sense of how much she's willing to help? You're the only one who has communicated with her. I realize none of this would have come to light without her; however, there is no guarantee she'll stay involved."

Max answered, "In my subsequent meetings with her she clearly indicated a willingness to be further involved. She is aware of the need for secrecy and knows she cannot discuss this with anyone, even her fiancé. She will be in NYC on Wednesday and we can assume she will attend both the lunch and the meeting.

"All we need to do is coordinate Peter's European inspections with Natalie's flight schedule. Once we know Natalie's bid line for the month, we can put Peter on an inspection that will pass through the city while she's there. Natalie will be told in advance when Mia will drop the Russian wish list at their apartment. Information in hand, she will then make a routine visit to Pietro's and transmit the wish list over the secure line."

Mr. Z was ready to wrap up. "This has been a very productive meeting—we have a clear path forward and, once Natalie agrees to be involved, it's a plan that can be implemented quickly. It all depends on the Russians acting as predicted. If they think they have Peter turned on the 11th, then we will be ready to act immediately. I'll have Langley schedule our flights to NYC. Any questions?"

There being none, the meeting was adjourned.

Virginia Beach
March 6th, 1973

Peter delivered Mia to the briefing room right on schedule at 9:00 a.m. The evening before, they had dinner at the Officers' Club at NAS Oceana. As usual, Mia turned a lot of heads. Since it was a naval air station, Peter didn't meet anyone he knew—which was just fine with him.

Peter was a bit guarded in his affection toward Mia; the hurt would take a while to subside. For Mia, the continued boyfriend/girlfriend relationship was humming right along and she adjusted to the situation. Peter held back in bed but Mia did her best to please him and he didn't resist her advances. After all, they needed to put on a convincing show for the camera at the Penn Garden Hotel — and practice makes perfect.

As usual, Mr. Z began. "Mia, this will be a short session. Our follow-up questions center on the hotel room where you will meet Peter on Sunday, and the method of transmission of information from you to your handlers." Z flipped open his notebook. "Tell us everything you can about the hotel room and how the Soviets have it rigged for monitoring."

Mia gazed up at the ceiling, biting her lip in concentration. "I don't know much but I'll tell you all I can. We always used the same room. Since it's a Pan Am layover hotel, and I'm an employee, I'm shown a certain amount of deference. In addition, the Russians gave me some cash to tip the reservations people to ensure we always got the same room. I know there is both video and voice monitoring, but I don't know where the devices are located. For the next session, I'm sure there will be active voice monitoring. If I can't turn Peter, they will intervene with a heavy hand and take control."

Z handed her a sketch pad. "Please note the room number and sketch the interior. Indicate where all the furniture is placed and pay particular attention to lights and appliances close to electrical outlets. We'll double-check with Peter and, between the two of you, we'll have an accurate sketch."

Mr. X took the lead. "You told us that the primary means of transmitting information are dead drops, brush passes and identical exchanges. In Peter's case, which methods were used or will be used?"

Mia took a sip of water. "The first time, I made a dead drop of the film in John Jay Park at the location I described. There were no additional exchanges — I assume all the information gathered came from the video or audio tapes. They didn't tell me what methods they would use going forward if I'm successful in turning Peter."

Mr. Z wanted to know more about the Stork Club. "Can you give us the names of others whom you suspect, or know to be, members of the spy network managed by Ivan?"

"That's a tough one. At the School for Scandal, we all used code names. They separated those that were going to be part of the network and had special briefings for us; I never learned any real names. That was strictly forbidden, and there were serious consequences if we violated the rules. I have seen some of them here and there over the years; and to the best of my knowledge, none of them is based in New York. Considering the number trained, I would assume there's at least one at each of the Pan Am bases I mentioned yesterday."

Mr. Z had an idea. "We want you to keep your eyes open. Pan Am flight attendants wear name tags. If you see any of them again, discreetly note the name and pay attention to conversations to try to determine anything that could help identify them. Don't make a direct approach or draw attention to yourself. For now, just do the best you can to give us bits of information and we'll do the rest."

Mia was relieved that there was no additional active involvement on her part. "I understand and will certainly do my best."

Z looked around the room. "Any more questions? No? Mia, that's all for now. We're going to have Peter come and get you in a moment. We'll have him review the sketch of the room. He will check in with us every four hours while you are in the Norfolk area. You and he will remain together at all times and will act as if you are down here on vacation until your departure Thursday morning. Peter will take you to the airport and stay with you until you actually board the flight. Once back in New York, go about your normal routine until Peter arrives on Saturday. Peter will be your handler from here on out, and you will probably not see any of us again. All direction will come from him. If an emergency arises, Peter will provide a method to provide an alert. Any questions?"

Mia shifted in her chair. "None at the moment. If something comes up, I'll ask Peter."

Z concluded on a somber note. "Mia, by now you have figured out that this is a very sensitive operation, and we expect your total loyalty and cooperation. If you do otherwise, you will regret it and things will end very badly for you. In return, we will assess your father's situation. The path to freedom for you and your father lies with us, not the Soviets."

Mr. Z stood, extended his hand to Mia, and told Mr. X to summon Peter. The gravity of the situation was not lost on Mia. She stood, looked Mr. Z straight in the eye, and said, "I understand completely."

Chapter 50

Pietro's staff greeted the team from Norfolk like old family friends. A table for six had been set up in a quiet corner of the restaurant. Natalie arrived, glowing with enthusiasm and dressed in a black-and-white jacket with red trim and a flared white skirt—a wonderful combination of tailored and feminine. She was wearing the pin Max had given her those many months ago when they had lunched at Pietro's. When he saw it, his heart skipped a beat. She greeted Max with a hug and a brief peck on the cheek. He introduced her around the table and saw the approving smiles her presence elicited from the team. They clearly thought she was special, too.

"Daddy will join us for the main course. I helped him plan the menu and we included all Max's favorites, so—if you object to the choices, blame Max." Chuckles all round.

The lunch alone would have been worth the trip to New York. Pietro's famous chopped salad followed by cannelloni with a velvety chicken filling and covered with tomato-tinged béchamel. Next came scampi, followed by the main course of double prime New York strip steaks, creamed spinach and baked potatoes. For dessert there was a choice of rum cake or tortoni ice cream cup. The men agreed it was one of the best meals ever. Natalie blushed with the group's effusive praise; Nat acknowledged the compliments with a gracious smile.

Nat suggested a move to the third floor. His office was small, with no frills—just a large, scratched desk and chair and several filing cabinets. Typical of his Italian roots, Nat had four beefsteak tomatoes ripening on the windowsill. Cramped as expected, they managed to wedge in the five extra chairs.

Mr. Z took charge. "First of all, thank you both for agreeing to meet. There isn't much we can tell you about why we need your help but, simply put, we require a confidential means of communication between New York City and our base in Norfolk. If you allow us to install a secure communication system here in your office, it will contribute significantly to our operational effectiveness. Natalie is generally aware of the significance. She cannot share details, but can assure you that our need is of paramount importance."

Natalie spoke up. "Daddy, I've known Max for over six months now; I can assure you he is a trustworthy and reliable naval officer. In a way, I created this whole situation by bringing to his attention several strange things I noticed which had to do with Mia. He and the others determined that the information warranted immediate follow-up. I think we should help in any way we can."

Nat's body language was receptive, but he understandably had questions. "Exactly what is it that I will do? Will it interfere with my business?"

Mr. Z answered, "No interference at all—we will only use your office when you are here or the restaurant is open. Our requirements are simple. We install a secure communication line here in the office. Natalie or others on our team will use the line to communicate with Norfolk. We haven't briefed Natalie on her potential role as yet, but our impression is that she will be willing to help."

Nat got right to the point. "If I agree, what happens next? Will my family be in any danger?"

Mr. Z said, "No danger—the communication with Norfolk

is two steps removed from our operational activities. We call this compartmentation. The result is an isolated and safe environment for you at all times. With respect to our equipment needs, sometime before the end of next week, a communication team will visit. On the surface, they will look like regular Bell Telephone guys. Work done will be primarily in your office but they may need access to your telephone line, which I assume is in the basement. It will take half a day at most. If you agree, Max will contact you to provide the installation schedule."

"Based on my daughter's recommendation, I'm going to let you install your system and will wait for Max's call. I want to do whatever I can to help, especially if my daughter approves. Is there anything else?"

"No, that's about it. Your country thanks you," said Mr. Z with unusual warm sincerity. Nat smiled, obviously proud of his daughter's crucial involvement. Z went on, "Please feel free to get back to your dinner preparations. We have taken enough of your time; there are a few things we still need to cover with Natalie."

Nat shook hands with everyone and left. Max took the lead and approached Natalie.

"You have a general understanding of what's going on with Mia. We know she has compromised Peter, and there may be a situation where Peter will appear to be cooperating with the bad guys who will need to pass information through Mia. However, Mia has agreed to cooperate with us. We will need a copy of what the Russians give to Mia before she delivers it to Peter. That's where you come in. Mia will give a copy of the information to you at the apartment and you will then deliver it to us over the secure line here in the office."

Natalie gave a little frown. "But what if I'm not in New York when the information needs to be transferred?"

Max smiled. "We have that figured out. Once you get your

line for the month, we will coordinate Peter's inspections accordingly. You will always be here in New York when he is on his way to Europe through JFK. If there's any last-minute change to your schedule, we'll work with Mia to arrange the transfer. That will be our problem, not yours."

"How will I know when a transfer is set to happen?"

"Mia or I will contact you," said Max. "You'll have plenty of advance notice. You'll have to arrange your schedule to stop by the apartment, pick up the information, and then get to the restaurant. The whole process is very efficient. You know you can't share any of this with Scott. If that becomes a problem, we'll address the issue. It's essential to limit the number of people involved. We're using you for the transfer to avoid arousing suspicion. If Mia is being surveilled, a solo trip to Pietro's would look odd; but for you it would be perfectly normal."

Natalie put her hand on Max's forearm and smiled at Mr. Z. "In my earlier conversations with Max, I did agree to consider helping. Since Daddy is now on board, how can I do otherwise but hop on the bus? My involvement sounds low risk and straightforward. I'm in."

Mr. Z provided more details. "We are very grateful to you for bringing this to our attention. It is, as you will understand, impossible for us to lay all our cards on the table, but I know you have a pretty good grasp of what's going on here. You have our sincere thanks for your continued cooperation and willingness to be involved. All communication will go through Max by way of the secure line here in the office."

Mr. Z rose and offered his hand, indicating the meeting was over. All three shook Natalie's hand; Max got a hug and a parting kiss on the cheek. The touch of her kiss caused Max to reflect, *This will be interesting, to say the least. I just knew she would come through for us. I hope Scott understands how special she is.*

Chapter 51

Norfolk, Virginia
March 8th, 1973

Thursday dawned with a flurry of meetings to tie up loose ends. Mr. Z would meet in the secure room at 0800 with X and Y and designate the respective responsibilities of the CIA and Navy. Max and Doug were scheduled at 1000, and at 1200 Peter would join the group after seeing Mia off at the airport.

Promptly at 0800, Mr. Z kicked things off. "Today we're going to ensure we are all on the same page. First of all, let me briefly outline what the CIA is doing. I have instructed our NYC team to monitor the room that Peter and Mia will be using on Sunday. They will book one of the adjacent rooms and we'll have our equipment in place long before the Russians do their final preparations. The sketch provided by Mia and Peter will facilitate installation of our listening devices. Any questions?"

Mr. X weighed in. "Will the NIS be involved with the operation in New York?"

"This will be strictly CIA," Mr. Z said. "We're not giving Peter any details other than telling him we'll be close by if things begin to go south. Our agents at the hotel will be on the lookout to determine how the Russians intend to monitor the room 609 meeting. We won't interfere, of course, but seeing which Soviets are involved will give us insight into their New York operation. Our agents will be disguised as hotel staff."

If Mr. X was disappointed that NIS would not be involved, he didn't show it. "Looks like you have all the bases covered. We have trained resources available to assist if needed. However, I do understand the need to keep things inside the Company."

With a nod, Z continued. "Thanks for the offer, X. The second thing to organize is a technical team who will prepare bogus information in response to the Soviet requests. We will be in direct contact with Naval Reactors in Crystal City and Submarine Operations at the Pentagon. There's nothing we need in this regard from NIS. However, we may want a designated NIS resource at the advanced tender. Possible duties would involve help in preparing the false documents we will be giving to Peter. All they need to know is that LCDRs Millen, Pritchett, or Y may be in contact for assistance. That's about it until Max and Doug get here. Any other questions?"

X and Y shook their heads, and everyone adjourned to the coffee pot.

Peter loaded Mia and her luggage into the 'Vette, and they headed to the airport for her 10:00 a.m. departure. Although Peter wasn't flying himself, they were greeted warmly at the National lounge. The staff confirmed Mia's standby status and issued her boarding pass. The couple ordered a pair of Bloody Marys and nestled into a quiet corner of the lounge.

Mia took Peter's hand. "Darling, when you arrive on Sunday everything in the room will be just as it always is. You have to act completely normal, despite how you might be feeling about me. Fortunately or unfortunately, depending on your point of view, I am an experienced agent and have been in situations like this before. When I propose that you work for the Soviets, you must look completely dumbfounded. You know what we have to do and we don't want any of those other chaps coming into the room."

Peter looked into her eyes, which shone with tears. Whispering, he said, "I do know how important this is to both of us, regardless of our mutual feelings. We can't afford to screw this up: I'll follow your lead and behave in just the way they'll be expecting. Don't worry; I'm not going to let you down."

For the next thirty minutes, they sat holding hands. Hearing the call to board, they walked hand in hand to the gate. Hugging each other tightly, they kissed tenderly before pulling apart. Mia started down the jetway and then, turning back towards Peter, smiled and blew him a kiss.

Fortified with coffee, Z was ready to roll when Max and Doug arrived. "Doug, we need to bring you up to date. Natalie and her father have agreed to help us and if the Mia-Peter meeting goes as planned on Sunday, we'll install a secure system in Nat's office on Monday. If things proceed as expected, Natalie will act as the conduit to get the information from Mia to us via the secure communication system. This will in turn be sent along to Navy and CIA analysts to prepare the fake information. Once completed, it will be transmitted to you, Y, or Max at the inspection site. As previously discussed, one of the three of you will assist Peter in the preparation of the final documents and participate in the on-board inspection. Any questions?"

Doug asked, "How much will Peter and Mia be told?"

"Everybody involved with this operation will be told just what they need to know," said Z. "Only we at this table, and a few at the very highest levels of the CIA and Navy will have all the pieces of the puzzle. Peter will be told next to nothing; Mia will give him the Soviet ask, and when he arrives at the inspection site, one of the three of you will help him prepare the documents and photographs to be given to the Russians. This is for his own protection and the safety of the entire operation. As far as Mia is concerned, if the Op goes forward as anticipated, she will be told to copy the information the Soviets have requested and to leave the copy in her apartment. Neither of them will be told of Natalie or Nat's involvement. Everything has to be compartmented — knowledge of the individual pieces will be strictly on a need-to-know basis.

"One final thing," said Mr. Z, getting ready to close. "The three of you need to know about the drop in the apartment because you will be Natalie's emergency back-up to carry out the retrieval and transmission if she is unable to do so. We have taken steps to ensure that Natalie should always be available, but are prepared in case something unforeseen should arise to prevent her from making the transfer." Z looked around the room for questions. Since there was none, he said, "Let's take a break until Peter gets here."

Max and Doug decided it was too early for lunch, so they went to the compound gym for a game of squash. On their walk over, Doug asked Max, "How are you doing with Natalie's engagement and impending marriage?"

Max took a deep breath. "It's the best thing for everyone. Yesterday she was just as lovely as ever — I'm really going to miss her. Since I'll be a handler of sorts, we'll still be in contact for the foreseeable future. Kind of a consolation prize…she won't be totally out of my life until the current mess is cleaned up — certainly beyond her wedding day."

Doug put his arm around Max's shoulder. "You seem to be holding up pretty well; I think it's time for us to make a trip to the Little Creek sing-along, or the Body Exchange, and get you back into circulation."

"Not a bad idea, Doug, but Norfolk just ain't New York. Maybe I'll implement Plan B when we're back on the Big Apple social scene." Max knew it was a pipe dream as soon as he said it. New York just wouldn't be New York without Natalie.

It was a hard-fought match with Doug winning three games to two. They showered quickly, and just made it back to the room by noon. As they were arriving, Peter was right behind them, and X, Y, and Z were munching on the last bites of Chinese take-out. Doug decided to get things rolling as the others finished lunch.

"Peter, I assume all is well with Mia—was her flight on time?"

"Signed, sealed, and delivered to National Airlines and on her way. I expect we won't communicate much until Sunday when I land at JFK; no time for idle chatter. All that has to be said has been said."

Max, parched from squash, filled his water glass. "Peter, what's your sense of how things will go down on Sunday and Mia's mood in general?"

Peter considered the question. "Funny you should ask. During our time at the airport, she told me to just follow her lead—that she is an experienced operative and will ensure everything stays on track. All I have to do is act normally and when the offer comes, react appropriately. My sense is she certainly doesn't expect to be treated with kid gloves. She is one tough cookie. I've got a few days to figure out the appropriate response to an offer to betray my country."

Mr. Z jumped in. "Peter, she is well aware of the stakes involved. You have addressed one of my concerns up front—good to get that out of the way. Remember, she is a trained operative and if she holds up her end, the flip has a great chance of succeeding. Obviously her head is in the right place. Before your final brief, do you have anything else to add?"

Peter shook his head. "Nope, you guys have my take on the

situation with Mia. Let's get on with the final instructions. We leave for New London later today and I'm sure everyone has some final preps before we travel."

"Ok here it is, short and sweet." Z lowered his voice and spoke deliberately, "Peter, in no case go off script or try to be creative or overly cooperative. Remember, you are being dragged into this situation kicking and screaming. Mia knows exactly what she's doing, and once you are ostensibly turned, she will become your handler and will be running the Soviets' Op. Just follow her directions. Ask reasonable questions at the Sunday meeting, but don't be overly inquisitive about how their Op is going to work. If serious problems surface, we'll take immediate action for your safety. If for any reason we do have to get directly involved, we'll respond appropriately. What are your plans post-meeting?"

"I told Mia that I could spend a few days in New York. I'm scheduled out on a late flight Tuesday. Once I'm theoretically turned, I'm sure there will be an indoctrination period. After two days of that, I'll be ready to get the hell out of there."

"I can appreciate that," said Z, with obvious sincerity. "That's it for now. Good luck with your exam in New London, and the meeting with Mia on Sunday. You know what's expected, and so does Mia. Anything last minute, we'll contact you through Max or Doug. One last thing—if, when you get to the hotel room, something seems out of kilter or unsafe, just make some remark to Mia about cows on the farm in Wisconsin. If you use those three words in a sentence, we will be able to bail you out without exposing the Op. It should be just Mia in the room as usual—with no surprises. I don't want to overwork this; the simpler the better. I'm ready to send you into battle."

Hearing about the bail-out protocol was a little unsettling to Peter. "I will certainly remember the special phrase and will use it only if the situation warrants. I'm good to go if everyone else is. I am determined to make this thing work—it's too important to our national security.

Z stood up and offered his hand. "Again, good luck, Peter. We're banking on you to do your best." Peter shook hands with X, Y, and Z and everyone filed out of the room.

Max saw the apprehension on Peter's face and thought, *This could turn into a bunch of monkeys humping a football or one of the coolest fucking counterespionage operations ever*—only time will tell.

Chapter 52

Midtown—New York City
March 11th, 1973

"**H**ello darling," Mia purred, opening the door of Room 609. "Welcome back!"

Even with so much at stake, Peter was still excited at the sight of her—V-neck cashmere sweater, red miniskirt, black leather boots. She threw her arms around Peter and gave him one of her unforgettable kisses. "I've missed you, even though it's been only a few days." As Peter pressed against her and playfully slapped her tight little bottom, he realized she wasn't wearing any underwear. *Never a dull moment,* he thought with a grin.

Piper-Heidsieck brut was open and waiting in an ice bucket. Mia filled two glasses. "Here's to us, and to New York." They clinked, sipped and took their usual places on the loveseat. Both tried hard to act perfectly normal; Peter put one arm around Mia and his free hand down her sweater. He caressed her breasts and kissed her long and hard. Wasting no time, it was on to the bedroom for act two of their little drama.

Mia lay flat on her back and Peter hovered over her. "Let's get you out of these clothes, but leave the boots on. I noticed your little bag of tricks on the night stand. Let's see what's in there to get the party started." He pulled off her skirt and sweater—as he thought, she had nothing on underneath. He gave her a long, admiring look; he particularly liked that she was a natural blonde all over, and her soft look contrasted excitingly to her black leather boots. He found a velvet cat-o'-nine-tails and a giant feather in the bag. He chose the feather first. Like an artist with a soft brush, he worked the feather over the canvas of her entire body. Her nipples sprang to life and she moaned softly as Peter teased her with soft, slow strokes.

Quickly, Mia was ready. "Please, darling—no more. I want you inside me now."

Peter needed no further encouragement. He lifted her legs and placed her ankles on his shoulders. The leather felt strange and erotic against his face and shoulders as they moved in unison. With mutual concern about act three yet to come, it took longer than usual for them to finish. They both finally managed a mild orgasm, but the apprehension remained.

So far, so good, thought Peter. The ball is in her court, and I sure hope she doesn't string this thing out. He lay beside her, kissing her softly and caressing her breasts. He looked into her eyes as if to say, OK, baby—let's get this show on the road.

Mia got the message. "Peter, we have some very serious things to discuss. There's something I have to tell you."

Peter decided a short delay would be more realistic. "Hey, babe—I was just getting started. Can't it wait until we have another round? The cat is just yearning to be used on your delightful bottom."

"No, Peter, I'm sorry. We must have this discussion right now."

Peter picked up her vibe and went with it. "OK, fire away. You have my undivided attention."

Mia held his head and looked into his eyes. "I need your help. Several years ago, the Russians arrested my father for helping with the German unification effort. He was very harshly treated, and his health began to fail. They came to me with a proposition—if I would work for them, they would treat him better, release him from jail, and allow him to live under close surveillance. His work at University could continue. Reluctantly, I agreed."

Peter immediately interrupted. "Whoa — slow down! This is a lot to swallow. If what you say is true, we have to end our relationship immediately. You know about my career — I can't have a Soviet spy for a girlfriend. That just ain't going to happen."

"Actually, that's not all of it — you're already involved even though you don't realize it." Genuine tears formed in Mia's eyes. "They encouraged me to develop an intimate relationship with you after we met, precisely because of your career. I was so worried about my father; I went along with their demands."

Peter surged out of control. "What the hell are you talking about? I'm getting dressed and getting out of here. Do you really think I'm going to flush my entire naval career down the toilet just so I can have sex with you a couple times a month?" Peter was off the bed, pulling on his clothes.

Mia dragged him back to the bed and screamed at him, "It is far more complicated than that — the Russians have pictures, audio and video recordings, and certain documents that would completely compromise you — and they have ways of leaking that information. You and your career will be ruined whether or not to agree to cooperate."

Peter threw her violently on the bed and slapped her across the face. A small trickle of blood appeared at the corner of her mouth. "You silly bitch — what the hell were you thinking? Do you think I give a shit about you and your little problems? I'm going to take my chances that my government will protect me. I've done absolutely nothing wrong, except making the mistake of falling for you. And this is the thanks I get? You want to turn me into a Soviet spy, too? No thanks. Like I said, I'm out of here."

"Peter, you must hear me out." Mia's voice was quivering, pleading. "You have no idea what the Russians have in store for you. You can't just walk away from this, expecting your government to protect you. The Soviets have contacts in the opposition media all over the world, as well as here in the States. They will leak and publish pictures of you accepting money, transcripts of recorded conversations and excerpts of sensitive nuclear navy documents. They showed me copies of what they can use against you, just to prove that these things exist. You and your picture will be world news for weeks on end. A United States submarine officer spying for the Soviets will be very big news. No matter how hard you or your government try to turn things around, the lies are going to stick. Once the ball is rolling, there is nothing that will stop it until it gains enough momentum to destroy you and your career—completely, irreparably."

Mia's words had a calming but devastating effect on Peter. Slowly, the color drained from his face and beads of sweat appeared on his forehead and at the back of his neck. "If only a tiny bit of what you're telling me is true, my life could be ruined forever."

Mia looked at him sympathetically; tears streaming down her cheeks. "These are very, very bad people. If you don't listen to me, all three of us will lose. My father will be back in prison, heaven knows what will happen to me, and I guarantee your naval career will be over. I hate to tell you this, Peter, but the first night we were together, I copied the documents you were carrying and gave them to the Russians. I am truly sorry, but I didn't understand the implications at the time. If those documents are released to the public, absolutely nothing will save your career.

Peter started pacing the room. "I still can't believe you fucked me over like this. There must be a way out. I can't just betray my country and work for the Russians for the rest of my life. You got me into this—let's have some ideas as to how to get us out of it—or we're all screwed."

Mia wiped her cheeks, "It won't be for the rest of your life. Sit down and listen to what they propose. There is a beginning and an end…it won't be forever. In about a year, it can all be over. All you have to do is cooperate. At the end, you'll be on to your next duty and your career can go on. I'll be finished with the Russians and my father will be free to leave East Berlin. If you still want me when all of this is over, I'll be there for you. I know how it looks, but the real truth is that I do love you, deeply. It's a complicated situation, but at least there's a way out."

"Complicated? That's an understatement." Peter sneered. He shook his head and slumped back against the pillows. "Dear God, how did I ever get mixed up in this? OK, I'm listening."

Mia took Peter's hand. "First of all, you must understand that if I can't convince you to go along, the Russians will take matters into their own hands. They are listening to every word we say. If you refuse, I will have no choice but to leave the room and they will confront you directly. Things will get much harder and the deal won't be as good. They don't tell me everything, but the potential outcome could even be worse than we imagine."

Peter considered this. Would the CIA want to roll up the bad guys while they are in here trying to muscle me? Then he remembered Z's admonition to avoid any creativity and stay on script. He looked at Mia. "I understand. Keep going. Of course, I would rather negotiate with you, if I have to cut a deal."

"OK, here's their offer." Mia looked beseechingly at Peter. "They want you to do six missions that will coincide with six inspections as you pass through New York. They will give me a list of information they want you to get during each inspection. They may want documents copied—if so, I will provide you with a miniature camera. In other cases, they may just want questions answered, based on certain characteristics available from a particular submarine. At the conclusion of the inspection, you will pass back the information collected.

"It will be up to you and me to make our schedules as compatible as possible and get the six missions completed in a timely manner. When the missions are over, my life will return to normal—my father will be free to travel, and your involvement will be at an end. In addition, the Soviets have indicated they would consider making payments to you depending on the quality of the information. I know this is a lot to process. Do you have any questions?"

Peter scratched his head. "First of all, taking money would only complicate matters. I'd rather get this over with and keep it as simple as possible. What guarantee did they offer that six missions would be the extent of it?" Mia thought she was getting close to closing the deal, but the issue of the end game needed to be addressed. In the real world, somebody as intelligent as Peter would never accept an open-ended situation.

"They didn't offer an end game proposal; it could get very complicated. Do you have something to propose?"

"Based on the time I have left on the Board, it will be tough, but possible, to get six missions completed before I'm transferred. One thought does come to mind—following the sixth mission, there could be a mutual exchange of mission information in return for your father. It'd be tricky, but I can't think of anything else. Maybe the Russians can put something on the table. Once he's released, it seems their hold on you will be at an end. Maybe they could just release him in good faith after the fifth mission. They could still threaten to expose me if I didn't cooperate and perform mission six. At some point, they would have to operate in good faith; difficult for people whose stock and trade is lying."

"Peter, I must have your answer." Mia knew she had to press

for his decision. "As I told you, if I can't get you to cooperate, my instructions are to leave the room and you will then be totally at their mercy."

Peter thought, *Should I cave now? Have I resisted enough to be convincing?* It was a tough decision, so he decided to interject a little humor. "Suppose we have the sex I counted on an hour ago? If it's fantastic, we have a deal. If not, I'll decide whether to roll the dice with the bad guys."

Mia knew he wasn't serious and the bluff was for the benefit of the watching Soviets. Peter was toying with them by making them wait. She said, "In that case, it sounds like a done deal to me; our sex is always fantastic."

Peter's tone turned serious. "You know I hate all of this. I hate what you've done to me, and I'm disgusted at being co-erced like this. I am really sorry about the situation you and your father find yourselves in and I really don't like the Russians. However—as you said, I'm not stupid; the only logical choice is for me to cooperate. But I want to hear from the Soviets as far as the end game is concerned and their guarantee that I'd be out after six missions."

Peter thought, *That will give the Ruskies something to chew on. In the end, the joke will be on them. Long before the end of the sixth mission, the CIA will have Mia's father safely ensconced somewhere in the States. The Soviets probably won't even tell her that he's no longer in East Berlin, just so they can keep their hold over her. But we will all know the truth.*

Peter, partly dressed, looked over at the naked Mia, who was partway under the covers. With a smirk, he said, "OK, Ms. Soviet Spy—what's next?"

Chapter 53

Midtown—New York City
March 11th, 1973

The drama in 609 continued to unfold as Peter waited for Mia's answer. With Peter's counter- proposal coming out of the blue like that, she was uncertain how to respond. This was certainly not something the Soviets had anticipated.

"You ask what's next," she said. "First of all I'll let the Russians know you will accept their proposal, contingent on a defined end game. It'll be up to them to respond to your request. You may have to meet with them, or they might want me to deliver their reply. I will communicate with them tomorrow; after that we'll be told what comes next."

Mr. Z could not have been more pleased with Peter and Mia's performance. Their interplay and dialogue was close to perfection. Peter's counter-proposal should not raise any undue suspicion; on the contrary, it would confirm his intelligence and quick thinking. The Russians knew the navy nukes were a smart bunch of guys, so it made sense that Peter would not just roll over without some pushback. Since the Soviets had not planned for a counter proposal, Mia did the only logical thing she could — buy some time and tell Peter she'd let him know what the Russians thought of his proposal.

Peter remembered his proposal that sex should be a part of his decision but decided that, under the circumstances, it was more important to move on.

"I guess there isn't much more to discuss, for the present.

Let's go out and have a nice dinner and put this behind us for now. Tomorrow is another day."

Mia picked up his vibe. "You're right, darling—I think that's best. You've had a lot to absorb in a very short time and you need time to process it all." She kissed him on the cheek and they got out of bed and started to get dressed.

Peter suggested, "How about a trip down to Mott Street? Let's wander around Chinatown and see what appeals. It might be fun to eat Chinese food, for a change."

Somewhat surprised, Mia said, "What a wonderful idea—I love Oriental food. I know a couple of places I think you'd enjoy. Most are BYOB so let's take a bottle or two of white with us."

They were soon out the door, leaving the CIA and KGB with their respective postmortems. To his credit, Peter had thrown a slow curve ball to the Russians. There was no point in prolonging the discussion with Mia; the ball was now in KGB's court and besides, he was very hungry and more than ready for dinner.

Mr. Z was in complete agreement with Peter's decision. He shared his thoughts with the other two operatives. "Well, I suppose there won't be anything worth recording. Let's ease off until tomorrow but keep the listening devices running. We don't want the Russians to pull a fast one on us."

The CIA determined that the Russians' method of eavesdropping was through a relay man posing as a mechanical maintenance contractor. The walkie-talkie he was using was actually monitoring the hotel room and relaying the real-time situation to KGB operatives in a nearby room. CIA agents posing as hotel housekeeping staff photographed the phony maintenance man and then tailed him to a Midtown apartment which was clearly serving as some kind of KGB operational base. The unintended consequences of the operation had yielded some very useful information.

With the couple on their way, Ivan left the KGB monitoring room and directed an operative to remain behind and tidy up loose ends. He had promised to call Gorsky as soon as there was news, no matter the time. In less than thirty minutes, he was in the Soviet UN Mission and on a secure line to Moscow.

Gorsky answered on the third ring. "Well, Comrade—how did it go? I hope you have good news; you know that this is of paramount importance."

Ivan said, "From outward appearances, things went as we had hoped. Neutron agreed to our proposal of six missions but requested a defined exit strategy. I'll get to that in a minute. At first everything appeared completely normal until Songbird put our proposal on the table. He got furious and hit her at least once. I have not yet analyzed the video to confirm the violence. He objected vigorously, and Songbird had to push hard to get him to agree. He finally did come around, but I think their romantic relationship could be damaged. A certain degree of sympathy for her father's situation certainly helped the outcome."

Gorsky pushed back, "Do you have any concerns? What is this about an exit strategy?"

"No concerns, I think we have Neutron right where we want him. But, as we suspected, he's not stupid. He wants assurances that right before or after the sixth mission the father will be released. He dangled two proposals—either a good-faith turnover of the father at the end of the fifth mission, with the promise that Neutron will deliver on the sixth, or a much more complicated swap of information for the father after the sixth mission, with the method to be determined."

Arrogant as ever, Gorsky said, "That is not going to happen. There's no such thing as good faith in the world of espionage. But let's humor him. Have Songbird propose an exchange here in New York at the conclusion of the sixth mission—then, at the last minute, we'll tell him something came up and things will be delayed. One way or another, we'll get the information and still have him on the hook."

"If I read you correctly," said Ivan, "I am to deliver that message to Songbird to pass on to him, and convince her we are sincere. Next, she needs to get his exam schedule for the coming months so our technical team can prepare the list of information we hope to obtain from his first mission. Getting the list to him through Songbird won't be a problem, but getting the response back must be worked out on a case-by-case basis. I'll meet with her tomorrow—she knows to call early in the day. Anything else?"

"Be on the lookout for anything suspicious. Things are going as predicted except for this counter proposal. It's up to you to put her under surveillance if needed or if you detect out-of-the-ordinary behavior. This operation must succeed."

The line went dead.

On the American side, Mr. Z made his own set of calls. From a Midtown apartment set up as a CIA operational base, he called Langley and directed a technology team to visit Pietro's as soon as possible to install the secure communications system. He instructed Langley to schedule Doug, Max, X, and Y for a briefing at 1000 the next morning in Norfolk, and to confirm with the technical team at Naval Reactors (NR) that the mission was a go—and that they should be prepared to quickly analyze the Soviet ask and create plausible but erroneous information on a 24-hour turnaround.

Mia and Peter found themselves at Hop Kee on Mott Street, two bottles of white wine in tow, packed in a plastic laundry bag with hotel ice from the dispenser on the sixth floor. Peter's imagination never failed him when it came to making sure some form of alcohol was readily at hand. They navigated the steep steps of the below-ground restaurant. When seated, another diner entered and sat alone at a nearby table. He appeared very interested in what was happening in their booth.

Show time, Mia thought. *Let's give that obvious idiot something to think about.* She needed Peter to avoid any discussion related to their espionage activities. A distraction was in order. She discreetly unzipped and removed the boot from her right foot, reached her long leg under the table and massaged Peter where it counted most.

Peter took a moment to process what was going on. "Are you trying to tell me something? I promised to have sex with you before giving you my answer on your business proposal but I guess I forgot all about it."

"You figure it out," said Mia with a devilish smile. "I'm not going to stop until something happens or you agree to hold up your end of the bargain in a manly and proper manner."

Peter unzipped his fly. "I'll give you about fifteen minutes to stop that—or until I tell you it's time to leave and go back to the hotel room." He thought, *It's difficult to stay angry with Mia with all her sexual creativity. I guess espionage does have a wide variety of unexpected fringe benefits.*

Chapter 54

Norfolk—New York City
March 12th, 1973

As a result of the drama in Room 609 the day before, all the performers would have a very busy Monday. Mr. Z was up early as usual and hit the ground running. He had talked to Langley from his CIA-arranged apartment, his first call ensuring the technology team was on its way to New York to install the secure line at Pietro's. The plan was to meet for a noon briefing at the apartment and to arrive at Pietro's no later than 1400. Mr. Z decided to stay in New York to introduce the team to Nat and oversee the installation process.

Promptly at 1000, he called the secure room at the Comm Center, where the team was assembled. "First off, I want everyone to know that Peter and Mia performed to perfection. As far as I can determine, nothing was said or done that would raise any suspicion on the part of the Russians. This operation is a total go; I want to make some preliminary assignments and provide an update. Regarding the installation at Pietro's—I will take the team over to meet Nat at 1400 today. Max, give him a call at the restaurant and tell him I'll be bringing some friends for a late lunch.

"My intention is to get this whole thing up and running as soon as possible—I'm sure the Russians will be pressuring Peter to make a European inspection. Max, call Natalie and get her line for the remainder of the month so we'll know the dates she's available to participate. No need to make a secure call; just keep it light and social. She'll understand the reason for the call. Once you have the information, pass it to Doug so he can schedule Peter to Scotland or Spain with a start date corresponding to Natalie's being in New York. When Peter returns to New York, give him the inspection schedule for the remainder of March, so he can pass it to Mia. Any questions?"

Max said, "No — this is pretty straightforward. It's great to know that Peter and Mia performed so well. I think we all knew that their verbal interaction was a potential minefield. One wrong step, and we'd be sunk."

Mr. Z continued, addressing X and Y. "I've contacted NR and confirmed the Op is a go. I need you to travel to Crystal City, if necessary, to ensure they have their elite team in place to do a 24-hour turnaround on the fake information. X, you need to alert your NIS contacts in Rota and Holy Loch that we may need their help before the end of the month. Tell them only as much as they need to know, but ensure we get their complete cooperation. Y, you need to clear your schedule for the remainder of March. You will probably be the advance man for the first mission. Any questions?"

Norfolk confirmed that everything was a go. Mr. Z said, "If anything comes up, X knows how to reach me. Well done, all. The Op is off to a great start."

Peter and Mia afforded themselves the luxury of room service for breakfast, to reward each other for a job well done. Their conversation was banal, and they intentionally avoided any kind of intimate exchange. To keep everyone guessing, the night before their lovemaking had happened in silence, except for an occasional erotic utterance. Around the same time that Mr. Z was talking to the guys in Norfolk, Mia excused herself, telling Peter she had to make a call. She dressed quickly and went down to the lobby.

Ivan was waiting for her call and answered right away. "We are all pleased with the job you did yesterday. We understand about the end-game proposal and are considering the options presented. We can meet at some future time to confirm the preferred option, but for now, we want to put your friend to work as soon as possible. Our preference is that something happen before the end of the month—please encourage him to make the necessary arrangements as soon as possible. When you have confirmation of the date, let us know when your friend will be visiting. As our way of thanking you, we have arranged a special gift for you at Bloomingdale's—please accept it with our sincere thanks. Do you have any questions, or do you think there is a need for us to meet?"

"No questions, and I don't see a reason to meet," said Mia. "Thank you for your thoughtfulness. As soon as I know when my friend will be visiting, I'll be in touch."

"Very well. I look forward to hearing from you soon. Goodbye."

The line went dead, and although the conversation had gone well, something was nagging at Ivan, though he couldn't put his finger on it. Mia had done exactly as they asked, and it had not been easy to turn Neutron. He had responded with end-game conditions, which was to be expected. He smiled to himself at the cleverness of the Bloomingdale's code—for a fashionable young woman like Mia, talk of Bloomie's was the perfect red herring. Telling her that a special gift awaited her was her cue that the information for her to give to Peter would be provided during an identical exchange of Bloomingdale's bags.

When Mia returned to the room, she found Peter lying naked on the bed. He motioned for her to join him. "How did your call go? Any problems?"

"No. My friends would like you to visit again as soon as you can. Do you think you can arrange that?"

"Yes, but you'll have to wait until I get back to Norfolk. The change in my inspection schedule early in the month created a need to revise everything. However, I do have a problem that requires immediate resolution." Peter's intentions were obvious, as he showed her that he was fully erect. *Let's keep the audience guessing*, he thought.

Mia needed no further encouragement; with the lights out, all the surveillance teams heard was the removal of Mia's clothing, the rustle of the bed covers, and squeaks from the bed springs.

As soon as Max was off the phone with Mr. Z, he called Natalie at 8L from one of the secure lines in the Comm Center. Based on their conversation at Pietro's the week prior, Natalie expected Max's call sometime during the day on Monday. Since she had essentially moved in with Scott, most of her time was spent at his apartment. However, she had decided to retain her share of 8L, at least until she was officially married. Caroline quipped that Natalie was paying rent for closet space. This arrangement conveniently coincided with the needs of the CIA operation.

"Hi, Natalie. It's Max. Everything went as expected yesterday, and things are moving forward. Mr. Z and some of his friends will be having lunch at Pietro's today, as we anticipated. How is everything with you?"

"As you can imagine, I'm in a bit of a tailspin with the wedding less than two months away. When I'm not flying, I'm doing wedding planning. However, I'll always find time to talk to you and hear what you're up to."

Both of them understood exactly what was going on. Max

continued, "I called to find out your line for the remainder of the month. All of us may be coming up to New York soon, and we were wondering when you would be around." Natalie dictated her schedule through the end of the month, and Max wrote it all down.

"Got it," said Max. "I'll be back in touch to let you know when I'll be in town with the guys. I know they would all love to see you and offer their congratulations and best wishes."

Suddenly something occurred to Natalie. "Max, I just thought of something that I think you might be interested in. I'm happy to help with your project, but I'm wondering if upper management at Pan Am might like to know about it. There may be something they can do to help. I'm sure they would be OK with me participating, but my thought is that someone should be told. Just an idea."

Max was impressed. Mr. Z and the CIA seemed content just to plow ahead, without considering how this might affect Natalie's job. "I'm pretty sure Mr. Z has already done something about this, but the next time I see him, I'll bring it up. As you are aware, he plays things pretty close to the vest, and we Navy guys are told things only on a need-to-know basis. But please be assured that I'll deal with this on your behalf—I won't just let it hang there." He paused for a moment and then asked, "Other than that…is all going well for you?"

Natalie melted at the tenderness in his voice. "All is well, and I feel confident in my decision. However, I'll never forget the time you and I spent together, and I hope we can continue to be good friends."

"I hope so, too. I'm sure we'll see each other from time to time, and we'll stay in touch. Talk to you soon."

Natalie didn't want the conversation to end but knew it was for the best. She said simply, "Goodbye, Max. Take care of yourself."

Chapter 55

Norfolk—New York City
March 13th, 1973

The five members of the primary team were assembled in the Comm Center secure room at 1000 to put the wheels in motion for Peter's first mission. His presence was not required, since his role was already well defined, and he did not have a need to know how the back end of the operation was going to work.

Mr. Z got things rolling immediately. "OK, Max—let us know what you have regarding the options to schedule Peter's first mission."

"I've got it all worked out with Doug, and we're ready to rock and roll, as soon as you choose a start date. Here are the options: Natalie will be in NYC March 19th through the 22nd, so we have scheduled Peter to spend the night of the 22nd there and then leave from JFK for London late on the 23rd. The following week, Natalie will be available the 28th and 29th, so we have scheduled Peter to overnight in NYC on the 28th and leave for Madrid on the 29th."

Clearly satisfied, Mr. Z laid out the plan. "Doug, tell Peter to give Mia both dates that he will be in New York. Here are my thoughts on personnel selection for the first mission—Y will be on the advance team to assist in Holy Loch. Doug will be part of the inspection team and will meet Peter at JFK on the 23rd. Max, I want you to be in New York on the 22nd to act as a safety net in case anything does not go as planned. Any questions?"

Body language from the group indicated in the negative, and Z continued. "I'll get NR on board and tell them to expect the Russians' wish list sometime on the 22nd or 23rd and be ready to deliver the basis for the phony documents to NIS in Scotland on the 24th. This seems to cover all the bases. Does anyone see any flaws in scheduling, or other issues?"

Max saw his opportunity to present Natalie's concern. "There is a potential problem looming—not with the first mission but with the overall operation as we go forward. Natalie has expressed concern that she is acting as an arm of the CIA, and her employer knows nothing about what's going on. She has concerns about her employment status if anything should go south now or in the future. I told her I would raise the issue with the team."

Z thought for a moment. "Her point is well taken. We can't go forward unless we loop in Pan Am. I've made a preliminary overture to upper management to let them know we have something to discuss; now that we've started the Op, I propose we meet with Pan Am at their offices in New York on the 19th or 20th. I will set up the meeting and want only Max and Natalie to accompany me. That will give them two points of contact within our primary team—me and Max. Any objections?"

Max spoke first. "Natalie will be very happy that you are out in front of this issue." Max did not know whether Z was telling the truth about already having made contact with Pan Am, but as the overall person in charge, he needed to give the impression of being in control, and even if he had neglected such a crucial point, he couldn't admit it. Max continued, "She's in town both days and will be busy with wedding planning. When the time and place are set, just let me know and I'll pass on the information to her so she can plan accordingly."

Doug said, "I agree with your reasoning, Z. I'm always up for a trip to New York, but the fewer players Pan Am can identify, the better. I assume the Agency will pick up Max's travel costs?"

Mr. Z nodded. "Of course. I'll meet Max at the National lounge the morning of his trip and have his ticket with me. For preliminary planning, I'll suggest to Pan Am we meet at 1100 on the 19th. As an aside, the installation at Pietro's has been completed. Since we'll be in New York, we'll have an opportunity to check out the system. After the meeting at Pan Am, I suggest Max meet Natalie at Pietro's for lunch. Max, after lunch, have her make a test communication run. I'll give you some typical information for her to send to the folks at the Agency."

Max felt a warm rush of pleasure at the prospect of a one-on-one lunch with Natalie. "No problem, Z," he said. "All I need is cash for the tip. They never let me pay when I dine with her." Then he forced himself to say, "We'd love to have you along— any reason you can't make it?"

With a half-smile, Mr. Z said, "I'm sure you can handle things without me. I have some issues to take care of at the Midtown apartment. I'll meet you at JFK around 1700 for the return flight south. Max, as soon as I confirm with Pan Am, I'll give you a call so that you can arrange things on your end. Most likely, I'll see you on the 19th."

Later in the day, Mr. Z confirmed the meeting on the 19th. Max called 8L, but as expected, Caroline answered, since Natalie was now spending most of her time at Scott's. He asked Caroline to tell Natalie to call as soon as she could. Natalie went over to 8L after dinner and phoned Max.

"Hello, Max. Caroline told me to call," she said.

"Well, I got right on top of your little problem. You and I and Mr. Z have a meeting with Pan Am upper management at 11:00 on Monday the 19th, in the president's conference room. I assume you can arrange your schedule?"

Natalie knew Max could get things done, but this was more than she'd anticipated. "OK, Mr. Efficiency, tell me what really happened."

"I'm dead serious. You're going to meet the big boys, so make sure you dress for the occasion. But wait, there's more—we're supposed to have lunch afterward at Daddy's place to check out his new office equipment."

Natalie felt a tingle at the thought of lunch alone with Max. "No problem," she said. "I'll see you at the Pan Am building on the 19th, and we'll take it from there. It will be nice to see you."

Nice to see you, indeed – that's an understatement, thought Max. "The pleasure is all mine, I assure you," he said. "Have a great weekend. I'll see you on Monday." They dragged out their good-byes and reluctantly rang off. There would be plenty of time for conversation the following week.

Pan Am Building
New York City
March 19th, 1973

The Pan Am president's conference room reflected the company's prestige: beautifully appointed, tasteful, and stylish. The select group of six sat three on each side of a spalted maple table polished to a mirror-like gloss. In a few minutes, it would be apparent to all why a flight attendant would be given a seat at such a high-level meeting. Natalie had taken to heart Max's advice to look the part—she wore a fitted camel blazer over a white silk blouse, with a Burberry plaid skirt and brown suede Gucci pumps. The men all wore business suits and ties—unusual for Z and Max. Natalie had hoped that Max might wear his dress blues, but the teams always traveled in civilian clothes.

On Pan Am's side of the table were Chairman of the Board

Najeeb Halaby, Pan Am founder and honorary Board member Juan Tripp, and the current Head of Pan Am Security, Eugene Kelly.

Mr. Z got right to the point. "The Agency sincerely appreciates all of you at Pan Am taking the time to meet with us. At the outset, I need to tell you that what we are discussing today is at the highest possible level of national security and sensitivity; as far as the government is concerned, this conversation is top secret. I assume and request that no recording is being made of this meeting; any notes you take should be cryptic and understandable only to you. Most of what we will be asking for at present is cooperation and possibly increased involvement in the future. However, we were unwilling to proceed with our operation until we provided you a general sense of what is going on at present, and what we may need going forward."

Juan Tripp spoke first for Pan Am. "Based on your preliminary discussions with Mr. Kelly, we clearly understand the need for absolute secrecy and that those who may be asked to help in the future need know only what they are supposed to do. The why is never to be supplied. Only those in this room will know and understand the why, to the extent that you can share it with us. Let me assure you that you can rely on Pan Am for 100% cooperation."

Mr. Z was equally gracious in his reply. "We appreciate your assurance of cooperation and secrecy. At this point, I am going to share with you where we are at present and what our current and future needs may be. We have reason to believe that certain Pan Am flight attendants have been recruited by the Soviet Union to act on their behalf, contrary to the security interests of the United States. These suspicions came to light as a result of some very astute observations by Natalie Tommasi, the Pan Am flight attendant seated on my right and based here in New York.

Because she was personally acquainted with LCDR Millen, seated on my left, she shared those concerns with him as a sounding board. He in turn contacted us at the Agency to see if any of her suspicions amounted to anything. Suffice it to say that our preliminary analysis indicates there may be validity to Natalie's concerns.

"However, we need Pan Am's buy-in for her to continue to keep a watchful eye and let us know if she continues to observe things of a suspicious nature. Since we seek to absolutely limit the number of individuals who are aware of these suspicions, Max will continue to be Natalie's point of contact for the Agency. Both will continue to perform in their existing capacities as a Pan Am flight attendant and a naval submarine officer. Mr. Halaby, as a former naval aviator, you may think it odd that we chose a submarine officer to participate, but I can assure you there are valid reasons.

"What we anticipate asking for in the future is some alteration of Natalie's flight schedule. Again, I must emphasize that our suspicions are not to be shared outside this room. There is to be no rational explanation attempted or offered for changes in her schedule—'It came from upstairs' should be sufficient. If there is persistent questioning by other Pan Am employees regarding anything discussed today, then Mr. Kelly and I should take it up on a case-by-case basis. However, I will say that requests to alter Natalie's schedule will not be frequent, which should help to avoid undue questioning by staff. Any questions so far?"

Mr. Kelly smiled. "Mr. Z, this is a simple need, given the thousands of flight attendants working for Pan Am. One special request here or there shouldn't raise eyebrows." Halaby and Tripp nodded their agreement.

Mr. Z continued, "The second area where we may need help is also simple. We may give you just the name tag worn by a flight attendant, possibly with information as to when and where the individual was identified. We will need your help to confirm the identification of the person wearing the tag. This may take a little work, but if you can limit the list to two or three individuals and give us all the background information available, we may be able to narrow the list to just one. A possible story to avoid questions from personnel could be that this person was particularly helpful on a flight and a passenger wanted to bring the information to management's attention so that she could be recognized."

Mr. Kelly again agreed to help and indicated that Mr. Z should continue.

"The next area of potential involvement will be the last, and it's pretty creative. We may need to train a Navy or CIA agent as a flight attendant on an accelerated basis. We are not yet sure whether this will be a necessity. One way it might work is that we would provide you with a qualified individual who fits the Pan Am profile; you could accelerate training through a fictitious test program in Miami, but we would actually use Miss Tommasi as a one-on-one mentor to compress the training process."

Since this was the first time Natalie had heard this idea, she could not hide her look of surprise. She felt it was not her place to say anything; she would do whatever was required of her — and it sounded like it could be fun. Halaby considered for a moment and then said, "That's a unique idea. It might even benefit us if we ever get in a tight squeeze and have to quickly train some people. Certainly as a test program, we could probably compress the usual six weeks to four, or maybe a little less, particularly if the person had medical and/or emergency procedures training."

Mr. Z said, "We could do things the other way around…

train a flight attendant to be an agent, but that would be the more difficult path, for a number of reasons. Are there any questions or concerns?"

Halaby leaned forward to shake hands with Z. "My obvious concern would be for the safety of our employees, but in Miss Tommasi's case, it sounds like there will be little or no risk. It is not clear where the Agency is headed with the identification exercise, but I know you have your reasons. I guess we'll just have to see what we turn up and how it might be useful. If the compressed training comes to pass, it will be your agent rather than our employee at risk, so I have no real concerns there."

Juan Tripp was ready to wrap things up. "I think we have a clear understanding of your needs, and as stated at the outset, we will continue to cooperate in every way we can. Mr. Kelly has considerable experience with our company, and I know you can rely on him to deliver what you need. I assume that no further meetings will be necessary, and any needed communication will be between Mr. Z and Mr. Kelly."

Mr. Z stood up, a clear indication that the meeting was over. "Thank you again for meeting with us and for your pledge of support. As things develop, I'll stay in touch with Mr. Kelly. We do understand your concern for the safety of your employees and will keep that interest paramount as we move forward."

Of course, this was a flat-out lie. The danger to Mia was considerable—one false move, and the Soviets would be capable of anything. The real purpose of the meeting was to assuage Natalie's concerns, rather than to give Pan Am full disclosure. Everyone got to their feet; there were handshakes all around, and Juan Tripp made a special point of taking Natalie aside and thanking her for her excellent performance record to date and her service to her country. She glowed at the sincere compliment.

However, the best part of the day was yet to come—lunch at

Pietro's with Max. Enough time had passed since Natalie's engagement that things would be relaxed and not a bit awkward. Max also looked forward to it with great anticipation. Precious and few indeed were the moments to share, especially over lunch with a glass or two of wine.

Chapter 56

March 19th, 1973
New York City

Natalie had called ahead and talked to Leo, the maître d', to ensure that the table she and Max had shared many months ago would be available for their lunch meeting. As they entered the restaurant and were seated, Max looked at her and simply said, "You remembered."

Natalie had also pre-arranged their lunch selections, relying on her memory of what Max liked best. There was serious business to be conducted, and she knew they didn't have all day to get up to the office; training on the secure equipment awaited her.

Max forced himself to begin the conversation with the real reason for their lunch meeting. "We appreciate all you have done to help our little project. I don't want to talk specifics here at lunch, but I do want to make sure you are comfortable with everything that's going on. Although I told you that you can't share any of this with Scott, if he becomes suspicious or starts to ask questions, we may need to revisit that restriction. But for the time being, if you can keep everything on the QT, that would be best."

With a look of understanding, Natalie indicated that she was aware of the ramifications. "First off, I really appreciate your getting in front of the issue with my employer," she said. "It's clear they don't have all the facts, but that's by design. As far as my continued involvement—I brought all of this to your attention because I thought it was the right thing to do. I never anticipated being part of the project, but I understand the need. As far as Scott is concerned, he hasn't noticed anything out of the ordinary. He's busy with classes and studying, and I have a lot of time to myself. I still keep some things over at 8L, since his place is too small for all my stuff, and Caroline is my best friend, so it's not unusual for me to go over there from time to time. If the situation becomes awkward, I know you and the team will figure something out."

The waiter arrived with a bottle of Bolla Soave and their first course, prosciutto and melon. Glasses were filled, and Max offered a toast. "Here's to future success in all we do." Natalie clinked his glass, and Max went on, "You know if there are issues, all you have to do is tell me. We're all behind you 100%."

Natalie understood the double meaning of what Max had said; it applied to her marriage as well as to official business. They did not need to discuss their feelings for one another; however, they both knew that feelings lingered between them. They enjoyed light conversation over veal saltimbocca and chopped salad, finishing with spumoni ice cream. Max left a substantial tip, courtesy of the CIA, and suggested they move things up to Nat's office.

Upon arrival, Natalie noted there was a new cabinet in the corner. Max retrieved a set of keys from his pocket, removed one, and gave it to her on a Naval Academy key ring. He told her to unlock the cabinet. Inside were a phone, facsimile machine, some printed instructions, and the CIA's version of the Polaroid SX-70 camera. From his briefcase, Max removed a set of documents stamped TEST.

"OK, let's get moving with Espionage 101," he said with a chuckle. "The team gave me a set of documents to use for instructional purposes. I'll fax the first one and show you exactly what to do, and then you can practice. After transmission, you need to call the top number on the instruction card and verify that the transmission was successful."

Natalie proved to be a quick learner. Max talked her through her first test; she successfully completed the second on her own and made the call verifying the transmission. Max told her that if there were problems, the guys on the other end were always there to help. Also, if for any reason the transmission was not clear, it was possible that the guys would ask her to read portions of the transmission to clarify the information on the document.

Then Natalie asked, "What's the deal with the camera? I thought photography would be Mia's responsibility."

"This is the CIA's version of the latest Polaroid camera—much faster and more compact. It's a backup, just in case something happens to the one we gave Mia. This is pretty nifty, and I'll show you how it works. We want to prepare for every possible contingency."

After taking two pictures of Natalie, Max gave her the camera and suggested she give it a try. She took a snap of Daddy's tomatoes on the windowsill, and one of Max, which she put in her purse. When she finished, Max said, "Well, that's about it for Espionage 101. Sometime during the day on Thursday, Mia will make copies of the Soviets' documents and leave them in the bottom of the armoire in your living room. All you have to do is pick them up, bring them here, and fax them, just as we practiced."

Max made a conscious decision not to tell Natalie that he would probably be in New York on Thursday. He wanted her to have the feeling that she was on her own, that the responsibility for the transfer was all hers, and that the team had full confidence she would do her part. Natalie put away the camera, locked up the cabinet, and said, "Well, that seems to be it. You're a very good teacher, Mr. Max. I'm pretty confident that everything will go as planned."

They moved toward the door of the office and stopped for a moment. They faced each other, and Max took her hands in his. He wanted so much to give her a serious kiss—not in a sexual way, but as an expression of the deep affection he felt for her. Instead, he gave her a brief kiss on the lips, then put his arms around her and gave her a big hug.

"I know you're going to do a great job. Don't worry about anything."

She returned the hug. "LCDR Millen, you are the best. I really am going to miss you—I'm sure our paths will cross from time to time." They stopped by the kitchen on their way out of Pietro's, to pay their respects to Nat. He paused in stirring a pot on the stove and took Max's hand. "Nat, we appreciate everything you are doing for us—and the loan of your beautiful daughter."

Nat hugged his blushing daughter and replied sincerely, "I'm happy to help in any way I can."

Max and Natalie stood on the corner of 45th and Third, where Max hailed a cab for Natalie, to take her uptown to her apartment. After a brief hug, Natalie hopped in and Max closed the door behind her. He looked after the cab until it was almost out of sight, then grabbed a taxi for his ride to the East Side Airline Terminal, where he would catch the bus to meet Z for the flight south. During the ride, he took the picture of Natalie out of his briefcase and smiled at it, just as Natalie smiled back.

The previous week, when Peter returned to Norfolk, Doug let him know that they had arranged for him to be in New York for overnights on the 22nd and 28th for inspection trips to Holy Loch and

Rota. Peter passed this information to Mia, who in turn told Ivan, as previously agreed. Ivan had the thought that this double opportunity could work to their advantage, for a number of reasons. Accordingly, he called Moscow on the 15th to discuss the matter.

"Gorsky, we have the dates for the first and second missions. As requested, Songbird was able to get Neutron scheduled quickly, and the second date is just a bonus, based on the Navy's operational schedule. I think it is in our interest to take advantage of the opportunity and provide Neutron some suggested activities that he might be able to include in the work-up of the second mission."

Gorsky replied, "He may be able to arrange for some drills to be run that will yield the specific information we seek. It is worth the effort. Our technicians will prepare instructions for Neutron for the second mission and provide a list of priorities for the information to be gathered. Will you transfer the information to Songbird yourself, or utilize an identical exchange? This information is too important for a dead drop."

With confidence, Ivan offered, "Songbird thinks she has things under control and a face-to-face meeting will not be necessary. An identical exchange is the best option—the less physical contact, the better. I still have to work out the details of getting the information back from Neutron when he comes through New York on the 27th. I'll have Mia set that up when she sees him on the 22nd.

"I will also tell her that Neutron's proposal of an exchange for her father after the sixth mission seems to make the most sense."

"Do you see any flaws in our plan?" asked Gorsky. "This whole thing is pretty simple, as long as Neutron gives us what we want. Is everything between the two of them as it appears on the surface? Will he deliver for us as requested?"

"I had them followed and observed at dinner after he was

turned on the 11th, and we may continue to monitor their conversations when they are in the hotel room. Their relationship is a bit strained; however, for all intents and purposes things appear to be as expected. We will continue to keep an eye on her from time to time."

Gorsky grunted, "OK. It is in your hands. Keep me informed." And the line went dead.

Mia's father, Karl, lived in a modest efficiency apartment at Behrenstrasse 47, about four blocks from the edge of the Humboldt University campus and just five blocks from Checkpoint Charlie. The university itself had been left pretty much intact since 1945 and required little restoration so that it could be opened in 1946 under Soviet control. This was not the case for some of the surrounding area, which suffered significant damage from Russian artillery during the closing days of the war, after which the Russian soldiers engaged in the rape and pillage of the once-beautiful city.

The apartment building where Karl lived had been hastily restored and was sufficient for his needs. It paled in comparison to his prior residence closer to campus, which had been left untouched but was seized by the Soviets for their use after he was imprisoned for anti-Soviet activities related to the envisioned reunification of the German state. Karl was completely oblivious to the fact that most of his daily routine was observed by a team of "watchers." This included his morning walk along the banks of the Spree River and his daily commute to the academic buildings on campus. Even if he had noticed the watchers, it would have been of little consequence. He knew he was essentially under house arrest and they could do all the watching they wanted. He wasn't going anywhere.

Little did he know that plans were underway to change his life dramatically in the coming weeks. His main focus was his research and teaching at the university—he had little time for anything else. He was not interested in doing anything that might rock the boat and had no control over those who might pull the strings that controlled his life.

Chapter 57

New York City
March 19th-22nd, 1973

Ivan began to regret he'd told Gorsky that a face-to-face meeting with Mia wouldn't be needed. He realized that the operation was just too important to leave things to coded telephone conversations and information passed through impersonal identical exchanges. He quickly put in a book club call to Mia and instructed her to meet him at the usual location in Van Courtland Park at noon on Monday, the 19th.

Mia immediately let Z know of her plans to meet Ivan, giving him the exact time and location of the meeting. Z told her she and Ivan would be under surveillance. He then alerted the operational team at the apartment to get the photographic evidence they would need. Z's overall plan was to confirm Ivan's involvement and start building his case against the Russians for their ongoing espionage.

Under the circumstances, Ivan decided that another call to Gorsky would be the best course of action. He would suggest it would be more efficient if Gorsky's team were to provide the package for both missions to Peter on the 22nd. Ivan didn't have to wait long for Gorsky to pick up.

Ivan said, "Comrade, I've been thinking. Since Neutron will be in New York on both the 22nd and the 28th, may I recommend that you provide packages for both missions at the same time, to minimize the chance of detection."

Gorsky thought for a moment, "OK, we'll get right on it and

have all the information to you no later than Wednesday the 21st. Do you foresee any problems?"

"No, I don't." Ivan said, "Songbird is under close surveillance and things appear perfectly normal. I plan to meet with her to emphasize once again the importance of the overall operation and tell her to expect both packages. To keep her on task, I'll tell her we are actively working on the swap of information for her father here in New York."

"All right—everything seems to be in order. I'll get the technical teams working on both packages."

With no goodbye, the line went dead.

Mia left for Van Courtland Park, discreetly followed by both the CIA and KGB. The CIA broke off contact after the last subway ride since they already had agents and hidden cameras positioned in the park.

Ivan was on his usual bench, feeding the pigeons. Mia took a seat next to him and offered some idle chit-chat about the coming spring weather. Just then, a nanny with a child in a stroller walked down the path discreetly snapping images of Ivan and Mia with her hidden camera. Mission accomplished. The KGB operative was far more conspicuous, sitting on a nearby bench reading a newspaper.

Ivan said in a low voice, "Good of you to come. Everything seems to be in order but there's one minor alteration in our plan. Since your friend's visits are so close together, we've decided to give you information for both missions on the 22nd. We'll use an identical pass at Bloomingdale's and you will receive a call early on Thursday to set the time. Any questions?"

"No. I assume my friend will still want to see me on the 28th. Our relationship is a bit strained at present, but I don't want to give any indication that he is not welcome to visit. However, I'm still worried about whether you will hold up your end of the bargain concerning the duration of the arrangement and the fate of my father."

"We are committed to keeping our promise," Ivan assured her, "and are planning to swap your father here in New York in exchange for the fruits of your friend's sixth mission."

"I'm counting on you to deliver my father," said Mia. "However, I do need instructions concerning how the package will be handed back after each mission. I have no information on that and we're set to start this week."

"That's one of the purposes of this meeting. In the Bloomingdale's bag, there will be a miniature camera, rolls of film and several empty Godiva chocolate bags and boxes. There will also be written instructions for your friend regarding the post-Op procedure.

"Since you may not be available to receive the information from him, we have arranged the following procedure: He will put any exposed film and written notes in the chocolate box and put it in the Godiva bag. Ideally, all the information will be photographed and our notes destroyed. As soon as he lands, he is to go to the lobby bar of his airline and take a seat. A man or woman will take an adjacent seat and ask for the time. He will look at his watch and say, 'I'm sorry, I'm still on European time.' The person will reply, 'No problem; I can do the math.' This will be a signal for him to make the swap of the Godiva bags. It's that simple. If there is no room at the bar, he should find a spot where there are empty seats."

"Pretty straightforward—I will offer to instruct him on the use of the camera. Anything else?"

Ivan looked off into space, his tone dead serious. "I know you are aware of the extreme importance of this operation. We are counting on you to keep him in line and ensure he delivers as anticipated. Stay focused and make sure you keep everything on track."

Pushing back a bit she said, "I do understand how important it is that all should go as planned but I'm very concerned as to whether you will keep your end of the bargain. If there's nothing else, I'll be on my way."

Ivan indicated that the conversation was at an end and continued feeding the pigeons. Mia stood up and walked down the path in the direction of the subway.

March 22nd, 1973

Mia waited in her apartment for the call telling her the time to make the exchange at Bloomingdale's. Natalie was over at Scott's and knew she was on call all day. When Max called she would pick-up the package at 8L, and then go to Pietro's to make the transmission. Conveniently, Scott was in class and at the library for most of the day. Natalie made an offhand remark about being in and out during the day, but definitely being home in time for dinner.

Sabrina was busy packing for her assigned flight later in the day. She chatted with Mia about the coming wedding and the need for a replacement roommate once Natalie moved out and no longer needed her "second closet." For now, though, it was nice to have her still paying a quarter of the rent.

As anticipated, the phone rang at 9:30. "Hello, this is Mia." The voice on the other end indicated there was a gift waiting for her at Bloomingdale's, and could be picked up at customer service any time after noon. "Thank you. Someone will be there today," said Mia. Translated, it meant she should be at the prearranged location precisely at noon for the exchange.

Mia hurried out and, using the local pay phone, contacted the CIA. She told them about Bloomingdale's and that her prepared package would be available in the apartment any time after 3:00. That would give her plenty of time to make the bag exchange, photograph the contents, and leave the package for pick-up in the armoire. After that, it was off to the Penn Garden to give Peter the originals.

With all wheels in motion, Max called Natalie and told her to make her pick-up any time after 3:00.

Mia's trip to Bloomingdale's via the Lexington Avenue subway was uneventful. There was no reason for either a CIA or KGB tail, since both knew where she was going. The CIA's team was waiting at Bloomie's to photograph both the transaction and the Soviet agent making the exchange. Afterward, they tailed him and photographed him going into the Soviet UN Mission. The CIA's case file was growing, much to Mr. Z's delight.

Shortly before 1:00, Mia returned to the apartment and got to work. She transferred the camera, film and Godiva bags to her overnight, and went right to work with the SX-70, copying the documents. There was loud music playing in the living room and she was so intently focused on what she was doing, she didn't hear the apartment door open. Sabrina dropped her luggage in the living room, took off her uniform jacket and made a dash for the loo. As she did so, she caught a glimpse of Mia busy photographing something in the bedroom. Sabrina slammed the bathroom door and Mia scrambled to finish photographing the documents. She quickly stuffed the copies in a large manila envelope, placed it on the bureau and put the originals and the camera in her overnight bag.

Just as she finished, Sabrina came into the bedroom, white as a ghost. Her eyes flickered toward the envelope on the bureau. "Sabrina, what happened to you? Are you OK?" asked Mia.

Sabrina explained that when she got to the briefing room for her flight, she had broken out in a cold sweat and started to experience nausea and stabbing pains in her stomach. She didn't have a fever, but did remember some questionable Chinese food from take-out the night before. Pan Am had diagnosed food poisoning and sent her home. Fortunately, she was in no condition to confront Mia about what she had seen in the bedroom. Sabrina had noticed some of Mia's recent unusual behavior and considered saying something to a guy she'd dated who had a connection to MI-6. However, she never got around to it and now she didn't know what to do.

Weakly she said to Mia, "I'll be OK. I just need to rest and let the worst of this pass. I'll go to the doctor tomorrow for a follow-up."

Casually picking up the manila envelope, Mia said, "I'll be at the Penn Garden with Peter, Room 609. We'll be around until he flies out to London late tomorrow. Please call us if you need somebody to make a run to the chemist."

"Thanks—there's not much to be done for food poisoning, unfortunately; it just has to run its course, so I'll be staying in bed until tomorrow. If I do need you, though, I'll call. Room 609, is that right?"

Mia nodded and picked up her overnight bag and the envelope.

A few moments later, Sabrina went to the living room to retrieve her carry-on. Just as she entered the room, she noticed Mia closing the door to Natalie's armoire in the living room—the piece that had served as Natalie's additional closet when she was living full time at the apartment.

As Mia walked out the door, she said, "I do hope you feel better soon. Remember; give us a call if you need help. Food poisoning can be serious, so if you think you need to go to the emergency room, let us know."

Mia closed the door and was soon on her way to the Penn Garden to meet Peter. She was uncomfortable with the situation, but any significant delay in getting to Peter would be suspicious.

Natalie arrived promptly at 3:00 and went straight to the armoire to retrieve the envelope. It wasn't there. Frantically, she searched everywhere it could possibly be in the living room, but the envelope was nowhere to be found. She tried to keep her emotions under control and then did the only thing she could think of — call the emergency number the CIA gave her. One of the agents at the Ops apartment picked up immediately.

Trying to be cryptic but accurate, she said, "This is Natalie. I'm at my apartment, and my friend was supposed to leave me a package, but it's not here. It's very important, and I don't know what to do."

The voice replied, "Stay right where you are. Don't do anything or call anybody. We will send help very soon."

Natalie answered, "OK, I understand. I'll stay right here."

In less than twenty minutes, there was a knock at the door — and it was Max. She threw her arms around him, almost sobbing with relief. "I'm so glad it's you," she said.

Max explained that the CIA called Mia, who verified that she left the envelope in the armoire as agreed. However, unexpectedly Sabrina had appeared at the apartment because she'd been sent home with food poisoning. Mia said she knew Sabrina had seen the envelope, but she didn't think she'd seen her putting it in the armoire. Max asked Natalie if she had searched the bedroom; she said she only checked the living room.

"Let's do the bedroom and see what we can find," said Max.

Sabrina was in bed, fast asleep. They quietly searched the room and bureau, but the envelope was nowhere to be found. Max motioned for Natalie to follow him back to the living room.

"Well, either she put it where we can't find it, or she's already given it to God knows who." Now Max was starting to panic. If the envelope were to fall into the wrong hands, the entire operation would be over. "Let me think for a minute. Before doing anything else, we should wake her and just ask her directly. I'll stay here in the living room, and you can gently wake her and ask her to come into the living room so we can talk to her."

Natalie knelt next to Sabrina and touched her shoulder. Sabrina rolled away from Natalie's touch, and when she did, Natalie saw the corner of a brown manila envelope peeking out from under the pillow. Carefully but firmly, Natalie slid it out. Sabrina did not stir, and Natalie crept back to the living room, where Max waited nervously.

"You got it! What happened?" Natalie told him where she'd found the envelope and how she had retrieved it. After checking the contents, Max's submarine training took over as he sprang into action. "OK, here is what we are going to do. I'll stay here and babysit until Sabrina wakes up. You make the transmission at Pietro's and get back here as soon as you can. I'll call the guys at the Ops apartment and tell them what happened. My goal will be to keep her here and not let her talk to anybody. I'm sure the agents will give me further direction; they may even come here to help get things under control."

Natalie threw on her coat, stuffed the envelope into a briefcase and started to leave. Max grabbed her shoulders, gave her a big hug, and said, "Good luck. Just act normal and do what we practiced. I'll wait for you here."

As Max opened the door for her, she turned and gave him a kiss on the cheek. "Max, you are just the best ever."

Max closed the door behind her, then leaned against it and let out a long sigh.

Chapter 58

In a flash, Natalie was off the elevator, out of her building and into a taxi. Settling in the back seat, she retrieved the photo of Max from her purse. *Well, Mr. Max, what did you get me into?* she wondered, looking at the picture. *But you did come through when it mattered most. I know I can always count on you to do the right thing.*

Arriving at Pietro's Natalie breezed through the kitchen where Nat was getting ready for the dinner rush. "Hi, Daddy — just a quick hello. I'll be up in your office for a while to take care of some things; I'll stop back when I'm finished. See you in a few."

Natalie sprinted up the stairs, bolted the office door and got right to work. She unlocked the CIA's cabinet, turned on the equipment and made three stacks of the Polaroid pictures provided by Mia. One was general instructions for Peter, next the requested information for the first inspection, and finally the Russians' wish list for the second inspection. Natalie made three separate transmissions — which took much longer than expected — and properly verified receipt after each one. Max told her to keep the Sabrina business on the QT with Langley. All communications completed, she shut down the equipment, locked the cabinet, and hurried down to the kitchen.

"Daddy, you can have your office back. I'm all finished and I'm going back uptown to my apartment."

"Wait a second, sweetheart—I have a few steaks and chops packed up for you."

Natalie was desperate to get back home, but forced herself to be cordial. "Thanks so much, Daddy. Your care packages are always such a treat." She gave him a quick kiss on the cheek and took the package. "I hate to run off but I'm on a tight schedule today. I'll talk to you soon." In no time at all, she was in a cab and on her way to the apartment.

About forty-five minutes after Natalie left, Max heard Sabrina being sick in the bathroom. He remained silent in a distant corner of the living room. It was far preferable if Natalie explained the situation and then questioned Sabrina about the documents she'd put under her pillow. The bathroom door opened, and Sabrina went straight back to the bedroom. Max breathed a sigh of relief.

An hour later, Max heard Natalie coming in the front door. He ran to meet her and put his finger to his lips. She got the hint, hugged him and whispered into his ear, "I did it! Everything went perfectly. I brought the package back; I know I was supposed to leave it there, but…this is a special situation."

Max smiled. "You are always a step ahead. That was exactly the right thing to do; I'm so proud of you. Let's adjourn to the couch and discuss next steps. If there's some wine opened, I think we deserve a glass after what we've been through."

Natalie went to the kitchen and returned with two glasses of white. They sat down and softly touched glasses as they began a sotto voce conversation.

"If you think she's feeling well enough, get Sabrina up and bring her in here to talk to us. She was in the bathroom again about an hour ago, but maybe things have started to settle down.

We have to find out what she did with the envelope, if anything, before she put it under her pillow. I'll take the lead, but you can back me up. In no case do we tell her what happened during the last two hours. OK?"

Natalie nodded. "I understand completely. Should I go get her up now?"

"Yes. I hate to disturb her, but time is really of the essence."

Natalie gently shook Sabrina's shoulder. Half-asleep, she instinctively put her hand under the pillow. She was startled fully awake when she realized the envelope was missing. In a reassuring voice, Natalie said, "Don't be upset. It's safe. We will explain everything. Let's go into the living room." She got Sabrina's bathrobe and helped her to put it on.

Sabrina was clearly surprised to see Max. He motioned for them to take a seat on the couch. "Sabrina, we find ourselves in a bit of a quandary. Inadvertently, you are now in the middle of a classified operation that will have serious repercussions for the United States, particularly if the contents of the envelope you found are revealed outside this room. We have to know if you discussed it with anyone, and what you intended to do with it."

Seeing an opening, Natalie spoke up. "Sabrina, you know that Max is totally on the up and up. He is a dedicated naval officer with only the best interests of his country in mind. I asked him here when a package left for me was not where it was supposed to be. When I tried to wake you earlier to ask you about it, I saw the envelope and took it back. Here it is. Can you tell us what happened?"

Sabrina put her hands on either side of her head, as if she were dizzy. "I got sick at JFK and was sent home. When I got here and ran for the bathroom, I saw Mia photographing something laid out in the bedroom. I didn't let her know what I saw. When I did come into the bedroom, everything had been picked up and apparently placed in the envelope." Sabrina stopped and leaned her elbows on her knees, her head in her hands. "Sorry. I'm feeling a bit faint."

Max jumped up. "Let me get you a glass of ginger ale. You're probably dehydrated—and we've given you a hell of a shock. Just breathe deeply." He went to the kitchen and got Sabrina a ginger ale. She took a sip and appeared to feel somewhat better.

"Thank you, Max. Well, the rest is pretty simple. I came back to the living room to get my carry-on, which I'd dropped in my race to the bathroom. I saw Mia closing the door to Natalie's armoire. After Mia left, I took out the envelope and had a quick look at the contents. It was obvious that Mia was involved in something far beyond a parlor game. Actually, I had been wondering about her unusual behavior of late, but this was beyond the pale. I knew I should do something, but I had no idea what. Anyway, I couldn't leave the apartment—I was too sick. So, I put the envelope under my pillow for safekeeping and that was that until Natalie found it."

Max sensed she was telling the truth. "First of all, let me be very clear Sabrina: Mia is working for the United States no matter what you may have seen in the envelope. Since you are a Brit, I can tell you that what is in the envelope will eventually serve the mutual interests of both our countries. However, because of national security, you cannot tell anyone what you saw or what happened here today. You must forget this ever happened."

Sabrina was too savvy to take anything on blind faith. Max couldn't help but admire her when she said, "How do I know that all three of you aren't working in concert for the Soviets and the KGB? I was planning to contact my friend Ian, who knows someone at MI-6…who is in and out of New York all the time. If I'm not to contact him, I need some manner of assurance that you two are telling the truth."

Max made a quick decision. Sabrina was not stupid so he decided to make an offer he hoped he would be able to fulfill. "OK—here's what I'll do. Someone from the CIA will contact Ian. They will tell Ian to contact his MI-6 friend and ask him to run your concerns up through his management and over to the CIA. MI-6 will then assure Ian's friend that this is something you must forget and leave alone. Closing the loop, Ian will relay that message back to you. I will not ask that Ian identify his friend. Will that work for you?"

Sabrina nodded. "Yes. With that proviso, I will trust you and Natalie for now. What happens next?"

"Let me have Ian's contact information and I will have someone from the CIA reach out to him as soon as possible. This is not something we can discuss on the phone so I'm going to leave now and meet with my contact to tell him about our agreement. Then I'll come back here and tell you if everything is copacetic. Please stay here with Natalie until I return."

Natalie picked up what was going on. "No problem. I'll give Scott a call and tell him I'm over here helping Sabrina out for a bit because she's not feeling well."

"I should be back in less than an hour." Max took the envelope and Ian's contact information and was out the door, headed for the Ops apartment. As soon as he arrived, they got Mr. Z on the speaker phone and Max laid out the plan. He apologized for taking independent action but explained he didn't see an alternative.

Mr. Z's voice came from the speaker box. "First of all, we received Natalie's transmissions. Tell her she did a great job. The wheels are already in motion at Navy and NR to generate the material for Peter's response. The beauty of the situation is that we started our work before Peter even got his package. Regarding Sabrina, that was good thinking, Max—particularly given the rather difficult situation. It was brilliant of Natalie to bring the package back; this ensured Sabrina would not learn what actually happened to the contents. It's always preferable for field operatives to make spot decisions rather than pass things on to management and get bogged down in bureaucracy We'll reach out to Ian immediately and tell him what he needs to do to reassure Sabrina.

"I'll contact my MI-6 counterpart in New York and set the agenda. I'll talk in generalities about the Stork Club and tell him it's essentially a courier operation. I'll tell him that we have a lead that will help us identify additional agents. Early information indicates they are based in London, Hong Kong, and other Pan Am bases. If we make positive identifications, we will share that information with MI-6 going forward. Obviously, the broader scope of our operation is off the table. Max, get right back to the apartment and assure Sabrina that she will hear something from Ian in the next day or two. In the meantime, urge her to sit tight. Good luck, Max—nothing ever goes exactly as planned. That's why I put you in New York; you and Natalie think fast on your feet and make a good team."

When Max got back to the apartment, Natalie was sitting comfortably in the living room, sipping wine and doing a crossword puzzle. Max's glass had been half full when he left, but now it was empty. "Wow, Sabrina must have made a quick recovery, to be drinking wine," he teased.

"Silly. I wasn't going to let that nice glass of chilled wine go to waste, so I drank yours. There's more in the fridge for you."

"You are as practical as you are thoughtful." Max went to the kitchen and poured out the last of the bottle. He sat down on the couch next to Natalie. "OK, it's all set. The ball is in Z's court and all we have to do is update Sabrina. She should hear back from Ian in a day or two. Any fallout after I left?"

"Not really. She softened a bit after I told her what a good guy you are, and a little more about our personal story. I think she believes that neither of us would ever do anything to hurt our country. Do you want me to get her up, or should we just talk to her in the bedroom?"

"Let's just go into the bedroom. She looked pretty weak and pale—I don't want to get her up again."

Natalie checked on Sabrina, saw she was dozing and asked if it would be OK for Max to come in and talk with her. Max poked his head in the door and said, "Sabrina, the wheels are in motion, and you should hear from Ian in a few days. My guys have a good relationship with MI-6, and things should work out just as I described. Any questions?"

"No—I think things should be all right in the long run," Sabrina said. "Natalie and I had a little chat after you left, and it seems you really are one of the good guys. I'll just wait to hear from Ian."

Natalie said, "Can we get you anything before we leave? More ginger ale?"

"Yes please, but with no ice. If you could just put it on the nightstand, I'll drink a little bit and try to go back to sleep."

Natalie got the ginger ale, and she and Max returned to the couch to finish their wine. Max knew Natalie needed to go back to Scott's and, much as he wanted to spend more time with her, he had no intention of taking advantage of the situation and prolonging their conversation. Both of them thought of the pivotal evening they'd spent on that very couch—but that was water under the bridge.

Max finished his wine and said, "Well, we've certainly had a busy day. I hope the next mission goes a little more smoothly. At least you won't have to do this again for about a month—Peter probably won't be back in Europe before then. The whole team is so grateful to you, Natalie, for what you're doing for our country. I hope that doesn't sound too corny."

"Not at all. This is important business and I'm happy to be involved, especially since you're a part of it. At least it appears there's an end game; it would be difficult to keep this up indefinitely."

Max stood up, took the empty glasses to the kitchen, rinsed them and put them on the counter. Natalie retrieved her father's package from the fridge; she would take it over to Scott's for dinner. They put on their coats and stood by the apartment door, as they had done so many times before. Natalie hugged Max and rested her head on his broad chest for just a moment. He cradled her face in both hands, looked into her eyes, and gave her a brief kiss on the lips.

Max said, "Hugs, goodbyes, and airplanes — seems to be the story of our lives."

They closed the door behind them, and Natalie did not resist when Max took her hand as they walked to the elevator.

"Take care, Max," she said, her eyes moist, as they parted in the lobby.

Chapter 59

New York City
March 22nd, 1973

Ivan kept Mia under close surveillance until she met Peter and delivered the mission instructions. She went straight from Bloomingdale's to her apartment and was in and out in about half an hour. Carrying her overnight bag with the Soviet's information she took a taxi to Penn Garden where Peter was already waiting for her.

Pulling her body hard into his, he kissed her with unfeigned passion. Reluctantly, Mia broke away and said, "Work before play." She placed the mission materials in three separate piles: one for general instructions, camera, and film; next, one for the first mission, and finally, one for the second mission. Peter reached deep into her bag and pulled out the velvet cat-o'-nine-tails.

Mia smacked him playfully on the hand. "Put that back my darling. We'll have time for treats later if you're a good boy and do as I say."

Peter stood smartly to attention and saluted. "Yes, ma'am—ready for training instructions!"

Very efficiently, Mia went over everything she had laid out on the bed. She demonstrated proper use of the camera, including loading and unloading, and how to stow the exposed film in the empty chocolate box. They discussed the procedure for the hand off at the end of the mission and rehearsed exactly what they would say so as to avoid any discrepancy.

"Read over the mission information carefully—if you are

unclear about any of it, prepare your questions and I'll try to get them answered. It's up to you to request clarification."

Peter read everything twice and made notes. "It all seems pretty straightforward. A few things are open to interpretation, though, so I'll make a value judgment on their real intent. I assume a face-to-face with the KGB is not a viable option. So, do I get my reward now?"

"Not quite yet." She gave him a peck on the cheek. "With the exception of the chocolate boxes and bags, put everything back in the locked canvas pouch and take it to the hotel house safe. It's to remain under lock and key until we leave for JFK tomorrow."

Peter knew the request to photograph interior areas of the submarine was a no-go; he wouldn't raise the issue with the Soviets before he left. Best to wait and see how the CIA wanted to handle the situation. When he didn't deliver, he would explain there had been no opportunity—operational areas of the sub were always occupied and the risk too great.

When he returned, Mia was dressed for the occasion in a see-through black and red number that left nothing to the imagination. She had laid out all her toys on the bureau. After greeting him with a body grind and a prolonged kiss, she led him over to the bureau and said simply, "Take your pick."

The Navy and CIA teams went right to work on the information that Natalie had transmitted. They formulated answers and created data to construct phony radiation, chemistry, and other engineering logs. LCDR Y was already in place on the tender in Holy Loch, working with the NIS agent to put together a package for Peter to photograph once he was on board the submarine. Everything needed to be completed by late afternoon of the 24th. LCDR Y would hand deliver the package that night and join Peter and Doug at the hotel in Troon where they normally spent the night. The entire team would board the submarine via tugboat on the 25th, leaving the Troon dock at dawn.

Late in the day on the 23rd, Peter and Mia took the Carey bus to JFK, as she had a flight leaving for Frankfurt at around the same time as Peter's flight. Peter met Doug and the rest of the inspection team at the Pan Am terminal. By 1830, all hands were out over the Atlantic on their way to the next chapter in the unfolding drama.

As soon as the planes departed, Ivan called Gorsky in Moscow. He picked up immediately. "Well, Comrade, how is everything going stateside?"

Ivan said, "Songbird delivered the package to Neutron as planned. Audio monitoring of their room continues. Neutron delivered the package to the hotel safe after his training session. Our hotel contact verified the package remained there until he picked it up on his way to JFK. There were no irregularities."

Gorsky interrupted, "Do you anticipate anything going wrong? Did they discuss the exchange for her father after mission six?"

"They did discuss it briefly, and Neutron indicated that New York would be an acceptable location. He has his instructions for hand-off of the information at the Pan Am terminal upon return. The method is tried and true; all he has to do is wait until our agent finds him at the lobby bar. A quick transfer and that should be it. He already has the material for the second mission, and the protocol will be the same."

March 25th-26th
Underway in the Irish Sea

Transfer from tugboat to submarine is notorious for its often hair-raising moments since the slippery, rounded hull of the sub was meant for speed underwater, not receiving personnel on the surface while already underway. Fortunately, the Clyde was calm on the morning of the 25th, and all five Board members safely made the "leap of life" onto the submarine's deck. The sub crew had been told to expect an extra officer on the team, but not the reason. They were also told to cordon off a corner of the radio shack behind a temporary curtain, ostensibly for administrative purposes. This area was going to be needed to evaluate and transcribe the Board's confidential notes.

In reality, Peter would use this space to photograph the dummy information which would be given to the Soviets. Doug would assist him with the photography and help create fictitious documentation on the ship's logs from the raw data provided by the CIA. Dummy pages of the reactor plant manual (RPM) had been created back in Washington, and Doug inserted them in a RPM binder to make them appear to be part of the on-board manuals.

For the questions to be answered in writing, Peter copied the phony information onto the forms provided by the Russians. Peter ignored the request to photograph various instrumentation panels; he would say that this was virtually impossible since the watch stations associated with the panels were manned 24 hours a day. The Navy intended to hold the line on no photographs. The information requested by the Russians was more specific than extensive. So, after two days at sea, Peter and Doug had easily completed the information package, with time to spare. The missing photographs would not make the Soviets happy — Peter decided that the Ruskies would just have to suck it up.

At the completion of the exam, the sub tied up next to the tender in Holy Loch and the inspection team off-loaded. A Navy van transported them to the hotel in Troon for the night. Alone in his room, Peter busied himself assembling the Godiva package to drop at the Pan Am terminal.

New York City
Midtown—Pan Am Headquarters

Mr. Z arrived at JFK around 1000 and went immediately to the Ops apartment for a meeting with the composite New York team. Their photographic expeditions were extremely successful, and the number of KGB agent photos was growing. Except for Ivan, already known to members of the UN Mission, code names were assigned to the various agents. As real names became available, individual files would be updated accordingly. After briefing his team, Z went directly to a meeting at Pan Am.

Mr. Z and Gene Kelly met in a secure conference room at the Pan Am building. As soon as they were seated Z said, "Gene, thanks for meeting with me on such short notice. I want to update you on the matters we discussed a few weeks ago."

"No problem, Z. My management is behind your efforts, 100%. What can I do for you?"

"First, we have identified a name tag we would like you to run to ground. The name is Inge, and she was identified at the Frankfurt airport on the morning of the 24th, around 0830. We are sure she is Scandinavian, but her country of origin is not known. See what you can do. If you can narrow it down to one or two women, their pictures will help us to make a positive ID.

"The next request will require some personnel shuffling. Tell scheduling it is a State Department matter and we need specific personnel to be available on specified dates. We anticipate running an operation on one of your 707s, and would like you to arrange to have these crews made available from April 9th to April 13th.

"Please choose three pilots, all US citizens, very experienced and preferably ex-military. As far as the flight attendants are concerned, we need Natalie Tommasi and her three roommates:

Caroline Bianchi, Mia Beck, and Sabrina Harcourt-Wood. You can choose the other two, but they must be US citizens, experienced, and ideally have some Eastern Bloc language skills. If this operation is a go, I'll fill you in on all the details and, prior to departure, I'll brief the entire crew. We anticipate a two-day turnaround somewhere in Europe. The final departure site is yet to be determined."

Kelly furrowed his brow; he didn't believe for a moment that Z didn't know the departure site. "That's a tall order on very short notice, but we'll get right on it. The good news is the dates do not involve a weekend and won't interfere with anyone's weekend plans. Anything else?"

"Just a heads up to start seriously thinking about the abbreviated training program we discussed last time. We are considering late spring or early summer. Ideally, it should be a four-week program — we have one or two individuals lined up to be trained. If the European Op is a go, I'll give you at least two days' notice to get the crew on board. They should consider themselves to be in a time-available status for those five days, subject to 24-hour recall."

The two men shook hands as they left the conference room. Z was really pleased with how the meeting had gone, and grateful for the ongoing cooperation exhibited by Pan Am. He asked Kelly to convey his sentiments to Mr. Halaby on behalf of the Agency.

March 27th, 1973
Pan Am Terminal, JFK

Peter's flight from Heathrow to JFK arrived right on time. He mumbled something to the team about maybe meeting Mia for a drink, and Doug covered for him as he separated from the rest of the team. Peter extracted the Godiva bag from his carry-on and took a seat at the terminal bar. He knew he wouldn't have long to wait. He'd been told his contact would already be in the terminal lobby waiting for him.

Fifteen minutes passed. Peter was getting restless and kept looking at his watch. Just then, a very attractive woman walked into the bar with a handful of duty-free bags, one of which had the Godiva logo. Just as he glanced again at his watch, the woman asked him for the time. Peter responded, "I'm sorry, but I'm still on European time." The woman put her shopping bags on the floor, adjacent to Peter's Godiva bag.

With a broad smile, the woman asked, "Oh, were you in Europe? I get so confused with the time changes and can never seem to get it right and adjust my watch properly."

Peter had been instructed that once given the correct reply, he was to pick up the other Godiva bag and just walk away. But her response was not the anticipated reply — what was going on? Why had she given the wrong counter reply? Just as he was about to drop his bag, grab the lady's Godiva bag and get the hell out of there, a man with a thick Eastern European accent approached and said, "I see you two are discussing the time. I'm running very late and don't have the correct time. Sir, can you help me out?"

The only thing the man carried was a Godiva bag identical to Peter's. With tingling fear at how close he had come to giving the Op documents to a total stranger, Peter replied through numbed lips, "As I explained to the lady here, I'm still on European time."

"No problem," the man said. "I can do the math."

Peter maneuvered his bag close to the one the man placed on the terminal floor. After a moment's delay, Peter reached for the other bag and exited stage left with a huge sigh of relief. As he walked briskly away he thought, *Can't these fucking guys even follow their own instructions?*

Peter had an hour to kill before flying back to Norfolk and was happy to join the others in the National lounge. He poured himself a stiff scotch and soda and sat down next to Doug who said, "Well? Did you get to see Mia?"

"Nope, but I did meet a real looker—you should have been there," smiled Peter. "That reminds me; I was supposed to call her if we didn't meet in the terminal." Peter went to one of the courtesy phones and dialed Mia's number. When she answered, he said in a low voice, "Everything seemed to go OK, but the next time you see your friends, tell them this whole deal is off if they can't fucking be on time. I almost blew it because their stupid guy was so bloody late."

"I understand you're upset, Peter. I'll pass it on. Settle down, and it will all work out. Have a drink and call me when you get to Norfolk. In the meantime, I'll see what I can find out."

Peter hung up the phone and returned to his drink, thinking, *I don't know if that was a test to see how well I follow orders, or what the hell it was, but I didn't like it one damn bit. The Ruskies better get their shit together, or I'm out of here.*

Chapter 60

East Berlin—Moscow—New York City
April 3rd, 1973

A violent explosion rocked the usually quiet neighborhood in East Berlin just south of the Spree River and west of am Kupfergraben. East German and American personnel located a few blocks to the west at Checkpoint Charlie had no idea what had happened. There was no prior warning of construction activities or blasting operations in the area. This created a state of high alert on both sides of the Berlin Wall. The East Germans feared some kind of a diversion, and the Stasi immediately increased the personnel assigned to Charlie. Surveillance activities increased regarding those going in either direction through the checkpoint. As usual, the Stasi did not trust the Americans and suspected some kind of trick.

However, at Charlie the Stasi found nothing out of the ordinary. It was determined later that a natural gas explosion blew off the top two floors of the building located at Behrenstrasse 47. A raging fire shot flames skyward through the roof of the building for over two hours. The tenement was a six-floor rooming house for working-class residents. When the fire department initially arrived, it was apparent that additional engines were needed. In addition to fighting the fire at 47, they took immediate steps to prevent the fire from spreading to the attached buildings on either side.

The site commander determined that emergency personnel needed to go apartment by apartment to evacuate the occupants of all three buildings. Fortunately, it was mid-afternoon and most of the residents were at work. The older and retired tenants on the lower floors were evacuated without incident. Efforts to extinguish the fire on the top floors of Number 47 were significantly delayed because of the priority assigned to evacuation efforts. The local fire station was undermanned and ill-equipped to manage such a large fire. Therefore, the tide did not turn until personnel arrived from other areas of the city.

Several hours passed before the fire on the top two floors of 47 was completely extinguished. When the area was inspected, fire fighters discovered a resident in the top-floor efficiency unit burned beyond recognition. Once cooled, the charred remains were transported to the city morgue.

Investigation revealed that the explosion was due to a gas leak in one of the upper floor units, ignited by an unknown source. Since there was a significant delay in securing the gas feed in the basement, the leak continued to feed the fire for well over an hour. Further inspection revealed the main gas cutoff valve jammed in the open position due to deterioration and poor maintenance checks.

As soon as the fire was declared officially out, conditions returned to normal at Checkpoint Charlie. However, the Stasi kept additional personnel stationed there and continued to carefully monitor traffic leaving for the American sector.

Moscow—New York City
April 4th, 1973

Gorsky called Ivan to discuss Neutron's data dump from his first mission, and what happened in East Berlin the previous afternoon. As usual, he was inclined to see the glass as half empty.

"Well Ivan, we have analyzed the production materials from

Neutron's first mission. Preliminary indications are that the data is exactly what the Navy and technical people requested; however, he was not able to take any of the requested photographs. My team is still interested in getting the photos. Lean on him to perform better on the next mission."

Ivan was ready to unload about the botched pick-up at the Pan Am terminal, but held off. "Here are my thoughts. I understand the difficulty. It would be like photographing a celebrity in a crowded room where cameras are forbidden, with lots of people watching, and pretending the photograph was never taken. There is a great chance Peter will be caught, and our camera seized. Neutron is not a trained spy and has about thirty minutes' training on the use of a miniature camera, with no instruction in clandestine photography. Turn this problem over to your most-experienced agents, and ask them for a solution. Then we'll teach Neutron how to proceed. Without an effective plan to avoid discovery — the entire operation will blow up, and we will be left with nothing."

Gorsky had to back down. He knew that Ivan was an extraordinary handler of his network, but was not expected to solve difficult logistical problems. "OK, Comrade, I see your point," he said. "I'll turn it over to our experts and see what they recommend. Without a solution, no more requests for submarine photographs." Before Ivan could raise the issue of the JFK hand-off, Gorsky shifted gears. "We have a larger problem. There was a huge explosion in East Berlin yesterday, and we fear Songbird's father was killed. A corpse burnt beyond recognition was retrieved from his apartment and spirited away to the morgue."

Ivan was furious. "When the hell were you planning to tell me about this? If or when she finds out, we can lose our hold on her. Not only is she important to your operation, she is a key member of the Stork Club. Have you managed the news?"

"We suppressed radio and newspaper reporting once we knew her father's building was involved. We reported minimal damage and that the building was safely evacuated with no fatalities."

Ivan was still steaming. "How long is that going to work? If her letters go unanswered, she will want to know the reason. Fortunately, we know they don't have a means of routine telephone contact. Once the first letter goes unanswered, she will use every means available to find out why. You must ensure her letters are not returned as undeliverable — that would immediately raise a red flag. Hopefully she will not receive news of the building explosion in East Berlin."

Gorsky said, "We'll keep her in the dark as long as we can. If she becomes suspicious, we can tell her we'll investigate the unanswered letters. It is important to hold out until the agreed-upon missions are completed. Then we'll tell her the truth. Or, if we want to try to get more out of Neutron, we'll create a myth that her father was caught at his old tricks. As a punishment, we shipped him off to a prison in the motherland. As a matter of fact, we might use that story as leverage to keep her and Neutron in line. This might not be so bad after all."

This new wrinkle caused Ivan to forget the botched exchange at JFK. "OK, Gorsky. I'll act as if nothing has happened. If Songbird asks questions, I'll tell her I'll check into it. As agreed, I won't lean on Neutron about the photographs until your brain trust comes up with a plan. A hidden camera might work, but it's still a big risk considering the close quarters. Anything else?"

"No, let's let the dust settle."

And the line went dead.

SPY IN THE SKY

Pan Am Base, New York City

Eugene Kelly met with scheduling and ensured that Mr. Z's request for three pilots and six flight attendants was met. When the nine people affected received their line for the month of April, they all thought it a bit odd. Some called scheduling, but they were all told the same thing—stay in the area the 9th through the 13th, and maintain a time-available status with 24-hour recall.

There was minor grumbling at 8L, since it was very unusual for all four of them to have the same consecutive five days off. Luckily, Natalie spent most of her time at Scott's, which eased the cramped quarters a bit. On the evening of the 3rd, Mia, Caroline, and Sabrina were discussing the situation when Natalie popped in to pick up some items from her spring wardrobe. She thought the shared time off a bit odd, and remembered Mr. Z's comments at the high-level meeting at Pan Am and his need to manipulate her schedule. After several glasses of wine, Natalie got an idea who might shed light on the issue. She excused herself and went into the bedroom to make the call.

Max answered on the first ring. "It's your nickel," he said.

Natalie quipped, "Hey, wise guy—haven't you noticed that phone calls now cost a dime?"

"How about that—a blast from the past. What's going on in Natalie's little world on the Upper East Side?"

"We were sitting around at 8L discussing that all four of us are off, but on call, from the 9th through the 13th. We're all on different lines, but have identical days off. We were told to stick around on 24-hour recall. I was just wondering if we can thank Mr. Z for that?"

After a brief pause, Max said, "Doesn't ring a bell, but with that guy anything is possible. Let me look at my calendar—there

is something unusual in this month's planning. Here we go...
Doug, Peter, and I finish an inspection at La Maddalena, Sardinia
on the 8th and were going to spend that night in Rome. My next
exam doesn't leave for Charleston until the 15th. By the way,—
I've been notified that Ian should have cleared the air with
Sabrina several days ago."

"She didn't say anything, but that doesn't mean much. We
told her to forget that the whole thing ever happened. If she
were still ill-at-ease, I think she would say something. If you
hear anything from Z about the scheduling issue, please update
me. You've really aroused my curiosity."

"Well, best to arouse your curiosity over the phone...if I was
there in person, we'd need to have...an interesting conversation."

Natalie responded in kind. "Well, since you are there and
I am here, that's not a good formula for success. I think we've
both had a few, so I am going to let you get back to whatever
you were doing, and I'll go back to the girls and my wine. *Bonne
nuit*, Max."

"*Dors bien, chérie*," said Max. There was silence on the line—
had he hung up?

Natalie returned the receiver to the cradle and went back to
the living room, to a lot of laughing and giggling. Caroline said,
"While you were on the phone with God knows who—not Scott,
we assume—we decided that the week of the 9th would be perfect for the bridal shower. We'll take care of everything, and I
mean everything. We'll nail down the details later, but for now,
tell Scott not to put anything on your dance card for that week.
He needs the time to study."

Natalie said, "A party that week sounds terrific. Nothing like
taking advantage of a target of opportunity, as the Navy guys
would say." *I wonder what's really going to happen that week*, she
thought. *Even if Max knows something...it's not as if he could tell me*

over an open telephone line. I knew better than to think he'd be able to tell me anything – did I just want an excuse to call him?

"I love a good party," she said to the girls, although she had a sense that the spooks had something in mind that would be even more memorable than a bridal shower.

Chapter 61

New York City—Rome—Warsaw
April 8th-10th, 1973

Max, Peter, and Doug were sitting around in Max's hotel room in Rome, doing significant damage to a duty-free bottle of single malt Peter had in his carry-on luggage. They were discussing options for dinner and late-night activities when the lobby called the room. LCDR Millen had a message at reception.

Max returned to the room and opened the envelope. "Listen up, guys—this is strange, but typical of Z. Rather than flying back to JFK tomorrow, we're taking a charter routed through an airport somewhere in the Eastern Bloc. The destination is not specified, but the Agency and Pan Am will ensure we get back stateside. Here's the kicker—we need to report to the Pan Am desk at Leonardo da Vinci Airport in Fiumicino no later than 0630. We're to take a taxi and bill the Agency."

Peter weighed in. "Well, that really sucks. We had one night in Roma to find a nice Italian girl for Max, but now we have to be bright-eyed and bushy-tailed by 0500. I wonder what the hell is up?"

"I knew something was fishy when the Navy asked us to stay in Rome an extra night," said Doug, ever the analyst. "There had to be a reason for the delay. Clearly this was not a magnanimous gesture from the Navy for a night of liberty in Rome. Let's pick a local restaurant and make the best of things. I'd recommend going easy on the wine; God knows what's in store."

Back in New York, the occupants of 8L had their orders—Mr.

Z needed them in Rome and ready to fly the morning of the 10th. Accordingly, Pan Am scheduling called and told them to dead head on the 110 from JFK to Rome on the 8th and then stay in Rome overnight on the 9th. Then they would work a charter back to New York on the 10th, with a stop in Warsaw to pick up additional passengers. As the four traveled across the Atlantic, the girls speculated why they were sent to Rome on such short notice, and the purpose of the Warsaw charter.

Natalie thought, *I know Z told Mr. Kelly that there might be changes to my schedule, but having all of us on the same trip on such short notice is really odd.* She couldn't share her thoughts with the group; but she wondered if Mia thought the trip was in some way connected to her. However, Mia knew Peter's next mission was at the end of the month, so this diversion could not be connected to the main operation.

The four roommates made small talk, each suppressing personal covert information: Sabrina pretending she'd never seen Mia photographing documents and that she'd received reassurance from MI-6 via Ian; Caroline trying to suppress her feeling that something very strange was going on; Mia carefully controlling her fear that the Op had gone in a direction about which she was uniformed. And finally there was Natalie, who had more pieces of the puzzle than the rest of them. She just flashed her Pan Am smile and pretended she was looking forward to flying a charter that might take them into unexpected danger.

Captain's Briefing, Rome Airport
Early Morning, April 10th

The Warsaw charter 707 was due to take off at 8:00 a.m. The four 8L roommates were in the hotel lobby five minutes early, shortly joined by two more flight attendants and three officers—the captain, first officer, and flight engineer. This rounded out the normal complement for a 707. Once at the airport, they filed into the briefing room. Natalie was assigned the forward galley with Sabrina and one of the unfamiliar flight attendants; in the rear of the aircraft would be Mia, Caroline, and the other new face. The captain explained that they would take the aircraft to Warsaw with a few passengers; the plane would do a normal turnaround of about 40 minutes and then fly the lightly loaded charter back to JFK.

Just as the captain finished, Mr. Z entered the room. A quick stare at Natalie and Mia reminded them not to offer any recognition. He got right down to business. "I work for the State Department. I'm sure you're wondering what's going on, but it's quite simple: we will have a few special passengers joining us in Warsaw. There might be some unusual things going on prior to takeoff. Just go with the flow and don't ask any questions, no matter what. Once the plane is fueled, catered, and ready for the passengers to board, things will return more or less to normal and proceed like any other 707 charter flight. Any questions?"

One of the flight attendants asked, "Who are our special passengers? Will they need personalized service?"

"I am not at liberty to discuss the particulars," Mr. Z replied in a tone that discouraged further questions.

Z asked the cockpit crew to remain behind and told the flight attendants to board the aircraft. Once the crew was on board, a handful of passengers started to dribble in. Last among them were Max, Doug, and Peter, all dressed as a relief cockpit crew. Happily, they took their seats in first class. Max caught Natalie's eye, shrugged, and murmured, "Don't ask. Just go with the flow."

That seems to be our motto today, Natalie thought, smiling at him.

The door was shut, safety instructions provided, and the aircraft pushed back from the gate. Upon arrival in Warsaw, the aircraft rolled up to the gate, where the catering crew and refueling operation were ready and waiting. All the passengers disembarked, with the exception of Max, Doug, and Peter, who hung around in the aisle in first class, talking about the inspection they had just finished. Then some unusual things happened.

As soon as the forward galley door opened, the catering crew, dressed in coveralls, got right to work as usual. Suddenly, the cockpit door opened and the flight engineer ushered one of the catering personnel into the cockpit, quickly closing the door. The flight engineer remained in the galley chatting up one of the new faces. The whole maneuver took less than 30 seconds. Natalie and Caroline exchanged knowing glances and said nothing. The boys ignored the strange goings-on and just continued their discussion about their visit to Sardinia.

Shortly afterward, the passengers embarked. Most were the same group that had flown from Rome and were joined by a similar number of new passengers. The flight attendants made an announcement to ensure the passengers remained in their assigned seats until after takeoff. Since the flight was light, the passenger load needed to be balanced for takeoff and landing. The door closed and just as they were ready push back from the gate, the captain made an unexpected announcement.

"There will be a delay before takeoff. Local government officials will board the aircraft and question some of our passengers. Please cooperate and have your passport and identification ready for inspection."

Four men entered the plane, two in uniform with submachine guns at the ready and two in poorly fitting business suits. The Navy guys and crew in the forward galley shot worried glances at each other and said nothing. The two suited goons briskly headed to the rear of the aircraft. Natalie thought to herself, *just go with the flow.*

At her station in the rear galley, Mia was the only one who had a pretty good idea of what was going on, but couldn't communicate with anyone. Since she had a working knowledge of Russian and also understood spoken Polish, she determined that one man was KGB and the other was SB, the Polish equivalent. They were looking for a male who was trying to illegally leave the country and had received a tip that today was the day of the intended departure.

The team of two went from passenger to passenger carefully reviewing the offered documentation and comparing the photographs with the passengers. Mr. SB rudely asked a few questions in Polish or very poor English and seemed satisfied with the offered answers. When the agents reached the forward galley, they indicated that Natalie should open the door to the cockpit to allow them access. Fear grabbed her. She froze in place not sure what to do. Natalie decided to stall for time and grabbed the intercom phone and buzzed the cockpit, "Two government civilians want access to the cockpit. Should I let them in?" The reply came back, "Roger, understood. Open the door."

Natalie took her cockpit key and inserted it into the door lock. Just as she was ready to turn the key in the lock and provide access, a frantic burst of Polish came over the walkie-talkie held by one of the uniformed guards. In an instant, the four intruders ran from the aircraft like they were shot out of a cannon. Natalie was right behind them and immediately closed and locked the front door. Grabbing the intercom she again buzzed the cockpit, "Front door shut and secured. Ready to get the hell out of here." Sabrina smiled and shook her head — Natalie had even surprised herself with her lack of formality.

Without further delay the 707 pushed back and was on its way to JFK. During the flight, Natalie brought beverages and food to the cockpit crew. When she got there, there were four men dressed as Pan Am pilots. A rumpled set of overalls was stuffed into a corner, and the new member of the crew sat in one of the two extra seats, quietly reading a book. She didn't bother to ask questions; she knew there would be no answers. *Just go with the flow,* she thought. During her routine trips to the cockpit, everything seemed perfectly normal…with the exception of the extra pilot.

Since the Navy boys were the only ones in first class, there was plenty of time for Natalie to sit and talk with Max. With a little smile, she thought, *I seem to recall that this whole thing started seven months ago on a flight back to JFK from Europe.* Max had similar thoughts, but neither of them mentioned that they'd come full circle. Peter spent most of the flight near the rear galley, talking with Mia. Doug spent a lot of time talking with Sabrina, since things clearly weren't going anywhere with Caroline. The thought crossed his mind that he should have paid more attention to Sabrina all along — she was pretty and smart, and he loved her British accent. He mentioned something about dinner when they landed, and Sabrina said she had no plans. Doug grinned; he was back in the game.

The flight was uneventful, and the crew was told there would be a short debriefing at the Pan Am terminal at JFK. This was a little unusual, but not unheard-of. The plane landed, the passengers left, and the crew assembled as directed for the debriefing. Everybody was there, except for the extra pilot.

Then Mr. Z entered the room. As usual, he kept it short. "Your government thanks you for your cooperation and assistance with our little adventure behind the Iron Curtain. Suffice it to say that you helped to bring a special passenger to the United States. We are delighted that everything went off without a hitch. I will make sure that Mr. Halaby is aware of your significant contribution. My suggestion is that you forget what happened today—it should not be discussed with anyone once you leave this room. Obviously, there's no way for me to enforce that request—however, you were handpicked for this operation due to previous military experience and/or your outstanding record with Pan Am, so you will understand the need for operational security. Again, thank you for a job well done. That's all I have. I ask that Natalie, Mia, Max, Doug, and Peter please remain behind. The rest of you may go."

Once the others filed out, another door opened and the extra pilot entered. He took off a shaggy grey wig, but Mia began to cry as she recognized her father, his bald head now gleaming under the bright lights, and ran to throw her arms around him.

"Daddy, how did this happen?" she asked. "I can't believe you're here!"

The room erupted in applause and little cheers. Max and Doug hugged Natalie, and Peter joined father and daughter in a three-way embrace.

Karl took Mia's face in his hands. "*Meine kleine Knödel*, I never thought I would see this day. I'm still not sure why I am here, but I am happy beyond belief. We will have plenty of time to talk about everything. The American government has been incredibly generous with me."

Mr. Z nodded, with just the slightest hint of a smile. He had delivered as promised. "I'm sure you all have many questions, but this is not the time," he said. "Doug, you are free to go. Everyone else is going over to the TWA terminal to board a westward flight. I'll conduct a mini-brief when we arrive. Please stay dressed in your uniforms."

Doug congratulated himself on having asked Sabrina to dinner. If he hustled, he could catch her at the Carey bus stop. He was happy his part in the little drama had ended for now—but the CIA adventure wasn't over yet.

Chapter 63

New York City—Chicago
April 10th-11th, 1973

Mr. Z had arranged for the use of a TWA briefing room. Pan Am provided a vehicle to transport the group over to the TWA terminal. Since they all had only carry-ons, there was no need to worry about checked luggage. Once assembled, Z started handing out envelopes.

"All right, everyone—in the envelope you will find a ticket to Chicago for today and a return to JFK tomorrow, as well as the name of the hotel where you will be staying. Your room has been prepaid. Karl's ticket is a little different; his is one-way, and he's been given the address of an apartment in Hyde Park where he will be living for the foreseeable future. You all might just as well stop calling him Karl, since he has an entirely new identity. Now he is Fritz Legenfelder, and if you all call him Fritz during the trip, it will help him get used to it.

"I'm sure you will get together tonight after the flight. I'm confident Fritz will tell you the story of his exciting journey. Do not discuss any of the information provided in this briefing until you're in a private place in Chicago. We have given Fritz a new identity and a job at Argonne National Laboratory at the University of Chicago. Once he's settled in, he will teach and conduct research, similar to his prior life at Humboldt in East Berlin; only now he will be free to come and go as he pleases.

"The Agency is determined that our other little caper will continue as initially designed. The four of you will continue in your current roles. It might appear that the Op should be over, but there are significant reasons for it to continue as if nothing has happened. There will be a status update back on the East Coast to discuss the situation. If there are no pressing questions, I suggest you be on your way; your flight leaves within the hour. Good luck to all of you."

Z thanked and congratulated each of them with a handshake. A TWA security officer came into the room and led them to the gate. They went through the routine of boarding and take-off for the third time in one day, but this time they were relaxed, all enjoying their seats in first class. Even before they reached cruising altitude, the entire group was dozing. During the flight, the TWA crew was most attentive since they assumed the little group were all Pan Am employees.

Upon landing, the group took two taxis to Fritz's new residence in Hyde Park. It was a modest two-bedroom apartment on South Kimbark Avenue. The furnishings were attractive and included a dining room table that would easily accommodate six. Natalie got out the Yellow Pages and called in a delivery order to a nearby Chinese restaurant. The envelopes from Z included a generous stack of cash, so everyone had ready funds to cover the cost of the meal. While they were waiting for dinner to arrive, they all sat around the table to hear Fritz's story of deliverance. He started right in.

"Late on the afternoon of April 3rd, I had no classes and was working at home correcting papers. Two gentlemen came to the door. They said they were Americans and showed me a picture of Mia. They told me they had come to take me to my daughter in the States, and since they were armed, I had no choice in the matter. I was told to change into coveralls and leave the clothes I was wearing in my bedroom. They brought an empty workman's bag and told me I was allowed to fill it with as many of my possessions as would fit. They provided me with some special boots that increased my height and had me put on the grey wig I was wearing on the plane. It was obvious that they intended I would never come back to the apartment or even to East Berlin.

"They told me there would be a workman's van at the rear of the building, with the same logo as was on my coveralls. I was to go directly there and was cautioned that I would be watched and must not attempt to go elsewhere. They told me to tell the driver that everything was repaired satisfactorily, and if he offered me a cigarette, I was to hop into the truck in the passenger's seat — which I did. Immediately, we were on our way eastward. We soon passed out of the city and drove several hours to a farm on the outskirts of Frankfurt am Oder.

"The truck dropped me off at a farmhouse where another team had a set-up to create a phony set of identification papers that indicated I was a resident of Poznan in Poland. I spent the night at the farm, and in the morning they hid me in an agricultural truck loaded with farm products. We crossed the Oder into Poland without incident. Poznan is strongly anti-Communist, so it was easy to hide me at a safe house in the city for a few days before continuing to the outskirts of Warsaw. At the safe house, my handlers created an identification badge to say I was an employee of the company that provides food service to planes at the Warsaw airport.

"This morning, they drove me to the catering company, took all my belongings and hid them in a food service box that was eventually loaded onto the Pan Am flight. I worked with the crew and provisioned several other aircraft, and then we finally came to the Pan Am plane. Those of you in the front of the plane saw what happened. Everything went smooth as silk. I entered the cockpit, took off my coveralls, and sat down. Earlier, they had given me the shirt, pants, and tie to put on under the coveralls; my jacket and hat were waiting for me on my seat in the cockpit. Before I knew it, I was properly dressed, quietly reading, waiting for takeoff."

The doorbell rang; the delivery man from the restaurant had arrived, and the conversation was put on hold while Natalie and Mia quickly set the table and readied everything for dinner. Chinese food was an exotic treat for Fritz, who was delighted by the wonton and hot and sour soups, egg rolls, and shrimp toast. Then they enjoyed moo-shu pork, beef and broccoli, General Tso's chicken, Szechuan shrimp, and pork fried rice. Fritz chuckled when he opened his fortune cookie.

"*A stranger is a friend you have not spoken to yet,*" he read aloud. He looked around the table at the group who had helped to save him from the Soviets. "How true—I wouldn't be here without the friendship of people who had never even met me."

Max then took the lead to put the pieces together for Fritz and the group. "You've had an incredible journey. During the coming weeks, I'm sure Mia will have many questions for you; however, at this time, I think it is only fair to let you know what has been going on over the past several months here in the States. There are some details I can't share, but I think I can answer most of your questions. As you are aware, Mia was pressed into service by the KGB, and in return you were given limited freedom in East Berlin. They sent her to the School for Scandal and then directed her to use the job at Pan Am as a cover to carry out her espionage duties.

"Several months ago, Mia became acquainted with me, Peter, and some other naval officers. She started dating Peter when I started dating Natalie. To make a long story short, we learned that Mia was working for the Russians and decided to try to help her out of that dangerous situation. The deal was that if she would help Peter and work for the United States against the

Soviets, our government would try to get you out of East Berlin and bring you to the US."

Max paused to take a sip of tea and think how to phrase what he wanted to say next. "Mia agreed, and along with Peter, we set up an operation to deceive the Russians. It is ongoing and will continue for at least three more months. I can't share the details, but everyone at this table is involved and it's a comparatively low-risk operation; not much deviation is needed from our normal routines. I'm sure you understand the concept of need-to-know, and that's where we are at this point. Mia did her part and took it on faith that my government would deliver. None of us in this room had any idea concerning the plan to remove you from East Berlin; what I'm going to tell you next is pure conjecture."

Fritz said, "Your conjecture is still more than what I've been told. I was given explicit instructions on what to do, and it was clear that I didn't have a choice. But any questions were met with blank stares and noncommittal replies. It was obvious to me that the team was professional and knew what they were doing, so I just let them take the lead. Please tell me what you think happened."

Max said, "Our troops at Checkpoint Charlie passed on a story from the daily intelligence brief that on April 3rd, there was a gas explosion and fire near the checkpoint...the day when you were taken from your apartment. There was damage done, but as far as we know, only one person died—supposedly. The Stasi were concerned that the fire might be some kind of -"

"Smokescreen?" Fritz joked.

Max laughed. "Yes, exactly. And it was. I think our people faked your death and took you out of Berlin in the opposite direction, to the east. Then something curious happened—the news of the explosion and fire was suppressed. There was little if any information from international sources concerning details or the precise location of the blast. My thought is that the East Germans and Soviets did not want word to reach Mia that the explosion occurred in her father's building."

Fritz was glowing with a wide smile. "So, the Russians may think I am dead and are suppressing the news so that Mia will not find out, so that they will continue to have a hold on her. Of course, it's no coincidence that there was an explosion at my apartment within hours after I was liberated from East Berlin. That's a pretty elaborate scheme, but consistent with the professionalism of the people who took me to Warsaw."

Max said, "I can't confirm or deny that theory; I just don't know for sure. However, your thoughts are in line with mine. If you just went missing from Berlin, the Russians would be immediately suspicious, and our operation would be in jeopardy. But now Mia will continue to do business as usual, sending a signal to the Soviets that she believes her father is still under their control."

Mia, Peter, and Natalie were speechless when they absorbed the scope of what Max had just outlined. Finally, Natalie said, "Well, all I can say is that our friend in the US government is a man of his word, and did deliver as promised. What a clever and elaborate scheme, if what Max said is true."

For the second time that day, Mia's eyes were filled with tears. "This is an unbelievable story. I am so happy and grateful — it's remarkable that someone cared enough to help Daddy and me out of a dreadful bind."

Max suddenly felt as if someone had run him over with a truck. "I'm exhausted, and would really like to hit the sack," he said. "I'm still running on Rome time. Natalie, let's grab a taxi to our downtown hotel. Mia, you and Peter probably want to spend some time with Fritz, and say goodbye. Our flight out of O'Hare isn't until noon tomorrow, so maybe we'll see you at a late breakfast."

Fritz took Max's hand and said, "How can I ever thank you and your government?"

Max put his arm around Mia. "Let me make one thing clear — if it were not for your daughter's courage, none of this would have been possible. It is she whom you should really thank." Mia kissed Max on the cheek.

Max and Natalie gathered their luggage; Fritz walked with them to the building entrance. The doorman called for a taxi, and Max and Natalie were soon on their way to downtown Chicago. Natalie put her head on Max's shoulder, took his hand in hers, and said, "What an unbelievable six months it has been. We've had more excitement and ups and downs than most people have in a lifetime. As I've said before, Mr. Max, I'll never forget you. When I met you on that flight from Prestwick, who could ever have imagined the impact we would have on each other's lives?"

Max was silent for a long moment, thinking of everything he wanted to say but couldn't. "I will never forget you, either," he finally said. "Knowing you has been an extraordinary experience in every respect."

When they got to the hotel, they checked in and found that their rooms were on the same floor. Tired and dragging, they got in the elevator and went up to their floor. Max walked Natalie to the door of her room, and his thoughts went back to that first night in Paris. His feelings hadn't changed since then, but he knew that the sooner he said good night, the better it would be for both of them.

Max took Natalie in his arms and kissed her briefly. He said simply, "*Dors bien,*" and broke their embrace. "We'll always have New York."

Natalie whispered, "*Bonne nuit.*" She started to turn away, then stopped, looked back at Max with a wink and added, "We'll always have Paris."

Epilogue

New York City—Norfolk Area—Chicago
April-May 1973

Apartment 8L underwent a dramatic change. The number of permanent residents had gone from four to two—Caroline and Sabrina. Natalie was spending most of her time at Scott's apartment, and now Mia was living with Peter in Virginia Beach when she wasn't flying. The CIA continued to pay Natalie's share of the rent, since they had designs on one of the four bunk beds if they found a suitable agent to train as a Pan Am flight attendant. In addition, they needed to use it as an exchange location for Mia and Natalie.

Mia and Peter enjoyed their relationship—what there was of it, with both of them traveling and still having to pretend to work as Soviet spies. She was not in New York very often, which made it easier to hide things from the KGB. When she was in NYC, she got the mission packages in the Bloomingdale's bag, took the photos at 8L, and then met Peter at the Penn Garden to do the hand-off.

Karl settled into his new identity as Fritz Legenfelder, professor at the University of Chicago and researcher at Argonne National Laboratory. Visits by Mia were carefully arranged; her trips to Chicago were under the pretense of a cultural or Navy event. At times, they would meet outside of Chicago, New York, or Norfolk, to avoid suspicion when she and Peter were on vacation or traveling together.

Doug and Sabrina were slowly becoming an item. He was

a frequent visitor to 8L whenever he was routed through JFK. Caroline now had a serious boyfriend and was rarely around. The little apartment that had once been a center for social activity and Upper East Side parties was now quiet and content...except for being the focal point of an ongoing Cold War operation.

Max and Doug continued to share their apartment in Norfolk. They were often on the same inspection team and went to clubs in New York or London whenever they could. Max took part in the usual Navy social activities, but it was hard to keep his mind off Natalie. Every other girl paled by comparison.

Messrs. X, Y, and Z ran the ongoing submarine disinformation campaign with the help of Mia, Peter, Natalie, and Max. Z's reputation at the CIA was on the rise as a result of his great coup against the Russians. The Agency considered the Op a great success, and it seemed the Soviets had no suspicion they were being fed a steady diet of flawed technical information. Mr. Z and NIS continued their search for suitable agents to train at Pan Am and infiltrate the Stork Club.

Gorsky and Ivan continued their deception to hide Karl's death from his daughter. When and if she discovered it, they would deal with the issue and devise other means to keep her in line. Mortin's little team met periodically in the basement of KGB headquarters to evaluate the success of their operation and formulate areas of inquiry for Neutron to pursue during the remaining missions. Their intention all along was that the Op would continue long after the agreed-upon six missions, and they were not going to let Neutron off the hook.

Natalie's wedding on Sunday, May 6th was everything that she and her parents could have hoped for. She was a beautiful bride, and it truly was one of the happiest days of her life. She chose Caroline as her maid of honor, and Scott's twin Jack was his best man. The quaint Gothic church, Our Lady of Peace in

Midtown, was at capacity with joyful guests, and the reception was an elegant affair at the St. Regis Roof. Nat oversaw the catering, which was truly a gastronomic experience. All the employees of Pietro's, even down to the busboys and dishwasher, were in attendance as guests of the family.

Natalie continued her periodic visits to 8L and Pietro's to perform her courier duties. Scott was so busy with grad school that he didn't notice anything irregular, so there was no need to let him in on her little secret. She occasionally spoke with Max, usually to set up her scheduled exchange with Mia. However, there was always time to catch up — they loved talking to one another. It was obvious their deep feelings for each other remained.

But they both knew she was fully committed to her marriage. That was just the way it had to be.

The End

Author's Notes

This novel weaves together actual and fictional people, places and events from the period 1972-1973. All locations in New York City, Norfolk and Scotland are accurately described as they existed during that period. The Penn Garden Hotel has been renamed the Affina Manhattan. Most of the restaurants described are still in operation today at the same locations; a separate note below is devoted to the history of Pietro's. The operational nature of the Nuclear Propulsion Examining Board (NPEB) is accurately described as the author served as a member from1972-1974. Pan American Airline's routine operations are also accurately described. Terry Hannah, who contributed to the writing of *Spy in the Sky*, served as a flight attendant during the period depicted in the story. The operational nature and cooperative effort between NIS (now NCIS), the CIA, Naval Reactors (NR) and Pan Am management are fictional.

The names of all Navy, NIS, CIA and Pan Am operational personnel are fictional. Juan Trippe and Najeeb Halaby were top executives at Pan Am World Airways in 1972- 1973. John Walker, convicted and now deceased spy, is also an actual person. When Walker served as the leading Communication Petty Officer aboard the USS Simon Bolivar, SSBN 641 (Blue Crew), the author served as the Communications Officer and his superior officer. The Russians did not turn Walker until he reported to the communications center in Norfolk, his next duty station after leaving the Bolivar. The dates of meetings between the Russians and Walker are accurate and are documented in Pete Early's book, *Family of Spies*; however, the nature of those depicted meetings is fictionalized to serve the purposes of the book's plot. The names of most of the Russian hierarchy are historically accurate; however, in general, the names of lower level Russian operational personnel are fictionalized. This would include the personnel aboard the submarine K8, KGB personnel, and individuals assigned to the UN mission in New York City.

Pietro's Restaurant was opened in 1932 by Natalino (Nat) and Pietro (Pete) Donini at 201 East 45th Street. The significant plot action depicted in the book takes place at this location. Nat was the father of Terry Donini Hannah, who contributed to the writing of this book. The description of Pietro's is accurate as it existed in 1972-1973. In the early 1980's Pietro's moved to its current location at 232 East 43rd Street. All the ambiance and recipes of the original Pietro's have been retained, and the current management shares a family connection to Nat and Pete Donini. Pietro's is currently managed by Bill Bruckman, whose additional historical perspective contributed to the scenes that take place at Pietro's.

Antipasti

201 EAST FORTY FIFTH ST., N.Y.
MURRAY HILL 2-9760

Prosciutto...........................
Prosciutto with melon or pears.............
Shrimp Cocktail.......................
Antipasto.............................
Onion Soup...........................
Minestrone Soup.......................
Tomato Juice.........................
Scampi (Half Order)..................

Steaks............................... 13.50
Chopped Steak........................
Steak Minute or Sandwich.............. 12.00

Shrimps Marinara..................... 8.00
Shrimps Fried........................ 8.00
Shrimps Broiled......................
Broiled Filet of Sole.................
Scampi...............................

Entrées

Pietro's partial menu from the 1970's

Nat Donini pictured in his environment

Memorabilia courtesy of

Terry Donini Hannah

Chicken: Broiled.........................
          Madeira.........................
          Cacciatore.....................
          Tetrazzini.....................
          Parmigiana.....................
          House Special..................

Lamb Chops...........................
Veal: Marsala........................
          Cacciatore.....................
          Scallopine.....................
          Parmigiana.....................
          Milanese.......................
          Veal and Peppers...............

Spaghetti

Spaghetti and Meat Balls.................
Spaghetti.............................
Shells a la Nat.......................
Spaghetti with Clam Sauce.............

Here, at Pietro's, all meals are prepared directly upon order and we ask your indulgence in giving us sufficient time. Our famed chef, Nat, will make anything you suggest not seen on the menu. Lobsters are available on a few hours' previous notice. For large dinner parties, a phone call will help us to render you the utmost in service and satisfaction.

Pietro's Menu

Tom and Terry Dressed for Work, Circa 1970
From Respective Collections

747 in Flight
Image Courtesy of Marilyn Christie

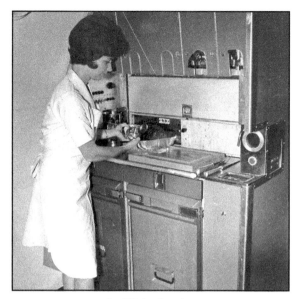

In Flight Service
Image Courtesy of Marilyn Christie

Pan Am JFK Terminal
Courtesy of Marilyn Christie

400 East 77th Street, New York City, NY
Author's Collection

Pietro's Today
Author's Collection

Exterior of Penn Garden Hotel Today
Author's Collection

Penn Garden Hotel Interior
Author's Collection

Pan Am in Viet Nam
Image Courtesy of Marilyn Christie

John Jay Park
Signal on Light Post and Dead Drop in Rock
Author's Collection

Boarding at JFK
Image courtesy Marilyn Christie

Hop Kee, Mott Street and Interior
Author's Collection

Pan Am Headquarters
Image Courtesy of Marilyn Christie

Terry at Checkpoint Charlie
Courtesy Terry Hannah

Warning Sign Checkpoint Charlie, Circa 1961
Author's Collection

Terminal Interior
Image Courtesy of Marilyn Christie

Captain's Briefing
Image Courtesy of Marilyn Christie

USS Simon Bolivar, SSN 641 (Underway)
The author and John Walker served together aboard this submarine
Author's Collection

About the Author

Tom Elsasser, Capt. USNR (Ret), is a graduate of the United States Naval Academy and a veteran of over 10 years on active duty as a nuclear submarine officer. He made 7 Polaris deterrent patrols and served as the Training Officer at the Nautilus prototype. His final active duty assignment was as a member of the Nuclear Propulsion Examining Board (NPEB), tasked with ensuring the operational safety of nuclear powered units of the US Navy's Atlantic Fleet. This novel draws from that experience. He currently resides in Philadelphia where he was born and raised.